ELEMENTAL

Amanda Curtin is a writer, book editor, and adjunct lecturer at Edith Cowan University. Her first novel, *The Sinkings*, was published in 2008 and a short story collection, *Inherited*, in 2011, both to critical acclaim. She has been granted writing residencies in Australia, Scotland, Ireland, and the United States, and the rest of the time resides in Perth, Western Australia.

www.amandacurtin.com

Elemental

AMANDA CURTIN

SCRIBE

Melbourne • London

Scribe Publications
18–20 Edward St, Brunswick, Victoria 3056, Australia
2 John St, Clerkenwell, London, WC1N 2ES, United Kingdom

First published in 2013 by UWA Publishing
Published by Scribe 2016

Front cover image: Shetland Museum & Archives, LS01916,
The foot of St. Olaf Street from the Sletts; woman standing on rocks

Typeset in Bembo by Lasertype

Printed and bound in the UK by CPI Group (UK) Ltd,
Croydon CR0 4YY

A CIP record for this title is available from the British Library

9781925228335 (paperback)
9781925307320 (e-book)

scribepublications.com.au
scribepublications.co.uk

If nothing ever changed,
there would be no butterflies
Author unknown

Contents

Notebook 1
1891–1905

WATER

That boy, Brukie's Sandy, he was a one for plucking the world from the sea. Driftwood, rope, slimy knots of net and weed, bonxie feathers, odd leather slippers, bits of wool, salt sacks, mittens, wax paper, eggshells, Dutchmen's caps, syrup tins, skeleton fish, the beaks and broken wings of gulls. Once, he scooped from the swell a hank of long yellow hair with the skin still upon it. Gave them gooseflesh, it did, those hard, tough fishermen, but the boy stashed it away in his bundle like it was worth something.

And once, Jeemsie had to stop him from pulling aboard a half firkin of sodden grain wriggling with rats. 'Ye gaakie lad!' the old man cried. 'What have I told ye about the long-tailed fellers on the Lily Maud!*' The kick of Jeemsie's seaboot busted up the rotting staves and flung the lot into the foam. And that boy, that Brukie's Sandy, he hung his sorry head, for he knew as well as any there were things a fisherman should never even say, let alone bring aboard a boat. But still he kept his eyes on the sea, for what it would toss up next.*

So there was none surprised at how it happened. Aye, none at all.

Do you remember when you were a wee thing, lambsie, and you begged for a story, a story true? Funny bairn you were, never wanting 'Cinderella' or 'The Three Bears', oh no, not you. You always wanted your grunnie to tell you about Fish Meggie, the Gutting Girl from the Top of the World, and at the end I would have to cross my heart and say, *And it happened so, true as the puffin flies or the sealie sings or my name's not Margaret Duthie Tulloch.* Years it was, lambsie, before you guessed that Fish Meggie was me.

I promised, didn't I, that I would write the stories down for you one day. You were right to be impatient, lambsie, you were right to roll your pretty eyes. *One day* is what mothers tell daughters, and daughters tell their daughters, and it just never gets to be one day.

But I have been to town, lambsie—given your mother the slip—and I've bought myself this case of pens, blue and red and green, these books of lined paper, fresh and white. I have things to tell you before they take me off to one of those places where people put their bloomers on their heads and you have to eat blancmange whether you like it or not.

It won't be what you're expecting, not the fairytales of Fish Meggie you used to love. Even if I could remember exactly how I used to tell them, they wouldn't sound the same, now you are no longer a wee thing and no longer begging for stories. And I *canna* remember them exactly, no. I used to make things up, hither and thither, or turn the details upside down, just to keep the smile on your face. I know there is much I left out. We don't tell children how sad the world can be.

Aye, and there are things I've never told anyone. Some things are not spoken of even when they are happening, and as the years go by it's like the words that might explain them have been taken by the tide.

I am past eighty now, and I have done a fine job of forgetting a good many things in my life. But when I look at you, lambsie, nearly twenty-one and thinking there's nothing of value you don't already know, I am ashamed of myself. You don't know who you are until you know where you've come from. Even when ... Ah, well. Even when.

So I will write my story, if I can find the words. I will pull the pictures from my memory and try.

I am seeing with the eye of a bird. There's a coastline, there are canvas sails, wee boats painted blue. Coming in closer, the boatie shore, the long stony sweep of it, and the soles of my feet are tingling. Everywhere, skinny children, barefoot on the shingle. I am blown from the shore, up the slope to a grid of four streets. Tiller Street—my street—crosses through them, rows of stone houses with their backs to the North Sea. The wind is a howl the likes of which I have never heard since. And in the air, a sea tang, fresh and sharp and rotten all at once, spiced up with old bait, fish guts, plumes from chimneys where the fish are hung to dry and smoke. I can see the stiff striped aprons of the women, the wifies. My mother's face.

If I spoke these words to you now, lambsie, they would sound shivery-strange, all shirred up on invisible threads, clipped of the Aussie vowels my voice began to grow when I came down here to this place from the top of the world. My ink is turning to water, briny and blue. I look at her, that girl I was, at all those people with her, and I see how easily it breaks, my will to walk away from them lean and free. Because when it comes to family, you can walk from the top of the world to the bottom and still not be free.

I will write them down, lambsie, the things I remember, and the things I have tried to forget. I will take my time, my own roundabout way, but I will do my best for you. It's your story, too, whether you like it or not.

And it happened so, true as the puffin flies or the sealie sings or my name's not Margaret Duthie Tulloch—no, I canna promise you that this time, lambsie. I've learned some things, see, and one of them is this: there's no-one can tell a story true.

I was born in a village as far north-east as you can go on the Scottish mainland, closer to Norway than London. Roanhaven was only two miles from the town of Gadlehead, and I'm told they're all the one place now. But back then, oh, we were a folk apart, we thought Gadlehead as much a stranger-place as Fraserburgh to the north, Collieston to the south, and all those inland villages where Ma would sell fish from the creel on her back.

Our house was a but-and-ben—a wee two-room cottage, that is—like the others in Tiller Street, squat and polished smooth by the wind. That wind! Ach, a force, it was, a furious spinning of salt and grit and sleet sucked up from icefloes, ashpits, the spume of the ocean. It could scour the hairs off your arms, freeze the mud on your boots. Every year it took a little more of the houses in Tiller Street, wearing them away grain by grain. Not the frames, no, for the pink granite of Gadlehead will survive more generations than ever I'll know, but the soft matter between that yields to the elements.

I was the youngest at number 8 Tiller Street. The others—well, there was Da and Ma, Granda Jeemsie, my brothers, Archie, Jamie and Will, and my sister, Kitta. If you had asked Granda, Da or Ma which of them was head of the household, each would have owned the name and looked at you as though it was the feeblest of questions, too plain to need an answer. Although my mother would not have been telling you this in words. No, Ma had Looks for that.

In the smallest but-and-ben in Tiller Street were Da's sister Unty Jinna, and her daughter, Liza. And next to us, Sailor Wattie, who had his own boat and a share in ours, the *Lily Maud*, Ma's sister Unty Leebie, and their children, Andrew and Elspet. Liza, Elspet and I were about the same age, so it was like having two more sisters. They could never come close to Kitta in my heart, though. No-one could.

We were sea people. We lived by its moods and rhythms as much as the fish and birds that were part of the order of things. From the time we could stumble along the boatie shore on our own feet, we'd be working—collecting whelks and limpets for bait, pitching stones at gulls pecking at the fish on our mothers' drying racks. Later, boys were expected to go to sea on the family boat or a neighbour's, while girls were put to service in the large estates thereabouts, or married young to another fisher family and made useful that way. *A fisher canna be in want of a wife*—that was the common wisdom and no-one quarrelled with it back then. When we children stood with our bare toes in the icy sand, gazing out to sea, I fancied there was freedom in what Archie, Jamie and Will saw, a ticket to the wide world, beyond the life I would know. To catch a glimpse of my future, I'd to turn in the other direction, to the land. There I would see the labour of the mending sheds, the worn tracks between the peat country and our fireplaces. Tubs of grey, soapy water where woollens were scrubbed on wooden boards. Roadways leading to the farms and estates where my mother and aunties walked to sell fish. For me and Kitta, for Elspet and Liza, the pattern of the years ahead would be plain and safe and all the dreary same.

It didn't stop me from yearning, mind. Even my earliest memory ...

I was a wee bairn when I tottered into the winter sea. Straight in, clothes and all. Folk said later I was blessed to be alive, that my heart didn't stop, nor my blood turn white. Jockel Buchan, an old fisherman, strode through the shallows to reach me. Waded in, he did, almost to the knees of his great seaboots. I remember this, aye, but I don't remember feeling frightened, or cold, though how could I not have been? Nor the sound of Kitta and Liza squealing like piglets all the while he was hauling me ashore. Nor Unty Jinna shaking my shoulders and calling me *a raickless bairn*. These things they told me later. What I remember—aye, even now, I remember—is struggling to be free of the arms holding me safe, twisting round to the water again, searching the sea for another glimpse of the huge white wings that had lifted from the waveslick and flown far away into the sky. The most beautiful thing, lambsie! Ma used to say my *pretty birdie* was a kittiwake or a solan goose that had strayed too close to the shore, *and what a foolish bairnikie who would droon herself for that!* But I knew it was something miraculous, and I cried to fly away with it.

Granda Jeemsie took on a rage about my little rush into the sea. He muttered for weeks and shook his head. He spat on the ground and marked a cross on the sand with the blade of his gullie knife. He gave a sixpence to the widow of Jockel Buchan when the old man and his yawl were taken by a storm that same winter. Jeemsie Neish giving away a sixpence! Now, that was a thing to remark on.

~

My people would have recognised you, lambsie, you and your mother both. You have the look of Ma's side of the family—the Neishes—on your brow and in your eyes. Aye, and in the set of your frame, too. *Wifie's bones*, Ma used to say, her proud claim to generous hips and a strength in the spine fit for fetching and carrying. I canna expect you'll think on it as any sort of blessing, but you'd have been given the nod back then, lambsie, the nod and the closed-lipped smile of those parts that was grim and smug both.

Me, now, I always had the Neish build, too, but there was not a soul who would smile upon on a *reid-heidit* throwback from some ancient Pictish kin. The Neishes would lay no claim to red hair, and nor would Da's side, the Duthies. Be thankful this curse passed you by, lambsie. Aye, I know you're smirking, thinking your grunnie fanciful with talk of curses, but it was not a thing to smile about then, no.

Imagine this:

In the distance, a little quinie—a wee fisher girl—is running up near the braes, her hands flailing about like stars, long hair whipped from her scalp in knots and skeins. It's dusk. No-one pays her any mind. Too much to do. Loaded murlins to carry to the boats, the boats to be readied for sea, no time for else but the business of setting sail this night.

Granda Jeemsie and Da are striding in front with coils of lines slung about their shoulders. Ma and Unty Leebie are behind, bent under the weight of floats and ropes and hooks. Then come the boys, laden too, but still green enough to be full of the thrill of Going to Sea.

Suddenly Ma freezes. *No.* The word catches a moment in her throat. *No, NO!*

Leather floats tumble from her murlin, skitter across the sand. She swings around. *Archie! Jamie!* But they have seen for themselves and are already running, though too late to stop it, too late, too late.

The little quinie has danced her way down to the boatie shore, flitting along, chasing after gulls, her fists pounding the air as they escape her. She turns away from the sea.

Ma pants, florid. It could not be worse. The quinie is right in front of the fishers now. She is all Granda Jeemsie's scandalised face can see.

He stops. And so does Da. And Sailor Wattie. And Buckey's John and his boys. All of them stopped cold by this *reid-heidit* child who has put herself between them and the sea.

And then Granda Jeemsie rips the lines from his shoulders. *Get from my sight!* is what he says, but the words are mangled up in rage. He stomps back to Tiller Street, pushing Ma aside with the meat of his hand, leaving the coils for her to gather and rewind. The rest of them follow, turning the dusk thick with spittle and mutter.

The fleet would not be setting sail that night.

I knew I'd done a terrible thing, and never would I do it again, but just what it was I'd done was a bewilderment that day. I made myself small on the sand, hugging my knees. Kitta will come, I told myself, Kitta will come find me. By the time I heard her calling my name, I was a wretched, whimpering, shivering thing. She dragged me to my feet and hugged me, and I wept into her plaited hair.

Kitta wiped away the snotty strings from my face with a scrunch of her skirt. *Ye're to be quiet now, Meggie mine*, she said firmly. *Home an' straight to bed, Ma says.* And when I nodded, she put a finger to her lips, took something from her skirt pocket and handed it to me. Turning the folded lump of bread over, I spied a pink sugar scraping inside. A jeely piece! I gasped, looked up. My sister was grinning.

Ma knelt by our closet bed later, and her voice was a gruff whisper. *The fishers say it's unlucky*, she told me, her fingers opening and closing as if trying to pluck something from the air. *And maybe they be right, quinie, maybe no, but isn't for us to say when they be the ones the sea plays with, a witch who can give or take at leastest whim.*

I listened, aye, and I learned, and from then on I stayed far from the boatie shore on the nights the men left so never again would they be cursed by the redhead crossing their path.

Mind, when it came to the things a Buchan fisherman thought cursed, the list was long. Pigs, rats, cats, hares, rabbits, salmon ... Even now it feels reckless to write that list of words, as any child of fisherfolk had it slapped into them, from the time they could point, that pigs were to be called *four-fitted beasts* or *grunters*, rats were *long-tailed fellers*, salmon, *the reid fish*. Pastors, now, they couldn't be named, nor seen near the boats, and we called the kirk *the bell hoose*. Strange, you think, that the work of the Lord should be held in such fear? Well, fishermen didn't like to take chances when it came to offending gods, the pagan and the Christian both. To show reverence to the Lord, well, that might upset the Witch.

I don't know, lambsie, just what it was about red hair that threatened the fishermen's pact with the sea. But I remember a day when our Archie was sending me dark looks as he dumped by the door a ruined twine of lines shredded by dogfish. Like the fault was mine. Ma took my chin in her hands and knelt down to whisper. *Don't ye fret, quinie, for if we end our days with hair at all, it all be the same colour.* But look, lambsie, see how wrong she was. Dulled with age it might be, but my hair has never gone the usual white or grey.

She could be soft at times, Ma could, when it came to me and Kitta, glancing around first to check there was none watching to mistake soft for weak. But she was a tough woman, aye, like all the fishwives of those parts, because tough they had to be.

Times were different then. You're rolling your eyes again, aren't you, lambsie. *That's what old folk always say.* But it's true. Time matters. You will know this when you look it in the face. Isn't a child alive today who could have survived back then. I don't mean the hardships of those days—the meanness of the food, the idea that children should work for their keep. Those are things that can be endured, and if a child now were to be cast back through the years and flung into a but-and-ben in Roanhaven, the wee thing would learn. Learn and survive. People do when they have to.

No, the thing I venture would befuddle a child of today is this: in the scheme of the universe—your family, your village—you were one notch north of a hindrance and two south of a help. *Loved* you were, aye, in the way of those days, a careless kind of love that took all manner of things for granted. But if you had a thought in your head there was none who would stoop to hear it and none to say you mattered the peeriest thing. And if you were a girl, you'd to get used to that, aye. You would forever be the last, the very very last, in a world where the words of men and the ways of shoalfish and the direction of the wind were what mattered.

I canna imagine a child of today taking it into their head that they were not the centre of all else. That the world was not waiting for the next thing they might say.

Ach, all the nieces and nephews of mine there might be in the world somewhere, all the family I don't know. Could be, lambsie, could be you are the first of the Neishes and Duthies to have your own special name, one that doesn't belong to a long line of those who have gone before you. *Laura*—that was your mother's choosing. Always a mind of her own, that one.

Maybe it seems I was going along with the past when I blessed your mother with a family name, but there's a thought to make me smile. It wasn't for tradition that I called your mother Kathryn, it was for someone I loved with all the beats of my heart. And because in the midst of so much forgetting, *this* I wanted to remember.

Kitta wasn't the name my sister was christened. Ma gave her Grunnie's name, Kathryn, but no-one ever called her that. Kathryn Duthie? Well, that wasn't any use to those who must know which Kathryn Duthie it was you meant when there were Duthies all about those parts, as far inland and along the coast as you could tramp in four days, and a Kathryn in every third but-and-ben besides. So they would make up tee-names. I suppose we would call them nicknames now. A stamp of ownership would be added, some little flourish to explain which Kathryn or Janet or Isobel, which of the Duthies or Buchans or Rosses, and that would be an end to it, whether you liked it or not. Me, I was Ginger Meggie to begin with. Ma was always called Jeemsie's Belle. There was Postie Andrew who drove the post cart. Net Tildie mended nets for the herring boats. Jinna's Liza—ah, now, that was a cruel one, for it told to all the world that there was no father to give a name to my cousin. Liza seemed always to carry that shame like a bundle on her back, like she was a child born to be sorry.

Kitta was a few days old when she saw Da for the first time. In he stomped, Weelim Duthie home from the sea, a six-foot bluster of seaboots and salty wool, and they say she opened her eyes and screeched herself pink and purple at the face peering down into her crib. *Like a kittlin at the stranglin'*, Da pronounced in disgust. So Kathryn became Kitta. And to most in the village, she was Weelim's Kitta. You see, you never could get by with just the name from the pastor's blessing.

My beautiful Kitta. I wonder, you know, about names. Are they just labels to make the everyday easy, or have they some special power to bestow luck, good or ill, on the head of those they tag? Did the name Kitta turn a placid Kathryn into the wild girl people thought her, or was it always destined to be so?

~

I remember the day Kitta announced she would not marry. We were all of us plucking whelks from pools near the boatie shore, and Brukie's Sandy lolloped towards us in his gangling way. *Pretty Kitty!* he called in a gurgle of laughing, his slack-chinned face full of light.

Kitta straightened up and called out *Ay ay!* and *Here's some dulse for ye, Brukie's Sandy.*

He took the treat from her and waved his arm like a windmill as he galloped away, grinning back at Kitta. His cheeks were fat and bulging with the chewy, briny seaweed we all loved.

Ooh-hoo, Will sang. *There goes the bridegroom and here comes the bride!*

And Liza piped up in her tuneless little whine: *Ooh aye, ooh aye, Kit-ta's get-ting ma-ar-ried!*

Kitta smiled back at poor simple Brukie's Sandy and waved and waved until he was just a speck against the sky. And then she turned to the others, scornful, and put them straight. Married? Not her. Not ever.

Such a thing to say! Foolish. *Raickless*. Of course, the pronouncements of a twelve-year-old girl were normally paid no mind, not even by other children—except adoring younger sisters. But this day, there was something convincing about the way Kitta tossed her long dark plait when she said it. Something fearless in how she stamped her heel on the rubbery weed.

Elspet blanched, and Liza snorted loudly, and both of them looked to Will, who was thirteen and soon to Go to Sea with Archie, Jamie and the men.

Don't ye be foolish, he said, and he seemed to be casting about for some reassuring word. *Ye're no bonnie clip, that's true, but ye're a hardworking quine an' there's lads who don't take poorly to a fat face.*

I opened my mouth. Closed it. Could find no words. My lovely sister! Her beautiful face, like farm cream and Sunday roses!

Kitta shut him up with a look, withered the pity right there on his face. She didn't stoop to answer but that night she whispered to me, *I'll not be stayin' put to be married, Meggie mine. I'm goin' to leave this place an' see the world!*

I put my hand in hers and tried to smile and she squeezed my fingers hard.

It was madness. We girls weren't going anywhere. We had only to look at Ma to see the map of the rest of our lives. Already we were in training, fetching and carrying for our brothers at sea, scraping the mud from their seaboots, reddin' the lines for the *Lily Maud*, cleaning before the men came in and after they went out again so our home was as neat as God's house. Good daughters who would become good fishwives.

And it was a sin to be caught hand-idle when we could be knitting. We knitted from the time we could master the simplest stitches—knit, purl, stockinette. Everywhere we went, no mind what else we might be doing, there'd be a ball of thick blue yarn and a pair of needles stuffed into our leather knitting belts—wiskers, they were called. And if there was a moment to spare, clean hands or not, we'd knit. Ganseys, drawers, mittens, scarves. Long seaboot stockings knitted in the round so there were no joins to rub the ankles of our fathers and brothers. It was a serious business, this, not just a thing to while away the hours before bed. We had to knit tightly, on fine needles, with never a dropped stitch: a gansey that let in the cold, the bite of that wind, was not a bit of use to a fisherman in a gale or a child gathering bait on the boatie shore or a fishwife tramping farm to farm across the heather moors. Those plain, workaday garments were all we had to keep ourselves warm, and everything we wore—*everything*, lambsie—we knitted ourselves. Oh, you canna imagine how scratchy they were, those woollen drawers and vests, how the fibres would chafe against your cold, raw skin! It would take years for them to soften, if ever they did, and I would take care to keep my old misshapen underclothes from Ma's eyes, so she wouldn't make me knit myself a prickly new set.

We girls were yanked from the classroom from time to time to learn from our mothers. I'd to help Ma on her rounds through villages inland, to farm women, to cooks in the big houses. The burden Ma carried in the creel on her back would change its load as we went, but not its weight. The fish would be replaced with grain and neeps, butter and cheese. Ah, a long time it's been since I've thought of those days—the rhythm of our walking, the swaying of the creel, the way Ma would haggle to get a good trade.

It was just the way life was. Our labour was needed by family, fleet and village, and the children we bore would be the labour for a new generation. Kitta's vow not to marry, her wish to see the world, was purest foolery.

But I believed her. I'd have believed anything Kitta said. And I understood, oh aye, I did. Sometimes when you catch a glimpse of the everyday, something happens and the view gets skewed, and in that moment the way you look on things is changed forever. That's what had happened to Kitta and me years ago, when we saw The Beasts that Go Down to the Sea.

Imagine this, lambsie:

It's the muddy hours of an April dusk, and Unty Jinna herds three little girls to a high point up above Roanhaven, skybound and windblown. It overlooks the curve of coast where the boats leave for the shoals. They say Jinna comes here to remember the laughing man who loved her, who set off in his boat one night and never came home.

Salt stings our eyes when we lift our faces from the nest of our woollen shawls. Liza grizzles until Unty Jinna pulls from her pocket a piece of dulse. Kitta glances at me, a slight raise of a brow. Liza will cry at the least thing, and loudest when her mother has a pocketful of dulse.

From our place above, we can see the *Lily Maud* and the other boats jerking at anchor in the shallows. And then come the fishermen, weighted down with lines, the womenfolk behind them, staggering in the onrush of wind from the sea. A watery procession blurring in our eyes.

A sleety wind lashes us from the sea, flattens our skirts against our knees. Kitta and I pull at the wool with our mittened hands but it sticks to our legs like wet sails. Our eyes are raw from the howling wind. When we look down again to the boatie shore a vapour has risen from the sea, swirling skyward in shrouds of white. We gasp, Kitta and I. We canna breathe. And when our breath returns we shriek and shriek like a pair of hooked gulls. For there below us, lurching about in the shallows, are two-headed monster-people, hunchbacked and many-limbed.

The sea is full of beasts.

What nonsense is this! Unty Jinna slaps our cheeks. And when we huff out the terrible words, Jinna slaps us once more, exasperated. *Beasts? There be no beasts!* she tells us again and again.

But there were, and for a long time I would carry them in my head. It was all the more terrifying because Kitta, older and cleverer than me, had seen it, too. After that, Kitta and I would speak quietly to each other of The Beasts that Go Down to the Sea—even though by then we knew it was a thing of the everyday we had seen: Ma and the other wifies rolling off their stockings, hitching up their skirts, ferrying the men on their backs from the shore to the boats. 'Floating' the men and their gear.

Ma was puzzled when we told her about the beasts, and talked to us as though to a pair of simpletons, spelling it out for us slow and plain.

The men must be kept fit for work, quinies. They must keep their seaboots dry for the spell at sea. No fish, no money, see? No fish, no food!

But it didn't seem right—no, it did not—and what I felt in my spine that night is what I saw in Kitta's face when she vowed to see the world and never to marry.

And I made a promise, too, lambsie, a promise to myself. Maybe I would marry, maybe not—I thought to keep my choices many. But my promise was this: I would carry no man on my back.

The year I turned eleven, the world began to change. Now that I look back on it, I know there were big things happening all over and everywhere. That man in America started up his motor vehicle empire. The war in Africa had just come to an end, with many a man and boy losing his life. Two brothers flew up into the sky in a fantastical machine, and flew down, too, which was more the wonder. And in the freezing north some silly explorer pushed off in a little boat to sail the Northwest Passage. That was World Progress in 1903, lambsie, a year that had its share of madmen.

None of that touched us in Roanhaven. And what Progress there was to speak of in Gadlehead town I couldn't say, either, because we didn't take much interest in the Gadle's world except for the market where Da took his catch. Or if the town happened to reach across to us in the village—which it was soon to do, with the curers and their wallets and their arling books. I'll tell you about them by and by.

In Tiller Street, Progress caught us by the scruff of the neck in 1903. For some years, fewer of the men had been fishing the home coast with longlines, returning with loads of mackerel and ling after days at sea. The way of their fathers and grandfathers was a dying thing. Herring now was King, making its stamp on towns and villages all along the north-east coast. Roanhaven had started to change, too. Our men began the wrenching business of beaching family vessels on the boatie shore and hiring themselves to the new steam drifters from Gadlehead's fleet; no-one from the village could afford to buy a drifter. Da held out longer than most, hoping the deepsea fish would take hold in the markets again. But the Age of the Silver Darlings had come, and fishermen, if they were to remain fishermen, had no choice but to tie their fate to the herring. Grudgingly, Da and Sailor Wattie said that come spring they and the boys would join the fleets doing the circuit from the Western Isles up to the Shetlands, down along the home coast and further south to East Anglia. For nine months of the year they would follow the shoals.

Kitta had learned the names of the faraway places that Da and the boys would go to, and she listed them for us, holding court. *Stornaway*, she said, her eyes mysterious, her fingers tracing circles in the air. *Castlebay, Scalloway. Lerwick, Baltasound.*

Will they see elephants? Elspet whispered. *Will there be Wild Injuns?*

And we laughed at her, Kitta and I, laughed at such foolishness. But you know, lambsie, there was something hushed and magical about those foreign names, and it seemed to us that our fathers and brothers had become strangers already. At school we begged Miss Birnie to show us on the coloured globe of the world. The speck she said was Aberdeen was the closest place to us, and we traced a line from there to where the herring boats would travel. It didn't seem so far on the globe, measured in bits of inches, but still we were in awe. And in time we would be jealous.

Only now, looking back, can I set my mind to thinking how jealous Granda Jeemsie must have been, how bitter to be left behind with the wifies and quinies. Too old for the drifters, he was, but fit enough still to take the *Lily Maud* out after cod and haddock off the coast—fish for those of us left in Tiller Street, and for Ma's creel. This he would manage with a makeshift crew—whoever he could find. Whoever was, like him, too old for the drifters, or perhaps too young.

Kathryn and her worry eyes came today. All this nonsense about salt, I canna abide it. *I have been eating salt all my life, one way or another*, I told her. *I will not be taking my eggs without it now.* But she has been to that fiend with the horse face and gloomy words and has booked me in, she says, to have my blood pressure checked and all manner of other things.

I looked at her this morning and thought: I have a daughter of fifty-two years. Why should this thing I know already knock the breath from me? But the age of a child seems a greater marker of time than a person's own age, and it holds a special grief that comes with having walked already the path they are coming upon, knowing, suddenly, there are not many paths, just this one. My Kathryn. Isn't that her face is lined overmuch, she is silk-skinned, and beautiful still, but age is doing the pushing and pulling it always does, aye, and she is no more the quinie I still think her. Her hands, though, I like to look at her hands, smooth from the clay she works with.

How suspicious she was when I told her I wasn't ready to take my books back to the library yet. She gave me a Look—oh, how like Ma she can be! Had I been going to town on my own again, she wanted to know, when I'd promised her I wouldn't? No, I said, and for once it was truth. I haven't been to town, nor anywhere. But I didn't tell her what it is that's taking up all my time, I haven't let her see me writing in my book. She wouldn't like that, no indeed.

But I am forgetting, lambsie, drifting off the track, writing as if to a diary of the day, instead of writing to you of the past.

What a strange thing it is, this looking back, remembering. There was this girl that was me, and she did this thing and did that, and I watch her in my memory. I know she was doing the right thing here, lost her way there, should have recognised dangers that seem so clear now. I wince when I see her do what she will regret, say things I know will hurt her in the end. I see her like a girl in a story. Someone a bit like me but more foolish, more wise, more brave, more this, more that. A bit like me but not me. And you're thinking: of course, that's how everyone remembers, like watching a film of their lives.

But sometimes I'm inside that girl, I'm inside the story. And I have no more idea of what she should do than she does herself—no wisdom to see from the outside—because I am the girl and the story will do as it will.

Meggie, Kitta whispers, her head low over a slate of chalky sums. *Meggie, hear. I'm goin' to the fish!*

Ye're not!

Am too, Ginger Meggie. And she produces a shilling from the pocket of her skirt, turns it over in the palm of her hand like it's a magic-man's trick. As well it might be for the way I gape at it.

She laughs softly. *Eh, hush your mouth, quinie, or ye'll swallow a bumblebee.*

But ye canna go to the fish. Ye know what Ma says: it's not respectable. She'll not let ye. An' Granda will … I stop. Am unable to imagine what Granda Jeemsie will say.

Kitta tosses her plait but doesn't look so sure. *Maudie Ross has signed—Maudie Ross!—and is there a livin' soul in Roanhaven would say the Rosses are not respectable? Ma will be pleased for the shilling.* She gives me a little push, looks at me anxiously. *She will, don't ye think?*

But Granda …

I've signed the book, Meggie. I've signed an' that's an end to it.

But no, it was Ma who put an end to it. Granda Jeemsie never even got to say his piece, for it was over before the *Lily Maud* came home next day. The shilling was returned and the whole of Tiller Street heard just what Ma thought of *chaifing snipes* who would take the pledge of a girl not yet fourteen and who didn't have her parents' leave to give it.

It was a wonder those arling men from Gadlehead kept coming back to sign up Roanhaven girls. They never had collected too many names in their books. Maybe the drift of fishers to the Gadlehead crews gave them hope, I don't know. But families slow to send their men to the herring were slower still to give up their women. It didn't pass the thoughts of those in the village that domestic life would not continue as it had, the girls doing the work they'd always done with never a glance to the world outside. Roanhaven families knew about the lasses gone to the fish, they'd heard how the crews travelled about by boat and by train, living far from their families—scandalous! It was no life for honest fisher girls, God-fearing and good.

But still the Gadlehead curers sent their hopeful men, offering girls the lure of a shilling to be arled for the season. And then, if a girl was a fast worker, she could bring home a little pile to the family at the end of the year. Those arling men were cunning with their silky words, aye, they knew just what to say, and every girl heard the word *escape* like a whisper. Becoming a gutting quine, well, it meant leaving the tight grip of family, travelling beyond the village, beyond even the town. A ticket to the wide world. Who wouldn't be gasping for that?

So Ma kept a narrow eye on Kitta, and let it be known—in Gadlehead, in the estates nearby—that she had a daughter ready to go into service. A respectable girl who worked hard and knew all she needed to and nothing indeed she shouldn't.

~

I remember that day, a week before Kitta's fourteenth birthday, like it's happening now. There she is, standing outside number 8 Tiller Street with her long braid looped up and tucked beneath Grunnie Neish's second-best hat. A flush is on her face, that sweet, lively face, and nervousness in the way she scuffs at the ground with the toes of her thick boots. A brand-new kist is by her feet, light as air to carry: Kitta hasn't much but underclothes and her needles and balls of wool. Rowescroft House supplies uniforms for kitchen quines, and she'll be given thread and needle and expected to make one of them fit her.

She has a little yellow daisy in her hat that someone has left on the lid of her kist. Brukie's Sandy, I think, and I wish I'd thought to do the same, I wish I'd picked her a whole bunch of yellow daisies to carry as she leaves.

I'll knit ye a scarlet gansey to wear at Hogmanay, quinie, she says lightly, flicking at my fringe with her long fingers. *Just the thing for a ginger head.*

I count up how many weeks and days to Hogmanay, when Kitta will come home.

Oh, now, don't blub, Ginger Meggie, ye mustn't blub, she says.

I look at her face, suddenly shiny, suddenly wet. *Don't ye blub yourself!*

She turns away as I hug the scratchy woollen jacket that my sister will wear on Sundays to a church that is only a few miles the other side of the Gadle but might as well be on the moon, or even in Aberdeen.

~

With Da and the boys gone, and now Kitta too, it seemed to be change, change, everything changing. But in truth, life coasted on for some time, in the way it had always done.

Da's goodbye to me was a short sermon on obedience and godliness. I'd heard him remark to Ma that I would be more useful now at home than at school and anyone in the parish with eyes could see that. She raised her brows but said nothing. From then on, I would push my palms together every night and pray to be given the two more years of school that the law allowed me.

How I loved that little schoolroom at the end of Hailness Street, with its long brown tables and wooden benches. It was there that I could read Real Books. I read them all, aye, every one the school had. *Kidnapped, The Dog Crusoe, Rob Roy, The Jungle Book, Romeo and Juliet, The Class Book of Physical Geography (New and Enlarged Edition)*, all seven volumes of *A Scottish Keepsake* and six of *The Willow Compendium of Prose and Verse*. What precious things, no matter their flaky spines and oily smudges smelling of fish. What exhilaration to open a book and disappear! My first notion, it was, that there were people in the world who didn't live like us nor think like us, who gave no heed to the will of the sea. I didn't care much for Miss Birnie reading aloud to the class. No, it was words printed on the page I wanted, the feeling there was a voice speaking just to me as if I was someone who might understand, a person with Real Thoughts in her head.

I read anything that passed my eyes within the small world of Roanhaven: labels on boxes of matches, on packets of tea, on all manner of things. The amber bottle of Lifegiving Balm kept at the back of Ma's dresser that promised to *gently infuse its Kindly Influence into those Parts in the most perilous Disorder*. I had my eye always on the hymn books at church, out of bounds to the young, and I swear I'd have risked a strapping to lay my hands on the family Bible in Ma's kist, wrapped in calico and shavings of camphorwood and not to be touched, not ever. Only school gave me the gift of the page, and for that I tried hard to prove myself worthy.

Miss Birnie told Ma I was a Clever Lass, clever enough maybe for the big school in Aberdeen, though Da would never have given me leave to go if ever he'd been asked. It didn't come to that anyway because of what happened. Still, for all the praise heaped on my head for reading, for penmanship, even for sums, I was found wanting when it came to the business of learning housewifery and practising needlework. That, lambsie, was the part of school I didn't like. It would wash over me, leaving no more lasting impression than the tracks of a crab across the sand at low tide. Instead of paying mind to my needles, I'd be listening to Mr McCrindle on the other side of the room, teaching the laddies. How could heel-darning and the barleycorn stitch compare to Astronomy? But the tracking of the moon and the constellations was the work of men-to-be who must know the way to the shoals and back. Girls? Pah. Girls were to keep their eyes down.

At home, there was always work to do, just more of it since Kitta had gone. Granda didn't go out to sea for days any more. He couldn't manage the lines without a strong crew; the weight was too much for him. But every few nights he'd take out the *Lily Maud* with his straggler-helpers and return next morning with a modest haul. Before school we'd scrape the fish clean of scales with twigs of birch, knife out the insides and take off the heads, and then split each fish to dry. If the weather was good, they'd go on racks outside, but more often we'd hang them in the chimney. Ooh, the smell of them there, smoking lightly, scented with fir cones burnt to ash in the grate! The dried ones were called speldings and the ones in the chimney were smokies. I wish you could taste them, lambsie. Nothing like that today, no.

Reddin', now, that was always women's work, and Granda left us to it. After school, Liza, Elspet and I would clean the hooks—a stinking job! Pinching off bits of rotten bait, checking the knots of horsehair that tied each hook to the snoods of the lines. And before Granda took out the *Lily Maud* again, we'd to gather bait for the wily bottom feeders: cod, haddock, whiting. Whelks were best, scraped off stones in briny pools, but even in April we'd oftentimes be breaking a crust of ice to find them. When whelks were scarce, we'd pluck limpets and mussels from rocks in the shallows. Shelling—another job I couldn't abide. Always there were enormous mounds of empty shells along Tiller Street and right down to the boatie shore. Whelks and limpets, those were parboiled first and then shucked, but mussels had to be prised out of a slimy sea syrup. Horrible! The smell of shellfish has forever made my nose run, my eyes itch. Agony, it was, not to scratch the burning till my lashes fell out.

And it was a job made the worse for the absence of my Kitta. Wasn't that I didn't like my cousins—oh, but that Liza! If she wasn't whining she was prattling fit to give us all a pain in the peenie.

One day she fixed us both, Elspet and me, with a wide-eyed stare I'd come to mistrust.

So, what d'ye think they told me, those tinkie lasses, up by the peatie bog?

I shrugged. Elspet looked at me and shrugged too.

Go on, think of what, Liza urged.

I rolled my eyes at Elspet and carried on shelling.

How ye get to be preggernant, that's what! And Liza sat back and waited, her bug eyes smug.

Elspet made a clicking noise with her tongue. *Everybody knows that,* she said softly.

I looked at her, surprised. Imagine Elspet knowing something like that, something I didn't.

Liza was crestfallen but, determined to gain ground, gave a startling account that seemed to grow more and more fanciful, more and more *naked*, by the word. It was instantly clear, from Elspet's face, that the details she'd been given were scanty, the picture incomplete. First she tipped her head to one side and looked at Liza sceptically, but by the end of the tale she was gasping and I was thinking: Aye, quinie, aye.

No drawers? said Elspet faintly when Liza paused for breath.

The bow of Liza's top lip creased and she snorted. *Of course no drawers!*

I threw an empty shell as far as I could in the direction of the boatie shore, and resolved to ask Kitta when she came home.

~

On the day before Granda's trips, we would bait the lines, and at night Ma and Unty Leebie would head off to the boatie shore, struggling with murlins loaded with lines and bulls' bladders bloated up for floats, or big flat ballast stones from the river. I was left to clean up after supper, to see to the fire, to knit, but while no-one was there to see me I would perch a wee while on the stone wall in front of the lean-to, looking across to the boatie shore. Something compelled me to watch, I don't know why. In the distance, in the plumes of mist lit by fishermen's lamps, were Ma and Unty Jinna and Unty Leebie, wading back and forth between the *Lily Maud* and the shore—the lighter murlins floating before them, the weightier loads balanced on their heads. But I would climb down from the wall when Ma crouched in the shallows for Granda to climb onto her shoulders, to be delivered to the *Lily Maud* with his seaboots warm and dry. As I shuddered, I could feel Kitta—far away—shuddering along with me.

Before the men went away to the herring, they would sing as the fleet left at night. *The Lord is my shepherd, I shall not want ...* I can never hear the words of that psalm without remembering the sound of their voices and the way the wind would blow them back to us from the sea.

There was a fleet no more at Roanhaven, no more that comforting choir. Whatever god Jeemsie might have bowed to as he set sail, he kept his prayers to himself.

All those pages filled up in my wee book and I'm not yet past 1903! At this rate I'll not be finished in time for your birthday, lambsie. But I'm finding as I think and remember, and try to write what I think and remember, that it's a funny thing about stories that are real and not fairytales. They are more than just the things that happened, aye. You think about one thing, and what came first, what next, and then you're off in another time and thinking of that. And then it takes you by surprise to see so many threads between them, looping in and out and all around—everything connected. Stories can't just tumble out like buttons from a box, clattering and random. You have to think of the order of things. What to tell. And what to leave out.

The family routine turned a little, weaved a little, to gather in the changes of that year and stitch them into the pattern of what had always been. But then things came among us, new things, and they pulled the pattern out of shape, this way and that. I used to think it began the day Granda came home with his leg busted and the poison in the palm of his hand, but that's not right, I can see that now. I have to go back a few paces to find the shift in the world.

And there it is, right in front of me.

Elspet grabs hold of my gansey elbow and pulls me to the lean-to between our but-and-ben and Unty Jinna's. Pointing frantically, she is gulping at the air. Such a meekling, Elspet, as scaredy as a cradle bairn, seeing fairies everywhere.

The shed smells of tarred rope and the must from old murlins that Ma won't toss away.

There, Ginger Meggie, there! Can ye see?

I drop to my knees beside a stack of rope, turn my head sideways to the ground. No fairies, no. But something. A shivering mass of wet fur.

Hello, wee doggie, I whisper, crawling forward quietly, my hand out.

Ooh, Meggie! Elspet squeals. *Ye shouldn't. Ye'll get yourself bit!*

The pup is as scrawny as a sick hen, matted up and ragged round the snout. It tries a growl that comes out all wrong, like the wheeze of Ma's bellows before she mended the split in the concertina bit. I reach again, I brace myself, for, much as it pains me to admit it, Elspet might be right. But the wee thing whines and slumps with its snout to the ground. Dead, I think. And then the twitch of an eye.

I cradle it close, willing the beating of my own heart to manage for us both, but at the door, I stop. I need food for the dog. I need a place by the fire to keep it warm. I need my mother's blessing.

Ma purses her lips.

I rehearse quickly in my head: The wee thing will eat scraps and sleep in the lean-to and I will do the gathering and shelling and reddin' just the same and go to school just the same and it won't get underfoot of anyone and when it's strong and big ye'll never know it's there and I will wash all Da's ganseys and seaboot stockings when he gets back for Hogmanay and the boys' too, all the smelly ones, and I will carry the heaviest murlin and the biggest creel … and … and … But it's a funny thing about dogs: they know a true heart. The pup looks straight at Ma and speaks for itself.

And that's how it comes to be that Granda Jeemsie finds us by the fire that night, me on my knees on the sooty rug, the dog licking at a bit of old fish head.

He stands in the frame of the door, furrowing and frowning. *What foolery has come to this house?*

I know better than to speak. Ma is knitting in the chair. She says nothing, too.

I give no leave for no fulpie. Take it out an' away! he growls, a scowl on me.

Ma carries on with her knitting. *I gave Meggie leave for her wee whelp, Da. I see no harm.*

Have ye stones in your head, quinie? Cloth in your lugs? Granda's punchy hands are jumping and twitching. *Out an' away, I said, out an' away now!*

I look at Ma, then back at Granda.

I don't see the harm, Da, Ma repeats and puts her knitting down. *An' I don't think Weelim will stoop to bother about a whelp.*

Mild enough, Ma, but if Granda had shifted his thundery eyes from me, he would have seen the Look, and maybe it wouldn't have changed what happened next but he wouldn't have been so surprised about it.

I'll not tell ye again, he threatens, reaching for a block of peat in the pail by the door. But Ma is on her feet and her hand grips the upswing of his arm.

I gather up the dog and hug him to me, both of us shivering from the chill in the room as Granda flings open the door, rattling the hinges, and stumps off into the howl of the night.

~

So proud I was, lambsie, to have a wee doggie of my own. I couldn't say what kind of dog it was—a bit gingerish, like me, with a white blaze on his side the shape of a wing. I called him Crusoe. Like Dick Varley's brave-hearted dog in that book Miss Birnie had read to us and I'd borrowed to read again myself.

How I longed to tell Kitta. Owning a dog, well, that was no common thing among fisherfolk. An extravagance, it was, a mystification. The only person thereabouts I knew of was Lady Ferguson, wife of the Laird of Pitfour, and she was gentry with idle time on her hands, and folk thought her an oddness anyway. I saw her once at Mintlaw, while Ma and the Fergusons' cook were haggling at the kitchen door. I peered through a gap in the hedgerow and watched Lady Ferguson parading on the cool green lawn with three terriers on golden leashes. Ma wouldn't believe it when I told her later but they were wearing *clothes*, those dogs! Aye, jaunty tartan jackets that buttoned under their bellies. Imagine! I wouldn't put clothes on a dog but the leash, now, that seemed a grand idea. I looped a rope over Crusoe's head but the poor wee thing almost strangled himself trying to pull out of it. It didn't matter, he didn't need a leash. Always he was close by my heels, except to chase gulls on the boatie shore. A good wee dog, he was, and a bother to no-one.

Crusoe thrived on whatever scraps Ma didn't want for soup, and I made sure Granda could have no complaint about the dog, nor me. But I had set something among us on the day I brought Crusoe into our home. Granda felt himself wronged, and his ill-temper had come to stay.

~

There came a time in the autumn of that year when I realised something terrible: I hated Granda Jeemsie. It was shocking to have thought such a thing. To hate, now, that was a sin. Ma had once given me a good hard slap to the side of the head when I said I hated milk pudding. Imagine, just imagine, the punishment for hating a person, and such a person as your own granda. No-one must ever know, I told myself. I will keep it inside my own head and none will know. But that very Sunday, Pastor McNab fixed his eye on me and bellowed at the congregation: *Be sure: your sins will find ye out!* Words from the Bible. I looked away from his turkey face. Pastor McNab had already decided I was Trouble that day in Sunday school when he heard me telling Liza which Bible stories I loved the best. *The Bible is not a set of STORies for your enterTAINment, Meggie Duthie! The Bible is the WORRRD of GOD!*

I never did hear Granda say the word *hate*, but he was a hating man himself, indeed he was. He hated to be kept waiting when he came home from the *Lily Maud*, hungry for soup and bannocks. He hated losing his pipe, a daily plague, and sulked at Ma when she remarked that he was the only one who would touch the filthy thing and whoever else but he could say where it might be? He hated the noise of children. And the singing of hymns on Sunday. And anything like singing, for that matter, even the whistling songs of Piper Stewie, which everyone thought pure and true, as sweet as a melodian. And I fancied he had now formed a particular hatred of dogs.

On that autumn evening in 1903, I watched the others leave the house. Forbidden, as always, from putting my accursed self in the way of fishermen off to their boats, I was to clear the plates and wash them in a bucket, but first I would scramble up the stone wall in front of the lean-to and tuck my boots under my skirt. From here I could see all the way to the *Lily Maud*. Ma pulling off her boots. Unty Jinna wading into the sea. Granda Jeemsie stacking ropes. All of them puffing white breath.

Crusoe usually waited at the foot of the wall, dancing on his stumpy hind legs and whining at me, *Come down, come down*, but on this day he trotted along to the shore, following a skimming guillemot. And he passed Granda. The old man gave him a kick with his seaboot. Crusoe yelped, he tumbled and rolled, and then he limped to the nearest safe place. By the time I had jumped from the wall to find him, he had hunkered down under a pile of nets in Net Tildie's lean-to. He wouldn't come out for me that night, nor next morning, or next. Days, it was, *days* before I could coax him out, poor bruised little thing.

Jeemsie knew I'd seen him. He probably heard my cry and then the sound of my running boots. But although he didn't turn back to be tainted by the *red-heidit quinie*, I'd seen him from Net Tildie's and I'll tell you this: a flush was on his face. He was pleased with himself, aye, pleased with his small disgusting victory.

It was wrong to hate, I knew that, lambsie, and very wrong to hate your elders, but that's what I muttered to myself that night. *I hate you, Granda.*

God was on my mind, God and Pastor McNab and how my sins would find me out. Well, they do, you know, lambsie, I suppose they always do in the end. But it was not *my* sin that God chose to punish. Or so it seemed, for a while.

~

He is trundled home, injured, in a cart down Skeel Street and into Tiller, one leg still with the seaboot on and the other flopping loose in his breeches. He doesn't look like Granda Jeemsie at all.

That florid scowl of his is pale as boiled cabbage. He breathes hard, panting sharply—just like I saw a seal do once before Da and Buckey's John knocked it dead. I cried for the sealie, cried for hours. I don't cry for Granda.

Mackie's Peter, spry old feller he is, older than Granda by a decade or more, wheels the cart into the but and eases himself into Granda's chair, stretching his stiff legs by the fire.

Rise, ye old gaak, an' get me out, Granda wheezes.

Aye, Peter says but he takes his own time, indeed he does, and looks down on him as though Granda is a large, amusing child.

By the time Granda is in the chair himself, bootless and wincing, Ma has boiled water and is mixing hyssop and mustard into a bitter-smelling paste.

An' how did a beastie manage to break your leg, too? she demands to know.

Never ye mind, lass. Just strap it up quick an' get that poultice on here. Granda thrusts up his big hairy arm and opens a palm already pussed-up and swelling.

Mackie's Peter snorts and Ma gives him one of her Looks. I can tell, plain as flour, that as far as she is concerned it is no laughing matter to have Granda laid up and helpless and generally in the way. But that old man, that Mackie's Peter, he has a funny way of looking on things, and in any case he would pay no more mind to Ma and her Looks than to his own wifie.

Old gaak, he is, he tells Ma. *Or maybe his eyes be gone, for it's purest foolery to grab the beastie by the fins of its back. Tripped hisself over his own boots with the shock of it an' fell half into the hatch. The poison got him. Aye, got him good!*

Mackie's Peter is enjoying himself.

Granda glares and probably has words of his own all ready to say, but it's then that Ma slaps the paste onto his palm. Such a roar! I clap my hands on my ears, and when I dare to look it's as though Granda's real face has slipped off like the skin of a hare boiled all the day, and left behind a punch of dough, all pink and grey and bloated.

Another snort from Mackie's Peter as he backs out of the door.

Me, I'm jumping to know what beastie has poisoned Granda's hand, so I skitter after Mackie's Peter.

Ah, was a dogfish, quinie—a greedy one, an' all, still latched onto a coddie as we was haulin' up the line. An' that old gaak, fool he be, he takes on a rage an' just grabs it without thinkin' ... And Mackie's

Peter shakes his head. *There'll be no fishing on the* Lily Maud *now, not for a wee while. Your da'll just about have a jamaica when he hears.*

I stare hard at the old man's back as he raises a hand and shuffles away. The prospect of the *Lily Maud* beached and no fish for Ma's creel and Da having a jamaica should have sent the cold through my bones, but when I turn back towards Tiller Street there's a smile shining up my face. So it was a dogfish that got Granda and made him howl. A *dog*fish! And doesn't that just serve him right!

~

Oh lambsie, if you could have seen it. Jeemsie Neish glowering by the fire, scumbling up for himself all the warmth from the smoking peat. It caused a gasp from every person who entered the but-and-ben. This was not part of the order of things.

He was a salty man, my Granda, with ears like whelks and brine in his eyes. Remote, like all those men from the sea. Silent on the land. You could hear their talk dwindling the further they got from the shore, as though the thing that was most alive in them, the purpose for their words, died a little with each step. By the time they reached their homes, stamping boots and discarding waterproof layers, scratching at scalps beneath thick woollen caps, they were silent. Men like that, they walked on land as though wary of the way the earth would not give with their weight. With people, now, it was different. They were used to people giving way.

There he sat, Granda Jeemsie, his leg propped up on the creepie-stool, a great clumsy presence among the knitting yarn, the pots and pans, the herbs hung up to dry. Above the mantel, like a rebuke from the grave, the small neat stitches of Grunnie Duthie: *My grace is sufficient for thee.*

He would glare at anyone who stopped to warm themselves by the fire, and there was no end to the things he needed while he waited for his troublesome leg to mend. *Fetch me this, quinie. Fetch me that.* Tea. His pipe. His woollen hat. The tin of tobacco whose words had all but rubbed way. Ma kept her face mild but I fancy I could always tell what Ma was really thinking behind her careful face. The aunties and the girls avoided us when they could. Why take part in Granda's suffering? I couldn't blame them for that, but I felt aggrieved just the same. Because it was worse for me than for all of them, aye, all of them put together. Just the sight of me made the old man broody, like a man with seven years' bad luck stitched to the hem of his gansey. Granda was not going to leave me to my own ill schemes, no, he was not: I was a thing to be ground down hard beneath the coarse pad of his thumb, to be run ragged till the air blew out of me.

You're a smart one, lambsie, you'll know, you'll be nodding your head already. I hadn't escaped the punishment of my sins at all.

~

When the day came for Ma to set off with the last of the fish, I helped her to fasten the leather strap across her collarbone. Only a little did she stagger as she took the creel's weight. She was strong, Ma was, and could carry heavier loads than this. I passed her a knitted piece I'd made for her to tuck beneath the leather, to help protect her skin from the worst of the rubbing as the creel swayed.

In truth, she didn't need my help. No mind how heavy, Ma could hoist the basket onto her back herself. But these small fussings gave me pleasure and pride, and I fancy Ma liked them too. And it gave her the chance to list off, one more time, all the things I must not do and all the things I must. Oh, how weighty they felt, my responsibilities, as weighty as the creel, for now I had the job of looking after Granda.

She squeezed my cheeks in her hands before she left. *We're relying on ye, Meggie, me an' your da, an' ye know what's to be done.*

Perhaps she knew what I was thinking too because she added: *Don't ye pay no mind to Granda Jeemsie's mumpin'. He's an old man, but he's ours, see? Family. But keep that whelp from his sight an' the reach of his one good footie!*

Lost, I was, when the grip of her hands relaxed. One last pat on the arm and she was away, into the grey of morning.

~

I'd no excuse for slipping off to the boatie shore for bait, or to the lean-to for reddin' the lines, not when the *Lily Maud* wasn't going out. And with winter nearly upon us, there was only so much staying away that could be done when the wind sliced its way through layers of wool. So cold, lambsie, you canna imagine, your fingers and toes bloodless white. And so every day when school was done, I'd be off home, walking with Liza and Elspet, envying them the friendly fireplace waiting for them at home.

Ours had become Granda's.

~

He held out his great paw, the fingers poking from the bandage a funny colour, like rotted weed. His face was sour as he waved the injured hand about. *Hurry yourself, quinie, hash, hash.*

But I was slow at unwinding the muslin strapping that Ma had applied so carefully, and it didn't help when he sucked in his noisy breath every time I tugged at his skin. Finally, when I had a foot or more of bandage coiled around my own fingers, I could see that the remaining piece was stubborn, gluey on the wound.

He was impatient, ready to pull it free with his other hand. Anyone could see that would rip away the beginnings of a healing skin and do more harm than good. And it would hurt. He was surprised when I raised my hand to stop him, and he drew back. It made me a little braver. I brought a bowl of warm water to soak off the bandage, and all the while Granda was giving me the eye. He grunted when I was done cleaning and drying, he waved me away as though I was something small and bothersome.

Later, when I sat with my knitting at the table, he spoke.

What nonsense did ye be learnin' away at school today, then?

It took me a moment, lambsie, to realise that Granda was not just grumbling at the world at large again. He was asking me a question. Inviting me to speak. I looked at him warily.

What cat caught your tongue an' run away with it, quinie?

We had Dictation …

He made a noise like a snorting horse.

… an' Musical Drill …

Musical Drill! Ye're kept from proper work for that! Pah! I give no leave for quinies to be bletherin' about with Musical Drill.

Now, I knew it was the law that put me in school, not Granda's blessing, but I did not say it. He simmered down soon enough, muttering at the fire, glancing at me by and by.

An' what do they learn ye at school about the ways of the sea?

I opened my mouth to tell Granda that it was only the lads who got to learn Astronomy and Seamanship from Mr McCrindle and the sea didn't seem to concern Miss Birnie overmuch. But then I closed it again and shook my head.

He slumped down further in the chair, wincing as his bad leg moved on the creepie-stool. And then, to my astonishment, he fixed me with his eye and said, *Hearken now, quinie, an' I'll tell ye a thing.*

The sea is a witch, a witch an' a mother. With a hand of plenty when she has a mind to be kindly an' a curse when she don't. She can sing a mannie to his death. To his death, d'ye hear? Aye, that's true, quinie!

And Granda checked my face for signs of doubt.

Aye, true as the tide. True as God. I seen it with my own eyes.

Granda settled back a wee shrug.

I seen her take young Tullie's Mickel, long time back, on the Kittiwake. Was a north wind howlin' all the long night, blastin' at our backs as we hauled in the linies, an' I could hear the trill of the Witch in it, all of us could, an' we huffed a wee bit louder as we pulled on the linies, an' stamped our boots against the cold, an' tugged the wool snug upon our ears—all to keep the lurin' song away from our minds. But that young Tullie's Mickel, he didn't know the sound maybe, he didn't take the care he ought. No, an' he was doomed, that boy. A goner.

Granda was not looking at me any more. His eyes were on the door of the but and I fancied they could see through the slats of wood worn smooth and shiny by mittened hands, beyond the houses on the other side of Tiller Street, beyond the street too, and way on down to the boatie shore and the witchy sea that sings from the depths and can make a boy a goner.

All the night that laddie let her in, he let his blood cool to the bewitchin' song, an' come the morning, when all the howl had died from the wind an' the edge of the sky was lit, d'ye know what that loon did? Eh?

He was looking at me again. I shook my head.

He goes an' takes a ballast stone under each skinny elbow an' he runs. 'Here I go!' That's what he cried, that daftie loon. 'Here I go!', all cheerful like, an' splash, straight into the Witch's arms, sunk an' gone. Befuddled to his death by her song.

Granda was out of breath now but his eyes were popping bright, daring me to disbelieve.

Just think on it, quinie, next time ye're bletherin' about at school with Musical Drill. Just mind what I tell ye about poor Tullie's Mickel an' what happened when he let music into his head. Nothing good, eh. No good can come from music!

After I made Granda a cup of tea, plenty of sugar, I sidled out to see Crusoe. A harsh afternoon, it was, a sleety wind about, but warmer for him in the netting shed than under Granda's eye. Crusoe raised his snout and swished his tail, but he stayed where he was, back from the draught. I pulled some old sailcloth around him.

Thump-thump from the but. Granda's stick on the wooden floor. He'd be wanting his supper. ·

Inside I took a smoky haddock and laid it flat on the table. Dry it was, tough to flake, especially with my fingers so dead and white, but dry and tough never mattered for soup. I kept glancing at Granda as I cut up the tatties. I couldn't tell if he was asleep, or dreaming-awake at sea again. A question was tugging at my mind.

Granda, I said finally. *Are ye not afraid, Granda?*

He jerked around at the sound of my voice, hauled back from wherever it was he'd been.

On the Lily Maud, *I mean. Are ye not ever afraid? Of the Witch? Of bein' a goner?*

He grunted and turned back to the fire. *Just get my soup, quinie.*

~

When I came home from school the next day, Granda was scowling and his bandaged hand was swollen, the fingertips bulging and dark.

What have ye done! he growled. *The very devil. Poisoned it be, just look.*

I don't know, I whispered. Whatever *had* I done? I'd used Ma's clean muslins, diluted the vinegar with sea water, wrapped the hand like Ma had shown me. And yet here was proof I had got it terribly wrong.

I poured warm water from the kettle into a bowl, and kneeled by the creepie-stool. *I'm sorry, Granda, I'm sorry. Does it pain ye?*

'Do it pain ye?' she asks. His voice was high and girly, mimicking me, and I almost laughed, swear to God, lambsie. But a second later I was paling before his glare and nothing funny on my mind.

Of course it pains me! he roared.

My hands shook a little as I stripped off the bandage. Both of us gasped. Sodden, it was, and the smell! Like the slime of a rotten mussel.

If Granda's poisoned hand pained him now, there was worse to come while I cleaned it out. I talked to him low and soft, like crooning, the way I shushed Crusoe when he whimpered. *Now, then, Granda … there, now, Granda.* But still he carried on his mumping and grumbling, snatching his hand back every time I tried to sponge away the evil-looking pus.

Granda, I tried, *Granda, will ye not tell me about the Witch again?*

He looked at his sorry hand and away, and then back at me. It was a look that said he knew what I was about, aye, he knew, true as the tide, true as God, but he would play along so I could get the job done.

He sighed. *A mannie be a fool if he's not afraid of the Witch. Bein' afraid is bein' alive. An' stayin' that way. Men not afraid are careless. They whistle the wind, wake the Witch from the deep an' bring their boats to ruin. Tullie's Mickel wasn't afraid, an' he were careless too. An' old Jockel Buchan, aye …* He snapped his head back to me—a strange look it was. Then he stared into the fire again. *Well, more of them as can be named or counted in my time. It doesn't do to dare the Great Mother. Ye can never say when she will turn her other eye on ye. Fishermen know to be canny, an' how to protect theirselves.*

He started fumbling in his vest with his good hand, fishing about inside.

See here, quinie.

He took something from his pocket, from the fold of a bit of paper, and laid it carefully on the arm of the chair. Grey and puckered, it was, something like leather thinned by time and worn down to a waxy nothing. I stopped my cleaning.

Go on, go on, he said, gesturing.

I touched it with the tips of my fingers. *Ugghh.*

Pah! said Granda. *Ye don't know, quinie. Ye don't know gold when ye sees it. Purest luck, this. Kept a wee babby safe for nine belly months an' your granda for near on fifty years. Safe at sea, safe from droonin'.*

I snatched my hand back. Now I knew what it was, this charm of Granda's. *How … how did ye come to have it?*

His eyes shifted darkly. *Purest luck, purest luck …* It was a story he was not going to tell me.

I thought about it, lambsie, as I sponged Granda's hand. Fifty years before, someone—some desperate mother, some greedy howdie wifie—had peeled the caul off a newborn's face and sold it to a fearful sailor. Purest luck, indeed, but that infant probably never did know about the precious gift they'd been born with. The shrivelled membrane on the arm of Granda's chair was a robbery from a babe.

~

For days, until Ma came home, it went on like this: me bandaging Granda's hand, cooking his supper; him glaring at me one moment and, the next, telling me about the sea in his faraway voice.

Those stories of his, or perhaps it was the way he told them—something changed the hardness of my heart for Granda. Did I still hate him? Aye, I did, for wasn't Crusoe banished to the netting shed still, and did I not remember the bruises from Granda's seaboot? And much else besides. But hate is a hard thing to hold upright and strong when pity starts to eat away at the edges of it. And the funny thing was: I thought I could see that same worrisome puzzle on Granda's face when he looked at me, his accursed quinie.

I don't think either of us knew what to make of the other any more.

Not long after Ma came back, something happened, something wondrous, that thinned the heavy fug that seemed to be all around me then. And it was to change all my days forever after. Aye, even this day, I've held its sweetness in my hand.

Miss Birnie told us girls to wear our best aprons to school and the boys to mind they washed the mud off their boots, because we were to have a Special Visitor, and Pastor McNab too. Whatever could it be for? we wondered, lining up from tallest to shortest and readying ourselves to sing 'What a Friend We Have in Jesus'. We always sang that for Pastor McNab.

The visitor was the Inspector from Aberdeen. Such a disappointment! He came every year, the Inspector did, to do his counting. That's what we called him: Mr Counter. He counted heads, he counted desks and chairs, he counted how many pieces of chalk Miss Birnie had, and how many slates were in the room, and the books in the library cupboard too. We always bowed and said Good Morning but he'd be too busy counting and writing numbers in his book to take any notice. But this day he stood at the front of the class, fidgeting on his feet, and looked around without counting. *Good Morning*, we said, and his face oozed out a smile—you know the kind, like you've a pain in the peenie that you're trying not to let on about in case someone brings out the castor oil. Miss Birnie, she was smiling too, but anyone could see she really was happy. Pastor McNab shifted his fierce eyes from one to the next.

Children, said Miss Birnie, her palms clasped together, *the Inspector has come from Aberdeen to give out a prize. Yes, for the student who has been the hardest-working of you all.*

Well! Nothing like that had ever happened before. We all murmured and looked at each other.

The prize, Miss Birnie went on, was to be a book. Mr Counter held up a box awkwardly, and oozed a bit more. A book! And Miss Birnie was smiling right at me! Liza, from behind, pinched the back of my arm and if I hadn't been holding my breath I would have yelped, it hurt so much.

Mr Counter said my name and Miss Birnie said, *Yes, you, Meggie*, and Liza pinched me again and Elspet squealed, *Ooh, Ginger Meggie, that's you, that is!*, and my classmates were so rough about pushing me forward to glory that I went flying onto my knees in front of old Counter's shiny boots. But I didn't care, I didn't care at all, because I was to be given a book!

Miss Birnie beamed at me as she helped me up. She gently took the box from Mr Counter so he could shake my hand, and then she invited me to choose. My eyes must have been popping in disbelief because she nodded at me and gave the box a little shake. Yes, I could really choose!

I was tempted by a copy of the Bible, the real thing, a book for grown-ups. There was a hymn book, too, in the same dark blue covers, and a handsome volume of *A Child's Illustrated Treasury* with a colour picture of Noah's Ark on the front. And then I saw *my book*, grand and green, a wreath of blue flowers curling around the title. My hand shot out. I glanced at Pastor McNab and his thundery brow and I took it anyway.

My first ever book: *The Girls Forget-Me-Not Annual of Prose and Verse.*

Pah, said Granda from his chair by the fire when I showed it to Ma. She looked flustered and pleased and patted my arm a couple of times, and remarked they were very nice, the flowers on the front. She wanted to wrap it in calico and put it in her kist with Grunnie's old Bible. *Ye'll be wise to keep it out of harm's way, our Ginger Meggie.*

But I begged her no. I didn't want to hide it away safe, I wanted to read it, to fill my head with its words.

She looked at me, and she looked across to the fire, where Granda sat, hunched and grumbling over his tea, and she put the book on the dresser next to the cornflower milk jug of Grunnie Neish's that was there for an ornament and not to be used. She patted my arm again and sighed and told me I was a Clever Girl, but she didn't look as though this was a thing to be happy about.

That night, before the lantern was doused, I took the precious book down from the dresser and opened it up to the list of names at the front. Some I knew already—Walter Scott, Robert Burns, John Keats, Mary Shelley. But there were many stories and poems whose authors remained a mystery: 'by the Eltrick Shepherd', 'by the author of The Legend of Genevieve', 'by the Sylvan Voice', 'by the Lily of Lorn'. I turned the thick pages, shiny like the inside of a shell, admired the flowery patterns around the edges. I stopped to read lines here, lines there. I memorised words I did not know, to ask Miss Birnie their meaning. *Sanctity. Melancholy. Indelible.* I whispered them to myself, like a spell.

A heather bough cracked in the fireplace. Sparks shot out.

I looked up. Granda's eyes, red like coals, were watching me.

When Kitta came home for Hogmanay, she would see how things were. That everything had changed. That's what I thought as I counted down the days.

Da and the boys were back already and would not be leaving again until the new season, in March. They brought home money for Ma—and something else, I don't know what to call it. Restlessness? No, it was more than that, and less. I couldn't have explained it back then, and even now I canna be sure. At times they seemed glad to be home. They would glance around, blooming, the warmth of fire and family on their ruddy faces. But other times, well, they were bleak, and only when they took out the *Lily Maud* would their mood change. I would catch a shadow passing their faces as they came up from the boatie shore, and when I see that look in my mind now I think I do recognise it. Something like that was on the face of the child I was when I stood on the boatie shore and resigned myself that this was to be my life.

The lighter in spirits Da and the boys were, the more Granda Jeemsie seemed to hunker down, shrivelled and sour. His leg still pained him when he walked, but the wound on his hand had healed into a raised, shiny scar—just tender enough to remind him he was getting frail, he couldn't do all he once could do. But while bone and skin were mending, not so Granda's dark rage about being the old one left behind. Oh no, not one bit. In truth, he probably didn't want to leave Roanhaven, nor be a hired hand on a drifter instead of master of the *Lily Maud*—it wasn't that, no. It was finding himself outside the centre of the family's breathing that drew out his misery and pasted it onto all who were sorry enough to look his way.

Hurry home, Kitta, I prayed every night. Hurry home for Hogmanay and the world will be put to rights again. Everything will be as it should.

~

Kitta did not bring her kist with her, just a new bag made from canvas. It looked heavy, or perhaps it was just the way she carried it—held away from her body, as though the bag was itself a body that might easily be bruised. Inside were gifts she had brought home: some apples *all the way from The Sooth*, some knitted caps and mittens. I didn't know what else was in her bag but I would have liked to find out.

There was little time for us to talk, Kitta and me, because Hogmanay kept us flurrying. All the day Ma had us sweeping and cleaning, taking out ashes, emptying buckets, and at night the whole village waited for the Auld Kirk bell to ring in the New Year. Then it was 'Auld Lang Syne', handshakes and kisses, and waiting for the first footing, the first to cross our door with a lump of peat for luck. Bannockies and black buns, a wee glass of whisky for the men and a well-watered thimbleful for the women, which they poured into their tea. The New Year day was for the rounds—visiting neighbours and having them visit in return—and for some in the village it was ceilidh time. But not at number 8 Tiller Street. We'd to listen to Granda's thundering on about the evils of singing and dancing, his judgment on those who *invite the devil in with music*.

No-one was up early next morning but Kitta and me. Even Ma, always first to rise, was still abed, her breathing riffled with the lightest snore. Kitta made porridge, and then inclined her head, a sign for me to follow. Out into the cold we went, up to the braes, Crusoe darting round our legs. I was slow about it, and she grabbed the sleeve of my gansey and jerked me along behind her like she would a dawdling child. Something was bubbling out of Kitta. She was distracted, her eyes sliding left and right as though looking for who might be watching. I couldn't find her. Even when I looked her full in the face, she slipped away, preoccupied with secrets.

Change. More change. First with Granda Jeemsie. Then Da and the boys. And now Kitta—a girl from the town and no more a fisher lass. And I thought: when things change, something new enters the space you live in, something you must move with, turn to, chafe against, until you ease a new shape for yourself. But something is lost, too, in the changing, some small piece of your world gone for good.

In the months between Kitta's fourteenth birthday and Hogmanay, I had lost a part of my sister that I could never get back. And for that I mourned.

~

There was a place up on the braes where we would go as children: the remains of an old sheddie. Oftentimes we put our tins of bait in there, our spare grapplie hooks, while we clambered about, digging up lugworms. But it was also a place to hide, sheltered from the sight of anyone with opinions on what a child should be doing every minute of the day. Kitta, Elspet, Liza and I would sit there a wee while with our knitting, talking, laughing about this thing and that—never for long, mind, for we had work to do, were expected back with our pails of bait. But it was a place to breathe, a brief freedom snatched from duty.

I can see us there that New Year day:

The wind is roaring through my hair, the cold biting through my gansey, as Kitta pulls me across the braes and bundles me into the shelter of the three-sided sheddie. We have the place to ourselves, no-one else is out in wind like this, not when it is the morning after Hogmanay. I flop onto a pile of hessian, shivering, and tuck the folds of my skirt under my knees, Crusoe leaning in to my side. But the cold is forgotten in an instant when a blast of wind rattles the walls of the sheddie and whips at Kitta's clothes. Her skirt billows and collapses like something demented. An unexpected rustling sound. There's something under Kitta's skirt. I yank up the hem to see.

Gasp.

Before I can reach out and touch the stiff, lacy thing she is wearing, Kitta has pulled my hand away and gives me a Look she's learned from Ma. My brows rise in awe, but I am worried too, aye.

Kitta peeks out either side of the sheddie, although it's clear there's no-one here but the two of us. Then she looks at me, really looks, for the first time since she walked in the door the day before. Kitta! Oh, I've missed her. My sister, at last, is home.

Da-dah! She whips a package from underneath her gansey and offers it to me with a swirly flourish—a gift wrapped in pale wax paper and tied with sisal.

Well, go on, she says, pushing it into my hands and dropping, all a-rustle, to hug her knees.

I trail my fingers along the smooth paper, admiring the sheen on it. Like something you imagine rich people might give, something bought from a shop.

Come on, Ginger Meggie, Kitta urges, and she pulls at a corner, tearing the paper a little.

But I'll not be rushed, no I will not, and pull the package from her impatient fingers. Something soft and puffy is inside the wax paper. I remember Kitta's promise to knit me a scarlet gansey, but it canna be that, no. This is smaller, and lighter, and I can tell, without even seeing it, that it is something I will love more than any old scarlet gansey, even one knitted by Kitta. Finally, it's too much for me and I slip the string off and peel back the paper.

Oh!

Kitta jumps up and pulls me up with her, and she is laughing, laughing at the breathy wonder on my face as I try to take in what I am holding in my hands, the most beautiful thing I have ever seen.

It's yours, Ginger Meggie. Truly it's yours!

I pinch a corner between my fingers and shake it free of the paper and a long streak of purple silk flies out of the sheddie, up into the icy white of the sky, curling and falling, whipping like a sail unloosed. Such a wild riot of colour as never before seen on the braes of Roanhaven.

I canna speak.

Well? Kitta demands, reining in the renegade silk and winding it round and round my throat.

But ... I stare at her, dumbfounded. Again that unease. *But ...?*

This is not a thing for a kitchen quine to buy with her earnings. A kitchen quine sends home her wages like a dutiful daughter, keeping only a tiny fraction for the things she needs. A kitchen quine has but a few pence to call her own, just enough to buy wool to knit her drawers. So how ...?

Never ye mind, Ginger Meggie, Kitta says, so pleased with herself, so mysterious and sly. *Just never ye mind!*

~

It was a kind of madness, delicious but worrisome, this secret I now held to myself. This precious thing that was mine, the second precious thing that now I owned. But this one I couldn't put on the dresser. I'd to keep the silk scarf well hidden, aye. It was dangerous, and I'd to protect my sister, and myself. Imagine what folk would say if I paraded about the place in such a blaze of colour, drawing attention to my wanton self and *offending the Lord an' all else*, for the blue stripes of the Roanhaven fishwives' aprons was thought to be the only uniform *fit an' proper for a sober soul*. And as for Kitta: still I didn't know how she had come by such a thing, nor what it was she was wearing beneath her skirt, but I didn't have to be told that it wouldn't please Ma, that it would give Da a jamaica and send Granda into a white-hot rage. Kitta wasn't saying. She would put a finger to her lips and lift her brow, but she wouldn't be drawn, no.

Isn't easy to hide a thing when you have no space that's yours. I had no bed, no cupboard for my clothes, not an inch of the but-and-ben that belonged to me. None of us did. Everything we owned—clothes, caps, boots, drawers, knitting wool, needles, pins, combs—was bundled in together, any which way, and the large closet next to the boys' box bed held all of this in its bottom part, while Kitta and I slept in the top. So until the boys left again for the fish, and Kitta went back to Rowescroft House, there was nowhere safe I could hide my precious scarf. I'd thought of Ma's kist, where linens were stored in camphor, and the Bible, but what if Da needed some rags for the *Lily Maud*, or Ma wanted muslins to dress a wound? Such a risk I couldn't take.

I folded the silk over and over, smoothing the frothy air from it, flattening it into the smallest square I could make and wrapping the paper around it. And I stowed it in the netting shed, right in the back corner, further back even than Crusoe would go when he was fleeing from Granda. From time to time, when the men and boys were out on the *Lily Maud*, when Ma was off with her creel, I would take the package out and unwrap the wondrous thing that Kitta had given me, trailing the lush fabric across my skin, examining the finely woven fibres—a world apart from the scratchy wool we used to knit our clothes. *All the way from India*, Kitta had told me in a hush of awe. *All the quines wear silk in India. Their dresses an' shawls, the scarves on their heads, even their drawers!* And we looked at each other, trying to imagine such extravagance, such indulgence, and thinking what a scandalous, *perfect* place it must be, this place called India. When I returned to school and traced a path between Aberdeen and India on the globe of the world, I took into my head the notion that the further you got from Roanhaven, the more startling, the more colourful, the more exciting the world must become.

And I made another promise to myself, lambsie. As I huddled at the back of the netting shed in the briny must, I vowed that one day I would wrap the purple silk around my throat and stride out into the world, with no mind to those who might look askance or think ill of me. One day I would be brave and reckless. I would wear Kitta's beautiful scarf like a brand.

When we ushered in that New Year, what I wanted to celebrate was the close of the last, a year when everything had changed, and so little of it to my liking. Surely 1904 could do no worse. Or so I thought as Ma and I kissed Kitta goodbye at the end of Tiller Street.

Kitta made every appearance of listening to Ma's words about *duty* and *respectable quines* and *hard work to please the Lord an' your da*, but I caught the lift of her eyes, even if Ma missed it. I didn't think her beaming face had the world to do with *hard work*.

It pained me to see Kitta undistressed to be leaving us this time, and I was beset with all the worrying things I had done my best to ignore while she was home those few days. Kitta had told me about Rowescroft House and the long days in the kitchen with the cook, Mrs McBrewan, and the other kitchen girls, Benff's Kirsten and Lally's Janet, but for all she had shared with me, there was much she had not, and was not likely ever to. I remembered the look about her when she first came home, the look that told me, plain as flour, that Kitta had a life now that didn't include me.

There were no tears on her face when she waved and tramped off in the direction of Gadlehead. But she looked back over her shoulder and gave me a wink that would have mortified Ma if she had seen it.

~

Come March, Da and the boys once again signed on for the herring. And again Granda Jeemsie was left behind to *complain an' fish an' complain some more*, as I heard Ma tell Mackie's Peter when he put his head around the door to see if the kettle was singing.

Mackie's Peter had been blind in one milky eye for a long time, and now his good eye wasn't so good either.

Where the old gaak be?

Ma frowned as she handed him a tin mug of strong black tea. *Boatie shore, an' thank the Lord.*

Well, tell him from me he'll be needin' another mannie for Lily Maud *this year. I be too dweeble-eyed to be goin' to sea no more. And another still, he need, for I hear young Bandy Rossie has signed to a whaler in Gadlehead and is bound for Faroes afore the week be out.*

Ma sighed. *I don't know, isn't hardly anybody left, anybody to go with him on the* Lily. *Bandy Rossie's da has been to see him already, aye, and he'll be down in the mouth to hear about your eyes, sure enough.*

Down in the mouth! Mackie's Peter cackled like a farmer wifie's broody hen. *An' just when has Jeemsie Neish never been down in the mouth, eh lass? Eh, our Jeemsie's Belle?*

So that was how our year began, just Granda, Ma and me, with Granda fretting on how he would take the *Lily Maud* to sea when Roanhaven's men and boys were leaving one by one, one way or another. And when Granda was fretting, that was reason enough for Ma and me to be fretting too.

~

I remained wary of Granda, never knowing how his temper would be. When Ma went on rounds, I would pick whelks after school until darkness forced me inside. And Granda, he was mostly content to leave me well alone, worrisome quinie that I was.

One night I crept in and found him nursing his hand, his face pained.

The tide is flowin', quinie. Fetch me some sea water.

I took the lantern and a bucket and trudged to the boatie shore, but I wasn't gracious about it, no. I was grumping and mumping all the way. Why hadn't I pulled on an extra gansey or wrapped a shawl around me? I barrelled my head to the sea wind, pulled off my boots, and waded in to dip the bucket into the icy sea.

When I returned, Granda sprinkled water on his palm and rubbed it into his hand, his arm, as though it were one of Unty Jinna's unguents and not just water from the sea. He had no time for Unty Jinna and her herbs and roots.

Ah, he sighed. And then he waved a finger at me. *Mind ye never draw the water but from a flowin' tide.*

I put the kettle on the fire to boil, shivering, shivering. I didn't want to sit there with Granda, so I pulled on another gansey, an old one of Will's. When I took Granda his tea, I could see, by the fire's light, that the gansey was on inside out. *Ach!* I went to pull it over my head, put it to rights, but Granda clamped a hand on my arm.

Stop it, ye foolish quinie! D'ye want to be takin' the devil to the inside?

I stared at his great lumpish paw, and pulled away. I should have held my tongue. I should have.

That's just superstition, that is. Miss Birnie says superstition is the friend of an ignorant mind.

A hush. A hush like I had never heard, ever. And then the rushing of blood into Granda's pasty face. He seethed and he boiled.

Iggernant! Iggernant! It's iggernant stranger-women with not an ounce of sense about them what will bring us all to ruin. The old ways is what keeps the devil from your red-heidit self, quinie. Isn't your Miss Birnie! Pah!

A spray of disgust hit my face.

Miss Bir-nie, Miss Bir-nie. His girly mimicking voice. *Wait till your da come back. We'll see about your Miss Birnie then.*

Bluster threats. Da wouldn't be back till Christmas. But I took care to open my *Forget-Me-Not Annual* only when Granda was gone from the house, and not to let him see the other books Miss Birnie was lending me to read. Books of her own, they were, from home.

He'd already taken on a rage when he found me reading with a lantern in the netting shed with Crusoe one night. He grabbed the book off me and held it up, swinging between his finger and his yellow thumb.

An' what kind of blether this be?

Oliver Twist, I told him. *By Mister Charles Dickens.*

Oo-hoo. An' what kind of story has Mis-ter Charles Dickens to learn ye?

I thought for a moment and then I said, *About bein' poor. An' about thieves. An' London.* And if he'd given me a chance, I would have thought a bit more and I might have said, *It's about what happens when ye want too much.*

But Granda was shouting. *Foolish quinies* and *folk from The Sooth with the devil in their soul* and *folk as'll take ye straight off to hell* and he dashed the book on the sand and waved a finger in my face.

Town folk an' fisherfolk never do mix. An' town folk from The Sooth are the devil's work.

He stomped into the dark and I rescued Miss Birnie's precious book.

Aye, I would have to be more careful.

~

He found his crew, Granda did, and a small gaggle it was, but he was content, even pleased, to have on board the *Lily* those who were blessed of the Lord. *Better a simple one*, I heard him tell Ma, *who doesn't question what be good an' decent than a mannie with too many thoughts in his head an' not an ounce of sense in any of them.*

And while Granda sang his hymn to ignorance, I tried to gather as many thoughts in my head as Miss Birnie could give me before I reached that line of chalk marking the end of my schooling. What would I do then? Whatever would I read?

My people were big on morality, lambsie, they prided themselves on that.

Even very young children in Roanhaven had a vague sense of what was proper and what wasn't, bred into them from the cradle. I think it was this that had made me hide the purple silk, and also made me anxious about Kitta. But I was thirteen, and it didn't occur to me that the hushed conversations outside the Auld Kirk, talk that stopped when Ma came out, had anything to do with my family. I just didn't put it all together back then.

Now, when I watch the past play out before my eyes, I understand something else: that morality and *what was proper* were not always the same thing.

Brukie's Sandy is galloping across the boatie shore with that peculiar rolling gait he has. I once asked Ma what was wrong with Brukie's Sandy and she clipped the side of my head and said, *Hush your mouth, Brukie's Sandy is a child of God, an' who are ye, Meggie Duthie, to sit in judgment on the Lord's work?*

I raise my pail of lugworms as he draws near. *Ay ay, Brukie's Sandy!*

He waves back, his arm whirling like a wing. I know what he's going to say. *Ginger Meggie cross your leggie.* Laughing like it's the funniest thing. He adores Kitta, Brukie's Sandy does, he always calls her *Pretty Kitty.* He gazes on her like she is some beautiful sea creature, something better than a human girl.

But a puzzlement is on his face. *Pretty Kitty look sad, Ginger Meggie.*

Sad? An' how would ye know that, Brukie's Sandy, when Kitta is far away across the other side of Gadlehead?

But he shakes his head and is off and away to the *Lily Maud.*

All the way home I am wondering what it is has put Kitta in Brukie's Sandy's head. I should have guessed.

The door is closed but voices leak from inside. One of them is Kitta's! But my joy quickly drains away. Kitta home? Without a message to say she is coming? Whatever it is that's happening, this I know: a kitchen quine home without being sent for is a kitchen quine who has been returned in disgrace.

I ease the door open a wee crack, peek through quietly, but

Granda has *the lugs of a loon*, so he always tells us.

An' ye can get yourself inside, quinie, or I'll have words for your sorry self an' all!

I sidle in and look from one to the next. Granda, his face as scarlet as the comb on a bubblyjock. Ma, upset but tight-faced. Unty Jinna by the window, keeping a wary watch for anyone passing by. And Kitta, my Kitta, still in her hat-for-best and travelling apron, fearless as always but the colour of bleached calico. I reach out my hand, but Ma is firm. *Not now, Meggie.*

My eyes are drawn to the fire. There, squat and bulky on the hearthrug, is the new kist Kitta had taken with her to Rowescroft House. That's when I know for sure that she will not be going back.

~

No-one would tell me what it was Kitta had done. Ma said I must pay mind to my own sins and leave others to theirs, which just made the worry worse. What sins?

When I asked Kitta, she told me she had done nothing, and since she had done nothing there was nothing more she wished to say on the matter. *So there, Ginger Meggie.* I wanted to shake her until all the secrets came spilling out, but she could be as stubborn as Granda Jeemsie when she felt herself slighted, and it seemed the whole village had taken to the task of slighting my sister. I couldn't really blame her for feeling set-upon.

There were rumours going about, each one worse than the one before.

Kitta was lazy at her work.

She had torn a linen shirt.

She had allowed a joint of meat to burn.

She had stolen a silver thimble.

It didn't seem possible that any of them could be right, but the village couldn't believe that all could be wrong.

The most shameful story came from Isobel Ross, who put it

about that Kitta was *in a certain way*, causing a rift between the Duthies and the Rosses that would never be mended. I huffed all the way home to tell Kitta.

I'm not pregnant, Ginger Meggie! Kitta said, but was disinclined still to confide in me.

I wouldn't be put off this time. *Then why are they sayin' that?*

I don't know, do I? she said wearily. *I'll tell ye this, Ginger Meggie: takes more than keepin' friends to get pregnant. Anybody what doesn't know that doesn't know anythin'.*

I frowned as she turned away. I remembered what the tinkie lasses had told Liza and Liza had told us. I knew more than Kitta thought I did about what *getting pregnant* involved. But what did Kitta mean? What *friends*?

I hugged to myself nagging fears about Kitta's disgrace. That it had something to do with the silk she had given me, the lace beneath her dull blue skirt, the look on her face that had made her a stranger to me. When the truth came out later, I learned a thing about myself: that my instincts for sensing the spine of trouble are as fine as the point on a gullie knife.

I didn't know what Kitta did in the hours when I was at school. She probably didn't want to leave the house at all, not alone, for there was none who would talk to her, not a quinie who would dare be seen to pass the time, not a loon who'd give her the eye of respect. But after school, the two of us were together, reddin' Granda's lines, collecting bait, splitting whiting to dry—and if it were not for the cloud of not knowing hanging over me, I would have felt complete. Like our lives had been wrung free and clean of their worrisome changes and put back to the place they were before Kitta left.

Come with me, I begged one morning. *Miss Birnie won't mind to have ye back in class. And we are reading* Rob Roy. *Oh, it's grand.*

But Kitta shook her head and Ma bid me to go, and I didn't like the grimness on her face as she said it.

When I came home, Kitta's kist was on the hearthrug again.

~

Although I thought I knew proper from not, it was a puzzle to me then, a mystification, *why* some things were thought proper and some things were not. And how it could be that a thing once thought not-proper could miraculously become otherwise.

It was Kitta's plan to go to the fish that had caused her to be taken from school, from home, from me, and put into service in that awful place. Going to the fish was *not respectable*. A year later, here she was, being granted her wish: arled to Messrs Nicol & Mair, curers of Gadlehead, and bound for the Lerwick season. And all with Ma's blessing. Was it because the span of a year had given Ma time to get used to the idea? Or because Da and the boys had seen *with their own eyes* how hard and long the gutting quines worked, the modest, decent lives they led? Or was it simply that the shame of Kitta's sins, whatever they were, was greater than the shame of her being a gutting girl? No-one would say. Ma was busy with packing Kitta's kist, the things she must take for a spell in the Shetlands summer of three months—longer if there was work beyond that. And Granda was souring by the fire, disgusted with the whole affair. *Let it be on your head*, he told Ma. *I wash my hands on ye all!*

All I knew was that Kitta was leaving again, going to the fish, and that I wanted to go with her.

~

A telegram came. A telegram! It was not the first ever to arrive at Roanhaven: this was the way all the curers notified their quines of the time of departure, and there were several local fisher girls now signed on to the herring. But it was a first for number 8 Tiller Street. It lay on the table, so much folded and unfolded and smoothed to be read that the faint words were in danger of disappearing completely. Granda Jeemsie glowered at it, as though it was the work of the devil come to his door.

SUNDAY 11AM STOP PORT DOUGAL PIER GADLEHEAD STOP ST NINIANS STOP

The season had been under way since March in the Western Isles, but Kitta was just in time to join the next leg, in the Shetlands, replacing a girl, sick, on a team out of Aberdeen. Then the boats would make their way to home waters in autumn, with the curers set up close by in Fraserburgh and the Gadle, until everything moved further south.

I read the words over and over, trying to make myself believe that, come Sunday, Kitta really was going to be sailing across the sea to the wide world we had both dreamed about.

She leaned on the table, her face close to mine. *Ye'll wear those words away, Ginger Meggie.* She flicked the long fringe out of my eyes.

St Ninian's *must be a big ship for all those lasses an' every one of them with a kist. How big d'ye think it will be? How many lasses will be on it, d'ye think?*

I don't know, do I? Kitta twisted her plait around her fingers. *I haven't seen the* St Ninian's, *have I? But*—and her eyes were round like pennies—*there are ships in the Gadle bigger than a dozen whales, bigger than anythin' ye can think of, Ginger Meggie. An' Clementina Slater says there be hundreds of girls sailing to Lerwick every time a ship leaves.*

Hundreds!

She reached over and took the soiled telegram from my hands. A fine line cleaved her brows for a second, and then it was gone.

I put my arm around her. *A ticket to the wide world, Kitta! Just think!*

She tossed back her plait, but that little line of worry threaded through her forehead again.

What if I canna keep up? she whispered. *I've seen them, Meggie, seen them at the yards in the Gadle. Clementina Slater an' the other quinies doin' the gutting. You canna imagine how fast they are.*

Ye've been to the yards? When? I demanded.

A few times is all. When I'd to go to the Gadle for messages, Mrs McBrewan sent me sometimes. An' on my Sundays, at the pier, Clementina showed me how to do it, an' I've been practising on dock leaves—ye know, holdin' them like a herrin', knifin' them with a gullie. But it's not the real thing, is it?

I stared at Kitta. Did Ma know she'd been to the yards? Or the pier when she was supposed to be in kirk?

Ye've been practising? Well, that's good, eh. An' ye'll soon be quick enough, quick as Clementina Slater for sure.

In, twist, flick. In, twist, flick. Kitta showed me the action, miming the fish held in one hand, the gullie knife in the other.

See? Ye've got it right already!

But those quines, they can gut fifty herrin' in a minute. Sixty, some of them.

I glanced at her, thinking she was teasing, but Kitta's face wasn't lightsome. Still I didn't believe her. Fingers canna move that fast, especially fingers holding a sharp knife, a wet, slippery fish. I looked down at Kitta's hands, still miming the action of gutting a herring: the plunge of the pointed blade into the throat, a sharp twist to remove the gills and guts, the toss of the gutted fish into the right murlin—all one stroke, smooth as can be. In, twist, flick.

I had something to give Kitta, warm in the pocket of my skirt. I took it out.

Here, I said. It was balanced on the palm of my hand, my other cupped over it to surprise her with this ordinary thing that I'd found on the heather moors. *A present for ye, Kitta. For luck. For protection.*

Oooh, show me! Come on, Ginger Meggie!

I unfurled my curved fingers slowly, one by one—ever the one for drama, me. There, on my palm, a wide feather, white, with a vein of blue running through the shaft.

Kitta smiled. Disappointed, probably, that it was just a feather. But she didn't yet know how extraordinary it was, this ordinary thing.

Guess where I found it. Go on, guess!

She shrugged. *I don't know, do I?*

No, an' ye'll never guess, neither. So there, Kitta Duthie.

She ran her finger along the glossy vanes of the feather, then looked up. *Well?*

Well! When I was walking over the moors, Crusoe chased a baby rabbit to its burrow and I'd to pull him out an' save the wee thing, an' when I put my arm in deep, right up past the elbow of my gansey, this is what I found. An albatross feather! An albatross feather in a rabbit hole!

She smiled at me again. *An' is that lucky, then, Ginger Meggie, is it? Will a feather keep me safe?*

Still she didn't see. *Just think*, I explained, *think of it. It's come all the way across the sea, this feather, an' blown up to the moors an' into a place it doesn't belong, never to be seen again, never to return. But I found it, Kitta, see?*

She was looking at me, looking hard, but I still wasn't sure she understood.

I found it an' I brought it back, back to be near the sea again. I couldn't stop beaming. *It means ye'll come back, Kitta. I will always find ye, no mind what stranger-place ye go. Ye'll always come back to where ye belong because I will find ye, see?*

Kitta took the feather and turned away, holding it up to catch a stream of sunlight slanting in from the door.

D'ye see? I asked, anxious I still hadn't explained it well enough. *D'ye not like it?*

She nodded, and when she spoke I could barely hear her. *Oh aye, our Meggie, I see. I do believe it's the luckiest feather that anybody's ever seen.*

Kitta crossed to the fire and threw up the lid of the kist, rummaging among the things that Ma had neatly packed, tossing aside clothes, wool, cooking pans, dishes carefully wrapped in bedding. She found a handkerchief to fold around the feather and stowed it safely in the shottle, the neat little compartment that held needles and buttons and her comb and pins.

There now, she said, *just the place to keep it safe, in a sea kist that will cross the sea with me.*

I helped her fold the clothes again, to tuck them in as Ma had done, and I wondered where it was, the lacy white thing that Kitta was wearing at Hogmanay. No sign of it among the thick, warm woollens she was taking with her. I wanted to ask but was afraid she wouldn't say, that it was something bound up in the puzzle of why she had been sent home, and was now to be allowed to go to the fish. Things she had decided I wasn't to know. It was too painful, the thought of being refused again when once there was nothing Kitta would keep from me.

When everything had been packed away, she gave me a hug, then took my face in both hands. *Bless ye for the charm, Meggie mine, an' ye'll bring me luck for sure, no mind what folk say about ginger heads!*

~

Did we know and had just forgotten? Or was it a story that somehow we'd never heard? When I look back on it now, it seems that our lives were so steeped in the lore of the sea that we must have heard the tale of the soulbirds. But if I had known then that when sailors drown, their restless souls fly away on the wind and find home in the bodies of albatross, I don't think I would have given such a charm to Kitta, nor she taken it from me.

~

Ma wouldn't hear of me going to the fish. *Ye've another year yet of school, at least, an' ye're too young, Meggie, too young by far.*

No surprise. And in truth I was torn between wanting to go with Kitta and wanting to stay in school. But I held my breath to ask for something else I dearly wanted.

Can I go tomorrow? Can I go to Gadlehead to wave our Kitta goodbye?

Ye'll not be going anywheres. A growl from Granda's chair by the fire.

No, quinie, no, I've to see the agent an' settle with him an' get Kitta away, an' ye've school—an' work to do here.

Work? Aye, and it seemed to me that it was always for Granda that I must work: baiting his lines, cleaning his boots, cooking his supper. *Pah*, I said under my breath.

That night Kitta tossed about next to me in the closet bed and I could not sleep. There was much I wanted to say, and more I wanted to ask her, but she wouldn't answer my whispers.

We rose before sunrise. Ma and Kitta were walking to Gadlehead. A cart had already come to take the kist with KITTA NEISH DUTHIE neatly carved into the curve across the top.

Will ye miss me, Ginger Meggie? Kitta asked, ruffling my already wild hair.

Course not, I told her, affecting a face as sour as Granda's. But then it was time for her to go. Kitta was leaving and this time I knew what leaving was. I knew it would make her someone else, that more of her would be lost to me for always. She was leaving again and I couldn't bear it.

Come, quinie, Ma said, and waited outside the door.

Goodbye, goodbye, Ginger Meggie mine, Kitta sang softly. She disentangled herself from me and looked around. Granda had his back to her and was saying nothing.

Hash yourself, quinie! Ma, impatient to get away.

Kitta squared her shoulders, blew me a kiss and marched out the door, turning only to poke out her tongue at Granda's back.

Later, when Granda stumped off down to the boatie shore, I slipped into the netting shed and stroked Crusoe's soft head, and wrapped the two of us in Kitta's purple silk.

~

Ma was not one for crowds but her description of the ship's leaving sounded like something from a storybook to me, a tale about kings and queens and parades. The pier thronging with a cheering crowd waving and throwing paper streamers to the girls on deck. A band playing, the girls singing, swaying arm in arm. Pedlars with pies and chestnuts and paper twists of cockles roaming through the crowds. People swarming, jostling, everywhere!

Ma seemed overawed still by the whole spectacle.

An' when the ship steamed away, oh, the tears. Hundreds of people cryin'!

Did ye cry, Ma? Did ye cry, too?

Course not, she sniffed.

Granda cleared his throat and I wanted to tell him, there and then, to hush his mouth. I knew I wasn't going to like what he had to say.

Godless, the lot of them. Town folk with no sense nor decency.

Well, I would, I declared. *I would have cried an' cried an' never stopped till I could see the ship no more!*

Foolish quinie, Granda grunted.

Crusoe howled outside, and it comforted me to hear it, as though the way I was feeling inside was pouring out of him for all to hear.

An' shut that beast up, that wretched fulpie!

He was bending over the fire, puffing it with the bellows, and in spirit with my sister I showed his back my tongue.

Every day it seemed that Granda Jeemsie's mood darkened a little more, and nothing could please him, if ever anything did. I was sorry for the crew of the *Lily Maud*—old Sailor Finney, and those boys, Turton's Jock and Brukie's Sandy. Sorrier still for Ma and me.

I envied Ma her tramp to the country, knowing I would be bearing the brunt of Granda's temper alone. And I told her so when I helped her load up with her creel.

Now, just ye mind, Meggie, she said vaguely.

Who could blame her, anxious to be away?

I was anxious for Granda to be away, away to sea on the *Lily Maud* this night, and I counted the hours till dusk. Unty Jinna and Unty Leebie would help him down to the boatie shore with the lines and I would watch from the roof of the netting shed and think myself blessed to be *the accursed reid-heid*.

But before then, there was much to do, to make ready for Granda to be away, and his temper was so bitter that I wondered how it ever was that I had thought to see a softer shade in it when he was laid up last winter.

I staggered through the door with washing just dried on the gorse up behind the village: Granda's blankets and ganseys, his thick seaboot stockings and woollen combinations. He was standing by the hearth, and watched as I unwound the clothes and linens that I'd wrapped around my arms to stop them flying off in the wind.

Need mendin', some of those ganseys do. An' where're my gloves, quinie? What have ye done with my gloves? An' ye've took my tobacco somewhere. New tin, just new. Where's that new tin, eh?

I don't know, do I? I said rudely, and got a raised hand for my trouble. A warning.

After sorting the washing and looking for Granda's gloves and tobacco, I sat by the fire with my needles, wool and a pile of ganseys.

Fetch me tea, quinie, he said.

And while I made tea, Granda was grumbling still about the tobacco, which wasn't the tin he wanted, and what had I done with the new tin?

Just when I thought I could take no more of his mumping, he fixed me with a sly look I'd seen before when he had something particular he wanted to say.

Ye needn't think to be leavin' like your sister do. Another limmer this family canna have. Ye'll be here, in this house, an' stayin' here, quinie.

I sucked in my breath, shocked. My ill prospects of ever leaving were enough to make me weep, but to call Kitta such a name! His own granddaughter!

Aye, ye needn't be looking like that, quinie. Your sister has shamed this family, shamed us all with her runnin' about with sailors when she should be in kirk and prayin'. Runnin' about an' takin' gifts. That's what she says, eh. Do she, eh. Gifts? Pah! A price like another, an' just another name for it.

I opened my mouth but he was gathering steam.

Gadlehead be no place for quinies, no place at all. Town folk, they be not like decent fisherfolk. An' sailors from stranger-boats—pah! They come from all round the world, godless places, an' think to sway a sober quinie's head with funcy things. Aye, I seen it afore an' it all lead one way, to trouble. Sooner or later, to trouble, aye. An' all from strangers with funcy things.

He was out of breath, Granda was, and a little froth of spit was in the corners of his mouth, and I had never before hated him as much as I did right then.

Ye shouldn't call our Kitta a limmer! My hands clenched as I spoke. *Ye shouldn't say that. Ye don't know anythin'!*

He looked at me, narrowing his small, pale eyes. *An' just what do YE know about it, quinie, eh? Eh?*

I checked my words. The truth was, I knew nothing much at all, but I didn't want to tell Granda that, to give him the smallest thing. I decided to show him my back, the greatest mark of disrespect I could offer, and as I marched out the door I could hear him shouting *The very devil!* and thumping the table with his fist, and I knew Ma would be angry with me because I had crossed a line.

~

Later, when I sat with Crusoe on the braes, looking out to sea, I realised that everything they had thought to keep from me, everything Kitta had refused to say, Granda had just told in his clumsy, savage way. I could put things together now and make sense of what had happened: his talk of sailors from stranger-boats and Kitta's brief mention of *friends*; his insinuations about *gifts*, and the mystifying finery. It was always in his nature to see a shadow and call it the devil.

Maybe I am being unfair, lambsie. Granda Jeemsie was a man of his time, and most folk then were inclined to see the world as he did, always to imagine the worst. Could be that Kitta's sins were no more than a bit of innocent flirting with foreign sailors when she went to the pier on her hours off, a few trinkets given to a pretty girl. I don't know. But word had got back to Rowescroft House. See, it wasn't only fisherfolk who would believe the worst of a girl.

As I sat up there on the braes, I thought of the purple silk hidden away in the netting shed, and how funny it is, the way things happen. Kitta had taken a gift from a stranger and made it a gift to me, and she had paid a price for the handsome thing. But you know, in a strange, roundabout way, the price she paid had also bought her freedom.

When Ma got back from her rounds, she could see at once how it was with Granda and me. But she was sick, too sick to press, too sick to scold me as she normally would do. Her throat was coughed raw, a rattle in the ribs, the curve of her spine worse than ever.

I wasn't talking to Granda, not since the day he called our Kitta a limmer. But our usual conversation was only ever thready, so the fact that I was ignoring him likely passed him by. So much for me taking a stand, lambsie. In any case, there was much to do with Ma sick, and I was too worried for her to let much else bother me. Even school had to wait. Unty Jinna had me scurrying into the moors, looking for roots and special leaves, and then I had to clean them just so and steep them in boiling water over the fire and strain decoctions for Ma to drink. And there were meals to be cooked, the house kept spotless, the clothes washed, and all that had to be done to get Granda away to sea. *Good riddance* was what I said under my breath, *an' don't come back*—soundless words that shamed me, for it was a terrible thing to wish of a fisher whose life was always at the mercy of the sea. *I didn't mean it, not really,* I told God. *I will be better, an' not complain. I will talk to Granda if I must.*

Ma regained a little strength. The racking cough eased to a dry scratching. But there was no question of her taking up the creel again, not for a good while to come.

We need neeps, quinie, neeps an' eggs, an' ye're ready now, aye?

How impressed I was, impressed with myself, to be given the responsibility of taking on Ma's rounds, even though it meant more time from school.

Ma suggested a short tramp. *Just to the near farms, quinie. Two days is all.*

~

The creel Ma gave me was smaller than hers by far and my weight of fish only a portion of what she carried on her rounds, but the load on my back, the drag of the straps on my shoulders, my blistered feet—aye, it was a sore experience. However did Ma manage?

There were gifts to ease the way. The smell of smokies, comforting, warm, and I minded what Ma always told me: *What's in our creel is good an' honest an' somethin' to be proud to sell.* All across the moors, the bright autumn yellow of the whins and broom was a lightsome sight. And for most of the way I had the company of other fishwives on their rounds, and then a tinkie wifie and her two quinies with their brass trinkets and armfuls of heather. Ma had never held with the bad feeling some had for tinkies. *They have their livin' to get an' their way to make, just like all of us*, she said. *An' if their wish is to roam in their gurdy vans an' mind their own ways, what's the harm of it?* One of the wee tinkie lasses chattered all the way, and I thought of Kitta, chattering with her girls far across the sea, all of them with soft white hands wet with guts and blood.

At night we made our wee camp and lit a fire in a circle of stones. Never before, all the times I'd gone tramping with Ma, had it worried me to sleep beneath the stars. I would creep as close to the fire as she would let me go, pull my shawl about my face, tuck my legs under my skirt, and drift to the sounds of wings flurrying and twigs snapping, owlies hooting and calling. Peaceful, and I was never afraid. But the tinkie wifie took it into her head to warn me as we shared a bannock and some strong black tea.

A lass shouldn't be on her own round here, nor any woman neither.

I thought maybe she didn't know the Buchan area so well. *Oh, we are never alone for long, there's always other wifies on their rounds. Or travellers. An' Ma says none will bother us on our way.*

She shook her head. *Don't trust there will be none to bother. There are bad men on these moors. Isn't travellers ye should fear, quinie.*

Oh, no, I hurried to say, though I knew most of the fishwives were afraid of the tinkie men, with their colourful clothes, their long hair. *We hold no ill will for travellers, no.*

Wasn't a traveller who dragged our Sarie away. She looked at the older of the two quinies, the one who, I now realised, hadn't spoken at all. *Fine, decent farmer loon, that one were, from a family what would say never a word against him.*

What the tinkie wifie told me put a different skin on the night. I slept with an eye open, one ear alert to footfall, human breathing.

Keep a sharp gullie knife in your boot, quinie, the tinkie wifie bid me as we parted in the morning, and she fretted when I told her Ma had not given me one.

~

I was not so good at haggling with the farmer wifies who bought our smokies. I had watched Ma do it, but it wasn't as easy as it looked, no.

Smaller than afore, said the wifie at Peterslie Farm, looking down her nose and setting her fists on her hips.

I frowned. *I don't think so …*

Canna give ye more than four dozen, an' ye can tell your ma so from Lochie's Katie. And she took a step back as though to put an end to the bargaining and I could go if I wished.

Aye, I said, knowing she'd not be budging an inch when she had one so green as me to deal with.

They had this way about them, those wily women, and I wasn't their match, not even near to it. How Kitta would laugh and call me *plucked like a chuckney.*

All the way home, I feared Ma would look at my load and think it less than it ought to be, but she unpacked it all on the table, the neeps and tatties, the butter, the eggs padded in straw, and pulled me to her, wheezing. *Ye've done well, Ginger Meggie, aye. Well enough for your first time out.* She reached over and smoothed my tangled hair. *Ye're our Fish Meggie now.*

It was the finest praise she could give me, and I couldn't speak for pride. I tried it on myself for the feel of it. *Fish Meggie.* And I wondered would it stick, this new name that spoke of what I had managed to do instead of the curse I was born with?

~

I couldn't find Crusoe that night. Ma had not seen him nor heard his bark for more than a day, and she'd been cross that I might have taken him with me to the farms when she'd warned me never to.

We searched all along the boatie shore for him, Elspet, Liza and me. We called his name, we clapped our hands, but we dared not whistle so close to the boats because of what the fishers always said: *Whistle an' ye never know what will answer!*

Nothing.

I stood up above the scaur where you could see right along the boatie shore and across to Tiller Street, and the other way up to the moors beyond. There was Elspet on her hands and knees, peering under a barnacled hull. Liza, kicking along the shore, her feet bare and her long skirt and apron tucked up into her drawers, calling for Crusoe from time to time when she remembered. A figure out on the water, on the *Lily Maud*, scrubbing the timbers with a stiff brush: Brukie's Sandy. Over there, Unty Leebie, spreading ganseys and seaboot stockings over the gorse to dry.

No Crusoe.

On the walk back home, I passed Granda. It was foolish to ask but I did it anyway.

Granda, have ye seen where the fulpie be?

It was in my head that maybe he'd kicked Crusoe again, but he wasn't likely to say so, now, was he? But I'd asked everyone else in the village, and none had a thing to tell me.

Granda spat on the sand. *Pah!* he said, folding his thick arms across his chest. *I don't know where your wretched beastie be. A long way from here if God be good!*

I didn't like what I saw in his face. Something mean, it was. Something satisfied.

Today your mother caught me, lambsie. It's a dismal thing to be old, always having to explain yourself.

I canna say she was encouraging about the birthday gift I am writing for you. She glanced at my book and frowned. *How long has this been going on?* she wanted to know. *Not long,* I said, though it's been months of *not long.* She didn't ask to read it, no, she just looked at me with that way she has and shrugged.

What's the point in raking up the past?

It made me wonder: what past does Kathryn remember?

And she told me I shouldn't be *upsetting myself.* Nor you.

It's her story, too, I said, and how prim that sounds when I think of it now. Aye, listen to me, taking the high moral ground, defending a daughter's right to know.

The truth is this: your mother knows only a fraction of the things it will upset me to write. She doesn't know because I've never told her.

I had nursed to myself hopes that Kitta would soon be home. That her spell away at the fish would be a temporary thing. That it was a way of getting her out of Roanhaven for a wee while and then she would come back. But it was a boom year for the herring, and the curers needed every team. Messrs Nicol & Mair sent word: Kitta's team would be kept on after the Lerwick season, following the shoals like the drifters did. Da and the boys were being sent to Rosehearty, Kitta's team to Fraserburgh.

Why the Broch? I grumbled to Ma. *Why could she not be sent to the Gadle, closer to us?* Even in Roanhaven we knew Gadlehead was overrun with fishworkers. The town folk were frantic, and gleeful too—it was one of the best herring seasons ever.

They go where they be told to, Ma said. *The curers have thousands of workers, they canna be bothered about families.*

Glum, I was. Kitta away. Crusoe still missing, not a sign of him anywhere. Every morning, every night, I would go looking, calling him—up and down the grid of streets, along the boatie shore, up to the scaur, all along the braes.

Picked up by stranger-boat, no doubt about it. Unty Jinna was inclined to blame the ills of the village on all but those in it.

Runned away, your wee doggie did, said Elspet, always one for the obvious.

Liza agreed, and she looked so smug that I thought for a moment she might know something, but no, she was just pleased that Ginger Meggie (Liza never called me anything but) had had one of her airs and graces knocked out of her.

Runned away … runned away … I loved Crusoe. I'd done my best to look after him. Why do the things we love have to run away?

~

After Fraserburgh, Kitta was sent south to Great Yarmouth on the train. The train! This was the last of the fishing stations for the season. By December it was over and the crews and teams had broken up, returned to their homes until the first of the New Year's run. Da, Sailor Wattie and the boys came back from Lowestoft, and Kitta would soon be home. Would she be staying, I wanted to know, or going back to the fish in the New Year? But Ma was busy with Christmas and Hogmanay and much else besides. *Hush your mouth, quinie,* she said, *an' get those neeps an' tatties scraped.* No answer? I took it as a good sign.

Oh, the joyous homecoming I had imagined. Kitta and I would escape to the sheddie up on the braes, wrapped up warm in our shawls, and she would tell me about the sea journey, the gutting, the quines she worked with, where she lived, what Lerwick was like, and the Broch, and the faraway Sooth—all about the wide world beyond the boatie shore. Her disgrace would be forgotten and she would be welcomed back, accepted, as gutting girls now were. Respected as girls who worked hard for their families.

There was still much I had to learn, lambsie. Life goes on, true as the tide, washing up old and new like wrack from the sea. For all that I had railed against the new that had come among us, I had begun to think it a good thing that in time the old would lose its grip. But here's the twist: sometimes the things you hope most will change are those, stubborn, that don't.

When other people were around, Kitta was her usual lively self. And defiant. Girls who overheard her funny stories were envious. Anyone who'd thought the worst of her, who'd thought to quell her spirit—well, they were disappointed. But up on the braes, it was different.

I watched her. What was she seeing as she gazed, so quiet, out across the boatie shore? I thought of the edginess in Da and the boys when they returned, like they were not all here, like they'd left the rest of themselves behind in some faraway place more to their liking than home.

D'ye miss it? I asked her eventually. *D'ye wish ye were back there? Somewhere else?*

She snapped back to life, my Kitta again, and half snorted, half laughed. *I don't miss the guts, Meggie mine! But this ... this place ...* She waved an arm, drawing an arc around the village.

What d'ye mean, this place? Home?

Home! That snorting laugh again. And then Kitta sighed, cupping her chin in mittened hands, and told me about her homecoming.

~

A gutting girl, rumpled and weary and hefting an overstuffed calico bag, kisses her friends goodbye at the station in Gadlehead and looks around her. She doesn't expect anyone to be waiting but she has discovered there is something about railway platforms, something about the bustle of people with straining necks and anxious faces. Something that makes you foolish and hopeful that someone will be watching for you.

No-one knows when she is to arrive, so no-one, of course, is here.

Jamming her woollen hat over her long plaits, she begins the walk home to the village. Her kist, well labelled, will follow her by and by.

As she nears Roanhaven, a bent figure joins the road from a seaward path, an old man burdened with a wicker basket of fish.

Eh, Piper Stewie! Can I help ye with your load? the girl calls, shouldering her own bag the better to free her hands.

The old man stops, glad of the prospect of help. He sets the basket down, he wipes his eyes with his sleeve and he looks her up and down to see who it is, this youthful traveller who knows his name. And then he stiffens, he takes up the basket again. Inclining his chin in the girl's direction, he spits on the ground.

~

There was no question about whether Kitta was going back to the fish. She was a gutting girl now. She was just biding her time until the season began again, like Da and the boys. But it turned out that her wait would be longer than theirs, because Da would not consent to her signing on for the early season in the Western Isles. *Too far from home*, he said, *ye'll begin in the Shetlands, closer by*, and that was his final word. All Kitta's tears and the stamp of her foot did no good at all. She was frantic she would lose her place in the team—such a good team, it was, one of the best—but luck was with her there. Clementina Slater, in Aberdeen, was laid low with measles, and the third member of Kitta's team had married a Gadlehead cooper at Hogmanay and was in no hurry to leave just yet.

What am I to do with myself till May? Kitta wailed.

Well, Ma had no intention, none at all, of seeing Kitta wanting for something to do. Kitta would tramp the rounds with the creel. She would do her share of shelling and baiting. She would make herself useful when Unty Jinna had sheets and fine linens from the big houses to wash and dry. And she would *get that mumpin' frown from her face for what did she have to be feelin' sorry for herself about?*

Whenever we could, we'd escape to the braes, Kitta and I, to lie on our backs and watch the grumbling sky. Sometimes I would read to her from the *Forget-Me-Not Annual*. Kitta liked the story of 'The Angel of Buccleuch House' but didn't think much of Mr Keats's poem with the *Frenchy name*, his sorry Knight palely loitering.

What mannie'd trifle about with GARlands, she sniffed. *And what do it even mean, Meggie, LOITERing?*

I wasn't sure I had it right, I had to check Miss Birnie's dictionary, and when I told Kitta, she pursed her lips and her opinion of Mr Keats took a plummeting. From then on, she would often affect a dramatic pose up on the braes, leaning against the sheddie wall, all mock wistfulness. *Eh, Meggie mine,* she'd say with a flutter of hands, *look at me, I'm woe-beGONE, I'm LOITERing!*

It was good to hear Kitta laugh. Things were hard for her. Even then, I could see that. My sister had had a taste of thinking for herself, making up her own mind without asking anyone's leave, and here she was again, being told what to think and what to do. And it was made that wee bit worse by the looks she got from some in the village who thought they knew who Kitta was and knew nothing at all.

I fancied, too, there were other things Kitta was pining for, things past my grasp, that she wasn't willing to share, no. But the more I searched her face for them, the more I asked questions and gave her the chance to tell me, the more her eyes slid from mine to a place I could not follow.

I walked into the face of the wind up on the scaur one night, alone and unsettled. *Crusoe! Cru–soe!*

I stopped. There was no use calling, was there? Crusoe wasn't coming back.

I turned for home, I pulled the shawl tighter around me, I bowed my head.

Change.

Again.

December 1972

Lambsie, there are moments in your life when it seems like the skin covering the core of you is peeled away and a new one, a harder one, begins to grow. The end of one thing and the beginning of another—aye, the old and the new again. While they are happening, you don't always see them for what they are. Only later do you say, *Ah, it was then.* But sometimes you look them in the eye, and you know.

It was not long, the space between Da and the boys leaving for Stornaway and Kitta's next season at Lerwick. But in that space were three terrible things. The world shifted, and me with it.

Such a cold winter it was that year. It was all anyone talked about, even Granda Jeemsie, who was never a man to feel the cold and scorned shivering as weakness. But this year he pulled an extra gansey over his head and blamed it all on *the poverty of knittin' skill among our womenfolk these days*.

With the cold came sickness. Ma had influenza again. Unty Leebie, too.

On a day Granda was preparing to put to sea on the *Lily Maud*, Kitta and I sat inside the doorway of the netting shed with the longlines laid out in careful figures of eight to prevent them tangling. Our fingers turned white, the nails purple, as we prised apart icy mussels from our pails and forced hooks through them, one by one. For a while we sang, to take our minds off the pain, but Granda shouted from inside for us to *halt that muckle racket afore the devil rises up to take us all to hell!*

We checked on Ma from time to time, taking turns with her hot-water bottle and a fresh brew to ease her cough. And to tend to Granda's wants. We were glad enough, for once, to see to them, just to escape the cold a wee while.

That night, when it came near time for the crew of the *Lily Maud* to be loading up and leaving, Granda stumped outside. He stood there, pulling on his gloves, his woollen cap down over his ears, and he barked at Kitta: *Hash yourself, quinie, your ma wants ye.*

Kitta poked out her tongue as she passed behind him, which would normally make me laugh, but the sight of Granda glowering doused all the laughter in me.

When Kitta came back, her face was the colour of the sleety sky.

~

I climbed up to my usual place on the stone wall that night, and I'd to steel myself to look across to the boatie shore. Guilty, I felt. Guilty that I couldn't help. Guiltier still to feel so relieved about it.

Unty Jinna, Liza and Kitta were unshouldering the loaded murlins and preparing to float them out to the *Lily*. I could almost feel the cold numbing their toes, freezing their ankles, as they pulled off boots, unrolled their stockings. The retreat of blood from the veins in shock, the cramping in their legs, while they ferried murlins from shore to boat. But there are worse things. How could I bear to watch the worse that came next?

Kitta looked up, in my direction, knowing I'd be there on the stone wall. All that had gone before—the disgrace of losing her position at Rowescroft House, the return to the village, the scandalous lies that were told of her, the secrets she'd not talk about—all these things were as nought compared to that moment when Weelim's Kitta Neish Duthie crouched in the freezing shallows to take Granda Jeemsie on her back.

A few weeks later, the next thing happened. I ...
I will have to tell it like a story, lambsie.

The red-haired girl is up on the braes, looking over the boatie shore. A skirly wind comes in from the sea, jerking the sails of the fishing boats and whisking away anything loose as it barrels through. An empty murlin and a brace of buoys, tied together with rope, tumble over the side of the *Lily Maud*. They skim the shallows. They helter-skelter across the shingle.

The girl runs down to gather them up, to drag them home behind her because she wouldn't dare return them to the *Lily Maud*. Oh no, not her, not the accursed quinie.

The buoys, ugh, they are disgusting things. She hates the sight of them, the feel of them even more. Inflated bladders, skins of small animals, cured and sealed with tar and corks. Skin and fur and gut. When she is nearly at Tiller Street, one of them breaks free of the rope and skitters off towards the braes again. She pulls the rest to the netting shed, shoving them roughly inside, and runs after the runaway float. It won't do to be the one to lose it.

She finds it up near the sheddie, its rope snagged on a jagged plank of timber. As she releases it, she sees it is a bloated torso, sewn up and sealed with tar where limbs had once been.

The girl swallows air. She slumps to her knees.

The fur of the leathery skin, stiffened by salt, is gingerish, with a white blaze on one side the shape of a wing.

December 1972

And then the world shifted again, for a third time, in a way that could never be undone, never be made right.

Ach, I promised to tell you everything, lambsie, but I told you too that I would have to take my time about it. Some things ... well, I just canna work out how to write them down. I picture your face as you read the words and I canna do it. I will have to find a way to make sense of it to myself before I can explain it to you, what happened next. On the *Lily Maud*. Brukie's Sandy.

But I will try, lambsie, in time. Indeed I will. Because I have been thinking about this for a long time now, and I have a theory: that everything else that has happened since stems from that one terrible thing I canna tell.

Notebook 2

1905–1909

AIR

He was a one, that Brukie's Sandy, a one with the grapplie hook, but this day the prize was just beyond his reach. Prize it was, too, the kind he always knew would come some day, if he was patient, if he kept both eyes on the sea.

A bottle.

And he saw, through the corked amber glass, that there was something inside it. A spiral of paper, a message from the sea. Imagine what faraway place it might have drifted from, what stories it might tell. Imagine!

So that boy, that Brukie's Sandy, he leaned out over the stern of the Lily Maud, *leaned out with the hook in his reaching hands.*

Dearest lambsie, a new exercise book, but don't be alarmed. I promise I'll not be writing the whole of my life in these pages—everything that happened, every month, every year that passed. But as I look out of the glass doors onto my wee patio of bay trees and rosemary, I hear the old carriage clock ticking on the dresser, and I have to keep writing, I have to return, while I can, to that place and time I've not been to in my mind for a lifetime. Call back the girl I was and find a place for her in the order of things. Retrieve the things I have chased to the blurred edges of memory, hold them to the light, see the shape of them now that I have older eyes. Ha, lambsie, aye, I know. It is as much for me I'm writing as it is for you, but you are a smart girl, smart enough to allow that it canna be another way.

It would have been simpler to write for you the stories I promised when you were a little girl—of Fish Meggie, the Gutting Girl from the Top of the World. But we are both of us past fairytales now, lambsie, each for our different reasons. The story of where you come from is real, as real as memory can ever be, and not so easy as fairytales.

When you discover something so shocking you canna even name it, you shut down, lambsie, you shut it out and yourself in. You walk through your days like a person asleep.

That was me in April 1905, when I left Roanhaven.

And then I found myself on the sea.

It was not as I had imagined it—the sea, when it was all around me. From the boatie shore, it had seemed, for all its restlessness, something fixed—a space to cross, with the wide world beyond it. I could never have guessed that the sky grows ever further away instead of closer and nothing is fixed at all. It was then I began to wake. Here I was, between one life and another. Between a girl of fourteen and in school, working at whatever her family said she must, and a girl of fourteen and about to earn money in her own right. Between a place of grim restraint and a place, I hoped, of freedom. I had been warned about the ruthless sea the whole of my life, but even at fourteen it seemed to me that nothing the sea could throw up could be as ruthless as what I had left behind. Kitta and I would have to return at the end of the season, but we would never go back there in our hearts. We didn't say those words out loud to each other, but it was a decision made, just the same, to close that door. Perhaps Roanhaven had taught us that. To believe that things could be made to disappear, simply through silence.

My leaving was not like Kitta's the year before, bundled off and away in disgrace. I could have stayed. But Ma saw how it was and would always be. Still, she gave me the chance to change my mind. *Are ye sure, Meggie, sure this be what ye want? To leave school an' go to the fish?*

I hugged her for my answer. I didn't want to leave school, no, and I wasn't sure I wanted to leave her, either.

She looked defeated, helpless, not like Ma. *I know, quinie, I know it be hard …*

Hard? Hard would have been easy, lambsie. But I couldn't stay, not when there was a chance to escape what had happened, and all those faces not really forgiving, not really forgetting, but pretending for the sake of loyalty to some dark past. Here I stumble with memory, numb to all but the fact that it was unbearable. And how could I say the word *unbearable* to Ma? She was giving me her reluctant blessing to leave, while she had no choice but to stay and bear everything.

~

Will your anchor hold in the storms of life
When the clouds unfold their wings of strife?
When the strong tides lift and the cables strain
Will your anchor drift or firm remain?

The girls' voices were jubilant when we left Port Dougal Pier in Gadlehead Harbour, accompanied by a brass band on the jetty. But as the SS *St Rognvald* steamed further from shore, the choir became thin and raggedy. And by the time the shadow of Gadlehead had dissolved into horizon, only one person was left on their feet. Me.

Too shy, I was, to join in the singing. But it's a funny thing, I became surer of myself the further to sea we got, because I discovered that I am a good sailor. Imagine that, lambsie! The red-haired quinie forbidden even to come within sight of the *Lily Maud*, to taint the fishermen on their way to the flighty sea, and here I was, standing on deck, while most of the others were lying wherever they could find space, groaning, crying, no mind to the Arctic winds whipping them into a freeze.

Some looked like a strange breed of animal, with a brown paper feeder over their faces. When we had our names checked off a list in Gadlehead, we'd each been given a paper bag, the kind that I'd seen the market sellers by the pier filling with hot, oily chestnuts and selling for a penny ha'penny. What was it for? I slit mine apart with my thumb and felt about inside but it was empty and flat as a griddle cake. I folded the edges into a diamond and tried it on my head, nervous but clowning. Kitta laughed, snorting like a horse, and some of the Highland girls giggled softly behind their long fingers. They glanced at each other but they didn't smile at me, no. I shrank a little and quickly pulled the bag off. *Foolish quinie*, said a voice in my head.

Clementina Slater set me straight. *It's for pukin', quinie. For the great return. Just ye wait till we leave the coast behind, then ye'll know what the sea thinks of 300 lassies runnin' away to the fish. And when we get to the Roost, ye'll dip your head an' pray for sea monsters, hurricanes, the very Witch herself to take your miserable wee body to the bottom, just to make it stop.*

Well.

It took fifteen cold, queasy hours to reach Sumburgh Roost, where the North Sea and the Atlantic crash together just off the southern tip of Shetland main isle. Those who had made the crossing many times braced themselves, but eventually every girl on board, even Kitta, was doing exactly what Clementina said: puking whatever was in her stomach. But not me. Aye, I felt the power of the Roost beneath me, flinging my body about like a thing with no weight, but I struggled to the aft railing and held on, my face straight into the blast of the wind. There were moments when the lurching of the ship seemed to fall in with the swilling of my blood, but I clamped my teeth, I wasn't afraid. I would not be beaten nor brought to my knees by the sea.

At last I could see the flinty grey of something more solid than cloud.

The wide world!

I kiss the air. It spins around me with the rush of something new, something that is white and clean and so real that I can touch it with my fingertips, feel it on my lips, on the skin of my face. It gusts through my hair, pulling it at the roots, and I am breathing it into me, this wondrous something new. And suddenly I know that I will never be the same again because I have felt freedom in my lungs.

Lerwick harbour was a mirror of Gadlehead, with its swarming sailors, ships from stranger-ports, holds of fish. As I stepped off the *St Rognvald* and onto the wharf, a truly wonderful new word I'd read in the *Forget-Me-Not Annual* came into my head. *Cacophony*. Such a word to try in your mouth, clicking from the centre, huffing from your teeth to your tongue. Ca-co-pho-ny. And that's what was all around me. A cacophony of voices and whistles, shouting and haggling, engine roar and the clang-clang of hammers on the hoops of barrels.

Watch your step, Fish Meggie, Kitta called as we followed Clementina to where a man with a pencil and clipboard was checking off names again. *Ye'll screw your head right off your neck if ye don't take care!*

Kists were being hauled off the ship and loaded onto carts and I hoped mine, brand-new with my name cut into the top, would arrive safe and sound and not fall into the harbour, as I saw happen to one. Inside it were three things so precious to me that my heart jumped about in my chest when the kist was collected from Tiller Street by the curers' cart. Kitta's purple scarf tightly rolled and stowed in the bottom of the shottle. The *Forget-Me-Not Annual*, wrapped up in my spare pair of drawers. And the third thing, a gift Miss Birnie had sent to me in a box when she heard I would not be coming back to school: another book. Dark brown, it was, old, and covered in waxy cloth, the edges of the pages the colour of tea. On the front and on the spine were curly letters of imperfect gold: *Underwoods by Robert Louis Stevenson*. Inside a square on the first page, the name *Mildred Birnie* had been crossed out and *Margaret Neish Duthie* written in its place. A message, too, in Miss Birnie's handwriting. My very own book of poems. *Please God*, I prayed, *keep my kist safe and dry and I won't bother Ye for a good long while*.

There were no carts for us girls. We'd to walk to a place called Gremista, where the Nicol & Mair gutting stations were. Most of the girls were pale and weak from retching the last two hours from the Roost, and many of them had suffered all the way from Gadlehead. I thought myself lucky—the luckiest ginger head ever to go to sea. However would the rest manage the walk? It was only a couple of miles along the shore, Clementina said, but some of them looked so poorly.

Ah, that's nothin', Kitta assured me. *If the cold doesn't set our bellies to rights, the smell of salt will do it.*

But the further we tramped along the road like a straggling trail of geese, it was not the clean, sharp tang of salt I could smell. Stronger and stronger, more overpowering with each step, a familiar smell blew into our faces. Fish guts. I held the back of my hand to my nose, and Clementina, beside me, rolled her eyes. To experienced gutting quines, *this* was nothing, either.

Ach, that first sight of Gremista! Already there were gutting teams at work in neighbouring yards. It was getting late, but the thrum of work was steady. I asked Kitta what hours we would work and she laughed. *While there's fish, there's work! We work till the cooper says stop. An' if ye need to piss, too bad, Meggie mine. Ye hang on, ye just hang on!*

Kitta's crude words shocked me.

Cacophony again. This time there was also the screaming of hundreds of gulls circling above the farlins, and calls of *Fill up!* and *Over here!* I had never in my life seen so many people working together. And it hit me with a great rush: I was a gutting girl now, and soon I would be among them.

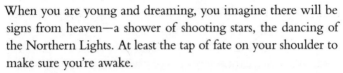

When you are young and dreaming, you imagine there will be signs from heaven—a shower of shooting stars, the dancing of the Northern Lights. At least the tap of fate on your shoulder to make sure you're awake.

But it doesn't usually happen that way, lambsie.

~

We met that night, my very first night in Gremista, over a splinter, a sliver of spruce hived off a barrel. The boy was one of the apprentice coopers given the job of helping girls clear out the huts up on the rise behind the yards, which were used as store sheds during the winter. These would be our homes, our *wee hoosies*, for the months to come.

Ach, the dismay of arriving at Gremista, tired and windravelled. No clean beds. No welcoming fires for a cup of tea, no. Those wooden huts were full of barrels and mice and the sticky webs of small black spiders. I looked at Kitta, at Clementina. No disgust. No surprise. This was just the way of it.

What's that? I whispered to Kitta, pointing to a shallow hole in the earthen floor in a corner of our hut.

Glory hole, she said, matter of fact.

Was she teasing? At home, all in Tiller Street had to share a three-seater laavie draining into the sea, but there were walls around it, walls and a door.

Kitta laughed. *Get that frown from your face, quinie! Is the same for us all. An' if ye want more privacy …* She jerked a thumb over her shoulder. *Well, walk over the hill an' ye can have all the privacy in the world. Miles of it. Just yeself an' the wind an' the rabbits!*

Six of us, it took, to make our hut fit to live in. We'd to light sulphur candles to chase out wee beasties, scrub it clean of mud and dust and scat, fetch coal from the yards and water from rain barrels. And we'd to make the two beds fit for six to sleep in, with chaff mattresses and linen we'd carried with us in our kists from home. The other girls in our hoosie had brought pictures in frames—Jesus on the Cross, Mary with her babe—and a wee pink china vase, which made it seem cosy. Kitta and I had nothing like that, nor Clementina. It would be hours before we could tumble into those beds, but at least our chores were lit by a sky that seemed unwilling to darken even after ten at night.

Before we could begin cleaning our wee hoosie, a dozen barrels had to be rolled out on their sides, down to the yards, and it was my howl of pain as a splinter drove into my thumb that drew the attention of the cooper boy.

Ee there, lass, let's see what ye is done ta yeself there.

I held out my hand obediently, then snatched it back when I realised he was just a loon not much older than me.

Ee, c'mon, lass, he said, laughing, *I won't sting nor bite ye.*

He grabbed my wrist, and this time I didn't pull away.

He leaned down and both of us peered at my thumb. Long strands of my fringe brushed his hand and, pffff, he blew them away. I looked around for Kitta, for Clementina, but both of them were down in the yards, rolling barrels to the coopers' store.

The boy still had me by the hand, his face so close I could hear him breathing. One of the Highland girls, passing by, looked at me in a funny way.

I tried to pull my hand back again. *I can fix it*, I said. *Only a splinter.*

But a big one, the boy said. *And ye canna take chances.*

What d'ye mean, chances? I can get it out easy with my gipper.

Now that's just what ye shouldn't do, he said. *I've a netting needle here, and that's the thing ta use. Just wait while I burn it clean first.*

Off he raced to one of the huts where the girls had their fire already alight.

I looked around, uncertain. Why couldn't I just dig out the thing myself? I'd done it before, plenty of times. I didn't like to be obliged to anyone, least of all a boy whose name I didn't know. Maybe I'd misunderstood him—his words had a strange rolling sound. I looked down to the yards again. Kitta and Clementina were still pushing barrels about.

I was proud of my gipper, my very own, sharp as could be in the pocket of my skirt, tucked into a leather sheath. I was just about to drive the point into my thumb and slit the layer of skin where the splinter was, when the knife was jerked out of my hand.

Ee, what ye are about? Ye be mad, lass? The boy was red and huffing, but then he relaxed a bit and folded his arms. *Aah, ye is new, is that it?*

Give me back my gipper! That's for my work, that is.

Aye. And he handed it back to me, offering it by the short wooden handle. *But see, give me your hand an' I'll show ye.*

I narrowed my eyes.

I'll not hurt. An' ye'll thank me tomorrow, lass, I promise ye that.

Ungrateful, unwilling, I held out my hand and watched as he slid the needle under the skin and eased the splinter out.

See? This way ye'll not open up the wound any more.

I realised Clementina was looking over my shoulder. *That's the way, aye. Ye know what the quinies say, Fish Meggie? 'Break the skin an' the salt gets in.' Good job, lad.*

He smiled at me and shrugged. I felt new and foolish and glared back and couldn't say the obvious thing, couldn't bring myself to thank him.

As soon as Clementina left, he kissed my thumb quickly, gave me back my hand as though presenting a gift and was gone before the shock had settled on my face.

What's up with ye, Meggie mine? said Kitta. *Have ye seen a wee ghostie blow out from the hut?*

Not a wee ghostie, Clementina barked. *She's only gone an' found herself a mannie already! Aye, a wee cooper boy—that's what she seen blow out from the hoosie!*

Kitta's eyes widened and the two of them were laughing and I turned my back in a sulk, annoyed to be singled out and teased. I kept my mouth shut: protesting wasn't likely to help, now, was it? But later, as I scrubbed a winter's dirt from the walls of the hut, I thought a little about the boy. He had been kind, if bold. There wasn't anything *wee* about him, no mind what Clementina said: he was tall, taller even than Da. And I flushed to remember how it felt when he kissed the place where the splinter had been, before I'd had the manners to feel shocked about it. In a day of confusions, one and then another, this was the biggest of all.

I tried to picture the boy's face, and it was his blue eyes I remembered.

Ach, how I wished it wasn't Gena Buchan's place I was taking in Kitta and Clementina's team. Gena was a legend among gutting quines. Girls said she could do seventy herring a minute. Seventy! What chance did I have of coming close to that? You're right, lambsie: none.

In truth, I was lucky to be in a team with Kitta. Once teams were formed, they stayed together. But twice now Clementina had lost a girl. Gena had married at Gadlehead last Hogmanay and was in a certain way—and not keeping so well with it. Clementina agreed to take me on because Kitta begged, but she was not pleased about it, no indeed. Nothing was going to be pleasing Clementina Slater that season. Losing Gena Buchan would mean fewer barrels done, and that would mean fewer shillings. Breaking in a new girl—well, that was just a broken toe on top of a broken leg.

She told Kitta that she looked at me at the pier at Gadlehead and knew, just knew, right then and there, that I would be a disaster. And so I was, lambsie. For a time I truly was.

~

That first morning in Gremista I'll never forget. Shouts at dawn: *Get up, get up, get up, quinies! Get up an' tie your fingers!*

I woke up crushed in a bed, with Kitta's arm across my neck and Clementina's ample self taking up a good deal of room. On the other side of the hut, groans from Isobel, Jeannie and Mary, a team from Cruden Bay. All of us scrambling for our clothes and gear, shivering in our wee woolly combinations.

In time huts would have a daily roster, each of us taking turns at lighting the fire, making tea and cutting bread and jam for all, but this first morning we were weary-slow. Nothing was organised. It was all we could do just to get ourselves kitted up, down to the yards and finding our places by six.

I followed Kitta's lead, pulling on skirt and jumper and seaboot stockings, tying a headsquare around my hair, grabbing rubber boots and an oilskin apron from a pile the curers' men had left outside. Other girls were quicker than me, and I'd to make do with whatever was left: boots so big that it was hard to walk without my feet lifting right out of them; an oilie that would have fit a girl as big around the middle as Clementina. Later on, we would swap our gear with other teams, sorting it out among ourselves so that no-one had anything too big nor small for them, but there was no time that first morning.

I struggled, too, with my clooties. I watched Kitta do hers: binding each finger with strips of cloth Ma had torn from flour bags, and tying them one by one with string. It was a complicated business and you needed to use your teeth, as well as the fingers you weren't tying. The clooties would be left on all day, so they had to be done right. I couldn't get them tight enough, nor tie the fiddly strings. Kitta noticed the dark looks Clementina was throwing my way and took pity on me.

Here, I'll do them for ye, Fish Meggie, but mind, tomorrow ye'll be doing for yourself!

I watched her bind and tie, bidding me to flex each finger to test the cloths—firm enough to hold but loose enough to keep my fingers moving. A picture flashed into my head: a girl binding her granda's hand. How strange life can be. Quickly I sent it away: I didn't want Roanhaven in my head any more.

It was even colder outside our draughty hoosie. I was glad of my thick woollens and oilie, the mittens over my tied fingers. The wind howled across the bay as we joined the crowd walking down to the yards. Even though I was stumbling in and out of my boots and clutching at Kitta to keep myself upright, I couldn't help but feel the crackling in the air. All those girls, those brave, strong quinies, with a job to do and the skills to do it.

I was not brave nor strong, and I had no skills at all, but on that cold Gremista morning I dared to think I might become like them. Someone new, someone better.

~

Kitta had been drilling me for weeks. The farlins would be in front of me, filled to the top with fish, and the sorting baskets in the middle. Gutted herrings got tossed into the baskets, according to size and whether or not they contained roe or milt. I went over and over it in my head, picturing how the sorting baskets would be arranged: fulls, large-fulls, matties, mattie-fulls, spents.

All that preparation was as nought when I stood there for the first time, gipper in hand.

The noise of hungry gulls overhead, of so many girls talking all at once. My head jangling so badly that I canna remember my name, hardly, let alone the difference between a mattie-full and a mattie, nor whether the basket for fulls is right or left. Herring and salt—fresh, wholesome smells overpowered by the reek of blood, the bitter dark of guts, blood and guts, blood and guts. Never have I seen so much, staining everything red, every surface slippery and wet. Soon it's all I am: red, wet, salted, gutted, blood in my eyes, scales on my skin. A fish hauled from water into air and struggling to find a way to breathe …

Meggie!

I snapped to attention, looked up from the silver-bellied fish loose in my hand.

What're ye doin', quinie? Kitta's hands didn't slow for a second—in, twist, flick. *Whatever is wrong with ye? Clementina'll have a jamaica if she turns round an' sees ye standing there like that, all gapin'.*

Sorry, our Kitta, I'm sorry …

Sorry! Ye'll be sorry if ye don't get guttin', true enough! C'mon now, Fish Meggie, let's see ye live up to your name!

And I began again. Bound fingers fumbling with the gipper, splattering blood as I tried to knife out the gills and guts clean in one stroke, concentrating hard on which murlin to toss the herring into. Clumsy I was, clumsy and slow, one fish to every eight, nine, ten of Kitta's.

But it was a beginning, and even Clementina admitted, *There has to be a beginnin' to everythin'.*

~

We were each allowed to take home a herring to cook for our tea, a lumpy or spotty one, unfit for pickling. Clementina stood over me while I gutted our three and then she begged our hoosie-mates to let me practise on theirs. Just the thing after the longest day on my feet, the hardest day on my hands: to gut another six herring. But Gena Buchan I was not, and Clementina wanted me to work on my *action*.

Ye're a disaster now, quinie, aye, but the speed'll come if ye get the action right.

She sprinkled the fish with salt, like the curers did in the yards to give us a better grip.

Move your thumb a bit. That's right. Now line it up with your middle finger on the other side. The back in the palm of your hand. See?

I did what she said, but I was too tired to see anything. If Clementina thought I might progress to be less of a disaster, then I was happy enough because it meant she might leave me to rest. But no, she'd not finished with me yet. I was to have my lesson.

Now, then, Fish Meggie, you won't be needin' to learn to pack for a good while to come—that's my job—but it's as well ye understand how the team works, eh?

I glanced across to Kitta by the fire. She was brewing tea and frying the herring I'd just gutted. She wasn't coming to my rescue. I looked back at Clementina and nodded.

Right, then, quinie. The barrels are packed all with the same type, matties with matties, fulls with fulls. They go in layer by layer, neat an' tight, salt in between. Bottom layer dark sides up, heads clockwise, next silver bellies up, widdershins. Dark then silver right to the top, an' we always finish with bellies. Eh?

I nodded again.

The girls from Cruden Bay were eating their tea and looking on as though I was the night's entertainment. Isobel called out, through a mouthful of fish, *Eh, Clementina, this one'll never make a packer with arms like that! No reach on 'em, eh?*

I looked at my arms. They didn't seem so short, but they were skinnier than Clementina's. Was this a bad thing? I couldn't tell.

Clementina ignored her and carried on with her talk.

Has to be neat, mind. If the inspector lifts a head to check an' the fish are slidin' this way an' that, he'll make us pack the whole barrel again afore we can get the Crown brand. So has to be neatly done, see?

She was waiting for me to say something, maybe a sign that I understood how important her job was. A nod was all she got.

Our cooper, he fills up with pickle last thing, and in the mornin' we top up with fish, see, 'cause they pack down a bit overnight. About ten days an' the cooper drills a hole in the side an' drains off the pickle. We top up again, more herrin' to finish, an' then the cooper pours in pickle an' seals the hole with a bung. Heads on an' then it's ready an' away. Eh?

Mmm, I murmured, hoping that was the end. A kirk bell somewhere chimed eleven.

Kitta saved me at last, slapping two tin plates in front of us on the wooden plank that was our table. *Tea's up!* she said. *Hungry, Meggie mine?*

I looked down at the thick slab of bread, the greasy fish. The last thing I felt like eating was a herring.

~

On that first wearisome night, I could have slept standing, sitting or on my head, aye, but first there were things to do. A roster to be worked out with the Cruden Bay girls. Food brought from home to be pooled. And we had to clean our gippers, sharpen them on the wheel, and wash out our clooties ready for the morning.

Kitta sent me to the rainwater barrel to fill our bucket. I stood there, eyes closing, slumping against the side. Footsteps passing, a voice close to my ear.

How is the hands, then, Fish Meggie?

The boy was already on his way back to the yards when I opened my eyes, but he turned and waved. *Ye can thank me at the ceilidh on Saturday!*

I looked down at my hands, red and raw from a day steeped in salt. Now I understood. What agony a slit on the thumb would be. But as for ceilidhs ... I tossed my head, like Kitta—she always looked so *imperious* when she did that.

A laugh in the distance.

I still didn't know his name.

Lambsie, I think if you asked your Unty Clementina's opinion on the matter, she would tell you I remained a disaster for a good while. But to me it felt that every day I was getting a bit faster with the gipper, a bit surer I knew what it was I should be doing, a bit less bewildered by the press of so many people. Disaster of another kind would soon catch up with me, but in those first days, those first few weeks, I felt I was making progress. Getting the action right, getting my speed up.

I was also getting used to another something new. The coopers were kings of the yards, and what they said was what we did for the hours at the farlins, but there was no-one fussing around with a list of what I must think or do. No men to cook for when we left at night, with boots to be cleaned and clothes to be washed. Sitting there, waiting for pots of tea. No work to get through one day so that men could do theirs the next. No fires to be lit and chairs brushed down to put others at ease. I looked around at the girls at the farlins and could not imagine any one of them carrying a fisherman on her back, although some of them probably had before they *ran away to the fish*.

When I heard that the drifters that Da, Sailor Wattie and the boys were signed to had been sent north to Baltasound for the Shetlands season, I could have danced a jig right there on the spot. They wouldn't be nearby in Lerwick, or joining us at Gremista. Oh, shameful, aye, to be wishing your family far away, but I'd had a taste of my own mind and I didn't want to be giving it up. I'd grown to like the idea that I was free to sing Sankey's hymns with the other girls as I fried our herrings for tea and our tatties for next day's dinner. No-one to watch me with a sour face. No-one to spoil the joy or thunder at me that silence is godly.

I could push Roanhaven away, even pretend it never was.

Isobel, Jeannie and Mary didn't seem to mind at all that their fathers and brothers were sometimes in port come Saturday night, but it looked to me a blighted blessing. After we'd finished on these Saturdays, off they would go, those girls, walking in to Lerwick for shop-bought cake, and then back to make tattie pie and egg custard—treats for their men. And when Old Boy Jackie and the other coopers and crew from the fisher boats got out their melodians and fiddles and played long past dark, the little knot from Cruden Bay would stick together, the girls dancing with their brothers and serving their fathers tea.

If Da and the boys had been here, Kitta and I would be doing the same. Bound to tend to them, to mind what they said. As it was, we could dance a reel with the girls as we pleased. Oftentimes the coopers and the fishers joined in. When I close my eyes now … ach, I can feel it, the stamping of feet on the wooden boards of the jetty, thump-thump in time to clapping hands. The cooling air on my clammy face as the girls swing me from arm to arm. The first time I felt a man's warm hand at my back, I flustered about, lost my step. Almost tripped over my own boldness. But a glance around at the neat-stepping fishers, all kindly and cheerful, quelled the urge to run away. There was none to call it wrong or even to put such a thought in our heads, none to call us names. If anyone had something to say at all it was just, *Eh, Fish Meggie is light on her feet*, or *Mary's Kirsty's Jeannie, ye've a sweet voice to hear*. I wasn't *runnin' wild*, I was no disgrace to my own, but what I chose to do with the hours away from the farlins was my say-so and no-one else's. What happiness to a fisher girl, happiness undreamed of.

The Highland girls didn't think much of the rest of us. Polite enough, aye, but kept to themselves. They spoke in Gaelic, the strangest kind of babble, and it drew a veil between them and us. They have the blackest eyes, those girls. Beautiful. And dark hair, thick, sheening like glass so you felt you might catch your own face mirrored there if ever they shook free the tartan headsquares tucked so primly behind their ears. Was that why they looked on me, on my wild flame of hair, with such pity? And sometimes, I think, with fear? They skirted around me whenever they could. Walked the long way round to avoid crossing my path. Or was I imagining that? Perhaps, but I fancied there was a special brand of wariness in how some of the girls looked at me. No mind. I was finding my way, and would answer no more to *Ginger Meggie*.

In spite of myself, I looked for the cooper boy, the one who said he would dance with me. But he wasn't to be seen. He'd been needed in the west, an extra hand at Nicol & Mair's Scalloway yards—or so I was told. I'd not asked, mind, but there were those who made it their business to say, apparently at the boy's bidding. I shrugged, indifferent—what was it to me? Why should I care? But I listened when the other boys spoke of when he'd be back. And I learned, from their talk, that the boy was older than I'd thought: seventeen. And that his name was Magnus Tulloch.

Singing and dancing in the starless dusk, warming our hands by the fishers' fires, sharing the griddle cakes we'd made, the tea the coopers brewed—these joyful ceilidhs at work's end every Saturday seemed adventure enough for me. But there were girls more daring. In little clusters, they'd walk to Lerwick to join the crowds of townsfolk, fishermen, sailors from ports all over the world, and quines stationed at yards within easy distance of the town.

One Sunday, while we tramped along the Gremista road to kirk, I listened to the talk about Saturday Night Lerwick. I hung on every word, and words became pictures. Dutch sailors in their clogs and baggy trousers. Men from Norway boats in dark dress, silver buttons on their jackets. Preachers gathering in Market Square, shouting hell and damnation—and here I thought of Pastor McNab, and didn't that make me shrink a little into my woollen shawl! Men atop wooden boxes, men with Things to Say, calling through cones of stiff paper. Groups of girls linking arms, swearing sailors, drunken shopboys, fishers in gangs, all of them dancing up and down Commercial Street, sliding on banana skins and twists of orange peel. A fiddler on each corner, or a man with a button accordion, or a makeshift choir. A babble of voices, foreign words. And the things you could buy in shops! Feathered hats, drawers with lace, dresses with ribbons. Icecream, marble cake, sweeties in rainbow colours, extra-strong peppermints. You could buy anything in Lerwick, the girls said. *Anything*!

Such stories. There was nothing like this in the *Forget-Me-Not Annual*.

Kitta was walking arm in arm with Bella Strahan, an older girl from Aberdeen. Clementina and I struggled to keep up.

They go mad for peppermints, those Dutchmen do, I heard Kitta say, laughing.

I nearly tripped over my own boots. I stared, open-mouthed, at the back of her head. I wanted to put my hand out, stop her right there. Blunder in like a little girl, the little girl they would all think me. Instead, I turned to Clementina.

Have ye ever been to Lerwick on Saturday night?

Course I have, she puffed.

I let this settle for a moment and then I fairly burst. *I want to go. Can we go? Next week, can we go?*

But Clementina, labouring up the rise, huffed a few words that the wind muffled up and tossed away. I made up my mind to be patient, to go to kirk and bow my head and think of *the word of God*. And I would ask Kitta later, back at our hoosie.

As if she'd heard what I was thinking, Kitta half turned and blew me a kiss across her shoulder.

~

The streets of Lerwick were alive with people by the time the gas-lamps had been lit.

Keep your hand over your pocket, Meggie, Kitta shouted in my ear.

I frowned.

Or they'll pat ye down for your money.

My hand flew to the pocket of my skirt. All I had was elevenpence in coppers and a silver sixpence and just let anyone try to take it, just let them try! I stared at oranges in shop windows, all polished up and shiny, and even though I'd never tasted one, swear to God, lambsie, just looking made my mouth flood, all sharp and tangy.

I kept my eyes on the oranges as Kitta shuffled me forward, but the next window—oh! Lemon drops. Licorice! For the first time in my life I felt a longing for things. Not sensible things, no, not things on a list—just pretty, delicious, extravagant *things.*

Kitta took one look at my face and reeled me back in. *Window shopping, quinie, that's all,* she said as we pushed our way into a narrow lane famous for its Shetland shawls.

Just look, Kitta said, draping white lace over her face like a veil and rubbing the wool between her thumb and forefinger. *People do say it's fine enough to be drawn through a wedding band.*

Kitta looked so much like a bride in the beautiful shawl that I felt I would cry, but the shop woman snatched it from her head and flicked her fingers at us. *Be off, away!*

Next door were soft ganseys too grand for the humble name, in stitches I didn't know and complicated patterns of leaves and crosses that I would never be able to knit. Granda Jeemsie's voice seeped into my head: *The devil do bide in funcy things.* I shivered myself free of that voice.

Kitta looped her arm around mine and pulled me further up the steep lane. I sniffed some luscious smell, unfamiliar. *Mmmm,* said Kitta, throwing back her head, breathing it in. *Cinnamon an' raisins!* And beautiful it was after weeks of fish oil, fish blood, fish guts, fish, fish, fish. We went into the bakery—heaven! You could almost eat the air. I was achingly tempted to sacrifice four of my precious pennies on a sugar biscuit fashioned into the shape of a butterfly, but a chorus of long-dead Duthies protested in my head: *Raickless waste! Extravagance!*

Back in Commercial Street, more than once I felt a light press of hands on my body. I spun around, tightened my grip on the pocket of my skirt, but never did I catch a guilty face nor a hand where it shouldn't be. Bella Strahan pushed roughly at a man in sailor whites and let fly with a crude new word that was shocking to hear but I thought would be a satisfaction to say.

She scared me a bit, Bella Strahan did, but I was dying to know.

Did he feel for your money, Bella?

She snorted, planting her fists on her hips. *He were feelin' for somethin', hen, aye, but it were not my money!*

Kitta had me by the elbow and was pushing me forward, but she slowed when we turned the corner. The rowdiest house on The Esplanade, and she was looking around, craning her neck above the heads in sailor caps and fishermen's hats and berets and tammies. There were people crowding round the door, leaning out from the balcony above and from every window. I stopped, rigid, when I saw the plate swinging above the doorway: *The Queen.*

Kitta tugged at my arm.

I stared at her. *But … but it's a public house!*

An' what if it is, now, Fish Meggie? Ye're not a wee cradle bairn no more, are ye?

I glanced around, uncertain, but the Gremista quines, all good girls from sober fishing families, were milling, mingling, in high spirits. I allowed myself to be pushed along with them. The Cruden Bay girls were there too—fathers and brothers not in port this night—and even they seemed at ease. I'm with Kitta and Clementina, I told myself, and Isobel, Jeannie and Mary. But it was too much, the pulse and heat of so much laughter, so much music, so many tuneless voices singing different songs all at once, a blur of foreign words. The air thick with a cloying smell, sour and yeasty, dizzying. Someone breathed stranger-words in my ear, and easy enough, it was, to guess what they meant from the way they were spoken. A glass I refused to take was thrust at me again and again, and two sailors bellowed some raucous song in my ear. *As red as red as a match's head* and they tried to ruffle my hair with their hands. I pulled at Kitta's sleeve, wanting to leave, but my sister was flouncing her hair and laughing, forehead to cheek with a man I'd never seen. I let go of her gansey. Inching my way to the wall of The Queen, away from the flow of people. Merging into the stone to watch.

So many men, and every one of them with a tankard or glass in his hand. Hardly any of the girls were drinking, but I could not take my eyes off those few who were. Quiet, serious Jeannie! She downed two tankards, one and then the other, and wiped frothy stuff from around her mouth with the back of her hand. Already she was glassy-eyed, staggering a little, giggling as a Dutch sailor caught her round the waist and landed a smacking kiss on her cheek. So this is the devil's work, I thought, watching Jeannie's sheening face. What happy work it seemed to be.

I shouldn't stare, I shouldn't, but I canna stop my eyes from flitting back to Kitta. No glass in her hand but she is every bit as intoxicated as Jeannie. I study the man. I do not think him a fisher, nor a sailor, from the shop-bought clothes he wears, his beardless face. His hands look soft—town hands. One resting on my sister's back.

I shrink against the cold wall. A pain welling in me. It is no accident, this meeting. And I had been so elated when Kitta agreed to the visit to Lerwick and invited the other girls along.

The pain grips, like something tearing from the inside.

Kitta throws back her head and laughs, and the halo from a street lantern shines up her face. She is a radiant, beautiful stranger, not a fisher girl from Roanhaven. But when I look again, I recall that expression of Kitta's each time she came home—something secret in it, something bubbling under the surface. It had been a mystery to me then.

Kitta laughs again, her face close to the man's. One thing is certain: for now, she has forgotten me.

~

It was past the tide of Saturday when we set out to walk home in the moonlight. No-one was talking much. Isobel and I were either side of Jeannie, to take her weight if she slumped again. She didn't look so happy now, and was sick twice before we were a half a mile down the Gremista road. Bella Strahan was unsteady, too, but no docile lamb like Jeannie. She flailed at

Kitta for trying to take her arm, and jabbed a nasty finger in my face for good measure: *An' ye can get that prissy frown from your face, Miss High an' Mighty Tighty.* Oh, for a mirror. I'd like to have seen what it looked like, this prissy face of mine. Kitta shrugged and rolled her eyes but kept a step by Bella, ready in case she stumbled. Kitta was always kind like that.

At last we reached our hoosies, ready to drop into bed with our boots still on. No point in taking off clothes that would have to be put on again in a few hours for kirk. Seldom had I been up so late, but how could sleep be possible this night? I lay open-eyed. My back aching. So many new things, troubling things, whirring around in my head. I looked across to the other bed. Even from here, the reek of old ale and vomit was overpowering. Poor Izzy, poor Mary, who couldn't help but breathe it in all the night.

I pinched Kitta's arm. I had things to ask her.

A crash against the door. Everyone woke, everyone flew to their feet, clutching at each other in the dark. Someone was roaring a song, with a bash to the door on every second beat:

> *Ay ay ay, ma quinies*
> *ma bonnie bonnie quinies*
> *Let's be having yer afore the banns are sung*
> *Ye're a peely-wally lily*
> *till ye've had ol' Johnny's wullie*
> *An' ye dinna wanna die a-won-der-in' …*

Jeannie giggled.

Hush your mouth, Clementina whispered fiercely in the dark, but all of us heard the crack in her words.

Fear.

Nothing funny about the threat in each thump on the hoosie door. We were shivering. Flinching with every blow. The chanty ran its course and I was thinking perhaps the singer was done. But as I tiptoed to the small square of glass that was our window, he started up again:

> *Ay ay ay, ma quinies …*

A bottle smacked against the pane, glass breaking glass. Izzy and Mary screamed.

Get back! Get back! Clementina shouted. *He's comin' in!*

And so he was. A pair of enormous seaboots kicking through the thin door. Kitta and Clementina herded us to the window and Kitta fumbled with the fire-iron, knocking out shards of glass to clear a way through. Clementina grabbed it from her, swinging it like a sword in the direction of the door. But by now there were other voices outside, a crowd gathering. The song petered out amid blustering and scuffling.

C'mon now, away with ye now, an' put down that wee glass afore anybody do be done a mischief …

They've got him! Clementina announced from the window.

Ee, an' here's a nice wee policeman come ta see ye off an' away.

I knew that soothing voice on the other side of the broken door, and wasn't surprised when a face with a long sweep of dark hair peered around the corner.

Everybody safe an' sound in here, then?

Magnus Tulloch was back from Scalloway.

Shaking still, we all nodded, but it was me he was looking at.

Ee, Fish Meggie, ye has been hurt, lass. I'll fetch some water for ye.

I frowned. What was he saying? But Kitta took my face in her hands and held it to the light of a lantern that someone had brought us.

Oh Meggie mine, let me see?

She brushed her thumbs across my cold cheeks and it was only then that I felt the wetness, the sting of the little slivers of glass that had only just missed my eyes.

Magnus Tulloch came back with water and some news. The drunken fisherman who had followed us home was being taken back to Lerwick and would be charged.

Why did he pick our hoosie? Mary wailed. Izzy began to weep, great rib-rattling sobs.

One of the older coopers was nailing boards across the window and the bottom panels of the door. *Don't know that he were that fussy, lass*, he said. *Prob'ly just lit upon the first one he saw. Just unlucky, that's all.*

But I could see Magnus Tulloch's face over Kitta's shoulder as she wiped away the blood, and he was grinning.

Nah, more like he fancied ta catch himself a pretty wee quinie with a touch of the russet about herself.

And as he turned to leave, Clementina Slater raised her brows and made a performance of fanning her face. *Ye've a right one there, Fish Meggie, my lass. Best not let your da hear about your wee loon, eh!*

It was a joke, of course, and I flushed to the roots of my unfortunate hair. But she didn't know the real joke: that it wasn't me who would give Da cause for worry if ever he knew the things I knew.

It was cold when we got back in our beds. The wind found its way through the hastily mended timber and we huddled for comfort as well as warmth. Clementina was snoring before I'd time to turn over the night in my mind. Now was my chance. I put my hand on Kitta's arm to see if she was awake, but she turned away.

Not now, Meggie mine, she whispered. *Not now.*

~

There was blood in the bed next morning when I woke, and not from the scratches on my face.

Oh Meggie, don't fret, Kitta said. *It had to arrive, and ye're prepared for the wee visitor, are ye not?*

I was. When Ma had packed two half-loaves in my kist, she'd tut-tutted that I was *taking my time about growin' to be a woman*. I'd eyed the thick wads of rag-cloth, folded over and over. I was in no hurry at all, thank you Lord. I'd seen it all my life, this *being a woman* thing, and I'd held to myself a wishful thought that the longer the wee visitor stayed away, the longer

I might pretend the world had other plans for me. But now my luck had run to nought. Well, that's it, I thought, I will be like the others every month now, shamed at having to wash out my half-loaves each night, each morning. Why we should be shamed when it was the same for all, I couldn't say, but so it was, an understanding. I was unclean now.

A funny thing, though, lambsie: the half-loaves stayed in my kist after that for a good while to come. The wee visitor always played games with me. But when it came, I was cast poorly.

All that first day, a dragging ache at my back, my insides clenching. I was glad it was the Lord's day and I could stay abed, curled around my pain, while the others tramped off to pray for God to keep drunken men far from Gremista.

That night, after the midnight bells, I heard the fleet sailing at the back of Sunday. I could not sleep, so I crept out to sit alone on the rise behind the station. Knitting in the cold moonlight, listening to the fishermen singing their prayers:

> O hear us when we cry to thee
> For those in peril on the sea

A crunch of footfall nearby made me shiver. How reckless to be out here alone. But as I scurried back, I fancied I saw a tall shadow padding noiselessly along the track, an outline of longish hair, and I was bold enough to wish I'd not been so hasty about leaving.

~

Next day was a long one at the farlins, on through dusk and into slow twilight. Drifters kept arriving, the farlins kept filling, and we didn't stop even for the broth and doughboys Izzy made for our tea. All day in blood and slime, with the pull at my back, my stomach bloated like a week-old fish, holding out, holding out. But even if there had been a break allowed for the laavie, I would have held out still. You'd to be desperate to use the rough shelter with its panless seat open to the sea and in full view of returning boats. If your belly muscles weren't strong when you arrived at Gremista, they were when you left. They had to be.

And much else besides. The stations were no place for weaklings. I was already having trouble with my hands, burning in the salt. I was beginning to think I would never toughen up, never be anything more than a disaster.

March 1973

Many things happened in that first season at Gremista when it was all so new to me, but I canna think they would interest anyone but those who lived through them, who share the same memories. Some have their place in the order of things that I want to write for you, lambsie. But you'll have to be patient a while still, because I am learning as I go that we don't always recognise the way parts fit together. We look back and it's not always clear that *this* thing was important, and yes, if it hadn't been for *that* …

I will just keep writing and hope the story will find its way.

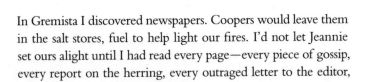

In Gremista I discovered newspapers. Coopers would leave them in the salt stores, fuel to help light our fires. I'd not let Jeannie set ours alight until I had read every page—every piece of gossip, every report on the herring, every outraged letter to the editor, and all the advertisements besides.

Oh, how I missed school, for the pleasure of reading. Word was that Miss Birnie had been angry to see me pulled from school before my fourteenth birthday. She'd wanted me to come see her, but I didn't go, and it was then that she'd sent me the book. Miss Birnie was an educated woman from Aberdeen. I didn't want to look into her face and see disgust. I'd have had to tell her it was me who had begged to leave school, leave the village, go to the fish. An educated woman might have understood how I felt about what happened, aye, but not what I'd chosen. Not my way out.

I read the newspapers aloud to my hoosie girls, none of them readers much themselves, and it sometimes turned out that they would rather do my chores so they could listen. Think of that, lambsie: I got to read instead of scraping potatoes for next day's tea!

Those newspapers, they gave us a picture of the world close by, news that concerned us. Sometimes was even *about* us. The roving reporter, his name not said, seemed very interested in gutting quines. To see ourselves through the eyes of the people of Lerwick was curious.

We fishworkers who came as strangers were needed but not always welcome. And some of us were less welcome than others. I read out the reporter's view that *among the girls from Aberdeen, Gadlehead and those parts is a rough, undesirable element that one does not find in lasses from the Firth of Moray or the Highlands.*

Clementina grabbed the pages out of my hand and thrust them on the fire outside our hoosie. *If my mother heard that, she'd have me on the next boat home*, she declared. *But first she'd seek out Mr Newspaper hisself an' give him somethin' rough an' undesirable to be gettin' on with!*

I found a letter to the *Shetland Times* from someone calling herself 'Modest Married Woman', who complained about *the number of stranger-women who were seen in Lerwick under the influence of drink and making a night of it.* I glanced across at Jeannie, sweet as can be with her knitting, and decided it was a letter best kept to myself. But happy I was to read to the girls that a certain John Noble, fisherman from the *Ivy Lass* out of Wick, had received a fine of four pounds for *drunk and disorderly conduct and disturbing the peace of the fishworkers at Gremista.*

All week Kitta avoided being alone with me. She knew I wanted to know about the man, and I couldn't ask when there were others around to hear. Did she plan to go to town again come Saturday? She didn't suggest it, and nor did I. Shawls and sugar biscuits aside, I was happy to leave Lerwick to the crowds. More lightsome it was, and safer, to see out the end of the week on station. Every fishing boat had a musician or two, and up they'd come to make a ragged orchestra for our reels, our quadrilles, our strip-the-willows. Music could be heard all over the bay and long into the night.

Still, when we were near to finishing at the farlins that Saturday, Kitta seemed jumpy, and slow with the knife.

Eh, quinie, ye great clumsy-drawers, what d'ye think ye're about? Clementina was pulling a dozen mattie-fulls from Kitta's mattie basket.

Perhaps Kitta was planning to walk to town, after all.

It was my turn to make griddle cakes—our hoosie's offering for the ceilidh. By the time I'd washed my face and hands, and changed into my pinafore-for-best, all the girls were there. I was praying Kitta was with them.

~

I had just about given up on Magnus Tulloch, thinking he must have returned to Scalloway or gone to Lerwick this Saturday night. I could have asked my cooper friend, Old Boy Jackie, but I did not want to seem overly eager. Or give the men cause to laugh at me. Or for word to get back to Magnus Tulloch and turn his head.

My mind was not on dancing, though I didn't refuse when the girls pulled me to my feet. All the time I was watching for Kitta. It seemed that she was sometimes here and sometimes not, and when I went looking I couldn't find her in the hoosie, or at tea by the fishers' fire. And then suddenly there she was, dancing with Clementina or Kipper's Tommy Buchan or Old Boy Jackie's mate Muckle Tam, and I thought: It's addled I am, she has been here all along.

I took a break from dancing to catch my breath and watch that Bella Strahan. She was standing in an empty farlin, calling a round of lancers, loudest voice on the station for sure. And then I heard from behind me:

I did not take ye for a wallflower, Fish Meggie!

It wasn't the same, dancing, when it was Magnus Tulloch's hand spanning my back. Warm, but a different kind of warm, and at first I looked at my boots to widen the space between us. When he spun me away to Kipper's Tommy, I gulped at the air, suddenly aware I'd been holding my breath all the while. Magnus Tulloch's hand caught mine and he twirled me back to him, closer, warmer, and when I chanced to look up—ach, those blue eyes.

He was a good dancer, light on his feet for a boy so tall. It got so I wished the coopers would stop swapping partners back and forth, but each time he reeled me back to him, there it was again, that smile.

Where have ye been all this night? I blurted once the polka was over. So much for me not giving him cause for airs.

Working still, lass, but all for good! Mr Sinclair bid me off into Lerwick for tea an' sugar. Canna be running out on ceilidh night, eh?

Aye. And I looked up at him, wondering how it was he had got taller since last I saw him.

Such crowds in the town! Could scarcely find a space ta put a foot down and then the other!

The fiddlers started up again, and Magnus Tulloch held out his hand.

For the rest of the night, I forgot my worries about Kitta. I forgot everything and danced.

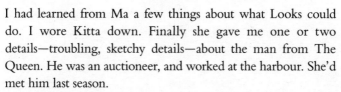

I had learned from Ma a few things about what Looks could do. I wore Kitta down. Finally she gave me one or two details—troubling, sketchy details—about the man from The Queen. He was an auctioneer, and worked at the harbour. She'd met him last season.

Where? I asked. Where would a gutting quine meet an auctioneer?

Kitta crossed her arms. *Only thing ye need to know, Meggie mine, is he loves me, so there! He do. An' Ma an' Da don't need to know about him yet.*

Well.

It seemed to me that the first was a thing of joy and the second of alarm, and the two did not bind together in any happy way. Why must there be a secret? Why could I not meet this man who said he loved my sister? Why did he not take her walking on a Sunday, the usual way of the gutting girls and their lads? Why and why and why again? But Kitta's patience ran out before I'd time to close my mouth. She tossed her head. She wouldn't say.

I resolved I would watch for her again on Saturday night, but every time Magnus Tulloch walked through the yards with a sack of salt across his shoulder, everything else in my head turned to dust and blew away.

~

By the time Saturday night came, I was fit to burst—from anticipation, and from dread. I demanded Kitta tell me: was she going to Lerwick? I actually stamped my foot, lambsie, swear to God. She put on a serious face but couldn't keep to it, and soon she was laughing fit to burst. I walked off in a huff, puffing the fringe from my eyes, and it was not till I got to the yards that I stopped short. That Kitta—she hadn't answered, had she?

I sat by the fishermen's fire with Clementina, mumping away to myself until Kitta sauntered down from the huts in her old shawl, obviously no plans for Lerwick this night. She waved and giggled, and then she pulled a knowing face, gesturing with her chin somewhere to my left. I turned around.

Magnus Tulloch.

~

We spent as much time talking as dancing, though for a while it was Magnus Tulloch doing the talking—and laughing so much that I had to laugh too. He described his friend Stivvy Ratter racing other fishers down the steep lanes of Lerwick, half running, half sliding, and tumbling every which way into the crowds on Commercial Street.

Did ye join in the race with them?

Nah, lass, coopers they be too fond of the seat of their pants for that!

And he jumped to his feet and swept his arms towards the dancing.

From time to time I thought to look around for Kitta, and saw her often enough to be at ease in my mind that she wasn't likely to be slipping off to Lerwick. Whenever she caught my eye, she'd point at Magnus Tulloch and pull her face into a pantomime of gasping and fainting, and I would pray he hadn't seen her.

Later, as we sat at the fire again, our hands warming around tin mugs of tea, I became a bit braver. I told Magnus Tulloch about my big trip to the town and the things I'd seen, though

I didn't mention The Queen. I liked the way he listened, head a little on the side, as though he didn't want to miss anything.

The fishers do say the town's no place for lassies. He was mock disapproving, waving a finger about. *And what do Fish Meggie say ta that?*

Someone wanted to hear my opinion! Especially wondrous when the someone was Magnus Tulloch. It made me braver still, or maybe foolish.

I say lassies can make up their own minds about where they should go and where they shouldn't.

He looked grave, and I thought my boldness not to his liking, just as it would be scandalous to Granda Jeemsie and would give Da a jamaica.

We-e-ll, Fish Meggie, he said slowly, *I've been wantin' ta ask ye somethin'. Would ye walk with me ta Clickimin Loch tomorrow?* He grinned. *An' I'll be very pleased ta know the answer—when ye has made up your own mind.*

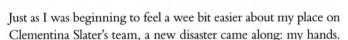

Just as I was beginning to feel a wee bit easier about my place on Clementina Slater's team, a new disaster came along: my hands.

The curers tossed salt into the farlins by the bucketful, and the burning on my hands had turned to infection. *Salty holes*, they were called, nasty green and yellow sores that itched and burned underneath the clooties. Nothing could stop the brine seeping through the wet calico. Every small movement hurt from the rubbing of skin against coarse fresh salt, the scales and gills and bones of the herring. There was only one cure—keep my hands out of salt. Which meant, for me, there was no cure.

I'd heard about the Mission to Fisherfolk lady deputies, who helped out with carbolic dressings, and bread and sugar poultices. The closest mission hut was at Garthspool, about halfway between Lerwick and Gremista.

Clementina Slater was beside her large self, pacing back and forth outside our hoosie. *Garthspool! That's an hour out of the day if they see ye right up, an' more if there be a line of ye!*

Kitta bit back, unusual for her. *She don't choose to have salty holes, now, do she! She just needs some dressings, is all.*

Clementina let fly. She knew exactly how many pence Kitta's *is all* was going to cost the three of us.

Wait! I said, interrupting. *Just listen, will ye. I'll not be going to the mission hut while there's work to do. I'll go between boats while the rest of ye are knittin'. Or next time we get a load of torn bellies an' have to wait. Ye'll not even know I've been an' gone. I'll not see us out of pocket 'cause of me.*

Clementina patted me on the arm. Kitta looked dark at her and none too happy with me, but I set a hard face upon her and she backed down. She was not in any position to take me on, see, not when I was keeping her secrets.

The mission ladies were kindly enough, and I think their ointments and poultices helped a little, but the truth was that I'd just to put up with the sores and the pain until the end of the season, the end of the year. And I'd to keep the terrible state of my hands well hidden from the curers in case they took it into their heads to send me home. Kitta said no, they wouldn't do that, they were too desperate for girls this season. But Clementina had heard of it happening. I would not be taking chances.

I would *not* be going home.

~

The other thing that ran a hook through the everyday was a good thing, aye, it was. But good things can be unsettling. So much heat and light coursing up and down and through you that you canna keep your heels on the ground. So much you don't understand nor think you ever will.

Magnus Tulloch was the other thing.

Every Saturday night I sat with him by the fire for the supper and singalong. And every Saturday night we danced. Oh, lambsie, you canna imagine what it was to dance back then. Apart from the pleasure of motion, the rhythm of music alive in your veins, dancing was an excuse—sanctioned, see?—for the twining of arms, for bodies to lean in to each other. For the touch of a face, for inhaling laughter. And a fine excuse for prolonged, shameless *looking*. I found I liked to look at Magnus Tulloch. Whenever Clementina Slater could be persuaded to sing, the fishers would beg her for a song she knew about Shetland mannies—something raucous about Vikings, I canna remember the words, only that her mother would not have liked them. I fancied I could see a touch of the Viking in Magnus Tulloch, with his long hair, his tall frame, and it turned my face the shade of my hair just to think of it.

But these loud, happy ceilidhs were no place for those sweet intimacies of learning what another thinks, who they are, the world they have come from. After kirk on Sunday—it was then I learned these things about Magnus Tulloch while we walked together to the loch, or along the sea road, or right up to the Knab.

He came from a crofting and fishing family in the south, near Sandwick. But the longline fishing was done, no future for him there. He'd apprenticed himself as a cooper to Messrs Nicol & Mair, and they would have him travel with the herring crews once free of his bonds.

So ye didn't care to sign on to the drifters yourself?

Nah, he told me, shading his eyes as we watched the bonxies circling, circling. *There be more than enough fishers already among the Tullochs.*

I said no more. Old Boy Jackie had told me quietly that Magnus Tulloch's father died at sea long ago.

Magnus Tulloch told me stories about his sister Grace, who'd once come to Lerwick on a bicycle *ta see the big city* and had managed to fall into Lerwick Harbour and had to be fished out by the Harbour Master's boy. *An' now she writes me letters every week, bidding me away from the evil city.*

Gracie had just married a boy he used to sit next to in school, Karl. Magnus Tulloch smiled when he told me this.

Have ye brothers? I asked, thinking of mine, somewhere to the north in the seas off Baltasound.

Aye, he said. *Whalers, they are, away at the Faroes.* They were older than he and Gracie by a dozen years or more, and he had not seen them for a good long while, nor expected to.

When he spoke softly of his mother's death from influenza the year before, my hand reached out before I knew it.

It was only natural that Magnus Tulloch would want to know what I had come from, too, and it made me anxious. I wanted him to like me. How could he like me if he knew? I kept my answers brief, my stories few, thinking that the less I gave, the less I would need to lie. Magnus Tulloch waited for more, and when it didn't come I think he was hurt a little. But he was patient, and he did not push, and I was ever grateful for that.

Since leaving home, I had always felt a needle of terror that someone, someone from Gadlehead, perhaps, would arrive on the station—someone who'd heard a whisper of what had happened. The Ross girls were not at Gremista, nor the Roanhaven fishers, and in any case they would be close-lipped about village matters. But people from close parts have a way of sensing scandal and will seek out scraps and hints and bits of fact to patch together into something to tell. If anyone had found out, if anyone made the connection between Kitta and me and what happened on the *Lily Maud*, gossip could hurt us. And facts—well, they could hurt us more.

The Knab is spectacular. You can see forever from its wild summit. Rabbits scamper this way and that among the gorse and marigolds, and the cliff face is home to hundreds of puffins, hunkering down among the small mauve flowers—I don't know their name—that cluster over rocks, sheltering burrows. *Ye canna look at a tammie norie without smiling*, Magnus Tulloch says, and I think: Aye, they are the strangest little things, birds that look as though they've been put together on the Lord's day off by someone with a sense of humour—a hodgepodge thrown together with the bits left over from other birds, some I've only ever seen in *The Class Book of the Natural World* at school. Fat, stumpy bodies in black and white penguin clothes. The brightly tropic-coloured beaks of toucans. Enormous orange feet, webbed like a duck's, splaying all ungainly as they come in to land on graceful eagle wings. Who could dream up anything as—what's the word? Anything as *preposterous* as a puffin?

We climb to the highest point. Here you can see right across to Bressay and Noss, and I slip, my boots sliding on wet moss. Magnus Tulloch turns and gives me his hand. I take it, then wish to pull mine back. My embarrassing, ugly hand, with bandages over three fingers, dressings the lady deputy at Garthspool has given me for the salty holes that won't heal. But Magnus Tulloch does not shrink from touch, and his care makes me numb to the pain. Once I am steadied, he relaxes his grip but does not release me, and here I am, walking hand in hand on the top of the world with this cooper boy as if we have always been meant to be here, doing this. How did that happen? I wonder. I glance down at his big hand, flecked with freckles like mine. My bandaged fingers are warm in his, and I dare to flex them a little so our palms meet, close that tender space between them. Something unlooses in me and I think: There are no words in books for this.

I remember that first day, the day we met, when he'd kissed my thumb. How shocking that was. These lightning moments, when all we have been schooled to feel is undone by sudden knowing … well, they are points along the measure of a life, lambsie. How much I had changed from that point to this.

On the upward swing of our arms, I gather to me the fist we have made together and kiss the back of Magnus Tulloch's speckled hand.

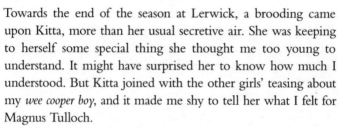

Towards the end of the season at Lerwick, a brooding came upon Kitta, more than her usual secretive air. She was keeping to herself some special thing she thought me too young to understand. It might have surprised her to know how much I understood. But Kitta joined with the other girls' teasing about my *wee cooper boy*, and it made me shy to tell her what I felt for Magnus Tulloch.

One Saturday, she was distracted at the farlins—a sorry thing, because Old Boy Jackie was doing the rounds with his wooden gauge. He stopped at Kitta's baskets. He chose the large-fulls to inspect, pulling out fish at random, measuring and sighing noisily.

There's trouble if ye don't take more care, lass, he declared finally, holding up a handful of ill-sorted herring.

Eh, sorry, Kitta said. *I'll fix it now, right as rain.* And she rapidly re-sorted the large-fulls and set about checking the other baskets, too.

Old Boy Jackie grunted and carried on down the farlin, but Clementina gave Kitta's arm a violent shaking.

What's wrong with ye, quinie? she hissed.

Kitta shook her off.

Troubling Old Boy Jackie is ill enough but now ye're losin' us time to fix it! Keep your head on your work, eh? Eh, quinie?

Aye, Kitta said, but she rolled her eyes and pouted when Clementina went back to packing.

I frowned. Something *was* wrong, but I knew better than to be the third person to take Kitta to task. And I'd an idea it had nothing to do with fish.

After a while I ventured, *Are ye goin' to the ceilidh tonight, our Kitta?*

An' just wherever else would I be goin'?

Where indeed?

It was not something unreasonable I'd asked. Kitta had been in to Lerwick with Bella Strahan the week before, and the week before that. Even when she stayed on the station she often seemed to disappear for a time.

But who was I to be calling anyone else distracted when all I cared to do on ceilidh night was dance? I decided I must pay more attention to my work. And to Kitta.

~

Town folk an' fisherfolk never do mix is what Granda Jeemsie always used to say. Suspicious, he was, of anyone from Gadlehead, more so of anyone from further afield. I always used to think it was a fisher belief, ignorant and shameful, jumbled up with the darkness I'd left behind. But on that Saturday night I learned something about people: that it is not just fisherfolk who believe they are the centre of the world, who shun all others as lesser works of God.

~

I see her leave the fishermen's fire where we have our supper. She gets to her feet as though to join in the dancing but veers off towards the hoosies. Anyone watching might think she's fetching a shawl. That's the excuse I give Magnus Tulloch when I leave, too, but I follow Kitta, creep behind her a little way distant.

She moves beyond the huts, up towards the rise. Look, I am blushing, ashamed of myself, of my prying. Kitta is going *over the hill for privacy*, unwilling to use the laavie on the shore when the boats are in port. So weary, we all are, of the crewmen's crude calls, the childish gestures they would never dare make when passing us on the way to kirk.

I sit outside our wee hoosie, shawl in hand, waiting for Kitta, but she is a long time gone. A long time.

Over the rise, in the fresh darkening of dusk, I stumble and wish I had thought to bring a lantern. I look up: the full moon is hemmed in but the clouds are alive this night, pummelling against each other, barrelling across the sky. It canna be long before the moon is freed to light my way.

I hear before I see them. Not far from me. Kitta and someone. A man. It can only be the man from Lerwick, the man who says he loves my sister. A cry of pain skirls into the wind.

I hunker down, afraid.

The wind tosses words at me. Partial conversation. Conversation that is argument. Argument that gives way to pleading. I string the words together. *Leaving. Family. College. No. The Sooth. Alone.* That cry again. *No!*

I want to run to her, cradle her pain. I want to spit at this man hurting my sister. This coward, this liar. Who says he loves and doesn't know the first thing. I want to shake them till their bones break, these town folk and fishers who don't mix, throw them into the sea to be pounded as one into food for fish and let the Lord and the Witch war over them. I want to curse Jeemsie Neish for his beliefs, and every last person in Roanhaven for what they condemn and what they let to pass.

I push the shawl to my mouth and weep.

The season at Lerwick that year—it was the best on record, and the longest. Nicol & Mair kept us there until it was time to go south to East Anglia; we weren't sent to Fraserburgh or Gadlehead in between. For myself I didn't mind, no. I'd every reason to stay on in Gremista, and the further I was from Roanhaven, the happier I would be. But Kitta, now, I wished for her to be in some new place, far from all that had hurt her and was hurting her still.

Something had bled from my sister. Maybe you wouldn't think it, to look at the way she was. Working hard. Chattering with the girls. Folk from our part of the world were good at doing that, unwilling to parade about with ill fortune pinned to their breast for others to see. Good at knitting a smile to wear. Kitta had not yet told the story enough to herself to be able to tell it to me, and she didn't know I had blundered upon part of it already. But I fancied I wasn't the only one who sensed something amiss. Clementina Slater—the last person I would have thought, then, a sensitive soul—was gentle with Kitta, and patient.

I stared open-mouthed as Clementina took out her gipper and silently cleaned up a handful of incomplete guttings from Kitta's baskets. *An' what ye be lookin' at, quinie?* she demanded.

I hugged her and she pushed me away, disgusted. But from then on, it was unspoken between us, Clementina Slater and me, that we would watch out for Kitta. That we knew there was *something*, if not the whole shape of what it was.

I said my goodbye to Magnus Tulloch on the Knab on a Sunday afternoon. We girls were leaving in the evening by the *St Siniver*. He would spend the winter in Lerwick making barrels.

We sat on the grass, high above the town, a sheer drop down a rocky cliff face to the sea below. I threaded weedy flowers, looping the stems together with hands that smelled of salt and fish no mind how much I scrubbed them.

Next year I'll have my papers an' I'll be coming with ye.

I looked up from my flower chain. Magnus Tulloch could see a *next year* for us! But it was next year, all the same. Such a very long time.

So, Great Yarmouth, Fish Meggie. The Sooth! Another big town, another big adventure for ye an' your sister.

Aye, I murmured, watching the waves far below us. *The wide world.*

I felt guilty that, while I was here, Kitta and Clementina and the Cruden Bay girls were doing the work. Scrubbing the wee hoosie, cleaning out the grate in the fire, returning oilies and rubber boots, packing up kists. They had given me leave to go, but hooted and called me *vain as a gobbler* when I unwrapped the dressings that the lady deputies had told me I must keep on all the time, whether or not my fingers were tied for gutting. I took care they did not see me take Kitta's silk scarf from my kist and stuff it into the pocket of my Sunday pinafore.

I could not bear to think of Kitta this day. Nor of what lay ahead. There would be time enough for thinking when the *St Siniver* left. For now, I just wanted to be here, free, with Magnus Tulloch.

I take the scarf from my pocket and let the silk warm through my fingers. There is this thing I must say to him, and I am finicking with words. Trying them out in my head, adding, taking away. How can a few words contain something so big? In the end I just blurt it out, like a child:

I don't want ye to forget me.

The wind howls around us, and I think it is a good thing he doesn't hear what I've said.

The outrageous purple scarf is whipped from my hands and Magnus Tulloch catches it by a corner just in time, so I don't lose it forever. It shoots into the sky, purple on grey, snapping like a mainsail in a gale.

I look at this magnificent gift that my sister gave me, wild as a seabird, and remember a promise I made to myself that I would wear it in public one day, that I would be brave and reckless. I am a gutting girl now, only somewhat short of a disaster still, with a job to do in the wide world, but is that a brave and reckless thing or does it just mean I have run away?

Scrambling to my feet, I take the scarf from Magnus Tulloch's grip, reel in the silk from the sky and wind it around me.

I will not forget ye, Fish Meggie.

And standing here, between the top of the world and the sky, I kiss the air.

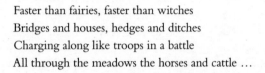

Faster than fairies, faster than witches
Bridges and houses, hedges and ditches
Charging along like troops in a battle
All through the meadows the horses and cattle …

My first ever train ride made me think of that poem we had recited in school, Mr Robert Louis Stevenson's poem, but it was night and I had to imagine the world rushing past. The lurching carriages rocked us 600 miles from landfall at the Broch to Great Yarmouth, a crush of girls singing and laughing, unable to sleep.

When we arrived, well. Another country, it was, and a shock. If we had thought Lerwegians did not much care for the flood of fishworkers to their town, it was as nought compared to our grudging welcome in The Sooth.

No wee hoosies here. The curers gave us an allowance and a list and we were to find our own lodgings close to the yards on the Denes, three or four girls to a room. Clementina shepherded us straight to Mrs Booth's. When I looked up at the house, with its flower-box windows upstairs and down, I gulped.

Very grand, I whispered to Kitta.

In the small back garden was a room with a stone laundry trough and a tin bathtub, and right down the back a convenience unheard of: a single wee laavie with a seat and a pan.

But the lodgings, they were not grand, no. We had a tiny windowless room underneath Mrs Booth's staircase, with brown paper hung loosely over the walls and covering the wooden floorboards. I opened the door and looked around outside, but the hallway walls and floor were not papered the same way.

What's all this for? I asked, flicking my fingers at the paper.

For us, Clementina barked, laughing, and then continued in a high, prissy voice and her version of an English accent. *Guttin' gels are dirty things, yew know. Greasy, fishy hands an' oil in their hair. All those nasty scales get over ev–ry–thing.*

An' they stomp in with nasty guts on their boots, yew know, Kitta joined in.

And, Clementina said, brandishing candles in my face, *they smell like somethin' horrid. Like … like fish!*

Kitta put a match to a wick and the room was filled with the reek of camphor. More to Mrs Booth's liking than the smell of four gutting girls.

The fourth was Bella Strahan, whose team was scattered, unable to find a room together. She was not her usual loud self, and lay spread-eagled on the horsehair mattress. All of the girls but me had had a bitter time of it on the *St Siniver*. But while most were feeling back to rights by the time the train drew in to the Yarmouth station, Bella was grey-faced still. Her travelling pinafore sour with flecks of vomit.

I eyed her, lying there on the bed in this brown-papered room we would share till near to Christmas. *She is harmless*, Kitta had told me. *Ye just don't know her.* But even like this, she made me nervous, Bella Strahan did.

Kitta was making me nervous, too, all Bright Carefree Quinie. Would I have my sister wretched and sorrowing? Of course I wouldn't, of course not, but it was a performance; she wasn't fooling me. The knitted smile again. I had been waiting all this time for her to tell me about the man, but now I knew she never would because of what it would cost her to unpick the stitches of that smile.

In the time it had taken to travel south, the sores on my hands had improved a little. Those few days had been a rest from the salt, but I liked to think it was the cradling of Magnus Tulloch's hands around mine on the day we said goodbye that had brought me healing, brought me luck. In Mrs Booth's windowless room, I peeled back the dressings and held my fingers under candlelight. *Look,* I whispered, *look, Magnus Tulloch.* The skin was pink and puckered at the edges—itchy, tender healing skin—and the yellow-green centres did not look so angry now. I took from my kist the little store of poultices and carbolic that the mission ladies had given me and hoped it would be enough to see me through.

~

Great Yarmouth was not so congenial as Gremista. The yards were on the South Denes, away from the heart of town, but were still more crowded. The work at the farlins was the same, but now the weather was getting colder. A frost was on the fish when we began in the morning. *That's nothing,* Kitta told me. *A few more weeks an' we'll be breakin' ice!*

I imagined myself describing the scene to Magnus Tulloch: The boats sail up the river, straight in from the sea, and unload the catch right at the station. You look up from the farlins, an' there they are, the boats, there in front of ye. And the noise! The gulls are smaller here but they swoop in like a shrieking white cloud. An' have ye heard about the cooper shops, the way they're in between the stations, right down near the salt stores?

I stopped to test my pulse. No, it was not helping, not comforting at all, this talking in my head to Magnus Tulloch. The distance between us was larger than my imagination. I could not put to rights the facts: he was not here, I was not there with him.

Old Boy Jackie had come with us, a familiar face, and some of the others from Gremista, but Nicol & Mair's English coopers were impatient, bad-tempered. They were resigned to all these stranger-girls coming in but they didn't feel the need to be cheerful about it, no indeed. They could never have cause for quarrel with our work. We knew what we were doing, aye, and were fast and clean about it. But something about us being here offended them.

Mr Samuelson, he was our supervisor, Old Bloddy, we called him. He did not like to see us knit in the times when we were waiting for a load to arrive. *You birds of passage is 'ere to work, not to idle about making bloddy socks!* Never mind that we were not being paid if there were no fish. One evening he sent us off to the salt boats, though it was not our job. *To make yourselves useful.* I stared at him, frowning. Me too? So close to where the steam drifters left at night? But he hurried me along with a jerk of his thumb.

An' what you be waiting for, Lady Carrothead? A bloddy copperplate invitation?

It was cruel on the back, hefting barrels onto the pier and rolling them the distance to the salt store. A fresh agony for my hands, too, newly inflamed since gutting began. But my work with the barrels lasted only until the crew of an East Coast drifter came down to load the boat. The Scottish master took one look at the redhead in front of him and declared he would not leave that night. Mr Samuelson was then set straight, he learned a bloddy thing or two about *ginger quinies on the watter.* And from then I kept my distance, knitting or reading from newspapers discarded on the pier.

Read us somethin' cheerful, Fish Meggie, Isobel bid me, and I ran a finger down a page of *The Yarmouth Independent.* The letters were always lively, especially the ones about us.

'*The Scotsman's Reception at Yarmouth*'? I read.

Ooh, aye, said Izzy, grinning.

'Sir:—*If I take my wife for a walk, along any of our main streets, during the autumn season when the Scotch visitors are with us, it is with considerable difficulty and discomfort we wend our way.*'

Con-SID-erable difficulty, Kitta said, mock serious.

'*Our Scotch fishing friends and the lassies monopolise the pavements, they have no consideration for other pedestrians, and rather than give*

*way for a lady, invariably they force the lady into the gutter in order to
pass along.'*

Ooh-hoo, said Izzy, *those lassies are no LAY-dies!*

'*The expectorations of the male sex are perfectly disgusting. They
show no regard to passers, and on more than one occasion, I have
personally observed the nuisance created by their filthy habits.'*

SOOO disGUSTing! Kitta said, her hand over her mouth.
Are ye disGUSTed, Izzy-lass?

Oh, aye, even more than ye if I knew what it were. Expori-what?

Expectorations, I said, looking up. *Spitting!*

And we laughed until Kitta wailed that she'd wet her pants.
Which made us laugh more.

~

I was glad to have Isobel by me at the farlins, and Mary on the
other side of her. I missed them at night, the Cruden Bay girls.
I even missed Jeannie's snoring. If it were not for my hands, the
mess it made of them, the sting of salt eating into the sores, I
would never have minded the nights when the drifters kept
arriving and we worked past twelve under the light of naphtha
flares, which turned our scaly arms as silver as the herring.
Exhausting, aye, but the routine was a comfort. We would send
Limpy Davy, a cooper boy, up to the Fishwharf stalls to fetch us
bread and jam and flasks of tea. But on days when we were done
by four, well, I was lost. I longed for the community of girls in
the wee hoosies of Gremista, our evening singing as we cooked
broth or fried some herring for tea.

Mrs Booth would not allow us in the kitchen. Too scaly, we
were, too smelly, *yew know.* We bought penny buns for supper
and then walked awhile in little groups, looking at *funcy things* in
shop windows. But the evenings were dark early, and the cold
was closing in, and there was plenty of trouble about in the port
side of town. Too soon we were back in the fuggy room under
Mrs Booth's staircase. Too much fuggy time for wishing we
were somewhere else.

Ye think too much, quinie, Clementina Slater said when I sighed yet again. *Be glad ye're here, eh! Just think of that!*

A picture of Roanhaven threatened like a sudden heavy squall. *Oh, aye, I am glad to be here. But Gremista … There's something … the air is not the same here. Don't ye think, Clementina? Don't ye think so?*

Ooh-hoo! Listen to this one, complainin' about the air now! Bella Strahan minced across the room, hands flouncing about.

I just mean … I stopped, flummoxed. I couldn't talk to Bella Strahan.

We-e-ell, Clementina said slyly, *I don't believe it be the Gremista air ye're pinin' for, quinie.*

Ooh-hoo, no, that's right! This one's walkin' out with a wee loon! A bairn an' a bairn!

Ach, hush your mouth. I'd had enough. *An' away with ye to Banff an' be boiled in a pot!*

Kitta had been half dozing, half knitting all the while. The whole conversation passed her by.

~

It wasn't long before Bella Strahan found herself somewhere more enlivening to go after supper. This would not have caused me any grief but that she was taking Kitta with her.

What place is it? I asked when Kitta told me to walk straight home with Clementina.

Not so far, the Wet Dock Tavern. An' ye needn't be givin' me that look, Fish Meggie. Have ye not been yourself to The Queen an' lived to tell? It's just for an hour of fun, an' all the girls from Aberdeen go.

Clementina doesn't, I thought.

Aye, an' ye can come with us, if ye like.

But she didn't mean it. She knew I didn't like. I opened my mouth to say all the other things I didn't like but she held up her palm.

Stop your worryin', Meggie mine, ye're not my mother!

I couldn't stop worrying. I worried when Kitta and Bella Strahan fair danced out of the yards and away to this Wet Dock place. I worried when the hours went by. I heard Mrs Booth come in from the laavie and stump upstairs to her bed. Clementina said, *Don't fret, quinie,* but she poked her head around the door to look at the hallway clock, even though we'd just heard it chiming nine. She pinched out the biggest candle and plumped herself onto the bed, but I don't think her eyes closed, no.

Not long after the chime of ten, we heard scuffling by the side door. Thank the Lord! I hurried to unlock it for Kitta and Bella before Mrs Booth woke up. What would she have said to Bella's whisky breath, the sour, sweaty reek on them both?

They were unexpectedly quiet, and shivering.

Clementina sat up, frowning, when Bella flopped beside her and then she heaved herself as far from Bella as she could.

Kitta climbed onto the bed and I looked her over carefully. Her clothes—something was amiss. The buttons of her blouse in mismatched holes. One of them missing. I pulled the blanket over her, rubbed her freezing hands. *Are ye all right?* I whispered.

She jerked her hands away from mine and curled them into her chest. A glance before she turned away. Dead eyes.

I drew a ragged breath. I had seen my sister's naked face.

~

One day Limpy Davy sidled up to me at the farlin with a grin.

Got summat for ya, I have, he said, all secretive, glancing left and right of him.

Well? I demanded, my fingers not breaking the rhythm of gutting.

Come from the Girl Bessie *in from Lerwick last night. The master's boy give it to me to dee-liver. Give me a ha'penny an' all.*

Lerwick!

He took from his pocket a small package tied with string, and I could see my name printed on the thick brown paper. Sizzling, I was, like a fish in a pan.

Want for me to open it for ya? he said hopefully, shaking the package and holding it up to his ear.

No, I don't, an' ye can just give it here afore ye go an' break anythin'!
I wiped my hand on my greasy skirt and took the package.
Come on, then, lass, who it from?
Never ye mind, Limpy Davy, just never ye mind!

All day it lay in my pocket, warm as a promise, the beat of a heart. I could not wait to open it, but there was a cran of herring in front of me, a yard full of girls, and wait is all I could do. And at the end of the day I had to wait some more. What foolishness to open a package when Clementina Slater was watching, when Bella Strahan would be itching to snatch it from my hands.

It was late, by the light of one of Mrs Booth's candles, when I untied the string and peeled back the paper. Inside were two more sheets of paper, folded one inside the other into a thick square. One was half a page of newsprint cut from *The Shetland Times*, with a circle drawn in ink around an article. I smoothed it flat, smiling, until I read the headline: ACCIDENT IN BARREL FACTORY. Then I raced through the rest of it: *cooper's apprentice injured ... piece of wood jammed one of the machines ... shield flew off and struck the young man on the back of the head ... rendered unconscious ... Gilbert Bain Hospital.*

Blood. I could imagine it everywhere, on the machine, on the factory floor, the barrel hoops, the doctor's hands. Magnus Tulloch lying there, not waking, awash in blood.

I grabbed the other page, handwritten in blue ink:

Dearest Meggie

Don't fret I am all right good as new since coming from the hospital but I did not want you to hear of the accident from others and think the news bad. Already I am back to work nothing left of the bruise but a yellowing now where the doctor shaved my head Nicol & Mair paid the doctor bill the hospital too and I am to be held only 2 day wages when I was away from factory 1 whole week!

Forgive me I am rushing to get this to Stivvy Ratter on the Girl Bessie.

I miss you promise you will come back Fish Meggie.

Yours aye

Magnus Tulloch

I let it go, my tattered breath.

He is all right, he is all right, I sang to myself over and over, shivering, until a new song took its place, and oh how feverish I was, and flurried and guilty all at once:

I miss you, I miss you, I miss you ...

I remember your hands when you were a baby, lambsie, always cold, your small fingers so white. I would blow on them with warm breath and wrap them up in woollen mittens, and I used to tell your mother: *She has her grunnie's hands, the North Sea instead of blood in her veins.*

And Kathryn would say: *Another thing she'll never thank you for.*

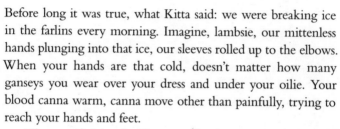

Before long it was true, what Kitta said: we were breaking ice in the farlins every morning. Imagine, lambsie, our mittenless hands plunging into that ice, our sleeves rolled up to the elbows. When your hands are that cold, doesn't matter how many ganseys you wear over your dress and under your oilie. Your blood canna warm, canna move other than painfully, trying to reach your hands and feet.

The work slowed. Clumsy, all of us. It was common for blades to slip, to nick the clooties, even slice through them. Those mission ladies were kept busier with cuts in the Great Yarmouth winter than ever I had seen them with salty holes.

In some ways, the cold was easier on my hands. It numbed the burning and itching of the ulcers. But the infection just got worse. I stopped going to the mission huts. What if the lady deputies took it into their heads to report me to Old Bloddy? Clementina said no, they wouldn't, it was not their job. *But best ye take no chances, aye, quinie, aye.*

I was moved wordless when she scratched the back of her hand with her gipper so she had an excuse to go to the hut herself to get dressings for me.

~

We are singing when it happens. Singing helps—I don't know why. Perhaps it gives our brains something to do other than send those little sparks of protest and pain to and fro. *What a friend we have in Je-sus ...*

Kitta screams.

I turn and there is blood pouring from her wrist, redder, fresher than herring blood, than the guts we are awash in up to the calves of our boots. She thrusts her hand into the pit of her arm, pulling away from Clementina, who has ripped off her headsquare and is trying to stop the bleeding.

Fetch Old Bloddy! Clementina yells at Limpy Davy.

Kitta shrieks anew. *What? NO!*

But Clementina nods at Limpy Davy and jerks her head, the signal to run. Clementina Slater has been in gutting yards long enough to know when it is best to *take no chances* and when there is no choice to be had in the matter at all.

I have to hold her round the arms, my Kitta, to stop her scrambling after the cooper boy.

~

Kitta was sent home to Roanhaven on the train, with a clumsy stitch in her wrist and a thick wad of calico around wrist and hand.

For all the days of my life, I have not forgotten the sight of Kitta's face against the window of the train. It seared me cold, lambsie, but I didn't know what it meant—not then, not straight away. But Kitta did. She knew right in that moment: all that stood between her and the end was a journey on a train. There would be no escaping it again, no escaping Roanhaven.

When I wept in the face of my loss, her loss, in fear for all she was returning to, when I watched her stricken face grow ever further from me, I had no premonition, no knowledge, that this was a distance I could never breach again.

~

For a while it seemed that Nicol & Mair might send us back too—Clementina was good, but not even the best packer could manage with only one gutter on her team. And then Limpy Davy turned up at the yard with a wee girl a step behind him.

Daisy, he announced. *Me sister.*

Clementina lifted a brow. *An' what are we to do with a wee bairnikie like this one? We're here to gut herrin', not play Knifey with bairns.*

But Daisy pulled a gipper from her skirt and said, *I can gut herrin' an' all, I can. Me Mam showed me how. Good as you I are.*

And so she was, although Limpy Davy had to set her on a box so she could reach into the farlin. It was a funny thing to watch, lambsie.

Me, I wanted to hug Limpy Davy's Daisy every day. I would miss my Kitta more than I could say to anyone, and I worried myself sick for her hurt hand and the hurting no-one else could see. But ... I am shamed to admit to such selfishness but ... This is the truth, lambsie: I didn't want to leave. There were weeks yet until the season was done and I did not want to go back to Roanhaven until the last herring of the year left Great Yarmouth in a barrel.

~

Less than a week later, another departure, unexpected. Bella Strahan disappeared, with not a word of goodbye nor reason—packed off back to Aberdeen, so it was whispered around the yards. I wasn't grieved to see her gone, I couldn't say otherwise, but I was curious, aye.

D'ye know? I asked Clementina that night, staring up at the staircase with its spidery shadows reaching into darkness. *About Bella Strahan? Did she leave word, or has anybody told ye why?*

She shook her head and snorted. *A cradle bairn, is it ye are still, Fish Meggie? Is no need for anybody to say when ye can use the two eyes God gave ye.*

I frowned helplessly in the dark. What was it I was supposed to have seen? But Clementina Slater was disgusted with me and pinched out the candle. The mattress rustled as she turned her ample self to face the wall of our little room. Which now smelled of camphor and only two gutting girls.

~

Christmas was near upon us and I was filled with dread. The herring season of 1905 was winding up with the year. In just a few months I had made my life over, left behind the wee quinie I had been. And now I had to return to Roanhaven.

You can never go back. That's what people say now, isn't it, lambsie?
Usually they mean it in a wistful way because their memories
are fond and they wish for simpler times, better times, gilded
times. If they truly could go back, maybe they would not find
the past so perfect as they had held it in their hearts to be.

For me, it's different. Roanhaven is a dark place in my
mind—not gilded, not better—and the but-and-ben at number 8
Tiller Street is the darkest place of all. But suddenly the angle
will skew, to shine like moonlight over that house of granite and
stone, and I remember something else: its *quietness*. You might
be wondering how a place could ever be quiet with eight people
crowded into two wee rooms. Perhaps it's because we ate there,
slept there, we clustered around the fire at the close of day, but
we lived our lives on the boatie shore, up on the braes, on the
Lily Maud, in the schoolroom, on the moors. Men, women and
children all with their places to be, their work to do.

And perhaps, too, because we were people steeped in the
ins and outs of restraint. It comes as a shock to me now, writing
these words, to discover this thing about myself: that there is
some small part of me that finds a thread of affection for restraint.

But not then, no. When I went back to Roanhaven at the
end of 1905, restraint was all around me—in the village, in my
family. And it ate away every kindly feeling I had for those sea
people I had come from. And what happened in the months
before I left again hardened my resolve never to return.

Kitta!

She drops the bundle of ganseys and stockings and hugs me. In her layers of wool, she is lumpish, heavy in my arms. The pallor of her face scares me.

I grasp her hand. *Let me see. How is it, your poor hand?*

A thick red scar snakes up her wrist, but although the skin looks to be healed, her hand feels loose in mine.

She shrugs. *Better than it were, Meggie mine. An' well enough to do for Ma now.* But her eyes slide away, avoiding me.

Where's Ma?

Asleep. Let her sleep while she can. The cough … Doctor's been.

A look between us.

I don't know. He shakes his head an awful lot. And Kitta begins to cry.

I peel off my shawl, my travelling apron, and make tea for her. Everything is in its place, the kettle, the pot, the tin of tea, the tea-cosy and spoon, just where they have always been. I pour tea into chipped cups, the same cups that have hung from rusty hooks beside the fire for all my life. My hand reaches for the tin of sugar on the cupboard, the old milk jug on the shelf above that, knowing they will be there. All is as it was, as it should be.

But the doctor has been.

The others are back?

Aye. She sniffs at the washing on the floor. *Back four days past an' already out on the Lily. I don't know how …*

I control my voice. *An' Granda?*

Silence. We have never talked about it, all this time, Kitta and me.

Well?

See for yourself when he stomps in.

What of the village? The others?

Them? Sayin' nothin'. Nothin' still. But the looks ... She exhales, pushing something bitter from her lungs. *Scared to think it really happened, scared to think they would have done the same themselves. So they say nothing. But they canna wipe it off their face, what they're not sayin'.*

I put a hand over hers and we drink our tea.

She touches the bandages on my poulticed fingers. *Unty Jinna has somethin' better. Go an' see her tomorrow. Few weeks an' ye'll be right.*

I know what she's thinking: Few weeks an' ye'll be gone.

Are ye all right, our Kitta?

She gets up and scoops the clothes off the floor, a great bulky armful. *Told ye afore, didn't I? Ye never listen, do ye? My hand's better now, better than it were.*

I pull my shawl around my shoulders again and step outside. The wind is howling through Tiller Street, a blast from the frozen north.

All this air, and I canna breathe.

~

That night, I sit on the wall, my skirt tucked under my knees, looking down to the boatie shore. The *Lily Maud* is in, and I smile to see how tall Will has grown. A man, now, like Archie and Jamie, but for the gangly legs and arms.

Da looks hunched, a muffle of lines and wool, and I canna tell whether it is just from cold or something more painful. He moves slowly up from the shore and I suddenly think: He is an old man already, my father, and a man I hardly know.

Granda Jeemsie stumps up from the *Lily* as though sure of his footfall on the sand, as though he has every right in the world and nothing indeed to be sorry for. He looks towards the village, slows a little, picks up his pace again. He canna see me, not from that distance, not in the winter dark with nought but the glow of a skinny moon, but I fancy he knows he is being watched this night. I fancy he knows I'm here.

~

It was a sombre Christmas. A holiday, a kirk day, a *family day*. But when we crowded into the pews of the Auld Kirk, it was not the spirit of Christmas I felt, no.

They turned their heads to look, our neighbours did, they were silent on this day of greetings and goodwill. Sailor Wattie, Unty Leebie and Unty Jinna, all of them came forward with handshakes and cheer. But the others, no. Buckey's John's Mary turned her face to the altar. She did not ask me about Ma, she did not speak to any of us. And Maudie Ross could hardly keep her bug eyes off Granda, until he set his scowl on her—and then she whipped around like she'd seen a selkie. All through the service, I kept thinking: The Christmas hymns sound different without Ma's piping voice carrying the tune. If Ma were here, it would be all right, it would be better.

After the service Unty Jinna and Liza came home with us, all of us trudging with our heads down, shawls and scarves clutched to our chin. The roar of the wind tore snatches of carols from a choir and tossed them round in the grey air.

~

We sat around the fire in silence, and I could hardly bear it.

I crept away to check on Ma. Her cough was worse, her skin red and dry. The sight of her there, lying on the bed, was a thing to catch at my breathing. Ma, my bustling, strong, always-working mother, just lying there. A ruddy, unmoving, unseeing thing.

It's Christmas, Ma, I whispered. *Listen, can you hear the carols outside?*

She pushed my hand away when I tried to stroke her damp hair.

What can I get for ye, Ma?

She moaned and pushed at me again.

Ma? What is it ye want? Ma?

Her eyes flew open, wide as can be, and she grabbed at my hand.

Snow.

Snow? Isn't snowing, Ma. There's no snow.

She turned to look at me and her face broke. *Ah, my Meggie, back from the fish.*

I pressed a wet towel against her head and she giggled like a little girl. *Ginger Meggie cross your leggie.*

I came asunder and wept.

~

Kitta refused help with the dinner. She'd boiled a rabbit and roasted it brown with neeps and tatties in dripping—a rare treat.

As she brought the big tin plate to the table and was about to set it down, it slipped from her fingers a little. Fatty juice spattered everywhere.

Consternation.

Eh, ah! Da jumped up.

Liza squealed like the ninny she was still.

Unty Jinna rushed for cloths while Kitta tried to mop up the table, dab at our sleeves, but Jamie waved her off.

No harm, lass, he said, picking a piece of stringy meat from Will's gansey and shoving it into his mouth.

I licked the back of my hand. *Mmm, good!*

Kitta relaxed and pulled a face at me.

Great clumsy quinie. Granda Jeemsie narrowed his eyes. *Ye'll not be goin' back to the fish now. Never.*

I glared at him. *She will. Course she will.*

Not with her hand like that. Canna gut herrin' with a hand like that.

Kitta was mopping furiously.

Her hand is better! All healed over.

Ah, he said, smug, *but weak, no strength in it. Eh, quinie? Eh?*

Kitta just kept mopping, tears in her eyes.

Granda Jeemsie was smirking. Cruel. Hard as glass. I know ye, I suddenly thought. I know what ye are because I've seen what ye're afraid of. I shone it onto him, the fullness of my hate, all of it there in my eyes, and he was the one to look away first.

Sinful, he muttered, *brazen quinies …*

But Da's fists thumped on the table, surprising us all.

Hush your mouth this day, Jeemsie Neish! he thundered. *None of us here be without sin! It's a day to be rememberin' that.*

~

In the hour between Christmas dinner and darkness, when Jinna and Liza had gone home, the men were asleep and Kitta with Ma, I wrapped up well and crept outside. The sky was blanched and grainy and I thought Ma might get her wish for snow.

In the sheddie up on the braes, I took from my pocket a brown paper parcel with my name on it in handwriting that was familiar now. It had come yesterday, delivered to the door by the post cart, and so glad I was that I was there to take it from Postie Andrew.

Inside, a box, plain-looking, small. I prised off the lid. A letter? No, there was none, just a wad of wax paper, light in my fingers. Gently I peeled it open.

Ohhh!

It was the most beautiful thing, lambsie, you canna imagine—a message without words.

A sugar biscuit in the shape of a butterfly.

~

Ma died in the early morning hours after Christmas night, as the first snow fluttered from the sky.

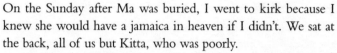

On the Sunday after Ma was buried, I went to kirk because I knew she would have a jamaica in heaven if I didn't. We sat at the back, all of us but Kitta, who was poorly.

I could see Isobel Ross eyeing me and whispering behind her smug, grey, stumpy fingers. I moved forward a pew to catch her scritchy mewling. *Ten months to the day since the boy*, I heard. *The Lord never forgets.*

I got up and walked out and I didn't go back, not even when Da sent Will to fetch me. And never again did I step inside that kirk. Wasn't that I turned my back to the Lord but I could never again believe there was space inside those walls for love. I did not think He would choose to shine His face on the Righteous of Roanhaven.

~

A Hogmanay in mourning. It passed us by.

~

In the New Year, Kitta was sick. I made oatmeal for her, with salt and some butter I begged from Unty Jinna, but she had no taste for it. All she would take was tea.

Whenever they were at sea, Da, Granda and the boys, I would find her in bed, clutching Ma's shawl. Grieving is what I thought. What a cradle bairn I was.

One day Postie Andrew brought two letters of condolence addressed to me. The one from Magnus Tulloch I kept to myself. The other I took in to Kitta, thinking its news might cheer her.

Well, I said, squeezing in next to her, *Clementina Slater hasn't much time for her brother Robbie's new bride.*

Kitta turned from me, curling her arms around her knees.

I held up the grubby letter, with much crossing-out and underlining, from Fitdee, Aberdeen. I skipped over the formal words of *sorrow for your loss*.

So, this is what Clementina says: 'She's a weak and peely wee thing from the city and no more sense than my grunny's goose, robbie goes off to sea and who do ye think gets stuck with miss goosey's complaining, not robbie that's who.'

Nothing from Kitta.

I wouldn't want to be Clementina Slater's sister-in-law, eh!

I tugged Kitta's arm and she grunted.

Clementina asked of Kitta's plans. Would she be going back to the fish? Now that Ma …? If not, we would be needing a third girl to step in, *and it isn't goin' to be miss goosey, she would be a disaster.* I kept this part of the letter to myself too.

I looked down at my hands, unbandaged, clean-looking since I'd been using Unty Jinna's washes and the poultices she'd given me to put on at night. But the scars on my fingers were red, tender to touch. What would happen when the gutting started and they were all day in salt again?

Clementina didn't ask about my hands.

~

When February came round, there was much to do. At the end of the month Da and the boys would be away to Lewis, the season beginning again. There was mending and knitting to be done, and lines and nets to be repaired for the *Lily Maud*. Ma's rounds, too—no longer Ma's—with our smokies. I would not let Kitta take the creel; she was tired and hunched and not strong enough. She didn't even argue.

I walked to the churchyard, to the stone engraved *Belle Neish Duthie*. There was nothing in me that believed this mound of earth was my ma, but I needed to talk to someone.

What do I do? I whispered, laying a handful of red clover at the foot of the stone. *She is slippin' away from us, Ma.*

But my mother's strength, the silent grace I'd taken for granted and did not ever think to need, was lost to me now. I listened for her voice. Nothing.

Unty Jinna was the only other person. I waited until Liza left with a basket of washing. My father's sister was pressing fine linen sheets with a hot iron and water, scenting them with dried rosemary. I gathered up some pillow cloths and folded them for her.

Is nothin' ye can do for Kitta now, she told me, frowning. *I done all I could afore your ma passed. But some things will be, no mind to wishing them otherwise.*

She looked at my blank face. Lifted a brow.

Ah.

I waited.

Steam hissed, rising from the sheets, and Unty Jinna breathed it in. The smell was sharp and sweet, both.

She will have to tell ye herself, Fish Meggie. She is the one to.

But Kitta would tell me nothing, no mind however many times I asked, and once again I reeled from the blow.

When I mentioned fetching the doctor, she gave me one of Ma's Looks.

~

I remember the sky that day, an early March sky. Dirty white, bruised with the grey of a storm heading in from the north-east. All through the morning, tramping across country, I watched shapes form in the clouds. A woman's face. A solan goose, the curve of its neck, its angel wings. The moon before dark has yet fallen. And then it was just the storm, a violence of wind and stones, almost too thick to see the way ahead. I stumbled with the creel laden with eggs and butter, sacks of neeps, and there was nowhere to shelter from the sting of hail on my face. Five minutes and I was drenched through every layer of wool, mud splashed to my knees.

By the time I reached Tiller Street, the hail had stopped but not the wind. I pushed the door shut behind me, and a roar of air shuddered through the chimney. Soot rained down on the grate.

The empty grate.

Four o'clock and no fire.

Kitta was not on Ma's bed. Not in the netting shed. On the boatie shore? No.

I checked with Unty Jinna, calm as I could be. She hadn't seen her.

I staggered up to the sheddie on the braes and she wasn't there, either, and then higher up to the scaur. And when I sheltered my eyes with my hands, looked down to the sea, I thought there was a speck of something, a long way distant.

But it canna be Kitta. In a winter storm, in water that will be a briny melt of ice. It canna be her. Our Kitta canna be in the sea.

But I have a bad feeling, the worst feeling, and it makes me run, run, and the closer I get to the speck of something that canna be Kitta, the harder the panic thumps in me. Because it *is* her. Kitta, floundering in the sea, up past her knees, and her back is to me, her *back* is to me, she is wading away from the shore, ever further away.

Kitta! I scream. *KI–TTA!*

She pauses at the sound of my voice, then moves again.

Come back! I am screaming louder, weeping. *Kitta! Come back!*

What is she doing? But I know what she's doing. And she canna … she canna …

She stops. She turns slowly. A girl-shaped sea creature, slippery and sleek and bound in human clothes. She is half gone from me, half gone.

I am running down to the sea. *Please, Kitta, PLEASE!*
She drags herself towards me. Stops again.
Come on, Kitta, come to me! It's all right, just come to me!
Another step, and then another, steps against her will.

By the time I reach the place where the sea is tossing itself onto the shingle, she is close enough for me to see that her skirt is hiked up, tucked into her drawers. That blood is streaking the inside of her thighs. That she has hardly strength to stand.

My mind is mush. I canna put together what I am seeing, canna make sense of it. So much blood, dark as roses.

Kitta is shaking violently. The sound of her teeth is louder than the waves. You will die, I think, die if I don't get to you, bring you in, make you warm. My feet go to move but then stop. I canna rush into the water that lies between us.

The sea is tossing it forward, rolling it back, forward and back in the pale green shallows, the bloody mess of a barely human thing. A skull, a face, a soft wrinkled hide yet to fill with fat and flesh. Born too soon, misborn, from a mother herself barely human. Barely alive. A mother half sea creature and half girl.

Nothing. There's a blank in my memory, lambsie.

I canna remember packing my kist, nor the journey to Stornaway with Clementina Slater and Liza, who was taking Kitta's place. It was a few weeks into the season, but Nicol & Mair needed every team they could get that year. Da had relented about the Western Isles, sending his permission by the *Three Bees* in from Castlebay. I don't think he cared overmuch about anything since Ma's passing.

Eight weeks, I was, in Stornaway. I know it is in the western isle of Lewis, I could show it to you on a map, lambsie, but I canna tell you a thing about it. It was a blur to me, a blur of guts and blood and scales and sores and sleep. Of forgetting.

I'd not have gone at all if Kitta was still abed but she surprised us, Unty Jinna and me, she was on her feet again. Cooking again, reddin' lines, washing clothes, aye. As though nothing had happened.

No-one had seen me half carrying Kitta home in the darkening dusk. In that small village where everyone thought they knew everything, no-one ever knew about that. Not even Granda Jeemsie, when he came back next morning on the *Lily Maud*. Influenza, as far as he was concerned, as far as they all were concerned. He didn't so much as poke his head around from the but—he had no wish *to be catchin' anythin' nasty*. Liza suspected, of that I am sure, but was never told to her face.

Unty Jinna had stopped the bleeding with the old herbs that knit and heal. I held a shawl over Kitta's mouth and turned my face away as Jinna pulled from my sister's body the bloody rope that had not passed.

If I had looked closer in the sheddie, lambsie, when I was searching for Kitta that day, I would have seen the bloodstained rags she'd left there. If I had looked down, I would have seen spots of blood on the sand, a speckled trail between the sheddie and the sea. But I hadn't seen what was there, only what was not. Later I burned the rags in the fire, kicked away the trail.

Kitta lay in bed a week, with no-one but Unty Jinna and me to see. And then she got up as though from sleep and stumbled weakly back into the world. Hardly sprightly, no, but no-one expected her to be, not after wrestling influenza. I cooked soup to make her strong, collected roots from the moor for Unty Jinna's tonics, and soon the ash faded a little from my sister's face.

If you asked Kitta where the fire-iron was, she would tell you. She would make a pot of tea and ask who was wanting a cup. She would say, *Pass the salt, will ye, Meggie mine.* If someone sneezed, her usual response: *Bless thee well.* Every small and trivial thing, like nothing had happened. But she drew a veil over everything I wanted to know. She never talked about it. She never really talked to me again.

I couldn't talk, either. Magnus Tulloch's letters came, and I put them away in the shottle of my kist. I suppose I was the same as my sister, doing what she had done. Sometimes that's just the way of it—we do what we must to put one foot after the other and keep on, keep on, just keep going.

~

It was me who buried the baby. High up, behind the scaur. As close as I could get to the sky.

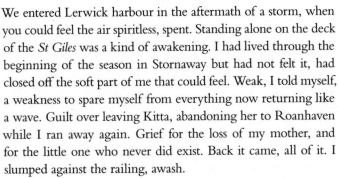

We entered Lerwick harbour in the aftermath of a storm, when you could feel the air spiritless, spent. Standing alone on the deck of the *St Giles* was a kind of awakening. I had lived through the beginning of the season in Stornaway but had not felt it, had closed off the soft part of me that could feel. Weak, I told myself, a weakness to spare myself from everything now returning like a wave. Guilt over leaving Kitta, abandoning her to Roanhaven while I ran away again. Grief for the loss of my mother, and for the little one who never did exist. Back it came, all of it. I slumped against the railing, awash.

Clementina Slater staggered up beside me, puffing a whitened breath none too sweet after all the roiling and retching hours from Stornaway.

Give me a wee look at your hands, quinie, she demanded, holding hers out to me. I held mine the same, palms up, and it was a shocking thing, proof of how much else I had managed not to feel. The dressings on my fingers were stained, the salty holes weeping.

Clementina's hands were beautiful. She'd never been bothered by salt, and oil from the herring—especially the roes—had made her skin as smooth as butter.

I flexed my hands only a little and there it was: pain. Like penance.

Ach, she said, disgusted. *Didn't I say it from the start? Ye're a disaster.*

It felt like a homecoming, walking to Gremista. Liza chattered away next to me, one question following the next, tweet, tweet. Clementina's patience with her was tattered already. She rolled her eyes at me meaningfully but I was too distracted to save her from Liza.

Magnus Tulloch's letters were still in my kist, unread. No response. What he would make of that I could not imagine. It was one more thing, a big one, among many for which I felt ill of myself. The thought of seeing him was stirring a soup in me. He might appear on the road up from the yards any minute, and what if he was offended? Hurt? What if he had no taste for chancing his feelings again with someone so flighty as me?

The wee hoosies of Gremista were just over the rise. The Cruden Bay girls picked up their pace, passing us. *Same hut this year as for last, aye?* Isobel marched ahead with purpose.

Aye. I didn't care which one we had but was glad for the company of Izzy, Jeannie and Mary. I was missing my Kitta more than I could say.

By the time we reached our hoosie, Izzy was triumphant, her sky-blue shawl across the door—a claim.

We cleaned out our hut, made it liveable and lit our fire for tea. While Clementina was slapping a rough batter on the griddle, I took the bucket and headed for the well, thinking: Here I am again, and how much has happened in a year, this year. I would be fifteen soon, and it did not sound so very old, but the space between Ginger Meggie and Fish Meggie seemed wider than the sea.

I leaned my head against the well pump, listening to gulls cry over the farlins down at the yard. All I wanted to do was sleep.

When the hand fell lightly on the back of my neck, I did not jump, I was not afraid. His voice was none of the things I thought it might be but as warm as I could wish it.

I knew I would see ye again.

~

Magnus Tulloch was the same and he had changed. How could that be?

He was free of his bonds now, a qualified cooper for Nicol & Mair. I watched his face as he told me, laughing, that he would be filling the barrels now, supervising the packers' work, *and how will Miss Clementina be liking that?* His usual long slide of hair was uneven, shorter at the back where his head had been shaved because of the accident, and I longed to reach out, run the palms of my hands over his skull, reassure myself—of something. What, I could not say.

Sometimes he would shake his head slightly, as though clearing something away. He talked and talked, news of the yard, who had arrived and who had not, and I thought: Ye have not asked, ye know it is not yet the time. But there were pauses in his chatter, and he was searching my face for reassurance too.

I am sorry for your loss, Fish Meggie.

Ma, of course, he meant.

I was tired, so tired, and my losses so many. I could make no proper reply. But suddenly, standing there at the well with a bucket of water that Clementina would be waiting for, I thought: Aye, Magnus Tulloch is the one I will tell.

I was the same and I had changed too. It is just what people do.

That summer at Lerwick in 1906—never have I sung so much. Not hymns, not Sankey's, no. I sang to put distance between the now I lived and the past I'd buried. I sang to take my mind from salt eating at the sores on my skin. I sang to get through exhausting days that sometimes turned into long, wearying nights. And for that I needed the mindless and the cheerful. Thank you, Harry Lauder, for 'Roamin in the Gloamin' and 'Doughie the Baker', for 'She Is My Daisy' and 'Stop Yer Tickling, Jock'. The girls joined in, ever willing—no need to be asked twice, them—but Clementina Slater often warned that if she was plagued with another round of 'It's Nice to Get Up in the Morning but it's Nicer to Lie in Bed' she would *take herself back to bed an' we could pack the herrin' ourselves*.

So purposeful, I was, about seeking out cheer that it took me by surprise when it turned into something else. When I stumbled upon the sublime.

~

Every night after tea, there were chores—washing out clooties, dressing my hands, sharpening my gipper. And then I'd sit by the fire, talking with Magnus Tulloch. On Saturday nights we'd dance, although sometimes we didn't because the music jangled him, set off the ringing in his ears. Oh, the disappointment after a week of waiting for that, for him … Well, I would scold myself for impatience—he couldn't help it, now, could he?—and blush at the strange and breathless ache in me.

Forgive me, Meggie, he'd say in a yearning way that would make me shiver and make me glad because it meant he felt the same.

On Sundays we'd tramp across the Gremista hill with a picnic of bread and jam that often we'd forget to eat. I know you, I would think suddenly, listening to him talk, watching him listening to me and not turning away. And when he spoke without words, with his fingertips on my face, I would have to tell myself, *Breathe, breathe.*

As I gutted and sorted and sang Harry Lauder songs, I would see him going about his work, topping up barrels with pickle, tossing salt into the farlins, inspecting the baskets with his wooden gauge, checking the packers' tallies against the number of barrels packed. Random glimpses of that long dark hair, a wry frown to tease Clementina and Isobel, broad arms encircling a barrel of salt. I found myself thinking about him, about those arms, and earning myself a few sharp words from Clementina for losing speed. Sometimes I would catch him looking at me too.

I know you, I would think again. I recognise you. Aye, you are *that* person to me.

And as the Lerwick season wore on, I began to wonder: Is this what love is? A force that makes you learn how to breathe again, breathe in a new way, because your heart is taking up more space in your body than ever it did, and nothing fits together any more, nor feels like it is human? Feathers in my lungs. Air in my blood. Bones as light as mussel shell. The core of me lifts on small beating wings and I know I can never be still again, nor earthbound, never again be just that girl.

And I remember thinking this: I don't know what to do. I don't know how to *be* like this.

How does any one of us ever survive love?

~

I am sorry, lambsie. Sometimes I forget I am writing to you and not just trying to explain to myself the things that have mystified me forever. But if I am making you squirm to think of your grunnie feeling this way, then no, I am not sorry for that. You must just get past it as best you can—pretend I am the girl in the story and not your grunnie. Because I will not rewrite the story to spare you. I will not dishonour love like that.

Love …

If there is just one thing you learn from me, I would wish it to be this: love can be as strong as muscle, as constant as heartbeat, but when you hold it up to the light, you must place it in the chalice of both hands, protect the butterfly it can also be.

Before I left Lerwick for Great Yarmouth that year, Mrs Leask, one of the lady deputies at the Mission to Fisherfolk, told me something I did not want to hear.

We canna just keep patching them up with dressings forever, lass. Ye'll not be gutting much longer.

I stared at her, then down at my hands.

Ye Scottie lassies are tough, aye, I'll give ye that, but there's not just the matter of pain. This finger be almost gone ta bone.

But that's what I am. A gutting quine.

Mrs Leask laughed. *That's not what ye are, lass. That's what ye do.*

But they were the same. Oh aye. How could they not be the same thing?

She ran her hand down my sleeve, rueful. *I don't know why it be so, but the red-haired lasses seem ta feel the salt worse, an' get poorly with the kidney pain too.*

Cursed and cursed again, I thought. Ginger Meggie cross your leggie.

~

Magnus Tulloch came with us to Great Yarmouth, with Old Boy Jackie and other Lerwick coopers. I hoped this would spare us from Old Bloddy but it didn't: he was one of the yard supervisors where our team worked. At least I was used to his temper. Poor Liza was terrified.

And I saw other familiar faces in the yards. Limpy Davy, still an apprentice, mixing pickle for Magnus Tulloch and Old Bloddy. Wee Daisy, now in a team of her own but still standing on a box to reach into the farlin. And Bella Strahan at the farlin next to mine, with a cluster of teams from Aberdeen.

Ma says Bella Strahan has a bairn now, Clementina told me, matter-of-fact, when we finished for the day. *A wee thing only a couple of months.*

I glanced at Clementina. No wonder she'd thought me feeble.

Home with her sister at Fitdee while she's at the fish. They need the money, Strahans do.

Bella Strahan stopped me one night when we were buying a pie for our tea.

How's your sister, eh, quinie? What news of her, eh?

She eyed me curiously when I told her Kitta was home since Ma had died and she could not go to the fish any more.

Well, that's sometimes the way of it, eh. An' she be well?

Aye.

She waited but I said no more.

Aye then. She shrugged as she turned away.

~

In truth, I could not really say that Kitta was well or not. I'd had no news of Roanhaven since leaving at the beginning of the season. Da and the boys—well, I'd have dropped in surprise if one of them had thought to write. They never had done it before. Granda, no. He could not write, nor read neither. Unty Jinna sent a note once, addressed to Liza and me, but it was short and plain and if there was a message for me there, buried among details of the weather and the number of whiting caught on the *Lily*, I could not find it.

Nothing from Kitta.

No news is good, I told myself, and I told Magnus Tulloch the same.

It's so long ago, lambsie, so long. What good is anger now? They probably thought they were doing right by Kitta, doing the right thing. We're supposed to forgive people for their ignorance, aren't we. But me? Even then, I knew it was wrong. I knew I should not stand by and do nothing, I should do something to make it right. I was worse, see, because I knew.

Aye, lambsie, it's myself I'm angry at.

One morning I was last down to the farlins because it took so long for me to pack the bread poultices on my fingers before tying on the clooties.

Ye've a visitor, Izzy announced, fit to burst.

Something of a hush came over our farlin. Visitors to the yards were few, and they were never welcome. If Old Bloddy were to catch anyone with a visitor …

I looked at Clementina.

She sighed, a huge gusting noise, sad and weary. *Aye, quinie.* She jerked her chin towards the salt store, away from the coopers' sheds.

I did not recognise him at first, tall and thin and gangly in sailor whites. But he started scratching his scalp under the close-fitting cap, jiggling about on his feet, and I knew him then. My youngest brother. Will.

He had left the drifters, hadn't gone south to Lowestoft with Da, Archie and Jamie at the end of the Gadlehead season. He was now with the merchant navy, and his ship, the *Veleteer,* was leaving for India tomorrow.

The wide world, I thought, awed. Truly the wide world. I went to hug him but he fended me off, and not until that moment did it occur to me: my brother had not come to say goodbye.

He looked down while he was speaking, shuffling his feet. He cleared his throat a lot. Will wasn't used to saying overmuch.

His little speech struck me mute.

Later I remembered how embarrassed he was—not by what had happened to Kitta, mind. No, he was embarrassed by *her*. I raged to think of it but at the time I just stood there, a great useless quinie, scarcely able to breathe. Until finally Magnus Tulloch rushed over from the coopers' shed to gather me up.

~ .

Maybe there's only so long you can go on putting one foot after the other before the thing you are pretending never happened pops in you like a seed and starts to grow, faster and faster because it has been waiting so long, bigger and bigger until it finds a way to escape and then there is no stopping it, it wraps you up, round and round like a winding sheet, until it is everything and you are nothing, you are lost inside and it is pretending you never happened …

~

It was a place called Birch Hill, a place on the northern coast, a distance from the Broch. An institution. Will said they took her there wrapped in a sail so she could not hurt herself.

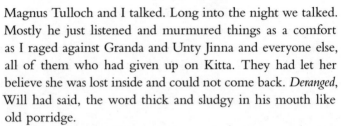

Magnus Tulloch and I talked. Long into the night we talked. Mostly he just listened and murmured things as a comfort as I raged against Granda and Unty Jinna and everyone else, all of them who had given up on Kitta. They had let her believe she was lost inside and could not come back. *Deranged*, Will had said, the word thick and sludgy in his mouth like old porridge.

Why? I kept saying, over and over. I could not understand what they had done. Always there had been those in the village who had lost their wits for a time, or for always, or were born like that, and they had been let to find their way, care given when care was needed. They had not been a bother. No-one ever talked of locking them away. God's own, Ma always said. Like Brukie's Sandy.

Brukie's Sandy?

Brukie's Sandy was the something I could not yet tell Magnus Tulloch.

I shook my head.

He went to speak, stopped. I looked up at him.

But could it be … he stammered, *do ye not think … could it be that Kitta is safer there? Safer in Birch Hill?*

Safe! How can it make her safe, bein' locked up with people who are witless, Lord bless them?

He shrugged, helpless. *Aye. But I just thought … maybe there is someone could help her there? A doctor. Someone?*

Only people can help her are her own, who love her, an' they have turned away. I've to bring her back, I promised her I would. I said no matter where she went, I would find her, I would bring her back.

I looked at him fiercely, daring him to say the obvious thing. That I was a fifteen-year-old girl: what could I do?

But Magnus Tulloch surprised me. He thought for a while. He shook the ringing from his head. And then he spoke of a plan.

~

I loved Magnus Tulloch, of that I had no doubt. But I could never be certain whether I married him so soon, in my fifteenth year on the way to sixteen, because I loved him or because, as a married woman, I might have more chance of making a home for Kitta. Or because I wanted it settled, for good and all, that I would never go back to Roanhaven.

At the close of the season, I sent to Da, by Liza, a letter and my year's wages from Nicol & Mair. It was the last the family would get from me.

First Ma, then Kitta, now me. Da and Granda would not be pleased to be losing the last of the family's female labour. Unty Jinna, already overstretched, would be pulled into the gap we had left. Maybe poor Liza too. And Archie and Jamie would be urged to marry, and soon. I should have felt guilty about Unty Jinna, but I could not forgive her.

Was there any other reason, I wondered, why Da might be sorry I wasn't coming back? A father was little more than an idea to me, an outline I saw on the *Lily Maud*, a man-shaped shadow by the fire. I didn't know what Da thought about anything.

No doubt about what Granda would think. He would be in a rage that I was announcing what I had done, not asking permission to do it, even though the law did not demand permission for me to marry. He would be bitter about my choice to marry outside Roanhaven, outside the fisher community. A stranger! He would curse me as a traitor for the loss of my three months of fisher work and nine of earning. But he would not be sorry to see *the accursed reid-heidit quinie* disappear, just as he would not have cried for Kitta. He'd called her a limmer, but now she was something even more shameful—a madwoman they'd had to lock away.

~

The wedding was in Great Yarmouth, just before we left. My memories ... oh, they are white, but not the white you might expect, lambsie, not wedding white, no.

A clergyman with a kindly heart for fishworkers read the banns at a church that neither of us belonged to, though we had gone there on Sundays during the season. Clementina and Isobel were my maidens. Liza had refused in a tight, frightened voice that made me sad and gave a presence of sorts to Granda Jeemsie's sour and certain disapproval from all those miles distant. Magnus chose his fisher friend Stivvy Ratter and Old Boy Jackie as gweedmen.

Inside the kirk, while the pastor spoke his solemn words, I looked at my boots and at Magnus Tulloch's. I looked at the scuffed, waxy floorboards, at drifts of sand caught between them. I looked, unflinching, at a mouseling scurrying at the edge of sight. I did not want to look up at the Lord's fine house where fine people prayed. It was only when Magnus Tulloch took my hand and bent to kiss the knuckles one by one that I raised my face, and then ... oh, then I wished I had set my eyes on his all along and never looked away.

As we walked from the kirk, the congregation of gutting girls and coopers and fishers showered us with small pieces of oatcake, a blessing they called the bride's bonn. Other wedding traditions—the bewedding giving of father to groom, the procession, fiddlers, the ale, the guizers—I was pleased enough to miss, but I was glad for this simple rain of plenty on my head. Those who were not so close to us whispered to each other curiously of the strangeness of the day, stripped of family and village blessings. But those few who knew what it was I had set my mind to do closed themselves around us with quiet and sombre joy.

I turned my face to the grainy white sky and thought of albatross feathers. And snow.

~

They contrived to give us space that night. Privacy. Clementina, the Cruden Bay girls, they arranged it among themselves to smuggle the two of us into the lodgings shared by Jeannie, Isobel and Mary—a wee sheddie at the back of a cottage in the same street as Mrs Booth's.

And then, giggling, they left us there, Magnus Tulloch and me, in a room hung about with sheets of brown paper. A jug of ale from Stivvy Ratter on an upturned box. A small bread pudding from my quinies.

Clementina had settled a wreath of holly in my wiry hair, and as I tried to disentangle it I watched Magnus Tulloch in the cold tallow light. Shrugging out of his shirt. Arms bare. Wrestling to pull off his boots.

Owwww!

He flung away the boot in his hand and scrambled across the bed to examine the puncture of a thorn on the palm of my hand.

Ee, what have ye done ta yeself now, Meggie Tulloch?

Meggie Tulloch. Me.

The perfect red pearl burst, and I held my breath as he smudged the blood away with his thumb.

And then I laughed.

A slow grin. *What?*

I didn't know what. It was like something had burst on the inside too. I kept laughing. I couldn't speak and I couldn't stop, and then Magnus Tulloch started too, both of us laughing, laughing till we ached, till we fell onto the bed, Magnus Tulloch with his hand clamped over his mouth to muffle the noise, me hiccuping and holding on to his shoulders. I collapsed against him—another wave of laughing, laughing fierce as crying, me still in my layers of wool, my crown of thorns, pressed to a naked chest.

When we had breath, I took his hand from his mouth. *Can ye help me get this thing off my head?*

The ale, the bread pudding, those rare gifts … wasted.

~

I didn't know about the gift of forgetting. This thing—what can I call it?—this rageful, tender thing, this body hunger, it makes you selfish, it makes you forget, for a time, scouring you clean like the North Sea wind, snatching important, unforgettable things into the howl of it and tossing them like plucked feathers, shaking you senseless like featherless skin, naked and open and many-limbed. For a time.

Of all the things unknown to me at age fifteen, this I'd not imagined, never guessed. A mystification.

It made me wonder, you know, lambsie. Wonder about God.

I know what you're thinking, lambsie, aye, I can see you with your fingers laced across your eyes, your face screwed up. Seems to me the young believe desire a thing of their own making.

Well.

I said I would not spare you, but perhaps I will spare you any more details of my wedding night.

Here's a funny thing, surprising. Thinking as I write these memories has made me feel a wee bit sorry for your generation, lambsie. New and free and unloosed from old ways. I don't mean I would wish for you the prohibitions of kirk and village, demanding so much, forgiving nothing. Making of something joyful a thing of disgust. Punishing its beautiful young people with shame. Never, my Laura-lamb, never that. But … maybe I am wrong, but I wonder if there's something missing, something given up for freedom. I remember what it was, that shiver to feel the brush of a hand. The gentle resting of an arm across a shoulder that made you impatient to be done with gentle. The sweet, clammy closeness of one body in a crowd, the one among many, the one whose heat you recognised and longed for, and knew to be as yours was too, and was for none but you, just you, just yours. Oh, lambsie … You canna imagine, you *canna*, and I am sorry for it, aye. Sorry you may never know that impossible, raddling thing. The sweetest anguish of *waiting*.

But I will say no more, and in truth it is for myself rather than to spare you. To keep for my heart alone those memories.

What I must write next is one of those things that comes from the blurred edges I have told you about. Sending it there all those years ago saved me from madness. Bringing it back … well.

I remember how I used to unwrap the dressings on my fingers. Fast. Without looking.

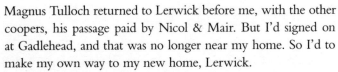

Magnus Tulloch returned to Lerwick before me, with the other coopers, his passage paid by Nicol & Mair. But I'd signed on at Gadlehead, and that was no longer near my home. So I'd to make my own way to my new home, Lerwick.

But I'd to do something first, the most important thing I'd ever done. Something only I could do.

Magnus begged me to wait. *We are new together,* he said, *we should get ourselves settled in Lerwick. Prepare ourselves, find out what is the right way, proper.*

But the thought of putting off any longer what I must do crazed me. I could not wait, I just couldn't.

Magnus turned to his friend Stivvy Ratter, asking for passage for me on Stivvy's drifter, the *Ann Rose*. Sorrowful, Stivvy bowed his head. He couldn't take a ginger on board, not even his mate's girl. But he knew crew on the passenger ship *St Siniver*, and I could work my passage, two passages, from the Broch to Lerwick.

I knew what working on the *St Siniver* would mean, cleaning the mess of three hundred seasick girls on their way back from the fish, but I was grateful to Stivvy.

Ee, just get back ta your man soon, Meggie Tulloch, he said, doffing his cap to me and nudging Magnus lewdly in the ribs, as men are like to do when one is newly wed.

So I took the train with the other girls from Great Yarmouth to Gadlehead and then I'd just to find my way to the Broch and along the coast. I was the daughter of a fishwife and had tramped the countryside with a creel on my back many a time. Fraserburgh was only twenty miles away. I walked.

I had to pass Roanhaven on the road above the scaur. I kept my eyes ahead of me. Wouldn't give it the turn of my head.

~

It takes my breath to think of it now. How foolish I was. Naive.

Hindsight tells the story—that's what people say, isn't it, lambsie? I had been shocked, and then angry. Then, desperate. I hadn't listened properly to all Will said. *So she could not hurt herself.* I'd not even listened when Magnus Tulloch gently ventured there might be another way of looking at what had been done. Oh no, not me. All I could see was a promise sealed with an albatross feather.

Had I patched up, remade, the picture of Kitta as she was when I left Roanhaven? And all those months before, the guise she'd worn, the things she had not said?

Aye, all I could see was my fearless sister who would throw back her head and laugh.

~

The red-haired girl shivers at the top of the steps, listening for the noise of weeping, blood-curdling cries. Listening for madness. But it is quiet in this grey stone building by the sea where her sister has been brought against her will.

A woman in a nurse's cape hurrying by directs the girl to a corridor on the left of a big arched door. Footsteps, heavy in seaboots, echo around the girl, bouncing off walls and from the ceiling high above. It is airless and dark, hard to see.

She finds the office she was told to look for—REGISTRAR. She waits to be noticed by the several people in smart clothes, pens in their smooth, white hands. Finally, she makes herself step into their space and sees surprise break on their faces. To be confronted so, in here, by a red-haired girl in country dress, a creel on her back, in hulking wet boots and smelling of fish.

Yes?

I am a gutting girl, she tells herself, brave and strong.

My name is Meggie Duthie Tulloch an' I am the sister of Kathryn Neish Duthie of Roanhaven an' there's been a mistake, she should never be here, an' I want to take her away with me now. Please.

The woman closest to her, wearing eyeglasses clamped onto her nose, stands up. She is looking at the girl strangely but gentle now.

Kathryn Duthie? Kitta?

The girl nods.

The suited man behind a desk says, *The girl who …?*

He stops.

The woman's face changes again, sympathetic. Sad.

The girl is suddenly too afraid to breathe.

~

She had been quiet and docile at Birch Hill, my sister. She spoke politely and answered their questions. She nodded at whatever the doctors said. After a while, they thought to let her walk in the garden. And still she was no trouble. Placid and calm. And then one day she climbed through a hedge. She found ballast stones on the shore and stuffed them into the pockets of her skirt. She tied a shawl around her eyes—why did you do that, Kitta?—and she walked into the sea. And this time, there was no-one to stop her. She just kept walking.

Oh, lambsie. There will probably be things you want to ask me now, but don't. I canna say more about it, no, not ever.

I could not bring Kitta back.

What else is there to say?

1907 was the first year of my married life, the first year of making a home far from the home that was not mine any more. A beginning. But a beginning that had to weave itself through an ending and find its way.

Magnus Tulloch gave me a wedding gift the night he brought me to the tiny fisherman's cottage, one of a cluster on the Gremista road, that would be our home together now.

I sat on the hearthrug by a peat fire, arms around my long grey skirt, hugging my knees. Would ever I feel warm again, would ever I thaw?

Magnus knelt down beside me. Wordless, he placed something on the floor between us. I forced myself to look.

A small package, the size of a hand, loosely wrapped.

My eyes went back to the fire, and I sank my chin further into the folds of my skirt.

He pushed it towards me. I felt it there, the edge of something. *Please?* His voice soft.

I turned a little, touched the wrapping with my fingers, looked at this man, my beloved. He had made his vows to another me, the one I was, the one before ... I did not know if or when I would be that girl again.

He nodded slightly, encouraging.

I picked it up, and the paper slid easily away. Inside, a small hairbrush, the wooden back dark and rich like honey, gleaming in firelight. The bristles felt soft against my palm.

I looked at him, a half smile.

Magnus Tulloch untied the ribbon at the base of my head, pulled the pins from the sides, unwound the taming twist of hair. Taking the brush from me, he began to pull it through thickly from crown to the ends, the long wiry sheets of hair heavy in his hands.

And then he kneeled forward to face me.

Is not just a hairbrush, not just that.

Then what?

A promise, my Meggie, a promise for every day. Every day an' always, Meggie, every day, this.

And I felt the weight of my hair in his hands, his hands gathering to him its burden, each stroke pulling me closer to him, away and to him again.

Magnus Tulloch was my heart, breath, blood, when I had none of my own. So much I do not want in my memory of those times, but that … I am grateful to remember that.

~

The season began in March. The comfort, the distraction, of work. Aye, I kept working. It never occurred to me not to, though Magnus Tulloch's sister Gracie gasped and fussed and glared at Magnus as if he was giving the nod to a great mistake. She delivered her pronouncement that what I needed to help me through my grief was rest and being looked after—what I needed, in fact, was her good self.

I liked Gracie straight away when Magnus Tulloch took me to Sandwick that Sunday to meet his kin. I took as a kindness when she invited me to stay awhile, *Safe an' sound in a nice wee village away from that city,* but the last thing I wanted was village eyes on me. Work, Clementina's bright, round, frowning face, the girls, familiar patterns—these things laid down a way to follow, a map for us, Magnus Tulloch and me. A constant in a blur of the new.

Being on the farlins was no easy thing, mind. I would let my eyes shift to the sea and think: She is just over there, just water hours, water miles, away. And Clementina would watch carefully, giving me a minute before prodding my elbow with a gruff *Hash, hash, quinie!* They'd buried her at the Broch, my Kitta, beyond the sacred churchyard, but she wouldn't care, she would snap her fingers to that, a nothing. The ground had been hard with snow, but an old man shovelling a path to the church door told me kindly there would be bluebells come spring. Kitta would like that, aye. Better than sacred.

The hardest thing would have been having to see Liza again, having to stand beside her at the farlins and listen to her small mind, her blethering on about Roanhaven and the people on whom I had closed my heart. But Clementina turned up that first season with Muckle Lally in tow, a girl from Fitdee. Word was that Liza was not to be allowed to the fish any more.

If ever I'd counted my blessings back then, I would have counted that.

~

I was a gutting girl for just one season more. And then, true to the lady deputy's prediction, the Lord above made a decision for me. The top half of my left middle finger, down to the second joint, had to be taken after the salty hole poisoning got into the bone. Mrs Leask gave me a note and it was done at Gilbert Bain as part of mission charity. No anaesthetic, just a swig of something hot that took the skin off my throat, and a cup of tea after to calm me down. I did not look while he did it, the doctor, but I remember he wore a white apron, like a butcher I saw in Great Yarmouth once. In that place of screaming, my pain curdled the air, loud and clotted thick and nothing to do with the butcher's busy work.

Once my finger healed, I got work at the factory where guts from the yards were mixed with seaweed and turned into fertiliser. Guts again, aye, but no salt. The work was not so tough as gutting, I could manage it with my awkward hands, and the hours not so long because fertiliser is just fertiliser, it hasn't to be kept fresh, no. But the smell—oh, it was worse, you canna imagine.

Gracie wrote me one of her letters, venturing the view that I was lucky. Lucky to be working in the factory now. *Best you be off farlins, Meggie Tulloch, before it be more than just one finger what's taken!*

But I was adrift. I could not stop thinking of myself as a gutting girl. I had been proud to be one, for all the mess and muck of it. When the girls came back next season, I went to the yards, the huts, when I could. I hadn't been to a ceilidh since returning to Gremista, but Magnus Tulloch was always suggesting we go.

Some Sundays Clementina or the Cruden Bay girls would walk with us after kirk. Oftentimes when Magnus, now foreman, was to be late at the yards, I would help Mrs Leask at the Mission for Fisherfolk hut, tending to girls whose hands were in as much trouble as mine had been, winding bandages onto cuts and sores after Mrs Leask had cleaned them up. Aye, I was a gutting girl still, just one who could no more hold a gipper in her hand.

I discovered something at the mission hut, something precious, something saving. Mrs Leask had a library! A small collection, it was, that she kept in a kist and loaned to any who showed interest in what she called Improving Literature. *Not too many takers*, she told me with a shake of her head.

After we finished with the line of girls, I would pull the books out of the kist. There were prayer books and cautionary tales for young women, a dictionary, an atlas, and a Bible, of course, but it seemed Mrs Leask counted poetry as Improving Literature, and it was these volumes I fell upon. One by one I took them home to read. Tennyson. Keats. Elizabeth Barrett Browning. And one that Mrs Leask's daughter had sent from her new home, far away, in Boston: Emily Dickinson. I copied poems I liked best into the blank pages at the back of my *Forget-Me-Not Annual*—in tiny letters, using every bit of space. I didn't always understand the words, but I would make a list of them, mark the pages with scraps of wool, and borrow Mrs Leask's dictionary to work them out. Reading those poems aloud put music in my head that found a place there, and stayed.

Magnus Tulloch listened as I read bits to him but he wasn't as much taken with the likes of Emily Dickinson.

> There is a word
> Which bears a sword
> Can pierce an armed man.
> It hurls its barbed syllables—
> At once is mute again.

Magnus Tulloch looked up at me, expectantly, from cleaning his boots, so I carried on.

> But where it fell
> The saved will tell
> On patriotic day,
> Some epauletted brother
> Gave his breath away.

Magnus Tulloch was frowning. *Does she say what word?*

I quickly read the rest of the poem to myself.

No.

No?

I thought about it. *Ye're to make up your own mind on it. That's what I think.*

Magnus Tulloch put a finger to his ear and shook his head, as though clearing away a clutter of noise, and then went back to scraping the mud from his boots. He was keeping his own mind to himself.

When I think of it now, I wonder what I would have done without Mrs Leask's books. Once again words poured into me, into all those yawning spaces. Wasn't that they could take the place of what was lost, but to feel them there was something, a comfort.

~

Magnus Tulloch and I were content. I wonder—is that the right word? *Content* sounds so small, so passionless and niggardly, for the way it was between us, everything we were. But words like *happy*—no, they are wrong, too. Because of the way our marriage had begun, there was a strand of sadness forever coiled into the skein of us. To say *Oh aye, we were happy*, well, that would be to unravel the whole to remove a part, and the thing left in its place would be shinier but lesser for that.

And I am finding it hard to think how to write about the way it was between us, everything we were. It's as if it was enough, of itself, and there is no need to record it. A strange contented restlessness, an easeful sadness.

Sorry, my lambsie, I am thinking on paper again, forgetting who I am writing to. Forgetting why.

~

One evening, Magnus Tulloch came home with light in his smile and hugged the breath out of me.

What's with all of this? I demanded, pretend-serious. *Have ye been pouring whiskey instead of pickle this day?*

Meggie … He stopped. A second thought, a worry, a cloud across the sun.

Well? I urged. *Go on. Tell me!*

His eyes darted about, his fingers splayed, closed, splayed again. He was a man plucking words like limpets from a jetty.

Just say!

Well … what would ye think of leaving this place?

A small pause and I jumped in firm with both of my feet. *I'm not goin' back to Roanhaven.*

No, no, lass, I'm not talkin' of Roanhaven. Nor anywhere nearby. Meggie … He leaned forward, his eyes were the glitter of a herring's back. *Meggie, I'm talkin' about Australia!*

~

The islands were not like Roanhaven, where things stayed the same until there was no choice but to suffer change. The Shetlands had always been a place of immigrants, Norse, Viking,

Scots, and ever since the last century had become a place of emigrants, too. Islanders left for far-off places to find work and opportunity, new lives in the new world—Canada, America, Australia, New Zealand.

Magnus Tulloch confessed he had been thinking on it—even saving—for a long time, but had put it from his mind that first day we'd met. But now ...

An' will there be work for coopers in Australia? I wondered.

Aye, he had heard so from the families of others who had gone. *But I am thinking, Meggie ... in time ... There is land in Australia, all that space, millions of acres of new land, an' if a man works hard, well.* He pushed back his hair. That shine again in his eyes. *We could have a different life, Meggie. Better.*

Going on the land was a something to me, not the Something I could see it was to Magnus Tulloch. But I hugged him, listened as he dreamed aloud.

The idea of Magnus Tulloch and I leaving for the other end of the world should have thrown into array the beat of a staid Roanhaven heart. But no. Straightaway it seemed right. I liked living in Lerwick well enough, and Gracie had firmly thrown the net of family over her stranger-sister. But this place did not have the stamp of home for me and I feared it ever would be so. I looked down at my hands, with their pits and scars, the deformed stump, and tried to imagine myself somewhere warm, somewhere young and clean. I thought: Of course, aye, that is what we are meant to do.

And the notion I could leave behind the darkness ...

Magnus Tulloch began to make plans, then arrangements, and the biggest thing to qualm me was the prospect of leaving Clementina—Clementina, who was my family now. She was not saying much.

And there was Gracie. Magnus Tulloch's sister wrote me wailing letters, begging me to make him see sense, change his mind.

The other side of the world, Meggie Tulloch! We will never see ye again, never see your wee bairns when they come!

Gracie and Karl had three little ones of their own already and she was ever hopeful for me, ever kind, always saying, *It will be your turn soon, our Meggie, don't ye fret on that.* She would never have understood, never, that we were *taking measures*, as it was called in those days, something I'd learned at the farlins. Because I did not want a bairn.

Back then, I could not explain myself, words stuttered to nought. My reason was a picture only I could see: waves tossing a wee creature back and forth in the shallows. It froze my heart, it was everything I wanted to forget, everything I could not bear, did not want.

Even now, when I have the words, they turn into questions. Was it that I couldn't allow myself to have what Kitta had lost? Or that what Kitta had lost had killed her? Maybe it was both. But maybe, too, I was frightened of loving someone so much again. The idea of having to keep a wee life safe, of never failing them, ever. A burden just too great.

On this, Magnus Tulloch was quiet. He would push the hair back from his forehead and his towering body would hunch down, shrink a little. I learned to douse the questions in his sighs with silence.

Maybe when we are somewhere else, he said. *A warm place, new. Maybe.*

Such a small, mean word. It was all I had to give him.

In 1910 we emigrated to Western Australia, a young colony in an old country. They wanted hard workers, wanted skills such as Magnus Tulloch had.

Every fisher and cooper family seemed to have a third or fourth cousin who had forged the way there before us, so we were busy, Magnus Tulloch and I, finding out what we needed to know. How to apply. What to take. Making our preparations for a journey of one way. Such a long way, lambsie.

In that flurry of months came a day that Clementina Slater would always after call The Madness. I have been thinking about this a lot lately, lambsie, how strange it is that sometimes we manage almost to erase the memory of pain to spare ourselves, and other times it's as though we've taken to it with a polishing cloth. That day in August 1909 is one of those memories. I can pluck it from the past, brutally whole and clean. All those years and I can still feel the sun on my skin when I think of it.

Many years later, Clementina would press, try to get me to talk about that day. *Ach*, I would say, *I was only eighteen, I canna remember, can I?*

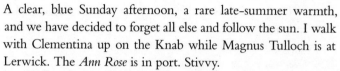

A clear, blue Sunday afternoon, a rare late-summer warmth, and we have decided to forget all else and follow the sun. I walk with Clementina up on the Knab while Magnus Tulloch is at Lerwick. The *Ann Rose* is in port. Stivvy.

The sky is the blue of Magnus Tulloch's eyes, I think, and Clementina Slater snorts.

I look down, embarrassed. I'd not meant to speak my thoughts aloud.

Blue skies every day, where ye're goin', she says. *Ye'll be sick of them, ye will. Ye'll be sayin, 'Eh, another bloddy blue sky, ho hum, yew know.'*

And we laugh, Clementina and I, with the sun on our faces and a wee pinch of panic that it is a long way away, this place of blue skies, and we won't have many more such times together.

The Knab is alive with people this day. Sailors in port. Groups of gutting girls from Gremista and Garthspool. Coopers and fishers enjoying the Lord's day. Lerwegians and the folk they call strangers alike. I remember what Clementina had asked me after I'd been here past a season:

So what are ye now? Are ye a Shetland lassie? A Ler-wee-gee?

I'd not be that if I stayed here for the rest of my life! I told her. I had come to know how Lerwegians feel about these things. *But ... I'm not a Buchaner either. No more. I don't belong anywhere now.*

She'd laughed her best barking, snorting Clementina laugh. *A flibbertygibberty bird—that's what ye are!*

And I think: Aye, I could be a bird.

Clementina and I rest awhile halfway up to watch the puffins. A scatter of them flying about the cliff face below, coming in to land, huddling in clusters by their scrubby burrows dug among the rocks. Bonxies circle, blunt and brown, their eyes sharp for unprotected eggs.

When we reach the top of the world, we sit on the grass with our jeely pieces. Clementina throws a few crumbs to a gull, and soon there are four of them waiting for the next. Rabbits dart about among the marigolds.

So, Clementina says, all no-care nonchalant, *he has a lass, then, has he?*

Who?

That Stivvy Ratter, of course.

Ooo-hoo! I whistle and she gives me a punch on the arm.

Two young boys clamber up the path, pushing and jostling and throwing clods of earthy weed at each other. A third, younger, stumbles behind.

Stivvy Ratter's a free loon, far as I know.

Eh, well. And she glances at me sideways and laughs.

An uprooted clump of campion lands beside Clementina, showering her with earth. She jumps to her feet, shaking her skirt.

— *Oi, young mannie!*

The two boys look aghast as the bulk of Clementina Slater heads their way. It's the third little boy who catches my eye. Now level with us, he is steadier on his feet and excited at seeing so many rabbits diving around him. He runs, clapping his hands.

Clementina is Having Words and, surprisingly, the boys are listening. Run away, lads, I think to myself, that's what I'd do.

I glance back at the little one. He is running towards me now, his eyes on a small black rabbit. I smile. No chance of catching a bunny, little loon, they're too quick for you. It dives left to right, the boy following, then back the other way to give him the slip. And the little one turns, too, running.

And I scramble to my feet.

And then I am running.

Running, shouting ...

Because the rabbit is racing towards the edge of the Knab and the little boy is running after it and there is no-one stopping him, no-one to stop him as he keeps running after the rabbit, straight for the space where the Knab ends, straight for the wide blue sky, and I know I canna stand by and do nothing, *it will not be me who stands by*, and I keep running to catch the boy, to catch him by his shabby blue gansey, his skinny leg, to pull him down to the earth, just one more step, one more ...

And I am downed from behind, crashing down, chin in the marigold earth as the little boy sprawls into the wide blue sky like a clumsy fledgling bird.

~

I dream of flying ...

~

Ca-co-pho-ny, I say to myself. People shouting, weeping. A screeching of gulls.

I am on my back, looking up at Clementina Slater's face and the blue of the sky. She is kneeling over me, shaking my shoulders. Her face is red. She is crying. Clementina Slater, crying, splashing me with tears.

Stupid, stupid quinie! Ye would've gone over with him! Ye were headin' right to go over, ye were, ye were goin' over too.

I was going over? Frown. I was ...?

With a great thump of panic, I remember. And I twist around, out of her grasp, to see the sky as blue as Magnus Tulloch's eyes. I am searching for the lift of wings, for something miraculous.

There is nothing. Nothing but air.

Notebook 3

1910–1932

EARTH

Made hardly a splash at all, that boy, Brukie's Sandy, when he lost his balance, reaching with the grapplie hook for a message from the sea. He toppled from the stern of the Lily Maud *in his gansey layers, his long oilie, his great hulking seaboots.*

As he fell, a rope from the stern. Snagging an arm.

A lifeline ...

Dearest lambsie, another new book, but your twenty-first birthday has come and gone. I pictured giving you these notebooks in a wooden box, a wee kist, but things got in the way of that. This tiresome disease ... I'd to settle for the silver earrings and cashmere coat. She chose well for me, your mother did. Kathryn has always had an eye for beautiful things. An artist's eye, I suppose that's it.

There weren't many beautiful things to buy Kathryn when she turned twenty-one. Everything was hard to get in the war, everything rationed. We had coupons for this, coupons for that, but just because you had a coupon it didn't mean you would get your this or that. I canna mind now what gift I gave your mother. Probably something practical for her glory box. Don't frown, lambsie—girls of your mother's time always had a glory box. I remember I made a cake ... aye, a marble cake, that's right. I gave some coupons to someone who knew someone who could get powdered sugar and cochineal. Imagine how frivolous, using coupons for cochineal! We didn't have a party, no, but that suited your mother. Never was she one for crowds of people. Well, you know this, lambsie, you know how she can be.

I wonder, would you have rather received a kist full of memories from your grunnie? Probably not. Ah well, you are young and that's as it should be. But one day. One day, I hope.

I've had time on my hands, lambsie, too much of it. Time to dwell on things. All those months to wonder about what it is I've been doing. After what the doctors said, I didn't think to be finishing what I'd started, but I am a tough one, aye, tougher than ever they thought. Well, they were not to know about the women of Roanhaven, were they? There is much yet to say, and it seems I am to be spared a while more to say it. But churning up the mud of the past, all the bones and stones buried there—is it fair? Some things are best left in the dark. So much sadness. I don't know.

I will carry on, for now, while I can.

But I forget things, you know, lambsie. Kathryn is right: I do. Even more since all that business in hospital. If I tell you a thing once and then tell you again—well, you've just to put up with that.

They are different, you know, memory and memories. Memory is the way you know it's Tuesday or what you ate for dinner last night, or that you've already bought a new pair of slippers so whyever would you go to town and buy another pair? But memories are the things that make you who you are, even the ones you are most afraid to look at square in the face. And the funny thing is, I am losing my memory but not my memories. If it was the other way round, you'd be getting a kist full of knitting yarn and last Thursday's shopping list, which still I canna find.

But will they remain, too, my memories? And will I remember how to write them? I am afraid that words I have loved all my life will be carried away from me like flotsam on the tide.

I must write faster, while I still can, and I must choose, lambsie, choose for you. I canna write it all, I know that now. After I came home from hospital, I made myself this promise: if ever I am well enough to go back to my notebooks, I will not just begin the story from where I left off, what came next, and next after that. No, I will try to write for you the things that matter. And I will try to write them all.

I had seen cornflowers and the North Sea and every kind of sky. I had seen Magnus Tulloch's eyes. I thought I knew blue. And then I saw Fremantle.

Of all the memories I have of arriving, finally, in this stranger-place, the furthest place on earth from the cold north, it is this one, lambsie, this memory that is the strongest, the brightest, the one to catch my breath even now when I think of it. Wasn't just that the sky was blue but that there was so much of it. A blue that began at the horizon and went on forever, deeper here, brighter there, but all blue, unbroken. I did not think of the word *relentless* then. Later, when I knew what blue could be, when I'd felt its heat, the jangle and glare of it—aye, then I did. But we arrived when summer had passed, and it was a while before I met this other blue.

On the weekends, Magnus Tulloch and I would walk from our hostel in Fremantle to the edge of the Indian Ocean, just to look, to exclaim to each other: Was there ever sand so fine, so white? Water so pure? *Black an' blue with fish, I'll wager,* Magnus Tulloch said, and I wondered what manner of fish they would be. I knew they would not be herring. No drifters here, no farlins, no gutting girls. It made me think of Clementina, her big laugh, the way she used to scowl … Clementina, my sister now. And I'd wipe the sun from my streaming eyes.

Magnus Tulloch liked to peel off his shoes and socks and let the bubbles left behind by waves foam over his toes, and he would pick up slippery ropes of brown weed and pop the berries between his fingers, a smile on his face. But not me, no. I did not want to look at seaweed swilling in the shallows. Look up, I told myself, look up and learn to unremember.

Magnus Tulloch would grab me by the hand and we'd run along the shore with the clean wind in our faces. Often there'd be no-one else there, it was like we'd the new world to ourselves. The wind would never leave my hair alone, no mind how well I tied or pinned it, and Magnus Tulloch would kiss me, gathering up the wildness in his hands. He'd pretend his palms were burning to the touch of it—*ee, ach!*—but it was gentle teasing, sweet and gentle. *Promise me, Meggie*, he'd say, *promise ye'll never cut it.* And I did promise, aye. I'd have promised anything when the wide sky was in Magnus Tulloch's eyes.

As we walked back through the dunes, Magnus Tulloch would stop and look at every plant—the spiky, the tough and weathered, the ones with furry leaves and clear green sap. He'd pick away at mussels on limestone rocks that crumbled easily into fine sand, and I would wonder could they last, how long could they last, the buildings made of this soft stuff, and before I knew it I would be thinking of pink granite houses with their backs to the North Sea, and having to stop myself. I did not want those thoughts. I didn't want Roanhaven in my head at all. But it seemed that every new thing reminded me of something of the old.

One clear day, while Magnus Tulloch paddled through the wavelets, I stood on the beach, looking across to the ripple of an island on the horizon. We had been told there were small animals that lived there and nowhere else—something like kangaroos but the size of hares. I walked along the beach a little further, where a woman and a young girl were sitting on the sand. Both wore dresses of well-patched worsted, and handknitted scarves. The woman smiled and I asked the child what she was searching for. She held up her bucket timidly. Inside, a collection of shells, shiny on one side, chalky smooth on the other.

Beautiful, I told her, *the whitest shells I ever did see.*

She looked pleased and put the bucket down, but then she noticed my hand, the stump of my middle finger. Children often stared.

Roisin! her mother said, embarrassed, a hand on the little girl's shoulder.

What name has the island over there? I asked the woman.

She stood up and shaded her eyes, looking across to the horizon where I was pointing. *Oh, Rottnest, that is.*

Do people live there?

Prisoners, she said. *And many have died there, so they have. Natives.* She made a cross on her chest and her head dipped. *Also the people at the saltworks. And the Governor hisself sometimes.*

I looked at her, confused.

Has a house there, he do.

Before they walked on, the little one offered me a shell from her bucket. *You can hear the sea*, she said softly, and held it to her ear. *Like this.*

Ah, the things you remember. Sometimes you know why they hook in your memory, sometimes not. That conversation with the woman I recall because it seemed a source of wonder to me that this was a place whose Governor lived with prisoners and saltworkers and kangaroo-hares. Did that make it a level sort of place for all? Of course not. It was just one more thing that added to the strangeness of being a stranger here, the feeling of not understanding how things were and how they fitted together. And after that, I could never look across to that island without thinking of prisoners dying while the Governor sipped his tea.

I took the shell with me and set it on the mantelpiece alongside my hairbrush. I would pick it up, that shell, from time to time, run my thumb across the surface. I didn't know the name of it, nor what manner of creature had lived in it, but it was some new thing to wonder at and to make me feel the distance between my old home and new, my childhood, not so long ago, and that of children of this time, this place. Shells there were aplenty in Roanhaven, leftovers from the baiting. Heaped up beside houses, along the paths to the boatie shore, up in the braes, everywhere. The idea of picking one up and taking it home! Like an ornament. Like something precious. How the Roanhaven child I was would have laughed at that.

I wrote to Clementina every second week and told her these things, and it soothed me, when I couldn't sleep, to think of her reading my words and smiling and frowning and shaking her head. Sometimes she would write a letter in return, but not so very many. Gutting girls never had much idle time on their hands, and Clementina Slater even less since she'd become Clementina Ratter.

Fremantle in 1910—oh, it was a different place to the one you know, lambsie. I wonder, can you even picture it? A small port town of lime streets and bicycles and horse-drawn carts. The public buildings were made of limestone hewed out of the ground by convicts in the century before, but everything else was flimsy and brokendown—shops, cottages. There were sea baths between the jetties, and people often said Fremantle was like an English seaside resort. Well, I wouldn't have known about that. We had plenty of seaside but no resorts where I came from, and I never did see such a thing but for the one time when Clementina and I walked to The Parade in Great Yarmouth on a Sunday afternoon, and it was November then, and bitter, so no-one was swimming or doing seaside things.

The hostel we stayed in was noisy at night, and I would lie awake listening to arguments and makings-up coming from the rooms on our floor. Through open windows came songs and the sounds of smashing glass and horses' hooves, the aching cries of gulls that were smaller and bolder than those in the north. I would run my hand over the ridges of Magnus Tulloch's arm, pull it closer to me, and he would murmur in his sleep and curl his body around mine. *This* is home now, I would tell myself. All the home I want. I will belong here one day.

There were reminders all the time that I did not yet belong. When people talked to me, I had to listen carefully. I could not always understand what they were saying, and they were just as puzzled by me—maybe more.

Magnus Tulloch told me to be patient, about this, about many things. *The further you go*, he would say, pulling the brush through my hair each night, *the longer it takes for the new ta take on the ease of the old.*

It helped when we moved from the hostel to a wee cottage in Martha Street. Just Magnus Tulloch and me. Our landlady lived in a larger cottage on the same sandy block of land, and I canna say she was the most welcoming kind of woman, no. But there was a sweetness to those days that could not be soured away by the stranger-ness, nor by Mrs Laskon, and it was something to do with … I am trying to think of the right word. *Possibility*, yes, perhaps that's it. Every morning when Magnus Tulloch left for work, I would watch his rangy figure from the window, shrugging into a gansey I'd knitted, and had washed and mended and folded so often that it felt like the shape of my hands was stitched into the olive green wool. After crouching to check the bicycle tyres hadn't softened overnight, he'd take his leave with that half-kiss half-wave he'd send flying into the sky like bird flutter, and it always made me think of some words by Emily Dickinson I had copied into the back of my *Forget-Me-Not Annual*:

> Hope is the thing with feathers
> That perches in the soul,
> And sings the tune without the words
> And never stops at all

I would watch Magnus Tulloch riding down Martha Street, the sun and my hands warming his back, and I would tell myself: there is nothing that might not happen in this new, bright world.

Even so, they lived together—the stranger-ness and the sweetness—one never sending the other away. I hadn't expected it would take so long for the stranger-feelings to go. I could never have guessed it would be two whole years.

~

On an early-autumn day in 1912, Clementina arrived from the top of the world. She and Stivvy had twins now, a girl and a boy. She struggled down the gangplank at Fremantle with a toddler's hand in each of hers, none free to swat the flies beading her sticky face. And so my abiding memory is of her squinting and scowling at Fremantle, her lips furiously puffing air.

Stivvy, in front, pushed and jostled to clear a way for his family through the crowd. He nearly stumbled, nearly fell, so eager he was to leap free of the gangplank and onto the earth of his home-to-be. Imagine that—and Stivvy a man of the sea! Magnus Tulloch and I called to them through the wire fence but they could not hear us. We watched the Immigration officers herding them into the big tin shed where they would be questioned and stamped as the latest in a trail of immigrants to this small, struggling foothold of the Northern Hemisphere in the south.

It would be hours before they were cleared to go, but I told Magnus Tulloch that I had been waiting a long time to see Mrs Clementina Ratter and I would put up with the dust and sand to wait a while more. And besides, it was Sunday, and a mild autumn sun was warming my skin, sparkling the ocean harbour and burnishing the sky blue and gold and silver. Wherever else would anyone want to be?

Finally they were through, the four of them with blinking eyes and a cluster of bags—their kists would follow later. Stivvy heard rather than saw us first, and then he ran, and he and Magnus clutched each other like men drowning. Clementina stood back for a moment to roll her eyes at their hand pumping and shoulder slapping, and then she thrust the wee ones forward and clasped us all to her in a lopsided huddle. I was weeping shamelessly in a mixture of great happiness to see her again and a breath-punching sadness that was something to do with all we had been through together.

Hush, quinie, she whispered, releasing us, *ye'll be scaring the bairns, ye great daftie lassie.* Just the same, she ran a sleeve across her eyes and cheeks and either side of her neck, and I did not think it was just to mop the sweat or send the flies on their way.

While I struggled to find a sensible voice for myself, I pulled out a straw hat from my basket and jammed it onto Clementina's head, insisting she wear it. Then I knelt to fasten bonnets on the tired, grizzling bairns, tying under their chins the soft ribbons I'd sewn into the bands. By the time they were all shaded with wide brims, I had composed myself enough to explain to Clementina: *Ye're not used to sun like this. Even in autumn, it can fry your skin like a bubbled egg!*

I threw my arms around her and Stivvy.

Welcome to Fremantle, welcome to Australia!

~

I had longed for this day ever since the letter had come saying Clementina and family were emigrating, too. Magnus Tulloch had grinned like a clown when I read it to him, but soon his little dance of excitement slowed into pacing. Back and forward, back and forward, the few steps between the Metters and the icebox.

What have ye told Clementina in your letters?

What d'ye mean? I demanded.

Well, is not a land of plenty, this, eh? Not a place ta make a fortune. Doesn't matter how hard a man works, is not enough, ever.

I looked at him, impatient, but sorry, too. He had arrived in Western Australia a cooper with hopes of going on the land, but now, two years later, he was a cooper still. It was not a thing of shame to me—I had married a cooper and was proud of it then, and could not be prouder now—but something needled at Magnus Tulloch's pride. So much so that no more was he writing to Gracie. It was left to me to keep strong that thread of family.

Not enough, ever ... He was not thinking of Stivvy.

I didn't tell her anything that isn't true ... I began. But what was *true*? I had written to Clementina Ratter of all manner of things.

I'd described the way the wind billowed rainless clouds and rolled them like puffs of rooed wool across the blue expanse of sky, and the strident birdcall that shook you awake from dreams, insisting you get up, get up, get out of bed and gaze upon the Lord's work. I assured her she had never yet felt the true warmth of the sun and how it found its way into that cold centre that never left us in the north. I offered her small exotic flowers on spiky leaves, brilliant white beaches, not a bit of shingle in sight. And I hoped she would want to see these things for herself one day—never really believing such a thing could be possible. But now my mind dwelled upon all I had not told her about this imperfect paradise. Was a story true made untrue when you told only part of it?

My voice trailed off. Magnus Tulloch was already frowning—why add to his worries?

Stivvy's cousin is nominatin' them, I said, *an' even puttin' up a loan to get them goin'. Ye canna begrudge them for havin' a better start than ours.*

No, never, of course not. That's not what I mean ... But Meggie, ye know where they'll be going? Ta the wheat. What do Stivvy Ratter know about farming wheat?

Not a thing, but then what do any of them goin' to the east know about farmin' wheat on land like that?

Well, that just made everything sound bleaker. But it was true. Most of those who'd gone out to the just-opened Wheatbelt at least had some farming experience from the old country, and still they were struggling to make a go of it. Stivvy was a fisherman—what chance did he stand? But I wanted to believe it would be all right, and Magnus wanted the same. Of course we would write and bid them welcome, but we decided on a few words of what we'd heard, too: barren land, lack of rain. The bitterness towards the people trumpeting this new scheme.

Neither of us remarked to the other that if anyone— *anyone*—had tried to talk us out of emigrating, no matter what tales of warning they told, we would have thanked them truly but scoffed to ourselves, certain our excitement for a new beginning would see us through anything.

~

Clementina, Stivvy and the children came home with us to stay until Stivvy's cousin Matty wrote from Merredin. Mrs Laskon grumbled about extra lodgers, but it was all show, I knew, nothing more. Another shilling a week we'd agreed to give her, and nothing she needed to do for it, no. And Clementina would keep the children quiet and out of the way. Good little things, they seemed to be, Haldane and Jessie. We didn't have a lot of space, but we managed, aye. Sugar bags and blankets folded up for mattresses, old ganseys for pillows.

On that first night, I thought we would never sleep, would still be talking at breakfast. Stivvy's pitiful accounts of the food on board ship—*dreich an' dismal*—gave way to the plans ahead. He bubbled away, boiling over with new words: *wheat strains* and *per acre, ringbarking, superphosphate*. He was keen to hear about the Castlemaine Brewery, but Magnus always managed to steer things back to Stivvy. *Nothing ta tell*, I heard him say. *Kegs for beer instead of barrels for herring.*

Clementina needed no questions from me to get her started. The news of every gutting girl and cooper we knew came rolling out, and it gave me a pang of the heart to picture them. Catches of herring still were high, seasons still strong. A thought strayed into my mind that Da would be getting on in years now—would he still be on the drifters with the boys? But I tossed my head like Kitta used to do, shaking Roanhaven thoughts away.

The story of the last two years filled the room, as light as air, as heavy as smoke, but at last sleep overtook us, one by one.

I was the last to bed. I picked my way across the floor of the sleepout, stepping over Stivvy and Clementina, both of them snoring. The bairns were curled into each other like sleeping kittens. I crouched down beside them. Look at them there. The full curve of their pink cheeks, so much like Clementina's.

I reached out to press a fingertip kiss on each, but drew my hand back quickly. That rough hand with its pits and ridges, its deformed shape. It was so ugly, they so pure.

A glance at the carriage clock that Gracie had insisted we bring with us—a ticking of time that once sat above the fire of the Tullochs' but-and-ben in Sandwick. Nearly three o'clock. In a couple of hours I would need to rise, to be at the factory by six.

Imagine it, lambsie:

A noisy place, and airless, hot in summer, freezing in winter. A tin-shed of a factory that sprawls across a whole block. But if you close your eyes and breathe it in, you might truly think yourself in heaven.

Hundreds of Shortbread Cream halves cooling on trays, slabs of Currant Lunch baking. The sweetness of butter and currants, vanilla and cloves, cinnamon and lemon peel hanging in the air.

Smell is more than a sense, lambsie. Did you know that? It has substance that settles, you cannot help but taste it as you breathe. Ask any gutting quine with the bitterness of blood and slime on her lips and her tongue. Girls at the Mills & Ware biscuit factory—always *girls*, no mind the age—they grumbled a lot about the heat from the ovens, the flour that made them cough, the concrete floors and windowless walls. But oh, that smell! No matter how hard the day, you couldn't help but smile when the rotation changed and some new deliciousness floated through. Chocolate Creams. Gingernuts. Macaroons. Even the plains—the Thin Captains and Milk Arrowroots, the Cabins used as ship's biscuits—they filled the air with something like … what's the word? Oh, just *goodness*, aye. As comforting as a pot of tea.

I used to listen to the grumbling, nod to be companionable, murmur to get along, but the memory of fifteen hours without a break at the farlins, knee-deep in muck, was part of me. I'd not speak of it—who would have believed me, eh?—but it was in my mind while the girls prattled on about *conditions*, because to me this job was a gift dusted in sugar like the Nice biscuits we made.

That day after Clementina arrived, I'd to jog the two blocks from home to get to the factory on time, and I left my apron behind on the kitchen table. No clean apron, no start. But Lois came to my rescue with a spare she always kept rolled tight in her basket. Lois had never forgotten an apron once that I knew of, but she was a careful person who liked to be prepared.

I rushed, sweating, past Forewoman Vi outside the Creaming Room, but aproned I was and late I was not.

So they arrived, then, did they, ya friends from Pommie Land? Ollie asked as she squeezed blobs of buttercream onto shortbread halves through the nozzle of a huge bag.

Good thing Clementina Ratter canna hear ye calling her a Pommie!

Ollie looked puzzled. *Well, isn't she? Same as you?*

What? Meggie English! Lois said, looking up from the lines of biscuits she was setting out for Ollie to cream. *A Scottie, her—no mistaking that accent!*

Ollie shrugged. *Scotland, England, all the same to me!* And she gave me a no-hard-feelings-you-can't-help-it hug with an arm already greased to the elbows with cream.

Ollie!

All right, all right!

I placed the top halves on each biscuit, lightly pressing down to sandwich the cream, and Vi ran the trays of assembled biscuits into the Packing Room for wrapping in paper and sealing with wax. We swapped jobs, the four of us, every week, to ease the boredom of the same old routine, and Vi kept a watchful eye over the whole operation. There was nothing to stop us from talking from start of shift till the noon bell.

So what was it like, seeing your friends after all this time? Vi said, grinning.

I hesitated. I'd been thinking of little else all morning, but there wasn't much I wanted to say just then. I liked my workmates at the factory—the girls from the Creaming Room, Enzia and Franca in Packing—and in time we became friends, but when it came to things that mattered, I was wary at first, shy of offering them up to be turned into fun, which is what the girls always did.

Clementina is the same, same as she always was, aye, an' Stivvy looks a bit fatter …

And they've got two young kiddies, haven't they? Ollie interrupted. *Twins? What a handful!*

I caught Lois's look, the little shake of her head at Ollie.

Oh …

Vi broke the clumsy silence, bursting through the door. There was a problem with one of the ovens and we were to take our dinnertime early, as soon as this load was creamed.

We finished the trays. The girls chattered about the state of the ovens, glad to have moved the conversation on.

That awkwardness, it was because they thought I could not have children. And even though their pity always made me squirm, I had no intention of saying otherwise, because it was what I'd told Management. See, when I first applied at the factory, I was turned away: *We don't employ married women.* Curt. No argument. But they were desperate for staff, and I tried again later, and this time the office manager gave me a second look.

Why d'ya want to work for, when you're married? Surely your husband wouldn't have a bar of that.

Where I come from, isn't any shame in married women workin', I told him. *Everyone does. Everyone has to.*

He'd looked at me sceptically, then down at my application form. *Says here you're nineteen. Ah. Well. You'll have a family on the way before you know it. What's the point in starting you?*

I took a huge breath and out came Lie Number One.

I won't. I canna have babies.

Shocking, but I told myself that there was some truth in it.

He blinked at me in consternation, clearly afraid of what embarrassing details I might be about to offer.

So, ye see, it's different for me.

He looked doubtful and I sensed a moment of chance. *Look, Mr Prentice, I didn't come all the way from the Shetlands to idle around on the beach. You need workers an' I need to work. An' I'm a good worker. Ye'd not be sorry if ye took me on.*

And ya reckon your husband will give his permission?

Permission. It summoned up memories I did not want in my head, and not one of them involved Magnus Tulloch. I looked at Mr Prentice and spoke firmly: *Aye. I mean, yes.*

Two years later, I was still the only married woman in the Mills & Ware factory, except for the widows, who were another kind of married. There were a few of them.

~

I was glad to take my break early and ran back to Martha Street.

Stivvy wasn't there—he'd gone for a look around—but I stood at the door of the cottage, panting, and took in the sight of the impatient, irascible Mrs Clementina Slater Ratter humming over two nearly-sleeping bairns. The look of tenderness on her face made me turn away with a wound in my breathing.

When finally she glanced up, she turned on me the full light of that tenderness, and in it I saw my mother and my sister and my best friend.

And something in me broke.

~

The problem with the oven was fixed by one-thirty, but we were behind schedule and would have to stay until the day's tally was done.

Any overtime? Ollie ventured hopefully.

Vi quashed the idea with a short laugh. *Y've had extra break time, haven't ya? That's what Management said.*

I was resigned to being late home on the last day I would want to be late, and had to remind myself, for the second time that day, how lucky I was to be working.

On the day I started, the girls had looked at me aghast, and no-one was shy about saying why.

How can you work in a factory without all ya fingers? Vi demanded. *Strewth! You're no good to me on a production line, luv, no offence, but we can't be standing round, waiting on you to catch up! I dunno, Management needs to take a good hard look at 'emselves, sending me someone like you, no offence, luv.*

Her outspokenness took my breath away, but I thought: So this is how it is. Well, then.

Management had in fact said much the same thing, until I produced Lie Number Two.

I've been workin' on production lines with half a finger missin' all my life, I told Mr Prentice. *Hasn't stopped me before an' won't stop me now.*

He'd scratched his brilliantined head and looked dubious but I stood my ground. On a less desperate day, I'd have been shown the door, for sure.

I told Vi the same lie and assured her that her production line would not be slowed down by me.

Well, by the time anyone found me out, I'd made good on my promise and was handling the heavy trays, lining up biscuits, even manoeuvring the cream nozzle, same as all of them.

I'd never manage with a knife again, I knew what my limits were, but you don't gut herring for three seasons, you don't knit the whole of your life, without becoming good with your hands. All of that could not be wiped out by the loss of a bit of a finger. And if anyone had ever asked me, I'd have told them straight: Creaming biscuits? A picnic compared to gutting fish.

Aye, I reminded myself again as the factory clock chimed six, I'd every reason to be grateful to Mills & Ware.

~

It was getting dark when I got home. I opened the door and found everything neat: the makeshift bedding folded, bags stacked in corners against the wall. Even Haldane and Jessie looked spit-and-polished and shiny-bright in a way only Clementina could manage in a place where all was new and strange. The teapot was on the sideboard, in a knitted cosy I'd never seen before. She had even managed the Metters. It'd taken days of wrestling with the old beast before I'd got it working, but even a Metters would bide its manners and behave for Clementina.

Ach, an' here's your Unty Meggie now, she crooned, pushing Jessie forward with one hand and hooking Hal by the breeches to swing him around to face me. *An' what d'ye say to your Unty Meggie?*

Jessie gave me a frown so like Clementina's that my face twitched with trying not to laugh.

Clementina pushed her again.

Ay ay, Jessie said. So grudging.

What's that, Miss Jessie? her mother demanded. *Ay ay WHO, d'ye care to say?*

The frown deepened, but Jessie said, *Ay ay, Un-ty Meggie.*

Hal, happy little thing he was, had been chattering away to himself but sobered at the sound of his sister's voice. He looked at her and up at me.

Ay ay, he echoed solemnly. *Un-ty Meggie.*

I am too young to feel old, I thought.

I reached out a hand to each of them but they shrank back. Clementina tsked.

Come with me, I said firmly, leading them to a big pinewood box in the kitchen.

Once a week, factory staff were allowed to buy a huge bag of broken biscuits for sixpence. I hefted the sack onto the table and scooped out bits and pieces by the handful: Cream Fingers, Nice, Gingernuts, Chocolate Creams.

Suspicion drained from Jessie's face as I filled her hands, and Hal's eyes widened. Both of them looked to their mother for a nod before stuffing their mouth with crumbs and buttercream and sugar. Not until they'd finished, and I was wiping their sticky hands and grinning faces on my apron, did I dare glance over at Clementina. But I wasn't fooled by the scowl, the shake of her head: she didn't begrudge me my shameless bribe. She was glad we were friends, me and the children, and never mind how.

Once they were cleaned up, she ushered them to play in the corner with a bag of things that rattled and tinkled, and poured two cups of lukewarm tea from the pot.

So where have they gone, Magnus an' Stivvy?

Her forehead furrowed. *Some place called … now, what did they say? The Anchor? Said they'd not be long, an' they better not be!*

Well, there wasn't much money for it to be otherwise, and Magnus was not much of a drinker then, so I expected they'd be turning up any minute. I fancied Clementina thought the same, and there were things she wanted to say before they did.

So ye're happy, quinie? she asked as I sat down opposite her. *Happy in this place?*

Aye. Happy enough. An' ye'll be too.

She shrugged. *Stivvy has his mind set on this farm. A fisher an' a gutting quine! All this way, an' I'm to turn m'self into a crofter's wifie now!*

She shook her head. *Show me your hands, quinie.*

I held them out at once and she tut-tutted and pulled a face. I sighed. *Herring hands …*

Salt an' gipper hands …

Biscuit factory hands …

A disaster! And Clementina's big snorting laugh set me off too.

She took my disastrous hands in hers and looked me in the eye. *Now, tell me, quinie, if ye're so happy, where are the bairns for Unty Clementina?*

The noisy arrival of Magnus and Stivvy spared me from saying what she already knew: that I wasn't yet ready. That there was still a frozen part of me that even the fierce Fremantle sun couldn't thaw.

~

I had brought home bread and cheese. But that Clementina, she'd conjured up a soup from nothing.

Good, Magnus declared, sopping it up with a hunk of bread, and Stivvy agreed with a nod.

I could taste dried peas and potatoes—all there'd been in our pinewood pantry—but as for the rest?

Whatever did ye find to make stock? I asked.

Potato skins. An' some green onion things from the Eye-talun mannie, your neighbour, what's his name? He called out to me an' passed them over the fence, nice as ye please.

I don't know. And I thought: How like Clementina to know more in a day than I'd managed in two years.

An' a spoonful of flour from that Mrs Laskon next door.

Mrs Laskon! Mrs Laskon gave ye flour?

I asked her for some, aye, and she did. She wanted to give me two spoonfuls, make it thicker, she said, but one's quite enough an' I told her thanks, one's all I need. And Clementina sniffed.

I was trying to imagine this conversation with our landlady, the same woman who wanted *a word, please, Mrs Tulloch* every time I saw her. Clementina Slater Ratter truly was a marvel.

The marvel looked at me curiously. *What problem is it ye have with her?*

Oh, no problem from where I see it, I said, looking across at Magnus, but he and Stivvy were deep in discussion again—*clearing* this, *fencing* that. I lowered my voice, all the same. *Problem's all with her. Turns up her nose, she does. At Magnus for the shame of his wife put out to work, as she calls it, as if I have no say at all. An' as for me—well, Mills & Ware, ye canna get lower. Factory girl—yew know.*

I laughed, but Clementina's brows disappeared into fleshy furrows.

~

It was late when I pinched out the wicks of the thick tallow candles. Mrs Laskon objected to electric lights after nine; she *wasn't made of money.*

My toes kicked something light that skittered across the floor. Something from the children's bag of trinkets. I picked it up, turned it in my fingers. A small cone, smooth inside, the outside pitted with tiny corrugations. I took it to the window but I didn't need moonlight to tell me it was a limpet shell.

How many limpets had I shelled in my life?

Faces in the dark—my beautiful sister, an old man, a slack-chinned lolloping boy ... Furiously I rubbed them from my eyes.

I held the shell to my face, breathing in the faintest smell of a cold, faraway sea, of all I had left behind. And left gladly, I reminded myself.

I turned to find little-boy eyes blinking, watching me, from across the room. I saw them all the time, eyes like these, in darkness, in the full glare of a blinding sun. Sometimes laughing at a runaway rabbit, sometimes crying from the blue expanse of somewhere I could not follow.

I reached out, but they blinked again. Were gone.

A catch in my throat, a violent shiver. Struggling to find a rhythm for my breathing again.

Haldane, I whispered silently, forcing a calmness I did not feel. *It's only wee Hal's face.*

I let the shell drop to the floor, then quickly scrabbled to pick it up again. It's like this, with memories, lambsie: you want to push them away, then you want to hold them tight. It makes no kind of sense.

I put the limpet shell with the one the little girl had given me on the beach not long after we'd arrived. The old and the new.

~

Only a few nights, it was, before Magnus cycled home with two bottles of Penguin Ale from Castlemaine and a parcel of river prawns, wrapped in newspaper, from the Greeks who used to drop their nets near the brewery.

What's all this, then? I asked. *Did ye find a spare pound flappin' in the breeze?*

He looked across at Clementina with a question on his face. *Have ye not …?*

We're off tomorrow! Stivvy cut in, singing. *Off ta Merredin in the morning! Off ta a new life! Say hello ta your farmer friends, lassie!* And he galloped to the kitchen and back, Jessie under one arm and Hal under the other.

Oh. Tomorrow … That's … that's … wonderful …

And Stivvy Ratter came to a halt and stared at the sight of the farmer's wife and the factory girl weeping silently into each other's hair.

~

It's a warm, clear Saturday in autumn 1912 when I summon up every scrap of strength I have to bid goodbye to Clementina, Stivvy and the bairns and wish them the happiness I long for them to have.

We are determined, Clementina and I, we made a promise the night before: we are done with crying, there will be no more of it. And so it was that we had busied ourselves with packing up, with cutting pieces for the long rattling journey east, with making lists of supplies to be sent on later once they are settled. And now we stand, hand in hand, holding on. And then she looks up and snorts, in true Clementina style, flicking her fingers at the sun.

Well, quinie, look at that. Another bloddy blue sky.

In the two years after Clementina left, things happened that could have made her bitter. They worked hard, the fisherman and the gutting girl did, they cleared and fenced, they ploughed and planted. But there were so many problems, unsolvable, one and then the next. Too little land for the farm to pay. Too far from the pipeline for water. Too little money to turn poor soil into rich. Much too little for a family and two wee children in a sheddie on a lonely block.

Clementina told me all this but wrote, too, of cheerful things, and maybe she did it to cheer herself, I don't know. What did she love most about her struggling little farm? Of all things, chickens! All of them named for gutting girls. *And which of my girls do you think is the best layer of all, quinie? Bella, that's who! And a muckle brown beauty she is!* And she would send me eggs by Paulie Garrioch's cart, carefully packed in straw, and always with a bag of brown and white feathers Jessie had collected for Unty Meggie.

In spite of the stubborn jolliness pasted onto the page, maybe even because of it, Clementina's letters were hard to read. But they reminded me of where we had come from, she and I. I would read them and think of my mother, of Unty Jinna and Unty Leebie, of all those strong women who bore and endured. Where did I fit in? They were all so much stronger than me.

But when I look at you, lambsie, there it is—a glimmer of something from that same stuff, the muscle from which spirit grows. You just don't know it yet.

~

For Clementina, for Stivvy, it all came to a head in 1914. As it did for the world. Anxiety stole over us like mist from the North Sea, and it stayed.

We Mills & Ware girls would often walk down to South Beach to eat our bread and apples. I would stand barefoot on the sand, my skirt hiked up in my hands, the cool green water rushing up to my toes, all fizzy with bubbles. How soft the sand, fine and white like baker's flour. How light the bleached shells that the sea threw up each night to dry in the sun next day. I had been born a sea child, spent all my early years with my feet wet or salted dry, but the Indian Ocean reminded me every day it was not the same sea.

One day I stood squinting into the horizon, the green of that crease between sea and sky, trying to fathom how many miles to land, and what land, whose land. Enzia ran past me into the shallows, where I never liked to go, and lost her footing. She landed on her bottom with a squelchy splash.

Ooowwww!

Lois helped her up and she twisted round to see the back of her dress.

Oh! Now look like I wee my selv. Embarrass!

No, no, ye canna hardly notice with that colour, I said.

Comforting murmurs from the others.

It'll be dry by the time we get back, pet, Lois assured her.

Enzia looked doubtful but flounced the skirt of her dress in both hands. Flap, flap, like a scarlet bird, up and down the beach.

The rest of us staggered up through sand and pigface to the lifesavers' shed near Marine Terrace, where we'd left our shoes. We flopped onto the stubble of grass.

Vi squinted at a puckered thread on her dress, easing it with her thumb.

Wonder what they'll look like in uniform? she said, all dreamy.

Who?

Our boys—who do ya think! Jack and Clarrie in Baking, Micky and Bob. They're all talking about enlisting when the time comes. Even Bruce and Mr Prentice, and they'd be in their forties if they're a day, I reckon.

Don't say such things! There's not a war yet, an' some are saying there will never be one. All that trouble in Europe—that's nothing to do with us here.

Vi looked at me, scandalised. *Of course it's to do with us! If England steps in, then we're in too. We're with the Mother Country.*

YOUR *country*, Lois added pointedly.

Your husband will be going?

Course he will. Ollie spoke for Magnus without so much as a glance at me. *Every good man will be going as soon as the call is out.*

I pulled on my shoes, quiet.

Vi sighed. It was the kind of sigh she usually reserved for chocolate sponge. *Well, I think Clarrie will cut quite the dash as a soldier.*

Ollie and Lois glanced at each other and giggled.

The dinner break was nearly over. I stood and brushed myself down, desperate to think about something other than the thing no-one could stop thinking about.

Enzia flew past, kicking up sand. *Come, hurry, or we late!*

~

Magnus was already home by the time I pushed open the door. His bicycle leaned against the wall, the leather seat still warm with the yeasty, malty smell that was on his clothes, his skin, his hair, even after he lathered it away in the tub. I never minded it, that smell.

Sometimes I recognised something like it on his breath, but it was sour, like rotten beet. The stale remains of Penguin Stout. *That* I never liked.

Inside he was sitting at the table, scaling a fish. His large hands worked quickly, scraping my old gipper against the grain, showering scales left and right onto sheets of newspaper. The skin of the fish gleamed red and silver-white, and I looked down at my hands. I could almost feel the salt gritty in the bitter syrup of guts and blood, my fingers closing around the shape of a herring in my palm, the diamond back as dark as wet slate, the white belly glittering.

Scales spat and flicked from the gipper as Magnus Tulloch worked.

He hadn't heard me. His eyes squinted in concentration and his lips were moving, as though trying out words he might later say aloud. Practising them on a fish that didn't have a lot to say.

Late afternoon light warms through the slatted windows. I have been given a new pair of eyes, or younger ones have been given back to me. He is beautiful, Magnus Tulloch, he has always been. Strong, and beautiful, and kind. The knife pauses; he pushes back with one elbow that long sweep forever falling in his eyes.

Look at you, the man you have become, the boy you still are. Do you love me like you did when I was your Fish Meggie? Do you love me now that I am a biscuit factory girl who works because she is too frightened of more loss to risk more love? Do you love me when I cry at night for a home I could not wait to leave, that no longer exists because everything that made it home has gone?

Yes, says the boy, his eyes never leaving the knife, yes and yes. The man is silent, has too many questions of his own.

I let the door close behind me and he looked up, and the history between us rushed in to seal all the little cracks.

I folded my apron and hung it over the back of a chair. *Cup of tea?*

Aye, he said, brushing scales from his hands and shaking them onto the newspaper. He held up the fish by the tail, and grinned.

Just look at this beauty!

The Greeks?

Aye. An' cheap!

I wondered what would be best: light the oven and bake the fish whole, or do a fillet and fry. But Magnus Tulloch had a better idea.

I could hang it in the chimney ta smoke?

Ooh, imagine! The taste of a smokie! Or Cullen Skink, the milky soup made with mashed potato and smoked haddock. I nodded, hungry for cold-water fish, fish from my mother's creel.

While he was splitting the snapper in two along either side of the backbone, I sat at the table, waiting for the kettle to boil, chin in the cup of my hands. I watched as he cut along the gills and scoured out the guts with my gipper.

So ye're a gutter now, are ye, Magnus Tulloch?

He clowned, bowing deeply and spinning the gipper in one hand, and for a moment the boy was all there was, and the two of us were laughing like nothing could possibly trouble us in this clear, bright moment in South Fremantle in June 1914.

The white flesh of the snapper was thicker than any haddock, and he threaded the two halves, one below the other, with thin wire, old style. As I watched his careful work, the sober face of the man came back.

Letter from Merredin on the bed, he said.

I raced to fetch it and returned with a sealed envelope.

What, ye haven't read it?

A shadow passed across his eyes and he shook his head. *It's Clementina's writing an' your name on the front.*

There was something about the way he spoke that made me think he knew already what it was I was about to read.

I scanned the letter quickly. The same story, but now, something new. Desperation. In every line. If the crop failed this time, all would be lost.

Magnus strung up the wire frame in the chimney. *Things are bad*, he said. A statement, not a question.

Mmm, aye. I put the letter aside, pressing my palm on it for a second.

We discussed what to use in place of fir and oak to smoke the fish as I lit the fire with spindly kindling. The knobbly, nutty banksia cones were the best we could think of.

Soon Magnus was fanning the fire and piling on the cones and we were hoping for the best, hoping for smoked haddock from a fish that looked and felt and tasted nothing like it.

I glanced back at Clementina's letter. Things were bad, aye, but her worry over the state of the farm was as nothing compared to her fear of what Stivvy might do if they were forced to walk off the land, in debt.

War is coming and you know what he'll do, he'll be gone for a soldier, that's what, the great daftie loon will be gone for the five shillings a day and to make himself a man again.

What had Stivvy told Magnus? They didn't write, the two of them, but sometimes Paulie Garrioch would bring news from the Wheatbelt after his runs from the ironmonger's store. He and Magnus would talk for hours down at The Anchor.

I would not ask him outright, would not talk about the war. I didn't want to hear him say it.

~

The next day Mrs Laskon came to the door, a pinched look on her face.

There's a … smell, Mrs Tulloch. A distinct odour of … something. Fish?

She looked faint when I told her about the snapper in the chimney. *As though we are beyond the pale*, I said to Magnus when she'd gone.

It really is too much, Mrs Tulloch, he mimicked.

Barbarians.

I sit one night with my hands around the tea-cosy Clementina Ratter has knitted for me. She is the best knitter I know, better even than Ma, and has learned some of the Shetland patterns that I could never have tried, not even before my finger was taken. The teapot is warm on my hands but canna bring comfort, no. Nothing can thaw the chill in my blood this night.

I listen for tyres braking on limestone, the scuffing of boots. Thud, thud, in my ears. Dull, like guns a long way distant. My own blood, is all. The drumming unease of waiting.

The gate scrapes. Magnus Tulloch half falls through the door. Rumpled up.

He fends me off with a blur of hands and lurches into the bedroom.

I follow. He is tearing at buttons, kicking off his boots, while I stand back, watching.

Finally I must ask. *Did you do it? Magnus? Did you? Did they take you?*

He falls onto the bed, still dressed, a hand across his face shutting me out. Silence.

~

They would not take him. The same war that was snatching men from all walks and dispatching them to faraway places did not want Magnus Tulloch. They turned him away, much to the satisfaction of Castlemaine Brewery, which had lost too many of its workers already. It was a terrible thing to think, and never could I say it out loud, to anyone, but I was glad of the ringing in Magnus Tulloch's ears, the dizzy spells he took on sometimes—leftovers from an accident in a barrel factory the year we met.

My duty, it be every man's duty, he had tried to explain to me. And when I refused to commiserate, something happened that never I thought would. His voice hardened. Aye, hardened against me. *Ye understand, Meggie Tulloch*, he said, *ye canna tell me ye don't. I canna stand by an' do nothing—an' ye know that, girl, ye know what it's like when ye have ta run at somethin' whether ye like it or not.*

I would not meet his eyes, and I would not discuss it, so it was one more little crack that came between us. Something that I tried to knit over with tight stitches of purl but never, never could.

Hal and Jessie were too young to see in the New Year, too young to understand the passage of one year into the next, but Clementina was stubborn.

Northern bairns they are, Buchan an' Shetland both, an' what were good for us is good for them as well. An' they need to know … Hogmanay is … They especially need to know now …

And so we put on happy faces for them, Clementina, Magnus and I—a pantomime of celebration we didn't feel. We did our best, but our best was a feeble thing, coloured with worry for Stivvy who, after only two weeks' training, had sailed for Egypt with the Australian forces the month before.

On the verandah of Mrs Laskon's little weatherboard cottage in Martha Street, we fanned the children's clammy skin and drank water with precious ice, waiting for church bells to chime midnight. The street was subdued. An odd peal of laughter from the direction of the Mandurah road, but it was a very different Hogmanay from last. Silence from Mrs Laskon's side: she was away in Perth with her daughter.

As the time drew near, Magnus poured three glasses of Penguin from a plain brown bottle, compliments of the brewery, and two tin mugs of orange cordial from a jug. And then it was crossing arms and 'Auld Lang Syne' and Jessie and Hal jumping up and down with no more idea of what was happening than you would expect from the bairns they were.

An' now we must watch for the first footing, Clementina told them, and their faces grew grave.

I feared they would be disappointed. No-one was around to cross our threshold, carrying a gift for luck.

But soon they were oohing, Hal and Jessie, at the arrival of a tall stranger in a fisherman's black hat and swathed in a long black cape that looked a lot like something I'd seen covering Mr Brescianini's chicken coop.

Look, here's a fine strong mannie to be first footing. It be the tall, dark an' weel-faurt ones that bring the bestest luck! And Clementina tugged at the stranger's hat, the better to cover his long hair.

A Good New Year ta one an' all, he announced in a singing voice, crossing the doorway. He turned and ceremoniously presented Clementina with a gift.

Half a pound of flour.

She was momentarily nonplussed but recovered quickly.

Ooh, thank ye, kind stranger. An' a Good New Year to yourself as well.

He kissed Clementina on the cheek, and then me, and I whispered to him, *Ye smell of hops, kind stranger.*

He appeared to change his mind about kissing the children, instead stooping only a little to shake their wee hands.

Goodbye! he sang. *An' many may ye see!*

Jessie stared after him, frowning, as he swished away, but Hal wanted to see the good-luck present.

Flour! He was crushed.

Clementina rescued the moment. *Flour, aye! An' what shall we do with flour, eh? Shall we make griddle cakies?*

Now?

Aye, bairnikie, now!

And Clementina took them inside on this stifling night to light the Metters and cook pancakes.

~

There were still voices in the distance when the children had gone to bed.

Magnus sat on the verandah step, his back to the house. Kneeling behind him, I put my hand on his shoulder, unsure of what to say. *Happy New Year?* Empty words. How could it be happy. The world was at war. And he still felt it keenly, the army's rejection. Tied to the homefront when he was itching to defend his old country, and new, both. Me, I could not pretend to be sorry the way it was. Such unspoken things kept him staring into the New Year's sky with his back to me this night.

I sat on the verandah, leaning against the weatherboards, and Clementina flopped down beside me. It looked like the effort at joy had cost her everything. I put an arm around her, rested my head against hers.

The New Year promised bleak for her—I couldn't say otherwise. Her husband away at war, the farm lost to drought and rabbits, a debt to Stivvy's cousin unpaid and nothing to show for two hard years on the land.

Clementina would be needing more blessings than a bogus first-footer could bestow on her with half a pound of flour.

She folded a jeely griddle cake and tore it in two, handing me half. We chewed the sticky, doughy sweetness in silence.

A last swallow, a deep breath, a sigh. *What am I goin' to do, Meggie?*

I took her face in my hands and told her straight: *Well, for one, ye're goin' to stay with us, your family; for two, ye're goin' to pay off that Matty with the army pay, just like Stivvy wants ye to; an' for three, ye're goin' to hug those bairns every time ye look at them, an' is that enough to start the New Year with?*

She buried her face in my damp, frizzy hair and cried, and I murmured over and over, *We'll manage, quinie, we'll manage, we'll just do what we can.*

~

On an evening in May 1915, when our shift had had to work on to finish the factory's army quota, it was nearly dark when I turned into Martha Street. Most of the cottages were lit already, some with electric lights, some lanterns and some, if times were bad, candles.

Why was our weatherboard cottage in darkness when Magnus must be home, and Clementina for sure? As I got closer, fear drew a finger up my spine. In the thin, uneven remains of daylight, Hal was playing some game with a broken picket for a sword, slashing at enemy sunflowers in Mrs Laskon's garden. Jessie was on the front step, elbows on her knees.

As I pushed open the low gate, Hal dropped his sword among the lacerated flowers, and Jessie flung herself at my legs.

I untwined her gently and lifted her into my arms. *Where's your ma, bairnikie?*

Clementina was inside, in the dark, staring at the unlit stove, and nothing—not shaking her shoulders, not the keening of her little girl—could rouse her.

I turned to Magnus, a heap at the table, and he lifted his head and pushed a piece of paper at me.

A telegram. Too dark to read it, but I didn't need to.

~

Our sweet Stivvy, hardworking, optimistic fisherman-farmer-soldier. He died on a ridge above a faraway beach a few days after the 11th Battalion landed there. The army told Clementina he was killed shielding a wounded man. That he was a hero. That he sacrificed his own life for a fellow soldier, for his country. That he'd been buried high on a hill overlooking the sea.

That's no good to me, is it? Clementina wept. *How does knowin' any of that help? He's gone. My Stivvy. Just … gone.*

Clementina was angry for a long time, at the army, at the war, but mostly at Stivvy for *not comin' back like he promised, the great daftie loon.* But when the anger passed into sadness, the shape of her grief changed. She became anxious.

He's lyin' there, she said, her voice cracking about the edges, sharp and clacking like knitting needles. *Just lyin' in some nowhere place. NO where he were born, NO where he lived, NO where his family must live without him. How can that be right, to leave a man in a place where no-one knows him?*

When I asked Mrs Laskon did she know the place, she brought over to us a big leather atlas. *Keep it, my dear, and God bless*, she said, her hands around Clementina's, gripping them harder with each word.

The two of us pored over the page headed 'Turkey', and Clementina found what she was looking for on a narrow finger of land between the Aegean and the Sea of Marmara.

See? she said. *Just a dot on a map.*

It was the tiniest label: Gallipoli. How much more that name had become to widows and wives, mothers and fathers, children, friends, the faraway bereaved.

But it isn't a nowhere place, I told Clementina. *That's not true at all. This place called Gallipoli is a somewhere place to you an' to us, to all with men an' boys they love. The place Stivvy died, that's Somewhere.*

But they canna even tell me about his grave; I don't even know if he has a cross with his name on it.

I didn't think we'd know while the war continued, maybe even after that, and it plagued Clementina, this idea of Stivvy without a proper grave, as if it made him lost, unremembered. So we made our own. A memorial on a ridge above the dunes a distance from South Beach, away from where the swimmers went. A slab of limestone, it was, soft—an offcut with rough edges that no-one would miss from a building block not far from the factory. We trundled it there in Mrs Laskon's wheelbarrow, dug it into the white sand, and took turns scratching the stone with a pointed chisel from Magnus's box of tools. All night we'd been, deciding. I read out loud verses from Clementina's mother's Bible, from my precious Robert Louis Stevenson, from the *Forget-Me-Not Annual* and the poems

I'd copied in the back, and she listened to them all. It had to be right, for Stivvy.

We sat on some sugar bags, Clementina, Magnus, the children and I, and toasted the sea and the sky and Stivvy's beautiful life with warm tea from a flask. Hal and Jessie dug for little crabs, and tipped buckets of sand over our legs, and strewed their hair and ours with dried seaweed. But we were silent, thinking of that place across the other side of the world, and hoping the words Clementina had chosen and we had carved so clumsily would keep his spirit with us:

> *Home is the sailor, home from the sea*
> *And the hunter home from the hill.*

June 1974

You never know when you're at the beginning of the end, lambsie. If you did, well. You'd never go on, would you?

War aged Magnus. First Stivvy's death. Then the stares and silent questions, the why-are-you-still-here? looks given to men who seemed able-bodied enough for war but remained in their jobs at home. *Shirkers*. And it was worse for someone like Magnus—a man not a father. A married man whose wife worked.

Ye canna walk around with excuses pinned to your chest, I told him.

If only. It would have been easier for him if he could.

I felt the eyes on me also. No more was I the only married woman in the factory. Many girls who'd worked at Mills & Ware when single had returned to fill in during the war, taking up places let go by enlisted men. These new ones, and even the girls who had been on my team for years, I knew what they were thinking. Why should you be spared? Why should you return home at night to your husband when our husbands, our brothers, fathers, sons, are away fighting for the freedom of us all?

Months went by, and Magnus wasn't sleeping any more. He didn't toss about, like I did, always pulling the blankets out from the mattress and trying to punch life into the pillow, but there was no sleep in his breathing, none of the steady rhythm that speaks of dreams. Just an occasional deep, wakeful sigh.

He was awake, I was awake, but our limbs curled outwards instead of towards each other, away from touch. Each day it grew, the pile of things we could not say to each other because too much time had passed now. It got so I could hardly remember what it looked like, the shape of us as we once were, the way we breathed together and moved as one thing, not two. It was my fault, I knew that.

But even though there was much that lay beyond my grasp, I looked at him, my husband, and I could hear what he was thinking, and I knew—just *knew*—it would not be long before he tried to enlist again.

~

One evening at the end of 1915, he came home from Castlemaine light as air.

Clementina was blunt, at her most scathing. *Ye're a fool, Magnus Tulloch, a gaak! Goin' away to war an' gettin' yourself killed is not goin' to bring him back. An' how is it ye're in now when they turned ye down last year? How did ye pass the medical?*

He waved the questions away as though they were a nothing. He would do anything now to go, anything it took, not because of what others thought but because of Stivvy. And not to bring him back but to take his place, carry on for him. They all felt it, the ones left behind. Each time they read a new report of casualties it maddened their need to defend and protect, no mind the cost.

And I didn't have to ask how he passed the medical. He'd learned, from before, what to say and how to bluff. He no longer had any of the symptoms that kept him from leaving with Stivvy, oh no. No headaches, no noises in the head, no dizziness, nothing. And the need for enlistments meant they were not so inclined to be vigilant now. The military and Magnus Tulloch had both got what they wanted, aye.

It isn't war, he told me, when we were alone, away from Clementina's anger. *Not for the sake of it, I mean. Tell me you understand that, Meggie. I am no lad, blind ta what it means. I'm not looking at war and seeing some lark an' adventure. I don't have a choice.*

Ye shouldn't say that. We all have to choose. Choosing is all we have.

And he twisted a wild ribbon of my hair around his finger and rested his forehead against mine.

I know.

He left in the morning, my wee cooper boy. He reported for duty and left for training at Blackboy Hill. A month later, he left again, on a troopship from the wharf at Fremantle.

I waved goodbye, one woman in a weeping crowd of hundreds, and I tried to feel proud of Magnus Tulloch. I did not want him to go, I didn't think it was the right thing, that there was any right thing about war. But aye, I tried to be proud. Not because he had no choice but because he did.

I was watching the news on TV not so long ago. Pictures of our young people being shipped off to Vietnam. All these years later and still we were losing them to war. Perhaps it was even worse, because of that lottery business. Their number was called. They went.

Your mother started crying once when we were watching together, and I knew what she was thinking—any mother would know. That if you had been a boy, lambsie, it could have been you going. Just like in the second war when lads I knew signed up, I would think: That could have been Steven.

There, I've written his name. My Steven. It would upset your mother if she read it. But something is scratching away at my memory, lambsie—maybe it's being old, maybe this disease—but I am afraid that if I don't write it down it will become one of the things that just disappears. And it's only now, now that I'm old, that I understand: if we don't speak the names of our dead, it's as though they never were.

Sometimes I wonder about my own brothers. Did they go to war? Did they join the navy with other northern fishermen? Die in enemy oceans or survive to have sons, daughters, of their own? Did they return changed, awake to the world beyond the village, or would it have always been the old ways for them, the fears we grew up with?

I don't want to remember them at all, but when I canna push those thoughts away I also wonder this: Did they ever think of Kitta? Did they ever speak our sister's name?

Clementina and I managed it all between us: the children, the rent, the cooking and shopping, the firewood and the dunny cans. The grief.

I tried to keep to myself the fear of what Magnus Tulloch might be doing at every moment of the day, a gallop in my blood that I kept checked, unspoken. But Clementina shared that too, with stray touches on my arm, my shoulder, to remind me she knew.

I longed for letters, and at first some came. The censor's stamp—APPROVED—a reminder of how things were. Once he left the south of England, Magnus Tulloch could not say where he was, what he was doing, so he told me about cocoa and bully beef and blankets crawling with lice, and sometimes the noise of *Old Fritz* in the night. He said he slept with my picture in his hand, and always he wrote, *It will soon be over, my Meggie.*

I wrote back each time, and in between, too, and I sent him socks and gum leaves and, once, a long curl of red hair.

While I worked at the factory, Clementina took in washing and starching and ironing for Miss Brown's private hospital, and the Sea View and Davilak hotels. She did her picking up and delivering on Magnus's bicycle after I got home. That bicycle! Clementina had never ridden before, but she plumped herself onto the leather seat one evening and wobbled her way up and down Martha Street until she'd beaten *the two-wheeler beastie*. Even after many months, the sight of Clementina Ratter perched on that bicycle, her chin balancing on a stack of linens to keep them in line and herself steady, was enough to give us all the giggles—Hal and Jessie and me.

We made an effort to laugh, for the children. We looked for any excuse when they were around. But once they were tucked into their beds ... ah, then our conversation fell to ash as we knitted socks for soldiers by candlelight. Sometimes Clementina would say, *Read us a pome, quinie,* or I'd read from the newspaper. Always the news of the war first, and we'd let it sink into the walls without stirring it with words. *The war just is,* Clementina always said. *Talkin' about it doesn't change the peeriest thing.*

Conscription was the Big Topic. At the factory, in the streets, in shops. But I was careful at home not to read aloud what the newspapers had to say about that, for I knew it would make Clementina teary and angry both. The arguments for, the arguments against—they raddled everything in me. I wanted every boy, every man, to be safe at home, away from the killing. But was this a betrayal of Magnus, my Magnus, who was risking his life for the world he believed in? And of all Stivvy had sacrificed? And then my thoughts would curl back on themselves, and I couldn't set them straight. How could anyone find the right thing, the noble thing, in something so terrible as war?

~

As we waited for peace and the war dragged on endlessly, I learned some things about myself. It's what happens when you canna control what is bearing down on you: you have to decide how to stand your ground, who you will be when it's done.

I learned how to live in never-ending anxiousness. All of us day after day with our hearts no longer beating a steady rhythm. Tuned in to static, news of death and damage. *The West Australian* would publish The Lists, state by state. Wounded. Killed. We took it all in, often without discussion, each of us reading the names in silence. There was no need to acknowledge what we all were feeling, it would only have made it worse.

I kept writing to Magnus, but few letters came back from him. *I don't know,* I muttered one day, coming in from the empty letterbox. *What does it mean?*

Clementina swallowed me up in a hug, but her words were blunt. *No news is good, quinie. No news means alive.*

It was another thing I learned: that nothing could mean everything.

I learned what I could do when Mills & Ware broke up the old teams in Creaming and Packing and moved the more experienced of us into areas of the factory where only the men had worked before. The huge mixing vats. The cutting rooms, with their stamping machines that had to be hand-fed, sheet by sheet. The ovens, which we would load and unload—trays so heavy they bent our backs. Before long the fingers of some of the girls looked a bit like mine, the skin scarred white and toughened from handling biscuits straight from the oven, the tips red-raw and bleeding from the sharp gritty surfaces of army biscuits. We used to say: *Poor boys, our poor soldiers, who have to eat the things!*

I drew a breath of courage I didn't feel and knocked on Mr Prentice's office door, and he sat back and heard me out as I told him my idea of having the girls tie their fingers with clooties, for protection, like the gutting girls used to do. I thought he would laugh, or be disgusted, offended. Here I was, comparing Mills & Ware with the dirty work of gutting. But he listened, Mr Prentice did, and I'll never forget what he said: that it was a fine day that day he'd *heeded his waters* and taken me on, *a very fine day indeed, Mrs Tulloch, married or not.*

Later he called me into the office and said Management had talked it over and the factory couldn't supply finger bandages because of the shortage of cloth. *But if you can bring your own, Mrs Tulloch, you and the other girls, then we have no objection. None at all.*

And that's what saved the Oven Room girls' fingers for the remainder of the war. I brought in strips cut from flour bags and showed them what to do, and although some were inclined to wrinkle their noses at first, soon they could see that it just made plain sense to do it. What a colourful sight in the Oven Room: the girls' fingers strapped in clooties made from whatever they could spare from the ragbag at home.

Not long after, Mr Prentice made me a forewoman, and then I learned another thing about myself: that I could guide and lead and keep one eye on the running of my team while joining in the chatter and singing that kept us all from going crazy. Aye, and that when I spoke, the girls would listen, and didn't resent me for it, either, because I was one of them, with as much to lose, now Magnus was at war.

But another thing I learned during those years was that somewhere along the journey from the Northern Hemisphere to this bluesky place, I had begun to feel the pull of the earth beneath me. Imagine: this from a water quinie from Roanhaven, a fisher girl!

Mrs Laskon had given us a part of the backyard for keeping chickens and growing what we could. *You need to keep those kiddies strong*, she said. *Everything in the shops is gone to blazes, and the Lord helps those who help themselves.*

How Clementina loved the scrawny yellow-white chickens we bought for next to nothing from Enzia's brother—pecky, skittish things, I thought. *Look at them*, she'd say, smiling as they squabbled and strutted about in the sand. *They lay eggs, they eat our leavings, they give us muck for the garden. Perfect creatures, chickens—what more could ye ask from them?*

I suspected there was more to it—a kindly feeling, a gentleness, among the hard memories of her time at Merredin. But she didn't tell me and I didn't press. Clementina had drawn a line under her years on the farm: finished, done, gone.

And while Clementina and the children fussed about with chickens, I turned to vegetables. The seeds were a gift from Mr Brescianini on the other side of the fence. What miracles! I held them on my palm—some like glossy beads, some as etched as limpet shells. I marvelled that from such dry, lifeless trinkets could come something as precious as food. Beans and peas grew up against the fence. The carrots and marrows I sowed into furrows, like those on Mrs Laskon's side of the yard. And from the first time I put my scarred, misshapen hands into the earth, to turn and prepare, to plant and water, I felt another of those shifts in the world. But this time it came from me. There she was, Fish Meggie, the Gutting Girl from the Top of the World, daughter of sea people, granddaughter of a fisherman with a caul in his pocket—insubstantial, like water, like air. But she was slipping away, aye, and in her place was someone stronger. Someone who, like Clementina, might be able to say *finished, done, gone.* And it seemed to me that it was something to do with the grains of sand between my imperfect fingers, fragments of all that is left when time wears away the living and the dead. I tried to tell Clementina how I felt, but she snorted, hands on hips. *I've had my fill of plantin', quinie, an' it's not my plan to be doin' it again. Ye can have the garden all to yourself!*

And so that's what I did. I turned the soil and planted seeds and began to feel a different kind of strong, the kind that belonged to me and not just to what I'd come from. And I started thinking: When Magnus Tulloch comes back, will he even recognise me?

Oh, lambsie, I don't know. I keep telling myself: Write the important things, there's not time to tell it all. And I'm feeling it more and more, that I am running out of time, running low on whatever it is that is keeping me going. But they are bound together, the everything and the nothing, and disentangling them often seems beyond what I can do.

Today your Unty Jessie came for a cup of tea and brought me some pink roses from her garden. As I sit here now, looking at them, the memory that comes into my head is not an important thing, no, but it is clear and bright before my eyes, and I want to catch it before it floats away, write it just as I see it there.

Ach, lambsie, you're probably getting used to me writing more, or less, than I promised.

A wedding is a big thing, an Occasion, and everyone is determined to grab it by the scruff and wring it for all the joy it can give. There are not many these days, with most of the men gone. Enzia's Joe has been sent home, disfigured but not dishonoured, with a small pension and a patch where once his left eye was. I remember him from before: a loud one, jovial, a boy still when he enlisted. Enzia says he is all the same Joe.

I've seen Joe since he's come home. Sometimes he cycles to South Beach to eat polony sandwiches with Enzia at dinnertime. He flirts, he laughs. He makes light of his injury. *Not need two eyes to catch fish*, he croaks in a voice like an old man's. *Not need two eyes to get married*, Enzia flings back at him. And the girls look on, smiling, cheered by the prospect of happy-ever-after in the face of so much life-cut-short. Vi's Clarrie, Micky and Bruce from Mixing, Lois's brothers Sam and Ted, Mr Prentice's son—all gone. So he's proof, Joe is, that men come back, they can be wounded and still come back. And still laugh. And still remember before. But I watch Joe, and I am frightened for Magnus Tulloch. For I know a few things about the stubborn kind of forgetting it takes to still laugh and still remember, and I fancy what I'm seeing is a fine performance of *all the same Joe.*

Enzia steps out of the bedroom to a chorus of *oohs*.

You're a sight for sore eyes, sweetheart! Ollie says, twirling her around.

Franca and I puff out the fold of white fabric that is a few yards short of a proper train, and Enzia's mother, Josepha, sighs proudly.

Enzia will be a beautiful bride on Saturday, in spite of the war. Others make do with calico prettied up with bits of muslin and whatever spangly beads can be finagled from heirloom pieces and friends' button boxes. But Josepha has been planning her only daughter's wedding since Enzia was a tiny girl, and long ago in Molfetta she'd put aside a length of Italian lace, laying it with care between cotton sheets and tablecloths in a tea-chest bound for Australia. And here it is, worked into the chaste bodice of this otherwise plain dress. I think Josepha is feeling a wee bit smug as she kneels on the floor with a tape measure round her neck and pins between her lips.

Enzia swishes around in the dining room of her parents' weatherboard house while Josepha tries to pin the hem.

Did you have a lovely wedding dress, Meggie? Lois asks, handing me a puffy pouch of fabric.

I turn away for a moment and canna speak. What rushes into my memory is not my wedding in the Great Yarmouth church, no. It's Kitta. My sister on a noisy Saturday night in Lerwick, fine Shetland lace shawling her braided hair. I push my fingernails deep into the palm of my hand before turning back to Lois.

Well ... no. I wore my travellin' apron an' scrubbed my hands an' Clementina pinned some holly in my hair because it was winter, nearly Christmas, an' not a flower to be seen.

Ollie and Lois speak at once. *Ooh, holly! Ooh, I never!*

How glamorous things seem from afar when you've never felt the everyday of them.

A bit prickly, holly, for putting in your hair. But at the time, I just let Clementina pretty me up as best she could. All I cared to think of was Kitta, and getting her back.

I tie the new sash around the waist of an old dress, and Lois, Ollie, Franca and I practise making our bows look the same, the ribbons even, so that we will be a set come Saturday, like proper bridesmaids. There's not enough fabric to be had for new matching dresses, but we do what we can with what we've got, and what we've got is some old blue sailcloth from the boatbuilder's shed where Enzia's brother works. Four blue bows to brighten up four tired cotton dresses.

Josepha wipes her teary face as she lines us up. *Beeyewdeefour*, she says. *An' on Satterdai the rosses*. And she gestures with her palms, waving spirals around our hair.

My excitement dims a little. Of course. I should have known I'd be wearing roses from Josepha's magnificent front garden. Pink roses in my red hair.

Beeyewdeefour.

~

Mills & Ware's gift to Enzia was her wedding cake. Not the traditional fruitcake—no sultanas, raisins, currants for that—but tiers of plain sponge, like we used to make before the war, with white sugar-water icing studded with little flowers handmade by Franca. We made it ourselves, the girls, we stayed back on our own time, listening to the night noises of the factory, the tapping, snipping sounds from the Tin Room upstairs, the low hum from the Jam Factory on the first floor. We promised Josepha something grand, a tall, handsome cake among a wedding feast of sandwiches.

It was beautiful when the four of us walked it down the Mandurah road to Josepha's early on Saturday morning on a white tray. But the day was a scorcher, it got up to 108 by afternoon, and by the time the wedding party got back to Josepha's after the church, the cake was lurching in a puddle of white icing and the sugar flowers had slid onto the tablecloth. Nobody minded, though, not Enzia, not Josepha, and for a few hours we pretended that the faraway war was actually far away. It was a time to laugh and dance, to toast to hope and happiness with warm lemonade, to eat sponge with melted icing and think it the finest wedding cake.

War has a habit of making you grateful.

I've been thinking about all those boys who have come back from Vietnam, who didn't ask to go in the first place. There were parades at first, a few of them—do you remember, lambsie? And then the parades became a place for people to throw red paint and shout. And then there was nothing. What must they think, those boys?

Aye, I know, lambsie, you have done your share of shouting, and you've the right, no mind what Kathryn says. Your mother has always been cautious. But these protests of yours—I just canna think you were shouting at the right people.

Doesn't mean I hold any ill-feeling to that young man, your friend's brother, who burned his notice in a kerosene tin. There's some who know, just know, they canna do it, and there's some who say they'll not let the government offer them up for something they don't believe in. And the ones who go—isn't because they want to kill, or want to die, only that they will do it, because they do believe. Seems to me they're all right, lambsie, if you can turn your head to look at the world their way.

I used to puzzle about those patriots in the first war—men and women both—who called the men at home cowards. I found a poem in *The West Australian* before Magnus Tulloch went. I cut it out and hid it away in my knitting. I would read it sometimes and wonder what manner of man, what father, what grandfather, what brother, could write such words. The poet whipped up a frenzy about all the killing to be done in the trenches and begged the boys at home to go and do their bit. And then, *then*, he told them they'd never get a girl if they remained behind.

Come and be killed, or stay and be shunned. Wasn't much of a choice, eh, lambsie.

They used to talk a lot about heroes and courage back then. Thing is, even now, when I think of the wars I have lived through, I canna put my finger on what these things mean. Is it more courageous to follow blindly or to make a stand for what you believe? To kill for the right reasons—is that what heroes do? What of the soldier who is reckless, selfish, but still saves a life? And if you do the right thing, and fail, if you cause damage doing it—do ill results cancel out good intentions, a good heart?

Your grandfather went to war with a good heart, lambsie. When he came home, his heart was broken.

Delays were commonplace back then. I didn't get the telegram telling me Magnus Tulloch had been wounded at Amiens until after the armistice in November 1918. He was in a French military hospital. Superficial injuries: that's what they said.

He would be all right!

And the war was over!

Clementina and I hugged each other, crying. Such joy, such unutterable sadness. When finally we could speak we told each other that everything—*everything*—would change now, although even then we knew it could never be as it was before. And somehow we buried the words *wounded* and *injuries* among the exhilaration of *He will be all right!* and *The war is over!*

Magnus Tulloch was shipped home in March—that miracle, that blessing. I can still see him, lambsie, walking to me down Martha Street, pulling the hat from his head. For a brief moment the sky was in his eyes, the sun in his hair, and he was there, nothing but the boy, and I thought: Through it all, you have found your way home. His lips moved but there was so much racket from a flock of twenty-eights flying overhead that I couldn't hear. What? I asked the boy. What did you say?

It was later that I understood: he had come back to say goodbye.

~

Inside our little cottage, Magnus Tulloch was besieged by a happy, weeping Clementina and a battery of questions from Hal and Jessie, who were eight years old and curious and avid for tales of adventure.

Leave your Uncle Magnus to catch his breath, Clementina scolded.

But I could see in her a need as keen as theirs to shake words from him, find again the man she had lost through the return of this one.

Magnus Tulloch smiled in a nervy kind of way, and begged leave to be gone a wee while.

Wait, I called, following him out, grabbing my hat from the hook by the door, *wait an' I'll come with ye, we can walk to the sea.*

I put my arm through his, but he disentangled himself. *Will not be gone for long*, he muttered. A clumsy kiss on the cheek.

The kitchen door closed behind me. Clementina's footsteps. She put her arm around my waist, and in silence we watched Magnus Tulloch wobbling down the road on the bicycle.

~

Of the thousand things I had missed in those years apart, the one that pulled most at my heart was that space in every day when Magnus Tulloch would unpin my hair, unravel its twists and curls, and we would talk. The rhythm of our lives seemed to live in those long, steady brushstrokes, reassuring and calm, commonplace, everyday. A promise made and kept. An always promise.

I thought of this when I heard the bicycle fall against the front wall that first night. It was late. Clementina had gone to bed already, the children long before her. I put the kettle on the stove. But when he let himself in, Magnus Tulloch's eyes were hazy, his step unsure. He slurred *sorry, my Meggie* and *goodnight* and clasped me in a hug that was over before I could lean into it.

Superficial. We did not agree, the army and I, on what it meant.

I heard the music of Emily Dickinson in my head.

There is a word
Which bears a sword
Can pierce an armed man.
It hurls its barbed syllables—
At once is mute again.
Now I knew. I knew the word.

~

Castlemaine took Magnus Tulloch back, and I was always grateful to them for that. But it did not work out as they had hoped. Less than a month, it was, before the coopering shop was too much for him—the noise, the light, the impact of hammer on hoops, jarring nerves that were never still any more. Mrs Laskon, Mr Prentice, the girls at the factory—people were sympathetic, they seemed to want to pat my arm and talk in hushed voices, but I didn't care about people, only that Magnus Tulloch was alive and had come back to me.

All that skill an' training, it canna be for nothing? Clementina whispered when Castlemaine put him in the store-room, a packer of bottles, a lifter of the kegs he'd once crafted with special tools brought out from home.

Nothing is for nothing! Fierce. Wishful.

He never slept much at night. I would hear him moving round the house late; sometimes the scrape of bicycle tyres on the limestone outside our window. He told me once that the army doctor's orders were plain: he must push everything he'd seen, everything he'd done, from his mind.

Just don't ask me, Meggie. They said it's best if ye just never ask and things don't ever get said.

It made sense to him. He had no wish to bring unsayable things from the dark to live with us in the weatherboard cottage in Martha Street. But they did, anyway. Of course they did. I had learned for myself that things like that had to live somewhere.

They took up room, so much space, all the space between us in our bed, space that had never been there in the days when he would sleep curled around my body like a second skin. Now there was no peace for him in snatches of sleep, no comfort in the touch of my hands on his back. Was he awake or asleep when he pulled away from me? Was it me or the world he did not want?

But there were other times when the dark things in him surfaced and I did not recognise the glass in his eyes, the rage in his body as it laboured over me. Was he awake or asleep then? I didn't know that, either.

I canna write more of these things to you, lambsie. I can write of love, but not that.

But I'll tell you this: nothing is for nothing.

~

For five months I denied it: the sickness, the gentle rounding of my body, the fluttering of wings that were not mine. I was never one to know when the bleeding would or wouldn't come, so I held to the notion it was late, was all, just late, and would be upon me still. Finally Clementina, who knew what she was looking at, had had enough. She took my face in her hands and would not let me look away. *Ye're pregnant, quinie,* she said, *an' the time for sayin' otherwise is gone!*

Dr Hamilton confirmed it. *Twenty-nine and married fourteen years! A miracle baby, this little one, Mrs Tulloch, because no prevention method is that reliable, believe you me. Just ask the mothers of the hundreds of little accidents walking around!*

I don't know. It's true there were many girls on the farlins whose *measures* ran aground, in spite of their canny efforts to plan which years they would be *in a certain way* and when they would leave the season. But I think back now on what the mission ladies used to say about the work and what it did to us, the toll on our bodies. Maybe the miracle was that any of us fell pregnant at all.

I didn't tell Mills & Ware for a long time. The girls had already guessed, but Management was surprised as I was still slight, little changed beneath the enormous apron. I looked at myself in the mirror and saw Kitta there—her body had barely shown, either.

I walked from the factory on my last day with a bunch of agapanthus and a large tin of Family Assorted and my two aprons under my arm. The end, I told myself. My factory life done.

~

I was afraid the whole time, all of those months, more afraid than I had been of anything. I could not explain it to Clementina. There were no words I could find to say what it was, all that it was, this huge nameless fear, and I never wanted to go back there to the place it came from.

But when Steven was born, in the first week of a new year, 1920, I knew I'd to make a choice between fear and love. And I chose love. I chose him.

Your uncle, lambsie. You never knew you had an uncle, did you.

~

We brought our baby home on the tram from the hospital and walked from the Mandurah road to Martha Street. Then Magnus took off on his bicycle for the late shift at Castlemaine.

Jessie and Hal made such a fuss of the baby, offered him little wooden toys of their own. But Clementina had the two of them tucked into bed by nightfall.

We sat in the hot kitchen, she and I, Clementina mashing vegetables for soup.

It's a sign, quinie, she told me. *A new life for a new decade!*

I don't want any talk of signs. Ye sound like the old ones at home an' there's no place for the dark things here.

But somethin' good has come, for a change. I've wanted to be Unty Clementina for more than a wee while.

I examined Steven's tiny nails, the perfect fingers.

So. Are ye goin' to call him … She stopped.

I didn't catch her meaning.

Steven. Are ye goin' to call him Stivvy?

No!

I'd not meant to sound harsh, and Clementina looked down while I rushed to explain, gentling my words.

He is named to honour Stivvy, aye, but he has a name of his own. I don't think it's right to saddle a new wee life with another's before it's even begun. D'ye not think so?

Mmmm. And then Clementina grinned. *So it's Fremantle Steven?*

I flicked a tea towel in her direction.

Seagull Steven? Milk Arrowroot Steven?

Steven Tulloch is good enough, Unty Clementina.

I thought we might be calling him Gingernut Steven, but will ye look at that. She reached over to tousle the baby's silken head. *Not a ginger hair on him!*

I inhaled the sweet smell of baby curls, dark like Magnus's, like Ma's and Kitta's.

Clementina picked up the masher again, though surely the neeps and tatties could scarcely need more. *So, quinie. D'ye want us to move now, ye an' Magnus? Give ye some space with your wee bairn without a pair of nine-year-olds an' an old herrin' girl?*

No! I clutched at her arm. What would I do without Clementina?

Well, good, that's all right, then, that's just grand, she said, her cheeks pink like apples. *We'll work it out, quinie. It will all be grand.*

~

Magnus Tulloch would shake silent noises from his head as he rocked the cradle that Mr Brescianini had made for us out of sheoak from his vineyard at Wanneroo. He was wary of holding Steven, Magnus was, in awe of his small body, afraid it would break.

But there isn't any doubt he loved him.

Did he love me still? I didn't know that. The boy would have loved me forever, no matter what, but the boy had gone.

~

When Steven was a few months old, a letter arrived, a few sheets of paper that made all three of us silent.

I had written to Gracie after the war, to put her mind at rest that her brother was safe. We'd had no reply, but that was often the way then. Things went astray, mail went missing. When I wrote again to tell her of the child, her nephew, that she had always believed would come, a letter came back to us soon after. Full of happy wishes, Gracie was, though wistful that she would never meet our little boy. And she wrote of how things were on the island.

The herring trade had shrunk almost to nought during the war. We'd known of this from Paulie Garrioch, who Magnus saw sometimes on his way home from the brewery. The government had taken most of the drifters, Gracie said, just a tiny fleet left at home, and Shetland boys had been as quick to sign up as those everywhere else. Karl came home safe, *and the Lord be praised for that*, but so many others …

Magnus Tulloch put his head in his hands. The names Gracie listed on the page were the names of boys he had grown up with, boys who had become fishers or sailors, or coopers like him.

Some boats are back to sea, but most are idle now, Gracie wrote. *And what did they expect? is what I said to Karl. Look at who it was who bought our fine Shetland herring! Who was our biggest customer all them years? Germany, of course, and Germany has its shameful hands full now, too full to be buying fancy things like pickled herring.*

I could imagine Gracie waving her finger in Karl's face, just a little shy of smug. She'd always been suspicious of the herring trade, the way it lured people away from villages.

Aye, she wrote, *it's plain bread that Germany will be wanting now, and all they deserve too.*

I pushed the pages aside. I looked up to meet Clementina's pale face. We both knew what Gracie's news meant. Fewer boats would mean no farlins, no teams. The girls would remain in the villages where they had come from, and would not be leaving for the season every year. Their lives, changed forever, now forever the same.

Dearest lambsie, weeks have gone by since I wrote about Steven. Kathryn is pleased, I think, that she's not seen me scribbling in my book. If only she knew it's not the same one, that I have two others in the kist put away for you already! Ach, she's very good to me, your mother, and so busy with her work, all those beautiful figures she does. I don't like to upset her—not too much, anyway, not if I can help it. But some things—well, she can be unreasonable. Whyever it is that she gets so fretful when I go to town on the bus, I canna imagine. Clementina says your Unty Jessie is the same. Kathryn keeps wanting me to promise I'll not go off on my own, but I forget. And I don't see what there is to be fretting about, no.

She has come up with a new way for me to remember things: a board stuck on the fridge door. I'm to write things on it with a marker pen, and she writes things for me, too. Lists. I've always liked lists. Ticking things off, knowing you've done what it was once in your mind to do.

I've written a list on the inside cover of this book: the things I still must tell you, lambsie. If I keep looking at the list, maybe I'll not write so many other things, things that are not important.

Influenza, 1921

So this is the first thing on my list, lambsie.

In 1921, Anzac Day was not a national day of mourning, not in the way we know it these days. The newspapers retold the story of heroism, and there were parades and services. It was a day for grieving, aye, but a kind of mourning closer to the heart. Wounds still fresh.

A Monday, it was—what silly details you remember. Magnus was on the day shift.

Go if ye want, an' whenever ye want. I'll not be going with ye.

I put my hand on his shoulder but he shrugged it off.

What's the point, Meggie? Whatever's the point of any of it? Tell me that.

Clementina waved a pot of porridge as he shouldered his way through the kitchen but he grabbed the bicycle and left for Castlemaine, long before he needed to.

It's all right, quinie, Clementina said, as if the one who needed comforting on this day was me. *We all have our own way.*

Around midday, we took the children up to the stone we'd laid in the dunes for Stivvy and looked out across the sea. *Home is the sailor* ... But Stivvy—he was not home, was he. Magnus was right: whatever *was* the point? But then I looked across at Clementina, looked for bitterness in her face, and it wasn't there any more; it had not been there for a long time now. While Hal and Jessie ran barefoot, chasing wavelets back to the ocean, she brushed her fingers across the words we'd scratched and what I saw was a kind of soothing I didn't understand. But I was glad for it, aye, so glad.

That was the point, the only point, and I wished Magnus could have seen it too.

~

Magnus Tulloch did not get home until the Beaconsfield Hotel shut its doors and sent them on their way, all those men with nightmares in their eyes and stories they'd been told to bury, for their own good. And then he and Paulie Garrioch sat outside on the verandah, drinking from bottles in brown paper bags.

Clementina kissed me on the cheek wearily and said goodnight. *Just let it be, quinie. It will all turn out.*

Shameful, but I listened by the kitchen door. And all I heard, for my trouble? An occasional rustle of paper, the sound of boots shifting on the verandah boards. Perhaps they had run out of words. Perhaps they had told each other what had to be said and there was nothing left now.

I made tea. And waited.

When Paulie left, Magnus came inside, stumbling a little. He said nothing and went to bed.

It will all turn out, I told Steven when he began to cry.

~

By the time winter came round, Magnus Tulloch was spending more time at the hotel than at home, and every night his dinner sat drying on a saucepan on top of the Metters. Sometimes he ate it, most times it was there on the plate in the morning. Congealed gravy, hardened lumps of dripping. What it was he did eat, I didn't know.

We were only just managing, only just getting by. A storeman's earnings were less than a cooper's, and to get a war pension a man had to be *incapacitated*. That meant damaged in some visible, obvious way. What's more, a man had to *ask*, and that was something Magnus would never do. I wonder—did any of them, the men from the far north? They were not ones to show their pain easily. Clementina had her widow's pension, small though it was, and between us we managed the washing for the hotels, but the sum of it all was no great amount. Not enough for us and the Beaconsfield Hotel too.

Clementina took Hal, Jessie and Steven to South Beach on the day I decided we must talk, Magnus and I. A Saturday, it was, and it had to be done before he cycled off to the Oddfellows, his hotel of choice on weekends. There'd be no point once he'd started drinking. I had my words prepared, in order in my mind, and they seemed reasonable when I said them to myself, but then I had to catch my breath because *nothing* was reasonable about this, nothing made sense. It was beyond imagining that I would ever have need to say such words to Magnus Tulloch.

I sat with him at the kitchen table, hating—*hating*—that he was fidgeting and anxious to be gone, and that I could not let him, no. I had to be the one to speak, the voice he didn't want to hear.

Look at him there.

Look at you.

When did you get so thin? What are you hearing when you jerk your head like that? You would talk to me once. I knew about the ringing in your ears that never went away. Is that what you're hearing now, trying to shake free? Or is it noise I canna imagine, that you never talk about, never have told me? When did you get so pale? Where are we, Magnus Tulloch, where am I in your face now, your face I have loved so long, your face that once held all we were, safe, to shine back at me, assure me that we were the thing that would always be? When did you get so lost? Now it is hollowed out, your young face old, empty like the shape left in bedsheets that speaks of someone who once was there. I was there, in your face, once …

I said what I had prepared myself to say.

He gave me scant hearing. Grunted to let me know he had heard, so I would not say it again. A conversation it was not.

And I didn't want to but had to keep going. Mrs Laskon's rent … the children … food … it couldn't be Clementina's burden alone, now, could it?

Mute, he emptied a trouser pocket onto the kitchen table, a handful of coins, but his wallet remained in the other. It gutted me—*in, twist, flick*—that look as he left. It told me plain, plain as flour, that if it came right down to it, he would be choosing oblivion over all of us.

One night a few weeks after that, Paulie Garrioch saw him home, leaving the bike chained to the iron railings outside the Beaconsfield. Magnus Tulloch wheezed all the way, Paulie said, *coughin' like his lungs'd bash clean through his ribs*. He walked him from the bus on the Mandurah road with a steadying arm.

Needs a doctor, he do, Paulie panted as they struggled through the door and Magnus collapsed on a kitchen chair.

Those words alone would have been enough. Men from the north never did think to summon the doctor without grievous cause. But when I looked at him, my Magnus, looked at him properly—the stewy damp of his florid face, the sunken chest heaving—fear wormed through me. This was more than a fever. This I had seen before.

~

In Fremantle Hospital they confirmed it was flu. Had it been the year before, during the epidemic, we would all have been quarantined, the whole household, but it turned out that none of us came down with it. Perhaps that spoke of how little time Magnus had been spending at home.

As I stood outside his room, my face a mask of gauze and cotton mittens on my hands, they told me he was malnourished and his liver wasn't functioning as it should any more.

How much does he drink? Is he anxious? Does he sleep well at night? Headaches?

I don't know. Aye. No. Aye.

The doctors seemed surprised that Magnus Tulloch survived at all, but gradually he got stronger, his breathing less a labour. He even put on a little weight, but it wasn't enough, no.

Have to get out of here, Meggie, he would say when I visited.

Hush, I assured him, *they'll not be keepin' ye longer than they need to,* but it wasn't the whole story. There was talk of sending him to a hospital for veterans, to have him *assessed.* I could only imagine what Magnus Tulloch would be saying to that.

But in the end, nothing came of it. He was discharged with a paper bag of bottles—aspirin for pain, bromide to make him sleep. And strict orders about what he'd to eat to build up his strength—milk and cheese, eggs and meat. I looked across at him, this man of water, so pale, so thin. Eggs—aye, we could manage that, thanks to Clementina's chickens. Eggs and vegetables from the garden were the centre of all our meals. But as for the rest? Well. If Castlemaine didn't take him back, there'd not be food like that on our table, but it never seemed to cross the doctors' minds, what food cost.

Clementina and I talked about it later. She flicked her fingers at the doctors' orders. *Oatmeal, neeps an' fish cheap from the Greeks—that's what will stick to his bones. Just like at home. An' don't ye be lookin' at me like that, Meggie Tulloch. There's some things from home is worth rememberin'.*

No alcohol was the other instruction they gave him. I caught myself feeling happy, for once, about our poverty: the poorer we were, the less Magnus could drink. And wasn't that a thought to make me ashamed.

~

Steven was not usually a nervous child but he was wary of Magnus when he first came home from the hospital—aware, in that strange, knowing way of very young children, that his father's smile was painted on, his jolly words as empty as the skin of a seaside balloon.

Dada's home! I winced at the strain in my own voice as I held Steven up for a kiss.

Clementina pushed Hal and Jessie forward, and they were cautious too, though less agitated than Steven. So it was up to us, Clementina and me, to ease the way back in for Magnus, welcome him to the home he was returning to for a second time.

The first thing Magnus Tulloch did next day was cycle to Castlemaine to see about getting his job back, or any other job. I put aside my worry about him, weak and wavering all over the road, and tried to take it as a lightsome sign. That it meant his priorities were clearer to him now. *D'ye think so?* I asked Clementina.

She patted my arm, looked at me hard, waiting for me to catch up.

I didn't, not straight away.

He came home with good news: a job in the store-room again. And wasn't that cause to be happy? Aye. But when the first pay packet came home, a mockery of what it was supposed to be, I knew the truth about Magnus Tulloch's priorities.

He was still as thin as kindling, in spite of Clementina's best efforts. His face stippled like Mintlaw mushrooms. Often he refused the aspirin. *What's the point?* he'd say. What was the point when never would it stop, like a mallet on barrel hoops, over and over, and he would shake his head, as before, as though trying to dislodge something, trick the rhythm of the clanging into another beat, to change it, or quieten it for a while. But other times, he would swallow more pills from his palm than could possibly be safe, and then he would shrug and say it again: *What's the point?*

The bromide, supposed to help him sleep, sat among the underclothes in its squat brown bottle. *Poison*, he declared it. Bromide had been used on the troops in Egypt, France, Flanders—to calm them down, was the rumour, to curb *behaviour unbecoming His Majesty's men*. Funny, really—not really at all—because the only time Magnus Tulloch ever made love to me was in his sleep, or a haze I took for sleep. A body is all I was, a faceless woman in a dream, but I was afraid to wake him, afraid of what it would do. And truth to say, I was grateful for whatever small intimacy might bring the boy back to me, if only for the space between dream and awake.

Humiliating, aye, to talk of gratitude. I know already I will read these words again and scratch them away in shame, lambsie. But in hindsight truly I *must* be grateful. Because from those sorrowful, bewildering times, when I knew that never would he be coming back, came a gift.

Your mother.

Ye're not still queasy about blood, are you, lambsie? Such a worrisome little thing you were, dizzy every time you skinned your knees. Fainting at school when that boy in class broke his nose—do you remember? I had to pick you up at dinnertime and bring you home with me. I never knew what to say to make it better, because I knew how upsetting ...

Jam, oh aye, that was the thing. You could always be comforted with a spoonful of jeely.

Maybe you still are that way with blood, maybe it's a thing you don't grow out of.

Me, I seemed to grow into it. All those years with blood up to my elbows, the smell of it in my mouth, the taste of it in my ears. Knowing it was a thing left over from life when life had gone. Maybe it was always going to catch up with me, that knowing. Because, in time, it became fear.

Kathryn, 1922

It's a funny thing, lambsie. Sometimes we fear something so much that we canna bear it, feel we might die from the effort of holding it down with a fist of iron. And then, like a miracle, the thing feared doesn't come to pass. And don't we think ourselves foolish then, to have been twisted inside, knotted like wool, to have felt our fingernails breaking skin, so hard have we held the fear at bay. And so we loosen our grip a little, let the knots unravel just enough.

My first time being pregnant, with Steven, was like that. Every minute afraid, consumed by it—and then nothing ill happened, all was well.

But. The second time.

Dr Hamilton, kind in his way, wasn't one for false hopes. *Go home, rest, but be ready. You'll not keep this one, my dear. And eat plenty of liver to make up for the blood you're losing.*

His words crashed on me, green like waves, dragging me under. *When?* I managed. He could not tell me.

Now, you're upsetting yourself with morbid fancies, Mrs Tulloch. Keep your mind on the child you have. There's those less fortunate than you.

That day, the day after next, I see it now through a wash of red:

There I am, shivering under the feather quilt, folded towels between my legs, dreaming of sea water, dreaming of blood. Clementina easing my knees apart to carry away the wet and replace it with new. Me clamping down on that, to seal and keep safe. Magnus pulling back curtains, letting in the light, and my arms fending it off, away, because only in the dark can you blot out the shape of a barely human thing tossing in the shallows, seabed grazing skinless face. Afraid of the pressure inside growing, wanting it out, *get this thing out.* Needing to hold on, hold it in, but knowing the pressure is too much and I canna stay here forever. The waves push forward, pull back, and as I rise from the bed, wet, sticky, something slips from me with a pop, like a slippery plum.

Clementina!

And she holds me up as it slides down my thigh, a great rush of red following.

Well, quinie, that's that. Gentle, final.

But when she'd settled me back on the pillows and peeled back the folds of towel to examine the clotted matter, Clementina frowned and puffed a whistle of air.

What? Keeping my eyes on her face.

Canna say, quinie, canna say for sure. But … I don't know …

And she took it away.

Dr Hamilton came to the house and never did send a bill. People can be surprising, lambsie. Lots of things surprise me even now.

But nothing more than when Dr Hamilton pronounced me pregnant still. The clot I had passed was not a foetus, no. Exactly what it was, I don't think he could say.

And as the months went by, he kept shaking his head because I kept bleeding, on and off, but I kept growing, too. The *something* in me would not die, though I was no less fearful for its stubborn resolve to stay.

When Steven stretched his small hands across my belly and wanted to know what was in there, Clementina swallowed a barking laugh.

What to tell him? What could a two-year-old understand?

A baby, Jessie declared confidently. *There's a baby in there, in Unty Meggie's tummy.*

How did it get there?

Clementina and I waited to hear what twelve-year-old Miss Jessie had learned in the playground at South Fremantle Primary.

Fairies, acourse! Don't you know anything?

Back home, they'd say …

But I stopped Clementina before she could turn my mind to Roanhaven and any opinion it might have about this strange, fragile presence that continued to fill me with dread and fear—but with awe, aye, awe as well.

Steven's question stayed in my head. *How did it get there?* Is that what Magnus Tulloch wondered during the sober hours? Is that why the sober hours had become so few? Part of it must have been, and that part was bound by ropes I couldn't see to all the other parts he would never show me.

~

The bleeding never did stop completely, and when Kathryn was born in the winter, early but not so early as to be unsafe, it was a cutting birth, caesarean. I woke groggy and sick and desperate to know: Was the baby all right? Was there a baby at all, after all those months of blood? But against the odds, those towering odds, I had a daughter, a beautiful strong girl. Wondrous. That I was still in pain seemed a fair price for safe delivery, and I didn't want to complain. I ran my fingers along the stitching line on the curve below my belly, cupped it with both hands when I retched so much that I feared the stiff threads would break.

To be expected, my dear, you've had major surgery, the nurse told me when finally I asked. I thought she meant the birth, and she thought I knew the rest. And when the doctor came he assumed I had been told. So it wasn't until the next day that I found out they had taken more from me than my baby. That Kathryn would be the last.

It made it all harder when I went home. Weak, I was, unable to lift and carry, with a newborn to lift and carry for, and a two-year-old who clung to me like wet weed. Clementina was impatient—not with me but with Magnus. Incapable of dragging himself out of the fog to pick up Kathryn from her cradle and hand her to me, or walk to the corner for milk, or any little thing that Clementina asked of him.

Best he stay away anyways, she grumbled. *Best he takes himself to the public bars like he's goin' to do anyways an' keeps out from my sight. I've bairns enough to see to an' no time to coddle another one.*

All of this I watched, wrapped in a blanket, from the little secondhand couch Paulie Garrioch had 'found' and wheeled to our house in a barrow. *I am sorry*, I told her so many times that she got impatient with me, too. But sorry I was. Sorry to be a burden when she had already so much to do that was because of me. And sorry about Magnus. My sorrow was about him and for him and on his behalf and was too big to be contained by words. It flowed from me into all and everything and never would it end.

Oh, lambsie, I don't want your mother ever reading this. What would she think? That I look back on her arrival in the world and all I can see is blood and sorrow? No, Kathryn, no. Such joy you brought to us all, aye. I remember that, too, and the gentle times when Clementina and I would sit by the stove at night, knitting, talking, sometimes looking back, mostly towards what would come for our children.

The future is all there is, I told her once, *an' the Lord make it a safe world for them.*

Clementina chuckled.

What?

I was just thinkin', quinie, about the safe world we've brought them into. Back home, Hal an' Jessie would be lookin' after themselves by now. None of this playin' with balls an' dressin' up dollies. Ha! Did ye ever in your life see a dolly in your village?

I had a wee dog once, a dog of my own.

Ooo-hoo! A dog! Well, wasn't a dog nor a doll in Fitdee, just a world of things to do an' not a spare moment to think it were a hardship, an' if ye thought a spare moment might poke up an' say boo ye'd whip out your needles an' knit a sock for it!

Oh, aye, the same, the same!

And we laughed and made promises, especially for our girls, who would never—*never*—hold a gipper in their hands. And there'd be no sock-knitting—oh no! As far as we were concerned, you and Jessie could collect spare moments in a jar and string them together like shiny beads.

Not you, lambsie. Kathryn, I mean. Your mother.

And Magnus, aye, he loved her. He loved them both, her and Steven, in his way.

Oh Kathryn, so much you missed out on. The war stole from us both.

October 1974

Dearest lambsie, I've just had a visitor. It was you, my Laura-lamb! You turned up on your way to the university with a shepherd's pie from your mother and a message she will be by tonight. A bag of shopping, too. I canna mind asking her to go to the shop for me but she's bought things I have run out of, so I must have. Aye, I think I did, I remember now.

I wonder whether you will remember when you read this. Maybe not. You were in a great hurry to be away. You sat there with the cup of tea I fancy your mother told you to stay for. Your fingers drumming on the table. How beautiful you looked in that long purple dress with the little mirror things sewn on the hems of your sleeves. Bless you, lambsie, never were you good at pretending to be happy about a thing when you weren't.

I opened a packet of Shortbread Creams and arranged some on a saucer. *Not a patch on the ones we used to make at the factory ...*

You rolled your pretty eyes. Do I always say that?

It was after you left that I got my book out again—the first time for a couple of weeks. I have been too sick to write, lambsie. And tired. I don't know how much more I can give you.

I looked at my list again, the list at the front, and scratched a few things out. Not in that way of something done but to be—what's the word? Ruthless. Aye. Now it's just the things I have to write, while I still have the words.

But the next thing on the list ... well. I keep putting down the pen, putting it off.

Forgive me if I'm brief, if I leave out the details. You are a smart girl, lambsie, you can fill them in for yourself.

Magnus Tulloch, winter 1924

Only name and dates are on your grandfather's stone in Fremantle Cemetery.

Magnus Tulloch

b. 1889 d. 1924

Every time I looked at that stone, I would say the words I wished were there: *With the breath, smiles, tears of all my life.* But there was no money to have them carved then, and later … well, it didn't seem to matter. They were in my head, and that was enough.

There was a time I used to go to the cemetery every month to hang chains of yellow flowers over those letters and numbers. I never cared that they were weeds because he never did, no. He told me once they reminded him of the Knab. *D'ye remember, Meggie, when we would climb up there on Sundays?* Aye, to talk and eat our jeely pieces in the sky. It made me yearn to take a sharp pair of shears to memory, snip away the pain from it and leave behind just those days when Magnus Tulloch's love for me was everything and bigger than it all. He used to say that the most beautiful thing he had ever seen was a flight of purple silk into the sky that carried his heart with it. That's what I wanted to remember, too. But I thought of the Knab and there they were, those small arms flailing like wings, that flightless bird flung from the edge and let to fall because I couldn't catch the fabric of his shirt.

As time went on I'd not go to the cemetery so often.

I took you with me once when you were little. Do you remember that? You walked through the stones as solemn as an owl, looking all around you, your head cocked as though listening for something.

Why do the dead people need flowers? you asked me.

Oh, it's just another way of talkin', I think. We speak with flowers an' hope the dead will hear us.

You helped me pick the dandelions and string them together that day, and when we hung the chains across the stone you asked me what they said.

I canna think now what I told you, lambsie. Some pretty thing to lighten the weight in your eyes. But what I thought as I swept the words clean and brushed my hands across the precious earth was this: If I could have chosen my memories, Magnus Tulloch, I would have remembered us, I would have remembered you.

Can Granda Magnus hear the flowers talking? you asked, scuffing the path with your tight little shoes.

I don't know. But we can hope, aye. And I took you by the hand and we walked through the stones, both of us listening.

~

d. 1924. Pneumonia. But your granda died years before that.

Mills & Ware again

When your grandfather died, lambsie, I packed my grieving into a box already weighed down with loss. Among the things I kept in there was the boy whose heart had never come back from the war, and when I stowed away this latest grief it was like they came together again, boy and man—Magnus Tulloch, love of my life. It made it harder to turn from, but I'd no choice. Sealing that box, it was the only way I could go on.

That's what we did in those days, and I canna tell you now whether it was a good thing or bad. Sometimes I wished again to have a dog that would throw back its head and howl for me, for all I had lost, all I had put away. I remembered what it felt like when Crusoe had bayed at the night sky, the sound barrelling through Tiller Street, swelling in the spaces between the granite houses and flowing back over me like a healing balm. But there was no dog now, just the cries of my children, and they just made me sadder.

At your grandfather's funeral I wore a scarf of purple silk to say my goodbye. Even Clementina looked a tiny bit shocked. But then I stilled everything in me and set about finding work. I am thirty-three years old, I told myself, I have a family depending on me. My children, Clementina, her children: that was the shape of my family now.

I'd not expected finding a job to be easy, but the factory took me back in the early summer. I was lucky. Mr Prentice was still at Mills & Ware and he remembered. When he looked

302

at me I think he saw not who I was but who I had been, a girl he'd taken a chance on, who hadn't let him down. A widow I was now, one of many—it seemed there was an army of us—and even among the single women there were those who probably felt themselves widowed. They'd lost to war the men and boys they had thought to make a life with.

At Mills & Ware, five years on, it was almost like I'd not been away at all. There'd been changes, of course: a wafer machine, a third oven, factory back to full production. But it was still the same place, aye, hot and sweaty, slippery underfoot, its floury air tasting of whatever sweet thing was baking in the ovens.

I was put on Cakes, icing the big squares of sponge once they had cooled on the benches—chocolate, orange, vanilla. I liked slapping on the buttery icing with big flat spatulas and smoothing it in circles over the top and round the sides. Satisfying, getting it even and a nice shiny finish. It was my job, too, to run the empty bowls to the Mixing Room and bring back more. I didn't know how anyone could see through the dust of the Mixing Room. When I went home at night, little wisps of icing sugar would puff from my hair whenever I turned my head, and Steven and Kathryn would fling their arms around my neck and breathe it in. As well as bags of broken biscuits, now I would bring home odd-shaped bits of sponge in a tin—thin offcuts and splodgy spills from the trays—always with a scraping of whatever icing was left on the spatulas at the end of the day. Clementina huffed a sigh as she squeezed an extra fold around her middle—her Victoria Sponge Layer, she called it. But no complaints from Jessie and Hal, Steven and Kathryn, sticky smiles on their faces.

The twins were so good with Steven and Kathryn, keeping them away from Clementina's hot iron, making games in the garden with balls and the chickens, picking up Kathryn when she cried. Can you imagine fourteen-year-olds today with such forbearance?

Ach, it's good to smile about the day-to-day of those times. Before long, the world—well, it was not a happy place, no, and those of us with jobs thanked the Lord for them every day. After it all came to a head in 1929, Mills & Ware was like most other places, it put us all permanently on a week's notice, and never did we know how long it might be before we were among the jobless. We worked hard, we weren't late, not ever, we minded what we said. We hoped.

Clementina's ugly man

Clementina Slater Ratter became Clementina Laing in 1929, and wasn't anybody more surprised about that than she was.

She met Jack Laing—you remember your Uncle Jack, don't you, lambsie?—when she caught him one Friday night crouching down by our doormat, tucking under it a brown paper envelope with her name typed on the front. Inside, six shillings. No note.

What's all this? she demanded, frowning at his striped suit and olive-green tie and very red face. *Who are you?*

I'm an Ugly Man … he began.

Her face softened a little. *Ach, don't be so hard upon yourself, pet, ye're not so bad.*

His red face got redder and he tried again. He got as far as *war widows* and *welfare* and *fund-raising* before she stopped him with an upturned palm.

There's others need charity more, she said, *and will be glad for your face at their door.*

She handed him the envelope and folded her arms with a sniff.

Jack Laing looked taken aback. He'd not met war widows like Clementina. The look on his face made me laugh, and he glanced over her shoulder and doffed his hat to me politely. And then he invited Clementina to Uglie Land the next night. That was a fairground down by Victoria Quay run by the Ugly Men's Association to raise funds for people in the community who were struggling.

It was late when Clementina got home from Uglie Land. I made a pot of tea while she shook with laughing and told me about the merry-go-round and the chairoplane and the roller skating.

Did you skate? I asked.

Course I did, she declared.

Really?

Aye! Then a confession: *But I'd to hang on to that Jack Laing's elbow to keep my feet on the ground an' my behind off it!*

I smiled as Clementina talked of sugar floss on sticks and ginger beer and *That Jack Laing* this and that. I'd heard about Uglie Land, it had a bit of a lively reputation. Huge crowds went there of a Saturday night. But Clementina said no, there were not so many now. *That Jack Laing, he says the place has gone quiet since the Crash an' there's talk of closing.*

And that's what did happen a few years later. The Ugly Men's Association had been going since the war, and had done all manner of good, keeping an eye on those in need and giving a helping hand when they could, no questions asked. But after Uglie Land closed, the Ugly Men went quiet too, although there was still the need for help like that in those years, more than ever before. Maybe that was it, maybe the need was too great, I don't know.

We saw a lot of That Jack Laing after that, and Clementina found herself going to stranger-places. The Saturday she came home and told me she'd been to *the horseracing, d'ye mind!* we stared at each other, scandalised.

What was it like? I asked in awe. *What kind of people there?*

Just people, she said shrugging. *But with money they can live without!* She sniffed. *Horses have more sense than those people!*

It was a wee while before Clementina realised Jack Laing was an SP bookie, but by then it was too late. I'd grown to like having him around, the children thought he was moon and stars, and as for Clementina, well, she'd fallen hard. He asked her to marry him and she couldn't help but say yes, even though it shocked her to think what her mother, Lord rest her, would say.

She won't know, I told her.

But Clementina rolled her eyes darkly at the sky. *Ach, she'll know, she will, she'll be stampin' her feet in Heaven.*

An' what matter if she does!

It was a light in the darkness all around, and didn't she deserve the brightest, my Clementina?

Wasn't any question of Clementina and That Jack Laing moving to a cottage of their own in the Depression. He'd been living at a boarding house for single men. I knew the day would come when they would leave, but it wouldn't be now. So that little house in Martha Street took in one person more, and we all squeezed around each other as best we could. As it turned out, we were not so crowded for long because Hal soon left for the wheatlands, looking for work clearing or fencing, and That Jack Laing was away for weeks at a time in the country, although never was I sure what it was he did there. So once again things changed, and they stayed the same too.

When I look back on that time, I try to shut out the Depression, the way the world was then. I like to remember Clementina's face on the day she became Clementina Slater Ratter Laing, a hat of everlastings on her bluntly cut hair. Clementina, my dearest friend, my quinie, as she always and ever was to me. It was the last happy thing that happened for a long, long time.

Aye, it's the last happy thing on my list.

November 1974

Dearest lambsie, I'm rushing through the years, through my list of things to say, but I don't know whether I will finish. Time seems thin and wearisome and I have this feeling.

> Under the wide and starry sky
> Dig the grave and let me lie
> Glad did I live and gladly die
> And I laid me down with a will …

To think, I've been reading Mr Stevenson's words all my life, and suddenly I understand them.

They used to call the *reid-heidit* ones fey. *Knows more than she ought to, that one*—aye, and they didn't mean it kindly. But it can happen over a long life that you lose your fear of things you *just know*—you even start to trust that knowing. So I canna ignore this feeling that my time is running low.

There are still some things I've not written down, and if I don't do it soon then they probably never will be told. But there is a reason they are last on a list. How heavy it feels, knowing I must dig up the stones I have buried and look at them again, gather them into the order of things. And then I must roll them on to you.

I am sorry, my Laura-lamb.

The well, 1932

People called him a hero, in that strange way they do when they canna bear the senselessness of a thing and need some special word to comfort them, take their minds from the waste. Not Clementina, no. Even in the midst of it all, she was blunt enough to ask: *Why?* Again and again, insistent. *Why? He were just a wee loon an' it's not like it were his da an' he must have known there was no a chance of savin' him anyways. Why?*

To anyone hearing her, it would have seemed cruel—pushing such questions onto the mother of a dead boy, questions that had no answers, the kind that torture you all your days and never do relax their hold. But Clementina had the right, Clementina was there, and for her it was The Madness again. Like that day on the Knab. The furious pumping of blood as she wrenched a body back to the world. Aye, she had the right to demand *Why?* and it was not an empty question for which there could be no answer. Not for Clementina. She believed there had to be an answer. And that I *had* to know what it was.

~

It happened at midday, as Jessie and I were finishing our Saturday morning shift at Mills & Ware. Clementina was in the little haberdashery store in Attfield Street, looking for cheap wool, and forever after she would curse the moments spent chatting with Agnes Davies about knitting patterns from Shetland and the inferior grade of three-ply since the war *an' stupid, stupid things like that.*

I pieced it together like a film with what Clementina told me and what the police said. And what I knew, *just knew*. I have replayed it so many times, lambsie. I will write it down for you the way I have been seeing it for all these years, and I will not spare you, or myself, not one thing will I spare, because this I need you to know.

~

In those miserying times, men would often knock on the door of the cottage. Some had armfuls of boronia to sell, picked in the bush south. Some would offer to chop wood or sweep the chimney, just for a place to sleep. Some came right out and asked for food or a cup of tea to warm them on their way. Depression made beggars of all manner of men.

When the stranger came to Mrs Laskon's door, she had sized him up straight away. *A worker, this one, you always can tell.* And she gave him a job and a blanket and let him sleep by the copper in the laundry out back. It would take him a few days, he said, and he would do the job for board while he looked about Fremantle for work.

Clementina shook her head. *There's no work to be had*, she muttered. *She's taking advantage of the desperate.*

But it seemed to me that the man had a dignity bigger than desperate, and being unemployed and on the move with the legion of others doing the same was not going to make a dent in his sense of what was fair and what was not.

He said his name was Alfred but we could call him Digger because everybody did. Was it because he dug wells, or because he was in the war? I didn't like to ask. If a man wanted to talk about the war, he would find some way to do it, but most of them didn't. Clementina gave me a sideways glance and I could tell she was itching to come right out and ask was there a Mrs Digger—always she was *looking* for me. I frowned at her and instead she asked, *D'ye have milk in your tea, then?* And soon it was one question after another, Clementina, then Steven, all three of them with mugs of tea warming their fingers while Kathryn listened from the door. Always shy of anyone new, Kathryn was.

Since Hal had left and Jack Laing gone to the South West again for a month, Steven had lost his bearings a little. But the presence of the stranger cheered him. He began to brighten, drawn to the masculine in that powerful way of fatherless boys.

Can I help dig the well? he asked me. *I'm twelve, I'm old enough. Digger says I can if you say.*

God help me, lambsie, I didn't see the harm.

~

There isn't a sense of danger when the strut shifts. A minor irritation. A little runnel of sand like the grains in an eggtimer.

If the man had seen it, he could have called for Steven to grab the wooden ladder and lower it while there was still time. Or to toss one end of the knotted rope down the well and loop the other round the trunk of the banksia, aye.

If he had seen it and realised what was happening, that the gathering could not be stopped and there would be no time, I'd like to think he might have called to Steven, keeping his voice calm, to fetch a glass of water from the kitchen. A ruse to send the boy away.

But the plank of jarrah bursts suddenly from the rough scaffold holding back the earth while he works. Digger—Alfred— knows nothing.

But Steven … oh, my boy …

Steven is aware of it all.

He has just emptied a bag of lime into the wheelbarrow when he hears the crack of splitting timber, a cry as the strut hits the stranger's head. *Digger!* he screams, scrambling across the grass to reach the collapsing mouth of the well. He leans in, reaching, but the loose sand is rippling like water. He grabs the rake, he tests his weight on the top rung of the scaffold, and then he does this reckless, senseless thing. He climbs down into the well.

Digger! he calls again. Nothing. *Can you hear me?* But there's no movement in the cavern below other than the steady flow of sand.

A bang from the kitchen door and Steven looks up. The shocked face of his little sister appears over the lip of the frame as it gives way.

The whole thing, it just gives way.

Steven, my Steven, is trapped down the well, his leg wedged between the rake and a lattice of broken jarrah beneath. He tries to move the other leg, but sand is pouring in on him, the weight of the earth is holding him fast. The sole of that one free foot grinds down onto something, the hair and skin of the stranger's head.

Already sand is gripping his little chest, pinning his arms, no time, no time.

Looking up, he can see a mouth of sunlight, suddenly cut in half as a plank of wood clangs across it. Then a dangle of skinny legs.

No! he screams into the rush of sand. *Kathryn, no! Don't ...*

His words are swallowed, his head locked upwards into the circle of light.

He blinks furiously, my little boy, he blinks until the end.

The last thing he sees is Kathryn's legs being hauled up and out of the well. And then his Unty Clementina's face.

November 1974

Kathryn … Perhaps you understand a little more now, lambsie. About your mother, the way she is.

When Steven died, there was a hole in the heart of me, and only two choices. Bleed to death or grow another skin.

It took a long time.

How much do you remember, Kathryn, of the day you saw your brother die? You were ten years old, old enough to understand dying. Old enough to struggle against the grip on your arm, holding you back. To feel, later, that guilt: you couldn't save him, couldn't stop it. You grew up in the shadow of that day, but have always refused to speak of it. My fault. My shame. I was not there to help you.

A thing I have noticed in my life: the effort of keeping a thing unspoken sharpens the pain of remembering it.

If I had been able to see past the loss of Steven, if I had seen you as I see you now, just *seen* you, I could have told you plain that every day for the rest of my life I would thank God Clementina was there to pull you back. If I had shown you my grief, maybe you wouldn't have bundled yours away. If I had told you about the little boy on the Knab I couldn't save …

I could have helped you, Kathryn. We could have helped each other.

But I sank, lambsie, sank beneath the skin of the sea. It was left to Clementina.

This thing has been worrying at me ever since I began writing, picking holes in my sleep. I don't know how my Kathryn grieved. And I don't know what she said of that day, if she ever said a thing.

I took it into my mind to risk breaking all we had sealed away. To ask Clementina. I canna say she encouraged me. Such a frown. Even now, a grand old lady of eighty-four, there is no-one on this earth like Clementina for slapping you about the face with no more than a look over the rim of her teacup.

Is that what ye're doin', quinie, with your books? Haulin' up such things as have been put to rest? Shaking her head. *I don't hold with it. If ye've a mind to write wee stories for our Laura, ye can do it without causing anybody pain, not Laura nor her mother, neither.*

Have ye been talkin' to Kathryn, then? I ask darkly.

She sniffs. *Always did have more sense than her ma, Kathryn.*

I look at her, lambsie, I look at my Clementina, who has seen the worst times, the very worst of me, the times I thought to die. She's seen it all, aye, and borne it all too, and stepped in always. Never have I been a wise woman—I've just blundered my way through it all. But Clementina, she is the wisest person I know, and she always tells me straight.

Ye don't think I should write it all?

All?

She holds my eyes while she drinks her tea, two hands steadying the cup, and then she looks down at the saucer. Finally, she exhales a gust of warm breath.

Well now, quinie, why would ye want to do that?

Christmas Day, and you have left us, lambsie. Whyever you picked this day to fly away, I canna imagine, but your mother has been grumbling ever since you surprised us with your plans. I have a wee suspicion, though. I don't think Kathryn is so very sad to be spared chickens and ovens and gravy on this breathless hot day.

A Christmas you will always remember, this one. You woke up in the skin you have had all your life and grew a brand new one. In one day, the old and the new. I have known days like this.

I watched you, lambsie, as we sat drinking tea with the air all around full of 'Silent Night' and cigarettes, boards clacking with times and destinations, jangle-voices coming from airport speakers. You in that long cheesecloth dress, forever pushing your hair from your eyes, those thin tinkly bracelets running up and down your arm like music. You were fit to burst, bubbling away like a little girl all grown up but a little girl still. Trying not to show it in front of your university friends.

Clementina and I share a glance. Proud of our granddaughters, fearless and brave. We can read that look on your faces, yours and Wendy's, both of you about to cut your moorings. Clear as a Fremantle sky, it is, what's in your eyes:

The wide world!

Look at this crowd come to see you off, missing their Christmas pudding to do it. Jessie and your mother deep in talk,

Kathryn dabbing at her eyes, a flash of white cotton scrunched up in her hand. Your Unty Jessie is probably trying to soothe her: *Wendy's a bit older, Wendy will look after her.* And wouldn't you squirm to hear that! I look at Jessie's lined face and think, as always, of Hal, forever thirty-four. You never knew him, lambsie. Sweet, funny Hal, your Unty Jessie's twin, a life wasted in the second war as his da's was in the first. Ach, so cruel on Clementina.

You introduce your friends, lovely young people, and that boy with the droopy moustache, a charmer, him. Forgive me, lambsie, I canna remember so many names, all of them clattering together. Look at Clementina, her generous self squashed into a hard plastic chair, a big snorting laugh at something one of the girls is telling her.

They are all here for you and Wendy, here to bid you a happy goodbye.

I've still to finish your books, lambsie, the ones you don't know about yet. Oh, when you told us you were going travelling! For a moment, my blood stopped, I swear it did. Thinking you might have plans to see the Top of the World, where the sea people come from. Your people. But you and Wendy, you have other plans. Asia—for now, that's your wide world. India, where all the quinies wear silk.

So I've time before you come back. Before you decide, per-haps, to turn the other way, look to the cold north, to that other place. When I can gather the things in my heart to write this one last thing, it will be done, and I will give the books to you when you return. Will ever you read them? I canna say, but I hope.

I drink my tea, I chat to your friends, hide my ill-shaped hand under my shawl. I watch the buzz of strangers, their hugs and laughter, their tears. I promise myself I won't embarrass you, lambsie. But when you kneel down beside this wretched contraption, your blue eyes smudged dark, your water eyes, those worry eyes that are your mother's and I've not seen so much in you before ... Well, they are gone, my promises.

Do you remember what it was you whispered? *Not for long, Grunnie, I'll be back by the spring. You'll be all right, you will, won't you?*

And so I will, my Laura-lamb.

~

When you and Wendy went through the doors with your passports in your hands and we could not see you any more, when your friends waved and left for their Christmas trees, when Kathryn and Jessie slipped away to blot their patchy faces, it was just Clementina and me. She huffed into a seat beside the wheelchair and sniffed, reached across to pat my hand.

I looked at her and all those years between us, swilling back and forth like the surge of the sea.

Well, quinie, she said, *here we are.*

Coda

2011

FIRE

That boy, that Brukie's Sandy, he took his time drowning, as is the way of the young and the strong.

Laura

The gathering is small. Laura glances around her. The older we get, she thinks, the fewer there are to remember. And Aunty Jessie was so very, very old.

A drizzle of rain. Appropriate. It *should* rain at funerals.

She trails the procession across the rolling green lawn, long black coats, like a winter uniform, speckled with a light mist. No-one has thought to bring an umbrella. In the distance, half a dozen kangaroos disappear into a stand of wattles. This place is more like a park than a cemetery.

At the grave, Laura's anxiety is louder than the minister's words. She hunches down, winds the pashmina round her throat. No-one likes funerals. No-one. But when one of your own has come so close to death, even *being* at a cemetery feels reckless, like you are tempting fate. She would have preferred to make her excuses, send flowers, a letter to Wendy—she'd even written out what she wanted to say. But in the end, well. What disrespect it would be to the memory of Aunty Jessie, this lovely woman who had been a presence in her life for so long. And to what Grunnie Meggie and Wendy's grandmother, Aunty Clementina, had meant to each other. The two families had drifted apart over the years; even the friendship between her and Wendy had dwindled to Christmas cards and a birthday call if one of them remembered. But the bond between their grandmothers, and their mothers, too, had been like family, like blood, and it is that she is here to honour. Under the circumstances, Wendy would have understood if she'd stayed away, but she'd thought of her mother, and Grunnie, and she just couldn't do it.

Even so, people seem to be avoiding her, trying not to stare. Or is she imagining it?

… Dust to dust.

A quintessence of dust, she thinks. The finest.

Thunder breaks on the horizon and she raises her face to look for lightning, forgetting, as always, the order of things: light before sound. A glance at the grave again. So Aunty Jessie had wanted a burial, or perhaps it's what Wendy had wanted for her. Not so her own mother. Kathryn had always been clear about that. *Cast my ashes on the sand*, she'd told her. *Somewhere out near South Beach. If the earth doesn't take me home, the wind or waves will do it.*

Where's home? Laura once asked.

Where it begins, she'd said, her mouth tight. Typically cryptic Kathryn.

She'd followed her mother's wishes, and there'd been no plaque, either.

A young woman in a burgundy blazer is walking from person to person, offering a canister of earth. Laura takes a handful, steps forward, lets the sand fall.

Goodbye, Un-ty Jessie, she whispers. *Rest in peace.*

The grass is spongy and the heels of her boots sink into it. When she turns, a woman is waiting for her, two open arms.

Laura …

She hugs Wendy, buries her face for a moment in the soft collar of her coat. When they pull apart, Wendy grips her hands.

Thank you for coming. Above and beyond, with everything else that's happening. And it's a long drive for you, from the hills. Ma would have been so touched.

I loved your mother.

You were so very precious to her. Wendy's smile falters. *And how … how is …?*

Critical, still unconscious. But stable. She hears the inflection of hope in her voice, a hollow flute.

Another squeeze of the hands before Wendy is drawn away by a young man Laura doesn't know. But she returns a moment later.

You'll come to the house, won't you, Laura? You remember how to get there?

Oh, Wendy, I don't think …

You don't have to stay long if you need to get back to the hospital.

Laura glances at her watch. No. She's been away too long already. Avril will need a break.

A hurried kiss on Wendy's cheek. *We'll talk soon. I'll call you.*

Laura

Two weeks later

Night persists in the 6.00 am sky, tenaciously black, lunar lit. Children draw the moon like this, a skinny rind in shiny yellow crayon, glowing like there's no tomorrow. *You could draw the full moon, too*, she'd suggested to Cooper many years ago, sketching it for him, *big and round like this*. But he'd told her, with five-year-old certainty, that that was the sun, and didn't she know the difference?

So beautiful, the night sky, its cold glittering, its trinketery of stars. Turn the other way and it's already vaporising, an aura on the horizon warming into day, all pastel watercolours, pink and indigo, god-gilded. She is a body suspended between dying night and dawn.

Laura tugs at the door to the shed, wrenching it free from the warped frame. Pushes it shut to keep the warmth in and the cat out, a slinky brown curl of fur resisting the barrier of her shin.

A quick check before she leaves for the hospital. No time to linger. This might be the last lot she sees into the world for a while, but there are more important things. Critical things. Cooper is her priority, and Avril, too. Laura's taken overdue long-service leave from the university so that everything else can wait for however long it takes. She shivers, hugs a hard truth to herself. Such a long, long time it is going to take. Does Avril have any idea how long?

She is careful where she puts her feet in the shed. The milkweed has been stripped, the leaves reduced to lace, and mature caterpillars are all over the place, in the process of migrating from food to shelter. Some have already fixed themselves to the stems and leaves of potted bay trees, to knotted orchid spears, even to lattice and metal shelving. Their fat, stripy bodies, curled into the shape of a J, will rest now, a prelude to transformation, preparing to grow a new kind of skin. As she fills the humidifier, checks the heater's thermostat, she talks out loud in this incubator where no-one can hear her: *There is a place for you in the world, beauties. We need you all, every one.* She keeps an inventory in her head of how many, and where, and will tell Cooper about them when she sits with him today. It will be good to have something to say, something new.

By the time she pushes the door shut, hears the latch click, the sky has ripened into dawn. Beautiful, yes, but she prefers the sky that was. There is comfort in darkness. You can tell the night all manner of lies, and it will believe you.

She sniffs the air. Again! There's a bag of floury peppermints in the pocket of her jacket, Gold Seal Extra Strong. She slips one into her mouth and crunches down hard. It cauterises her sinuses, vanquishing that smell. Imaginary, of course. Not the homely ash of wood fires and potbellies, ever-present on cold mornings, nor that other smoke, dark and rapacious, laden with the cinders of mortgages and memories—a smell feared by all who live in the forested hills. This is different, a false summoning of seared skin and flesh-smoke. It had begun four weeks ago after Avril's frantic phone call about Cooper. You don't need to be a psychologist to see it for what it is: a cruel trick triggered by anxiety.

The cat is still hanging round, nonchalant but hopeful. She reaches down and scratches his chin—a no-hard-feelings gesture. *Now, off you go. Gideon will be looking for you. If you run, you'll be in time for croissants.*

He gives her a baleful stare, a long, disgruntled yowl of complaint. Laura shakes her head. She still can't get used to cats like this. Cats that talk back.

It's colder inside the house than out. No point in turning on the heater when she'll be leaving soon. Every weekday she's at the hospital all day. Glad to be, so that Avril can go home for a while. Glad just to be there, near him. Though what good it does for Cooper, who could say? So much of what we do for others is really for ourselves.

She makes a sandwich to take to the hospital, banana and honey on grain bread. Tomato would be better. Healthier. But, she thinks wryly, it would taste of tomato.

When she locks the door behind her, she pauses. A breeze is rustling the eucalypts, hundreds of dry leaves shushing. She reaches for a peppermint. Nothing is burning. There is no fire. But the smell of burning is back.

Avril

The light, the half-light, the nebulous haze. It would cast an unhealthy glow on even the most perfect skin, and there's not much of that around here. Masks, caps and gowns, cotton booties and mittens. What does that leave? Eyes, only eyes. The alert, canvassing eyes of the staff. And those of the others, the loved ones, stricken.

Avril splays her fingers inside the gauzy mittens, greenish and pocked in this eerie dim, and counts them down, one to five on each hand. A nervous thing, a ritual. Here, where death hovers so close that you can hear it breathing, feel its pushy presence in the unnaturally warm air, she is almost guilty about being *intact* among the disfigured bodies, tubes, beeping screens. She counts her fingers again. Her hands are as they should be. Except in what they cannot do. She is allowed to be here, to sit by his bed during the long nights, to speak to him in whispers, but she cannot touch Cooper.

He is a grievous wound. Simply that.

Third-degree burns. Full thickness. Seventy per cent. Complicated by the invisible wound that has put him in a coma, a knock to the head by a piece of roofing timber. At first these terms were shorthand for *Not expected to live* and *All we can do is ease the passing*. But Cooper is strong, stronger than that. They call him Miracle Man around here and look at him in awe and admiration. Pity is something they reserve for her, and for Laura.

Avril's long, strong fingers understand skin. They are used to kneading muscles, manipulating seized joints, soothing, healing—all through the medium of skin. But when there is no skin …

Most has been debrided along with the dead tissue beneath. To look at him, to steel yourself and really look when the bandages have been peeled away, you could not say where the thirty per cent that remains was, unless you knew. You could not imagine there was an inch of Cooper's body unskinned.

Cold panic grips when she thinks like that. Still, now, calm. Panicking will not help you, Coop, will it. What *will* help you?

Another riffle of panic.

Ms Mathieson?

Avril, please, just Avril. New, this one. They are always busy, too much to do. She used to offer to help, Laura too, but both of them know better now.

Avril, yes. Why don't you take a break, a cup of coffee, maybe. You know where the tea room is? We need to change the dressings.

Of course. She is aching for a cigarette. *I'll be downstairs.*

In the pressurised chamber between the ICU and the nurses' entry, she sheds the gown and mask, the layers of cotton that protect his extraordinary vulnerability from everything that is ordinary about her. She pulls off the mittens, avoiding looking down at her hands, cracked from continual scrubbing that cannot keep them clean enough. On the other side of the glass, two nurses yank the curtain across, ready to begin the task of unwrapping Cooper's medicated dressings.

The glass is cold against her forehead. What to want? What to hope for? Come back, Coop? Patients with burns as bad as his are put *into* a coma, to spare them for a while, but Cooper's hasn't been medically induced. She wants him to wake from it, of course she does, and they say it's critical it happens soon. But how could you want him conscious while all of this is happening? The only blessing here is that he can't feel the pain.

Her forehead leaves a slick on the glass as she pulls away abruptly.

She's been here long enough to know. When Cooper is conscious, the screaming will begin.

~

She walks a few paces up the rise, away from the ambulance bay, and tries to flick her lighter but a nannying wind gusts at the flame, *put it out, put it out, you don't want that.* Her fingers shake. *I do.* Just one and then she will let the wind ransack her hair to the roots, scour the nicotine smell from her clothes before she returns to the ICU.

First one since Sunday, she says aloud, as if the wind cares. The flame lengthens lovingly, turns gassy green.

She draws on the cigarette, pulling smoke into her lungs, withholding until the last minute. Eddies drift about her face, hazing the moon. Smoke. For god's sake, look at her, choosing to let smoke in to her lungs. Disgusting. But still she does it, cannot stop herself; not even the thought of Cooper, not even that.

If the investigators have got to the bottom of what happened, they are not telling her. She'll phone again during the day. Yes, I'll wait. No, I'll wait. Can you ask someone to call me? No-one ever does.

Ben says they can't complete the investigation until they speak to Coop. (*Until*, he says. Not *unless*.) But she knows there would have been a debriefing weeks ago. She knows there's something he's not saying. And now he's avoiding her.

The cigarette burns down almost to the filter and she is tempted, as always, to pinch between her thumb and finger the tiny molten nub within the ash, let it burn through the dermal layers, feel the pain. *Feel.* But she crushes it, as always, with the heel of her boot, picks up the damage and tosses it into a bin outside the hush of hospital doors.

Sorry, Coop.

And although her mother-in-law has never spoken in judgment about her smoking, not even given a disapproving glance, she speaks to her, too, as she crosses the divide between worlds.

Sorry, Laura.

Laura

The early-morning streets are a mess. Her neighbourhood's annual verge collection brings out polite recyclers by day and ruthless scavengers by night. She swerves to avoid debris as she pulls out from the driveway, the contents of an up-ended tangerine suitcase from the house opposite spilling onto the road—videocassettes, mostly, boxless and broken. Shiny ribbons of drama billow and snap in the wind.

There's an elaborate-looking piece of exercise equipment on Gideon's verge, something with pulleys and steps and footrests. Laura blinks. Gideon? She shakes the image from her head. None of my business, she tells herself. The carpet-covered thing next to it—she knows what *that* is: a cat's scratching post, never used. *He prefers my armchair,* Gideon told her with a rueful *what-are-you-going-to-do?* shrug.

It was because of the cat that she'd met Gideon when he moved in a few months ago. A terrible noise was coming from her patio, like an animal in pain. She'd peeked out from the blind, expecting something more than one small cat. There he was on the table, green eyes blinking, beautiful, sleek and loud. He rumbled when she approached, tentatively patted his head and turned the collar round to read the tag: *Allee-Cat.* She squinted, read again. Definitely *Allee.* And the address—just two houses away. The Martins' old house.

Gideon had grinned when he answered the door, an ageing hippie in a long woollen cardigan and jeans. He folded his arms and shook his head at her awkward armful of purring cat. *Well, sir, look at you. Pretending to be lost again. Shameless!*

She'd asked him what was wrong with the cat. *Why does it make that howling noise?*

Gideon just laughed. *He's a Burmese, it's what they do.*

I couldn't help noticing ... She nudged the collar as she handed the cat over. *Allee?*

He grinned again. *Long story. Bore you with it over a glass of wine some time?*

~

The car pulls on to the main road that snakes down through the hills. Through the post-dawn grey, pinpricks of hazy yellow appear—lights of the city, the highway, suburbs in between. She nears that scar, that tract of stumps and stubble, she hates driving through. Where a wildfire rushed and twisted last summer, ignited ancient grasstrees steeped in resin, exploded flaming shrapnel across firebreaks, across the road. Mist collects in blackened stands of eucalypt bones.

She shrugs the coat off her shoulders and fans herself with yesterday's unopened mail. Calm down, she tells herself, breathe.

As Laura leaves the hills behind her, she thinks of her street again, the mess it's in. Gideon had left a message—*Anything you want carted out to the verge?*—but the clutter of her spare room will have to wait. No time, no energy. One day, too, she's going to have to deal with her mother's stuff. She sighs. A responsibility pushed aside shamefully long. And then there's Cooper's old room. How many years has it been? Ten, maybe more, since he left home, but he just laughs when she threatens to toss out his textbooks and posters, the clothes that don't fit, the cupboards full of *Star Wars* figurines. Even the dinky little sporting trophies with their tarnished shields. *Get rid of them, if you want—'s OK with me. They're more yours than mine,* he tells her.

Told her.

Is that true? she wonders. Who does childhood belong to? One thing's for sure: even if she had the time, she wouldn't be tossing out anything of Cooper's. And he's probably counting on that.

She swallows down the surge of panic before it swamps her. Calm down, breathe.

Ridiculous thought. Cooper's in no condition to be counting on anything.

Avril

A distracted smile as she passes the desk outside ICU, on her way to gown up again. Joley, with a phone pressed to her ear, raises her hand. *Hold on,* she mouths.

Avril tucks the cigarettes into her back pocket and waits for Joley to finish her call.

I was just coming to find you. There's a visitor.

Really? Avril glances at the clock on the wall.

She's asking for Laura. I've put her in the lounge.

Avril frowns. Someone for Laura. How long since there's been someone for Coop? Why are his mates from the station staying away?

Who is it?

Didn't get a name. Joley's voice crisp, I'm-a-nurse-not-a-secretary.

Thanks, Joley, thanks. Can I get you a coffee on my way back?

No, I just had one. But thanks.

~

The visitors' lounge is now as familiar as a room of her house. During the long nights, it's a place to go when everything presses in on her and she loses Cooper, her Cooper, the real Cooper who is in there somewhere, she knows it, safe and unbroken, floating like the yolk in an egg. She curls up on the armchair in the corner with ginger tea in a stained mug. Reads for a while. Dozes but never for long. Naps are all she needs, here at night, at home during the day. Sleep seems risky; she has to stay alert, whether she's beside him or at home keeping things together, keeping the bills paid.

In the lounge is an elegant woman, vaguely familiar, leaning on the back of Avril's favourite chair. She's twisting the end of a linen scarf into knots, a handbag and a large envelope at her feet.

Avril tucks strands of wayward hair behind her ears, pushes back the aubergine fringe. *Hello?*

Avril? Hello, we haven't met, but I'm an old friend of Laura's. Wendy Casley. You might know … Laura called my mother Aunty Jessie.

Um, yes, hello. She's seen Wendy in photographs at Laura's. Avril steps forward and offers a hug, brief, awkward. *Laura told me about your mother. I'm sorry for your loss.*

Thank you. Such a long life, but, well, it was still …

Avril pats her pockets for the wad of clean tissues and offers one to Wendy.

Oh, I'm sorry, it keeps catching me … It's been weeks, you'd think by now …

No need to apologise.

And I haven't even asked you about Cooper.

Avril steps back, wrapping her arms around her chest. *Not much change. But they were able to harvest some more donor cells this week.*

She stops. The woman has no idea what she's talking about.

Um, they take cells from the areas where he wasn't burned and grow them into a sheet of skin, and then they stretch it out over the burn, sort of like a fishnet. Cells are sprayed over that and eventually new cells grow in between and it all joins up. Incredible, really …

Wendy Casley is making an effort but she's obviously squeamish.

The energy dies from Avril's voice. *He's still unconscious.*

Wendy looks as sympathetic, as uncomfortable, as everyone else who has come to the hospital to offer support. I should be grateful, Avril tells herself, grateful for kindness.

You were looking for Laura? She'll be in this morning. Soon, probably.

Yes, the nurse told me. Could you give her something for me? She picks up the bulky envelope. *I've an early appointment next door, the Medical Centre, and then I have to leave. So I thought …*

Of course.

I found it … I'll explain to Laura. I didn't want to post it, after all this time.

Avril takes the package and immediately drops it on the table. Her hands feel gritty. She wipes her palms on her jeans. *I'll make sure she gets it.*

And will you ask her to call me when she can? Wendy is twisting the scarf again, knotting the ends, pulling apart threads. *I hope Cooper is …*

Yes, I'll tell her.

Laura

The wide glass doors at the hospital entrance are ahead. Laura stops suddenly, almost winded. There's a bench a few steps away, probably for the benefit of those with crutches, frames, IV drips. She sits heavily, brings her forehead to her knees, and waits for the feeling to pass.

Uh, excuse me …

She looks up. A young woman in a white uniform, a little breathless, clearly in a hurry.

Sorry, but are you all right?

Laura smiles faintly. *Yes … thank you.*

The nurse nods. A brisk smile in return. And flies on her way.

She's all right, yes, thank you, of course she's all right; she just can't, for the moment, imagine how she's going to stand up and walk through those doors again.

Avril's upstairs, with Cooper, or, if the physio is making an early call, sitting in the visitors' lounge, reading.

One of the night-shift nurses, Joley, leaves books for the two of them on the fake marble coffee table in the lounge. Little post-it notes stuck on the covers. *For Avril and Laura, this is my favourite, hope you like. Avril/Laura, another good one!* Kind of her. A Danielle Steel, a Jodi Picoult. Not her thing but she won't tell Joley that. Avril devours them in bursts—escape, she calls them. Good. Any escape is good.

Laura feels the hard edges of a book in the bag resting against her shin. The true story of a burns survivor. So far she hasn't been able to get past the first few pages. Motivational words displayed in boxes. Photographs. No. It's too soon for this, too much a rehearsal of all that is yet to come if—*if*—they are lucky. But she's brought it with her. And a much-loved copy of *Pride and Prejudice*—comfort reading. She can't face anything new. The pile of books on the desk in her study, untouched all these weeks, can stay there. With the computer she won't turn on.

She thinks of Avril again. Stands up. Loops the strap of her bag over her shoulder.

Cloying, the sudden smell of honey and banana as she heads towards the hospital doors.

Avril

Pressure on her shoulder, an awakening, momentary relief at being released from a dream of bacon frying on a hot iron—inexplicable, nauseating. Filmy grit clears from her eyes. Laura. Laura?

Avril pushes herself up from the chair by Cooper's bed. *Ohmygod, what's the time?*

It's all right. Laura's voice is gentle. *It isn't late. You must have just dozed off.*

Her mother-in-law, capped and gowned in white, looks older than her years this morning. Frail in a way that doesn't mesh with everything Avril knows her to be. Cooper would laugh. He'd say something like *My mother, frail? Ha! My mother always says she's from a long line of women who had to be strong because strength was all they had.* She wonders whether it's true. No-one is ever as strong as other people think they are. Especially their children.

Laura is brushing the edge of the bed with her mittened hand, the closest she can get to stroking Cooper's arm.

How is he today?

Avril shrugs. There is never anything to say, and Laura knows that. It doesn't stop her from asking—it's a compulsion both of them have, to ask each other these unanswerable questions—but at least she understands.

I'd better go. Appointments this morning. And I might phone Ben when I get a break. You haven't heard anything?

No. Laura shakes her head but her eyes are on Cooper.

OK, then.

A glance at the clock behind the nurses' station. Avril needs to be back home by nine-thirty. But she isn't moving.

Um, Laura?

Laura twists round to face her, her gauzed fingers still moving across the sheet.

Do you want, um, coffee in the lounge?

~

Avril watches Laura running her hands through her hair absent-mindedly, stretching out her legs—narrow black jeans and boots—as she drinks her coffee. She tries to concentrate on what Laura's saying. Something about caterpillars. Away from the ICU, out of the whites, there is a more natural colour to her face, but it's still drawn. She's anxious, and it's making Avril uneasy because Laura is always calm, always. Gravity is part of her very being—although it's a frustration as well as a comfort sometimes. Avril is sick of the mindless assurances from all and sundry—her sister Pascale, her clients, neighbours, even the lanky boy who delivers her pizzas, for god's sake—that Cooper will be OK, when it's far from clear that anything will ever be OK again. Laura knows this, and thank god for that. But. Perversely, Avril finds herself wishing Laura would just occasionally play along with the naive notion of restitution, that the life she and Cooper had once had might be made whole again. That his body will heal, his brain will wake. Recovery is still possible, the doctors have assured them, although they're cautious, evasive, about what *recovery* might mean. But increasingly Avril has the feeling that Laura knows, really *knows*, that it isn't going to happen.

They've told you something, Laura, haven't they? Something about Cooper's condition?

Laura looks startled. *No, of course not. They wouldn't give me information and withhold it from you.*

She's right, of course. Practical. Calm down, relax, Avril.
Really?

Really. Look after yourself, sweetie. Don't work too hard. Try to get some sleep.

A kiss on the cheek, a squeeze of the arm, real and warm. Avril leans into it, wishing everything else would just stop for a minute. She sees the envelope on the table.

Oh, you had a visitor last night. Wendy Casley? She left this for you.

Laura

Lunchtime, Cooper. Steak and lentil burger and a double-cream shake.

Martine leans in, pats the pillow lightly, before she hooks up one of the liquid food packs that push calories into his body. Same little joke every time.

A memory of Cooper and his mates. She'd caught them in the pantry once, after school, their cheeks stuffed with Twisties, their fingers ringed to the tips with Burger Rings and Cheezels. Leftovers from a party. Some game was going on, how many packets they could get in their mouths. All of them laughing and coughing gooey orange spittle. *Disgusting little critters*, Jarrad declared when she told him, the biggest grin on his face.

She looks at the feeding tube. Force-feeding—that's what it is. High-protein, high-calorie. Nutrition is one of the things his recovery depends on. Healing cells are ravenous, insatiable.

A pat on Laura's shoulder as Martine leaves. A smile meant to encourage but it's more like a grimace. A small regretful twist of the mouth that reminds Laura of her mother. She fights the urge to grimace back.

Her mother. If Kathryn were here, could see her grandson like this ... Kathryn, who'd always mollycoddled Cooper when he was little. *Be careful, Cooper, come back, sweetie, don't do that, be careful, don't jump on the trampoline with Twisties in your mouth.* It was not long after she died that he'd joined the service. Dropped out of uni to become what he'd told them all, at the age of five, he wanted to be when he grew up. They hadn't been related—her mother's death and Cooper's decision—but Laura had always been aware of how scandalised she would have been. Kathryn had been thrilled when he'd enrolled in Engineering, like his grandfather. There was security in Engineering. Respect.

Laura sighs. Somewhere she has a photo of her mother and Aunty Jessie at an exhibition opening, the two of them posing for the camera with old-fashioned champagne glasses in their hands. They stand in front of a piece of her mother's that Laura always loved—faceless, stringed hair, body curved like a cello. Aunty Jessie is caught mid-laugh, an arm around her mother, expansively gathering her in; Kathryn is stiff, spectacularly ungatherable. Critics often described Kathryn's work as *passionate, brave*, but her face … there it is. *Be careful.*

What's got into her today? Sitting here in silence, in a glaze of remembering, when *this* is what matters, all of this, the weight of now.

She thinks of the envelope Wendy left. Some memento of Aunty Jessie, probably. A little piece of the past.

Do you remember your Un-ty Jessie? she whispers to Cooper.

Avril

Parrots screech, busying the morning air, as the four-wheel drive turns into the long driveway bordered with a windbreak of Bushy Yate. Avril frowns. This time last year, she and Coop tried suspending brightly coloured nylon kites from tree to tree. They've also experimented with strands of bells, streamers. But nothing keeps the twenty-eights away from the mandarins, and in a few months they'll be demolishing the stone fruit and almonds, too. She draws the line at stringing up fishing line, like Murray next door does, criss-crossing the strands into a lethal web. She doesn't want to strangle the parrots, only to keep them away from the fruit.

It doesn't matter now. Fruit fly will claim what the parrots leave behind.

Her nine-thirty isn't here yet, thank god. There's time to let the stale air out of the treatment room, bring in fresh towels from the dryer, light the burner and add some oils—sandalwood and lemongrass, because Ewan doesn't like the girly stuff. By the time he arrives she has made a cup of instant coffee, resisted a cigarette and eaten two macadamia-chocolate-chip cookies.

She watches him get out of the car wincingly, not the way she's shown him.

Ewan, she calls from the verandah, *swing your legs around first, remember!*

A palm up to acknowledge and he shuffles towards the house, pinched and cold in the short sleeves he wears year-round. He'll never remember.

He's not in a chatty mood today, and Avril is relieved. She doesn't encourage conversation about Cooper with her clients, but Ewan sometimes persists, as though he has special rights. Perhaps he does. She's known Ewan and his spasming thoracic paraspinals, his reactive left sacro–iliac, longer than she's known some of her friends.

She feels his skin begin to relax under the warmth of the wheat pack resting on his back.

How have you found the new stretches? Managing?

A muffled grunt from beneath the towels: *Yeah, fine.*

She does the translation: *Haven't done them. Uh-uh. Not once.* He'll never do them.

In spite of the soft rolls of overindulgence in the way, it's easy to find the trigger points close the spine, out through the rhomboids. She applies pressure, easing off when she feels the grainy knots of muscle fibre release. Ewan's involuntary moans rise and fall in response to pain.

Usually she finds her work soothing, a temporary respite from anxiety, but today she's jittery. Too much instant coffee. The sense of being kept out of the loop. People who won't phone her back. And suddenly she's cranky. Cranky with Ewan, bloody Ewan, who is too apathetic, too lazy, to help himself. Why is she bothering, when he isn't? Her fingers dig into pink, healthy skin and she is chastened by a hurt whimper.

Sorry, Ewan, sorry. Roll over for me now, would you? Easy, that's right, good.

She gives the scalene muscles her full attention, drawing deeply along the sinewy ridges either side of the neck. It can be uncomfortable, this pressure, prompting resistance, and she checks his tolerance. *All right there, Ewan?*

The nurses are always asking Coop questions like this. *Comfortable there, Cooper? Everything OK, Cooper?* Pointless.

A barely perceptible grunt from Ewan. Translation: *Yeah, fine, I can take it.*

Can *you* take it, Coop? Can you?

She is about to finish in the usual way, with a rolling stretch of the posterior neck muscles, when she notices Ewan's closed eyes. A glimmer of tears at the outer edge, welling in the deep fold; a meniscus before the pool breaches.

Ewan? she says softly.

His silence tells her that the cause of the tears is not physical. And that he probably has no comprehension of where they have come from. He's embarrassed.

The towel around the wheat pack is still warm, and she uses it to blot his face, his neck, the tender muscles of his shoulders and back. Soothing, and sparing.

It can happen—she's seen it before—that working on the source of pain awakens something emotional, something embryonic and bewildering. The unruly return of a memory held down with the weight of a life; a beginning, or the beginning of an ending. Or perhaps it's the distillation of something unasked for, leaking into consciousness from the amnion of the world. Shapeless and formless, blindingly intense, it gives no clue, for now, of the course it would have you follow; all you know is that something has been released, and you are full of it, you are different.

He is subdued as he buttons up the cotton shirt, hands over his debit card.

Glass of water?

He shakes his head.

From the door, he manages the usual farewell in one elongated breath: *Right-then-Avvie-call-yer-Monday-when-I-know-me-roster-hope-yer-bloke's-on-the-mend-eh.*

~

A butterfly lands on the sill of the window by the washbasin. She recognises it's a Monarch, the type Laura breeds in her shed and then releases into the world.

Are you sure that's what she's doing out there? she'd asked Coop once. A wry smile, but she'd been incredulous that his beautiful, smart mother, who lectured in Lit Studies and read politics and poetry and serious novels, spent her nights messing around with weeds and humidifiers.

He'd roared out a laugh. *Whoa! Reckon she's got a crop going, do you? We all wish!* And he laughed again, shaking his head. *Nah, it's got something to do with that plant. Been declared a noxious weed; you don't see it much in the wild any more. Her butterflies need it to breed.*

But they're ... She hadn't wanted to say it, but he said it for her.

... only butterflies? Yeah, I know. But she says she can't imagine a world without them.

The Monarch flits away, lands on one of the dandelions in the thyme. Even from here, Avril can see their flat pugnacious bases, green among the silver, taking rude possession. The herb garden has already been colonised by couch and clover. She looks down quickly, saws at her nails with the scrubbing brush. Everything's going to seed and there's nothing she can do about it.

She'd spent two years improving the soil, breaking up the clay by adding lucerne, newspaper pulp, rotted manures. But now the thought of plunging her hands into it ... No, not even wearing the thick leather gardening gloves that skirt her forearms like medieval armour. That humus-rich earth is rank and alive, and for Avril there isn't a protective barrier sound enough, or an antiseptic strong enough, to alleviate her fears of transferring bacteria to Coop. He is so susceptible, so acutely, preciously at risk.

The water in the washbasin turns pink and she pulls the plug, runs her hands under the tap, blots at a bleeding cuticle with a tissue. Too vicious again. Maybe it isn't rational, maybe it's obsessive, but when you're in danger of being engulfed by things beyond your control you will grab hold of anything that floats by, just to keep yourself above the white water, keep yourself breathing. Disinfecting her hands, her nails, her hair, her clothes, scrubbing everything scrupulously clean, is one thing she can do. A ripple in a river of things she can't.

The photograph taped to the wall reminds her of what's at stake. Coop in uniform, laughing, his arm around her. A shot Ben had taken one morning when she'd stopped in at the station with a tin of fudge brownies that had, for once, turned out like the photo on the recipe. They'd had an argument hours before, at home. Same old thing. But not the same, because when she'd told him—again—that she wasn't ready—still—his long-stretched patience had snapped like elastic.

When will you be?

She'd felt cornered. Glared at him, mute.

Halfway through the door on his way out, he'd turned back, frustrated, wistful. *Will you ever be ready, Av?*

She'd turned up later at the station, with her wordless, entirely unsatisfactory offering, and he'd popped the lid of the biscuit tin and scoffed down two brownies. A silent exchange:

Sorry, babe. Not yet.

Yeah.

She touches the borderless edge of the photograph. Coop with a smudge of chocolate on his mouth, squinting into the camera with the bluest eyes, the whitest lashes.

She chokes down the thought that she hasn't seen his eyes for weeks. His eyelashes probably won't ever grow back.

Laura

It's dark at seven, true dark, long past the brief twilight that softens edges, makes spectres of eucalypts and basketball hoops and stop signs. On the table near the back door are two shapes that weren't there when she left this morning. One moves at her approach. Lithe, sure, across the table.

What are you doing out here in the cold, Allee-Cat?

He leaps down. The security light clicks on, old and clunky and only one of its floods working.

The other shape is a small foam esky, the kind Cooper used to take to the football, and in about the same condition—scratched and pitted, as though someone has picked away at the foam with their fingernails.

Laura tucks it under her arm with Wendy Casley's envelope and takes them inside, shouldering through the door and in the process failing to keep the cat from slipping through. Too tired to bother chasing him out.

She shivers and looks at the open fireplace, but it's no use, she can't bring herself to light a match. The single-bar electric heater is a poor substitute. She flicks on the switch and waits for the ticking bar to glow orange.

Allee-Cat bumps at her knees.

All right, steady on. You're not supposed to be in here, anyway.

Sitting on the sofa in front of the heater, she thinks of Avril, driving in to the hospital—or maybe already there, thin and stretched and gowned in whites for the night.

Dr Meagher is coming to see her on his evening rounds.

Laura realises her fist is pressed to her sternum, as though holding something in. Her ribs, a bony corrugation just beneath the surface. How much weight has she lost? It doesn't matter.

She glances at the esky.

Gideon had turned up on the doorstep a week after their first conversation. A petition in one hand, something to do with Landcare and the local council. In the other hand, the same esky sitting on her table now. Over a glass of Pinot Gris, their talk had moved from the shire's lack of resolve, to their work, families, and on to cats. A committed environmentalist who owned a cat?

He'd shrugged, palms up helplessly. *I've a theory we're each allowed one hypocrisy.* He jerked a thumb. *He's mine.*

When she reminded him he'd promised to explain the cat's name, he told her about Warder Clyde Allee. *A US biologist of the early twentieth century, and one of the first interested in ecology. A new science then.*

Laura was mellow with wine and the Margaret River brie that Gideon had brought over. She could already tell he liked an audience. *I haven't heard of him*, she said, prompting.

Wouldn't expect you to. I came across him light-years ago in my student days. He didn't have the panache of the Three Hs: Huxley, Haldane and Hamilton. But at a time when biologists were flummoxing about, trying to iron out the wrinkles in Darwin's theories, Allee persisted with the idea that animals were fundamentally cooperative beings, not aggressively competitive, as Darwin et al. would have it.

Was he right?

Ah. Well. Gideon grinned, tapping his chin. *Evolution isn't as simple as that, Dr Ellery.*

So you named your cat after ... an optimist.

Ha! A pacifist, too, a conscientious objector in the First World War. Not many of those around then.

Gideon settled back in the chair. *Just a good bloke all round, I reckon, ahead of his time.*

Laura smiles at the memory. Her neighbour—retired biology teacher, conservationist, reader of the classics, cook. A good bloke all round.

She releases the metal clamp on the esky and the room becomes oily with the smell of childhood, of Sundays at Grunnie's little house in Fremantle. A peek under the foil: chicken, gravy, onions. Allee-Cat yowls, stands against her leg, his paws stretching up to her thigh.

And who asked you to dinner?

There's a note inside, barely legible. She puts on her glasses and holds it under the light.

> Laura,
>
> Any change with Cooper?
>
> Will knock on your door on the weekend with a bottle of red—a new Merlot from Mt Barker. Nice. In the meantime, some sustenance. As Sancho says in *Don Quixote*: All sorrows are less with bread. The fact that it's said to a donkey shouldn't make it any less true. Or so I hope.
>
> Gideon

Half a stick of French bread is wedged between the foil and the esky wall. She breaks off a piece and puts the chicken casserole in the fridge.

The bread is sorrow itself, a lump in her mouth, expanding. She gives herself a good shake. What's she got to be sorrowful about? It's good news. Good. *Signs of elevated responsiveness.* It means Cooper might be coming out of the coma. She should be celebrating.

Allee-Cat rolls at her feet appealingly, purring loudly, still intent on chicken.

She's doing it again, trying to hold her heart steady in her chest. Cooper was struck on the head by a piece of roof timber. The MRI, CT and EEG aren't showing anything to suggest permanent brain damage but nor are they explaining his coma. The doctors are hopeful but the truth is: they don't know. And that's only part of Cooper's problems.

Multiple autografts, and more to come until he's ready for the pressure suit. A tracheotomy to help him breathe while inhalation burns heal. IV fluids, proteins through a naso-gastric tube, catheter. Pain that can scarcely be imagined, its constancy broken only by escalation when they scrub and dress the burn wounds. All of this he will awaken to. And to the grief of having to learn how to be Cooper again, or the new Cooper he must become.

And he will awaken to the questions.

Burning. She can smell it again.

So tired.

She looks at the envelope, unopened, on the table. It can wait. The past always waits.

~

The door creaks as she pushes it open, into the moist warmth of the shed. She loves being in here at night, the promise of metamorphosis by moonlight. A gentle anticipation bubbles along with the humidifier.

Crouching beside one of the metal tables, she watches the caterpillars, each suspended from a bud of silk. Not much movement yet. Too soon. Avril calls them *worms*, shudders at the sight, but Laura admires their brilliant tiger-striped bodies, smooth and soft and dry like the pads of a cat's paws. Who would believe that a speck of flydirt on a leaf of milkweed could become this gaudy creature, still less that there are other, more spectacular transformations to come?

Laura needs to believe in transformations of all kinds. That human skin can be regrown, synapses re-fired; that the millions of minute fragments that make up what it is to be not just *a* person but *that* person can be gathered like stars from the sky and reconfigured into a constellation just as beautiful so that the world may go on, please, as it was before, please, and surely it can be again.

On a bay-leaf branch, one of the caterpillars quivers, the slightest frisson of movement, and then begins to swing. Laura settles back on her heels to watch, never tired of witnessing this miracle. First the split—yes, and here it comes, the surprising bulge of green beneath the yellow and black stripes, which begin to peel back and fall away as the pupa contracts, eases itself free. And now for the feat that is pure alchemy: the pupa—wet, green and vulnerable—grows a cocoon for itself, a chrysalis in the shape of a perfect jade pagoda, collared with tiny studs of gold. In this, beauty itself will be created.

Laura struggles to her feet, her calf muscles cramping. Etching the silence now are faint scuffings as twigs move, leaves scrape leaves. Everywhere caterpillars are twitching. Poetry.

All this incipient life pulsing in the muted glow from the heater's light. It is soothing, like the snaking of narcotics through veins, an antidote to pain. Flushing sorrow away.

Avril

Avril is surprised to see Laura turn the corner from the car park in the grainy half-light, muffled up in wool. Early. She has a Landcare recycling bag over her shoulder and her hands are full. Avril grinds the newly lit cigarette under her heel, flicks it into a bin and waits, shivering. Calm, calm. Hands in pockets to keep them still.

Morning, Laura. That's what she intended to say. Instead:

The neurosurgeon's just been with him. They're doing more tests. They really think he could be coming out of it.

Laura tries to put an arm around her but is too laden.

Sweetie, grab these before I drop them, will you?

Avril takes two bakery bags.

I know, I know, Laura says. *We just have to stay positive. Come on, let's go up and talk.*

Avril peers into one of the bags. Chocolate croissants. Then the smell of coffee hits her. Cappuccino. The real stuff.

She falls in beside Laura.

It's good news.

Avril glances at her. Laura sounds emphatic but her face lets her down.

There's an argument going on in the foyer between a tired-looking security guard and a drunk with a cigarette. They skirt the scuffle, head towards the lifts in silence.

~

She waits outside the ICU while Laura pulls on the whites and covers her hair. She can see Coop from here, sees the way Laura goes to kiss him on the forehead, then checks herself—this same instinctive action neither of them can seem to stop. They can't kiss Cooper, no question of it; imagine the risk of infection if they did.

Avril turns away. Laura's back is to her but it's unbearable even to imagine the momentary anguish on her face when the reality of Cooper's condition descends on her again, the knowledge of what is yet to come. It's like watching herself, that renewed distress, every time she walks into the ICU.

Laura said she would say hello to Coop and then meet her in the lounge. A brief flirtation with the possibility of a cigarette, but no, there isn't time to go downstairs again. She picks up Laura's bags and takes a sip of coffee. Still scaldingly hot.

~

Avril perches on the edge of the couch, hunched over the table. She brushes flakes of pastry from her fingers onto a serviette, then folds it in half, in half again.

It isn't rational but I just keep thinking: it's not time, he isn't strong enough. Gut instinct.

Well, normally I'd never underestimate instinct, not about someone you love. There's something compelling, an antenna thing, a sort of wiring. But ... Laura reaches over, squeezes her arm. *But they told us from the start: it's unpredictable. Only Cooper knows when it's time.*

Avril nods, eyes on the napkin, folding it over again. *I'm staying today. This morning, anyway. I was going to call to let you know but you're early.*

Doesn't matter. We can take it in turns. The lines around Laura's eyes soften. *So you've cancelled your appointments?*

Yeah, only had one today. And Pascale. And they're both OK. Oh, and I forgot to tell you last night. Wendy Casley said could you call her.

Laura spoons froth from the bottom of the mug. *Mmm. Thanks.*

That thing she left, she said she didn't want to post it. Said it was old or something?

I haven't even opened it yet. She pulls the envelope from the Landcare bag, tears it open, turns over the package inside it. She studies the writing on the brown paper wrapping. An intake of breath.

Laura

When Avril goes back to the ICU to sit with Cooper, Laura leans back on the chair, spent. Just a few moments to gather herself. When she opens her eyes again, there's a moth flitting round the shade of the table-lamp. She waves it away, distressed, as always, at the prospect of fragile wings singeing against the hot light-bulb.

Why do they do that? she'd asked Gideon in despair one night, when one flew past her face and straight at the security light.

He'd pulled a beanie over his long hair and shrugged. *There's no definitive scientific explanation. We know it's phototaxic—automatic movement to the light. But as to why?*

He'd launched into a lecture, his fingers ticking off various theories: angles of light, mating, lunar migration … But Laura's mind had wandered. She was thinking of her butterflies, grateful they were spared whatever instinct drove these other hapless creatures towards self-destruction.

The brown paper package is on the table and Laura leans forward to trace the words with the tip of a finger. Her skin cools with the thrill of it.

For Laura
per Clementina Laing
Meggie Duthie Tulloch
April 1975

Blue ink, swirls and loops, a loose cursive that brings back other times, remembered through years of birthday cards and notes. Times when people wrote down what they thought on paper.

She gently peels away the brown paper and unties the string looped around three thick exercise books, worn at the edges, the covers spotted mouldy brown. She can smell time, and something sharp. Salt? More likely imagination. She always thinks of her grandmother when she smells salt. Grunnie's skin seemed scented with it, clean and pure like the sea. When Grunnie had told her, when she was a little girl, that she came from sea people, Laura had not been able to sleep that night, too fearful to close her eyes in case there were strange creatures from the past waiting in her dreams, seaweedy bodies dressed in the foam of the sea, staggering from the surf at South Beach to claim her.

The exercise books are inexpensive things, the kind probably sold by Woolworths long ago, but they feel substantial in Laura's hands.

She moves her coat, scarf and bag to the chair at the back of the lounge, furthest from the busy corridor. It's quiet, until other visitors arrive, but for the background hum of hospital noise. She takes off her boots and tucks her feet under her.

Do you remember when you were a wee thing, lambsie …

Tears fill her eyes. She hasn't been called lambsie for more than thirty years.

Avril

Ben stopped by earlier. Told a few off jokes that I'm not going to repeat. They all send their love, everyone at the station.

A minute movement of the dressings on his right hand—his forefinger maybe.

Coop?

She watches intently for another sign that her Coop, the real Coop, is responding to her voice, but it was probably just a random muscle movement. Dr Meagher has cautioned her to be patient. It could be days. But it could be hours—he said that, too.

Those guys. They're always here, always checking up on you.

Martine, busy unwrapping IV packs, eyes her curiously.

She lowers her lying voice. *Whenever they get the chance.*

A tap on the glass behind her. Laura. Gowning up. Ready to take her place.

Your gorgeous mother's here, babe. I'm going to go and have a piece of carrot cake for you.

Laura, pulling on mittens, looks rattled. Avril squeezes her arm. *You OK?*

Mmm. How's he doing?

We've been having a long conversation.

Laura looks like she's snapping out of a dream. *Pardon?*

Nothing. There's no change. So how's the reading going? What were they—your grandmother's diaries?

Not exactly. She pauses. *Recollections, almost like a long, long letter. Written in the years before she died. Her childhood, mostly, what I've read so far. Grim.*

Avril waits.

I ... Laura shakes her head. *She was a very articulate woman, my grandmother.*

Avril has seen photographs of Grunnie Meggie in Laura's family albums. There's one, in particular, one she remembers. A group of adults and children at a beach picnic. Laura had pointed out to her each person, explaining relationships, naming, but it was Grunnie Meggie who had caught her eye. Grunnie Meggie, looking straight at the camera as if the photographer had called her. Uncanny, like seeing Coop's features in an older face, a woman's face, the resemblance so much more than between Laura and Coop. Avril's own sense of ancestry is tenuous, at best, and she has always been curious about the things handed down through families, through time.

Laura?

Mmm.

Are they, um, are they very personal? I was wondering, if it's OK, could I——?

Yes. And yes, I guess. She was ... she was what you might call a character. There are things ... Maybe you'll see shades of Cooper in her. I do, sometimes.

Avril watches through the glass as Laura takes the chair beside Cooper. Goes to kiss his forehead. Remembers.

Laura

Laura rubs her eyes, sits up, alert, when the neurosurgeon arrives with a satellite of interns.

They run through the usual examination, notes, questions and answers. The students are focused solely on Coop, his chart, Dr Meagher's words. Only one, a slight young man with very white hair, throws Laura a sympathetic glance.

When they've finished, Dr Meagher looks directly at her.

Yes, Laura? You have questions?

The pain … how bad is it going to be?

Bad. But best you talk to the Burns Team about that. He softens his voice. *There are ways of managing pain.*

But not stopping it.

The interns look down, not one of them wanting to acknowledge what she is thinking, what is written all over her face.

No.

You've spoken to Avril?

Yes, I've just seen her in the lounge.

Her mittened hands stroke the sheets. She can't ask. Not again.

I'll tell you what I told Avril, Laura: Yes, he's strong enough. And no, we don't know.

~

Avril is in the chair in the corner of the lounge, twisted round so her back is to the door, her long legs looped over the arm. Sleeping, Laura thinks. Good. She needs it.

But when she tiptoes in to the lounge, Avril's head jerks up and she swings her legs round. Meggie's first notebook is open in her lap.

Ohmygod, Laura, isn't this amazing!

~

Two mugs of instant coffee. Two jam doughnuts from the coffee shop. Late dinner.

Eat, Laura urges. *Please. Not that it's healthy. I'm not even sure it's food.*

Avril pushes back the fringe from her eyes and bites into the doughnut. She examines the centre. *Did you actually get any jam in yours?*

Laura raises her brows. *Jam in a jam doughnut? Radical idea. If you're not careful, I'm going to have to make you something nutritious myself. Yes, cook! It won't be cuisine but it will be good for you.*

She watches Avril brush sugar from her hands into the white paper bag, get a disposable towelette from her bag and wipe each finger.

Avril, relax. There's nothing we can do.

I know. She is wiping her hands on a serviette now. Again and again. Eventually, she turns her attention back to the exercise book.

So obviously you never got these for your twenty-first birthday. That's kind of sad. Wonder what happened.

I don't know. She's written on the package 'per Clementina Laing'. Aunty Clemmie, Grunnie's dearest friend. She was Aunty Jessie's mother.

Do you remember when your grandmother died?

Oh yes. Because I wasn't there. Wendy and I were in India. 1975, so I would have been, what, twenty-two. She flinches. The brashness of her twenty-two year old self. *She was sick when I left. Leukaemia.*

And what about Clementina?

Hmmm. Laura frowns. *She died few years after Grunnie, I think. Must have been in her nineties, but nothing wrong with her mind—she was sharp till the end.*

Avril looks at the book again. *How much have you read, Laura? I'm about halfway through this. Can I keep going?*

If you want ... She looks at Avril curiously. *I'm about to start the second one.*

I ... Avril's fingers flex, and she looks down at them. *It's something to do with Cooper, you know?* She picks up the exercise book by the corners, careful not to let too much of its musty grime touch her skin. *What does it feel like?* She hesitates, her hand hovering over the cover. *I mean, this is your family story, where you've come from. I can't imagine ... I only ever knew one of my grandparents, and not for long.*

Laura feels flustered and shrugs. *It's ... I don't know. Ask me tomorrow when I've read more.* But when she glances at Avril, the awe on her face, Laura feels a rush of tenderness for the young woman her son married.

She puts the other two books in her bag and collects her things. *You'll call me if there's any news? Doesn't matter what time, OK?*

Of course.

And I don't suppose I can convince you to go home, let me stay tonight?

Avril shakes her head. *I'm OK.*

I'm worried about you, sweetie. You've had no sleep at all. Laura leans down, kisses the top of her head.

At the door, she pauses, turns back. Avril is already reading again. This is your family story now, too, she thinks. But as she strides towards the closing lift, other thoughts cross her mind, darker thoughts with lacings of superstition and silence and fear: Be careful what you wish for. What was Grunnie trying to tell her?

Laura

Laura rests the exercise book on the arm of the couch, stretches her hands before the weak shimmer of warmth coming from the heater. The watch slides loosely to her wrist. Thin, she thinks, downright skinny. So much for Grunnie's prediction of 'wifie's bones'. The smooth, white hands are unadorned but one finger still shows grooves made by the two rings she used to wear. Still, after all these years.

She turns up her palms, trying to imagine sores that would not heal, the speed of those ulcerated hands, the constant aggravation of salt and friction and freezing cold.

The phone rings, and she is there, panicking, panicking, but it's Wendy. A glance at the clock above the mantelpiece.

Sorry to call so late, Laura. I've only just realised how late. I don't seem to sleep much any more and I forget. I didn't wake you, did I?

No, of course not. I don't sleep much myself these days. And look, I'm the one who should be apologising. I meant to call you when I got home. Thank you for dropping off that package at the hospital.

I just wanted to explain about that, Laura.

My grandmother's journals. Laura looks at the exercise book facedown on the arm of the couch.

I thought that's what they must be, diaries or something.

Aunty Clemmie had them?

It looks like it. They were in a wooden trunk that had her name carved on the top, with a lot of other stuff of hers. I found it when I was clearing out Ma's house. I don't know, Laura … I don't think

Ma knew they were there. I'm sure she would have given them to you otherwise.

I keep wondering why your grandmother didn't.

No idea. But, Laura ...

Yes?

Where I found them. The fact that Ma didn't know. It's like they were hidden away.

~

Tea. More tea. She's her mother's daughter, all right. She used to chide Kathryn about it years ago. *Such an old-lady thing, tea drinking! So conservative, for an artist.*

Heavens, Laura, what's an artist supposed to drink? Absinthe all day? Kathryn's face wry and a bit impatient, her fingers circling in the air. *You've been watching too many French movies. And anyway, I'm practising to be an old lady.*

It had made her laugh. Her mother had always seemed old, even when she wasn't. It's probably how all daughters see their mothers. But with Kathryn, there was an anxiety, an overprotective fearfulness, that made her seem that way, as though ... As though what? It brings her to the same point she always reaches when she thinks of her mother. The point where she realises she never knew her from the inside. Maybe no-one ever knows their mother that way.

She picks up the cup and sips. It's a night thing, tea. During the day, she survives on coffee. But at night, tea, Russian Caravan, and always in a blue china cup that was her grandmother's. Another thing that was her grandmother's.

She opens the exercise book, with its lines of swirls and loops, some parts in blue ink, some in green and red. A gift of words her grandmother had knitted together for her more than half a lifetime ago. A special gift she had never delivered herself. It's a bleak world her grandmother is painting, bleak and strangely threatening, with things she's reluctant to tell. But it's a world Grunnie had wanted to pass on to her, for whatever reason, and it had been withheld—*hidden away*, as Wendy had suggested.

The line on the top of the page:

I will not forget you, Fish Meggie.

Her face softens. The words of Magnus Tulloch, her grandfather, Meggie's wee cooper boy. How Grunnie would have loved this accidentally wonderful naming of the great-grandson she never knew. He was born years after she died, but her mother hadn't said anything, had never reacted. Surely she knew? But maybe not. Laura has no idea what Kathryn knew about her mother's early life, or her father's.

Meggie and Magnus—love at first sight. How could anyone want to hide away something as precious, as miraculous, as that?

Avril

It isn't her imagination. It isn't coincidence. The movements are minute and sporadic, barely perceptible, but he is responding. A girl with an albatross feather is picking her way across broken synapses. A girl good at mending things torn and unravelled.

'It's come all the way across the sea, this feather,' Avril reads, *'an' blown up to the moors an' into a place it doesn't belong, never to be seen again, never to return. But I found it, Kitta, see?'*

She pauses to watch. No movement.

I wonder what her voice sounded like, Coop. I can't think of anyone we know with that kind of accent.

His limbs are still.

She reads again. *'I found it an' I brought it back, back to be near the sea again. It means ye'll come back, Kitta. I will always find ye, no mind what stranger-place ye go. Ye'll always come back to where ye belong because I will find ye, see?'*

She listens and waits. Sighs.

Oh, Coop, I love your great-grandmother.

Joley is suddenly beside her. *Avril, it's nearly three.*

I know. A yearning glance back at the bed. *I know, I'm going. And thanks, Joley, thanks for every blind night. I know I'm not supposed to be here so late. You're so kind, all of you, to let me stay.*

Both of them hear the noise. Like artesian water trapped within granite. Like subterranean pain.

Joley gives her a grim kind of smile. *A way to go, perhaps, but he's on his way.* She picks up Cooper's chart and writes.

Cooper is coming back! The little girl with the albatross feather turns around, to see if he is following her.

Avril is elated. Afraid. Panicking.

He's feeling it now, isn't he. The pain.

We're on to it. Joley is fiddling with the line, tapping a syringe. *What's that?*

Slow-release analgesics. He'll be on these continuously now. And ketamine, opioids, when we do the dressings.

Just words.

There are two kinds of pain, background and acute ... Joley stops what she's doing, rests a hand on Avril's shoulder. *Look, I know it's hard to stay positive but this is the best Burns Unit in the Southern Hemisphere. We know what we're doing, you know?*

Avril tries to smile and manages something that misses the mark.

Before she leaves, she leans in to Cooper and whispers. *Hear that, babe? The best Burns Unit in the Southern Hemisphere.*

His foot moves. That noise again, from the depths. Calm, Avril, breathe.

Follow the little girl, babe. Meggie's with you now.

Laura

Avril comes back from the Ladies' looking uncharacteristically pastel in a clean shirt of Laura's. *Thanks for this*, she says, putting a plastic washbag on the floor.

Deodorant, toothbrush, soap and washcloth, moisturiser for Avril's sallow skin. But no cigarettes, Laura suddenly realises. Not that she wants to encourage her, actually, but she should have thought to ask. It just never occurs to her.

She looks at Avril's too-long fringe, usually spiky but lank now from being clutched and twisted in her fingers, pushed back by her palms. Not much she can do to help there. But Avril won't go home now, not now, not until. And Laura can't blame her for that. She wants to be here if Cooper wakes. *When*, she corrects herself. When Cooper wakes. His brain undamaged. To all of this.

Avril has the exercise book again, holding it carefully by the edges.

Reading this, it's hard to believe she left school before she was fourteen. Did she ever go back? TAFE? Uni?

Laura shakes her head. *It wasn't like that back then. Not for women. But I remember she was always reading.* She smiles.

What?

Just remembered something Mum used to say: that when Grunnie discovered she could take out six library books at a time, she was like a woman who'd found religion.

Avril rests the book on the arm of the chair and gets a still-damp cloth from Laura's washbag.

Have you finished? Laura asks her, nodding at the book.

Mmm.

Laura waits, but Avril's scrubbing at something unseen on her hands.

Don't feel obliged to read the other books, she says gently. *There's a lot of ... sadness.*

Avril looks up in consternation. *No! I mean, please, I want to ... I really do. I feel like, I don't know, like she's talking to me, too.*

Of course you can read them, if you want to. It's just, with everything else——

She had guts, Meggie. Her sister, too. Do you remember her?

Kitta? I remember Grunnie used to talk about her a lot, but I never knew before now what happened to her. Laura's voice changes. *She died young.*

A nurse looks in, and they are on their feet.

They're going to do some more tests, Helena announces.

Is anything wrong?

Relax, Avril, it's a good thing. Really. But they've asked me to suggest you two go home for a while.

Mute, stubborn, both of them.

Helena smiles, resigned. *Yes, I told them it'd be a hard sell. At least go out for a walk, stretch your legs, get something to eat? It's a beautiful day out there, you know.* She half shrugs and leaves.

Avril slumps against the chair. *People keep telling me it's a good thing. What does that mean, Laura? I don't even know what 'good' would be for Coop.*

All Laura can do is hold her.

Avril

The little park opposite the hospital is still winter-green. Seagulls circle gracefully from the spire of the church, then land on the grass, strutting about like the litter police.

The sky is oceanic above them, white-capped waves of aquamarine. Avril lies on her back, head cushioned on Laura's rolled-up scarf, watching the sea in the sky.

Pretty cagey, isn't she?

Mmm?

She rolls onto her elbow, idly crumbling pieces of muffin on the grass. *Meggie. There's a lot she's not saying. Like this thing about the boy, Brukie's Sandy. She mentions him a lot. Have you found out what happened yet?*

Laura shakes her head. *No. She keeps promising to tell but I'm not sure she's going to. I was just about to start the last book. I'll read it tonight.*

Avril sits up, rasping her hands on the thighs of her jeans. She nods at the books in Laura's bag. *It's ... I don't know. Like she's standing next to you when you read. She's written not just for you but TO you. Like a conversation.*

With no-one talking back. I know. Poor Grunnie Meggie.

Why poor?

Well, I think she was probably used to me not talking back. Not talking at all. You know what it's like when you're that age.

Avril watches Laura picking at the label of a bottle of apple juice, shredding long curls of transparent paper.

I adored her when I was a child. I was closer to her than I was to my mother.

What happened?

Nothing, really. Nothing happened. But somewhere along the way I stopped noticing her. God, it's unbelievable. How cavalier we are about love.

Avril sees the sea-sky in Laura's face. *She would have known you loved her. Don't you think?*

Yes, and she would have forgiven me, too. But I'm ashamed, all the same. Love shouldn't be passive. You should be required to, you know, GIVE it. She was just there, always there, and it was like I forgot to love her.

Avril pulls her feet under her, cross-legged on the grass. *The second book—is it as dark as the first?*

The tide moves across Laura's eyes. *Oh god, yes. The things that happened ... And wait till you read about the gutting. Incredible, really. But it's not all dark ...*

Avril sees light cast upon the breaking waves. Laura looks almost transcendent. *What?*

There's a love story.

Laura

A sudden shower, and the windscreen wipers do their best to slap away the rain as Laura drives home along the highway, trying not to think about Cooper's next round of tests. She adds *new wiper blades* to a mental list of things that never get done, and by the time she reaches the turnoff she's thinking again of her grandmother and a grandfather she never knew. He is real to her only as a black-and-white image, one of those remote, colourless men who gaze stolidly from old photographs as though their duty to endure marriage, children, life, is a wearying thing. The Magnus Tulloch of Meggie's story is nothing like that. And to have had the kind of love when you don't just see the other but recognise them, know them to be *that* person, as her grandmother had put it. And to be recognised in return? *Imagine that*, she breathes, shaking her head. It must be why Grunnie never married again.

She slams the car door, and her boots crunch across wet gravel to the shed. A slight hum reassures her that the heater and humidifier are working, it's warm enough. She won't open the door, let the cold night in.

Inside the house, she turns on the heater and watches the bar slowly change colour. Grunnie's last book is on the couch. She's anxious to read it, hoping for light in her grandmother's life in the 'new world'. She hadn't told Avril about Kitta, or about the little boy who flew off the cliff. She'd hinted, she'd warned, but Avril was avid for a love story, and you could not have one without the other. What was it Grunnie had said in her quaint way? Joy and grief—you have to kneel to both.

She jumps when the phone rings.

Hello?

Hello yourself. Gideon. *Saw your car drive in. Could you stand a bit of company? A slice of spinach-and-fetta, perhaps?*

She hesitates only a few seconds but knows it won't be lost on him. *Come on over. I've just opened a bottle of that South African Shiraz I told you about.*

You sure? Because——

Yes, I'm sure. And Gideon? Wait till you see what I've just been given for my twenty-first.

~

Gideon holds a glass to the light. It glints and flashes, the bowl changing colour.

He takes a sip. *Mmm. Peppery?*

Laura's no connoisseur; she just likes it. *I thought of satsumas, god knows why.*

He swirls a mouthful, considering, as she puts a bowl of olive tapenade on the table. *Satsumas ... the blood-red plum, the Shiraz grape. A marriage of vine and tree.* He grins. *You've an interesting palate there, Dr Ellery.*

He spreads olive paste onto a cracker and offers it to her. He's baked his own sea-salt crackers. Who does that? she wonders.

She shakes her head. *They look delicious. But I'm not that hungry.*

You're never hungry.

You're never not.

Muthic? This through a mouthful of crumbs.

OK, surprise me.

A guitar riff as she puts the pie in the oven. Tom Waits. 'Downtown Train.'

He's watching her closely as she tells him the news about Cooper. You can't put much past Gideon. A warm, reassuring hand on her arm but he's cautious with his words.

Well, that seems … positive. An inflection. It's a question.

Mmm is all she's willing to say, but she's thinking: Will he be brain-damaged? Will he be able to handle the pain? Will he remember? Is it better for him not to remember? If she speaks aloud her fears about Cooper coming out of the coma, they will be released, out there, and it's better not to give some thoughts air to breathe.

She pours herself another glass, tops up Gideon's and changes the subject. Because, for once, there is another subject. Meggie.

He's fussing in the kitchen, and she's letting him, and all the time he's firing off questions about how Wendy found the package, about her grandmother, and she's telling him about Meggie's stories and all Grunnie is holding back. She hears herself gabbling, the rise and fall of her voice, and it's intoxicating to feel … what? Perhaps just to *feel*.

The spanakopita smells wonderful. She flakes the filo crust with her fork, tasting the air, its nutmeg and butter and poppyseeds, the rich, cheesy filling.

Gideon leans forward, puts down his fork. *So, what's wrong?*

Wrong? Nothing. This looks sublime.

But you're not eating. You're … you're playing with your food there, missy. A laugh but it's a Gideon laugh, a tell-me laugh, hard to ignore.

She shrugs. And she's grateful for the sudden racket at the door, an aggrieved insistence that *somebody* do *something*.

Allee-Cat purrs smugly by the heater as they eat the spanakopita and talk about the gutting of herring.

Sure you don't mind having him inside?

As if I have a choice. Persistent, isn't he?

Yep. Easier to submit to his every whim, I've always found.

And no-one will get hurt?

He throws a look at Allee-Cat. *She's a faster learner, eh, mate.*

Gideon doesn't stay late, and gives her a quick hug before leaving. The cat, trotting at his heels, glances back from the driveway. A wholly approving glance, she thinks. The cat equivalent of a thumbs-up.

She pours the last of the wine, picks up Grunnie's book and settles back on the armchair to read, but has trouble focusing. Her eyes are blurred. What's wrong with her tonight? Taking off her glasses, she looks across to the empty grate of the fireplace, and for a moment it turns red and amber-gold in her imagination. She remembers her grandmother's hair, a washed-out sandy ginger, a shadow of the flaming red of the young Meggie she'd never seen but had been told about. Hair down to her waist. Grunnie always said her grandfather had begged her never to cut it, and she hadn't until after he died.

Meggie and Magnus. Her thoughts keep returning to the story of a gutting girl and a wee cooper boy.

Since Cooper's accident, Laura's been feigning a calm she doesn't feel, for Avril's sake as well as her own. But now she's been jolted out of it—ironically, by something that has nothing to do with Cooper at all: the utterly surprising revelation that there might be a shred of truth to all those romantic fairytales about *the one*. Kathryn had been divorced twice and heartbroken too often, and Dad hadn't been lucky in relationships, either. As for her own brokenness … well, she and Jarrad had been a mistake almost from the start, and if she hadn't lost him to cancer when Cooper was ten, no doubt the marriage would have stuttered sadly to an end. And then there was Michael who, after their six years together, said he wasn't sure. She declined his offer to hang around until one of them had a reason to move on, and after that had withdrawn. Being alone seemed preferable to the prospect of repeating her mother's unhappy pattern. But now, here's Grunnie Meggie—of all people—not only reminding her what it's like to fall in love, but revealing this unguessed-at artery of blood shared by two hearts; something you can live your life perfectly well without, in ignorance of its existence, but with which you are made complete. It isn't the romance of it—at least, not *just* the romance; her grandmother's words touch in her a seam of regret, a longing, for something never had. Too late, of course. It doesn't matter now.

Laura sighs.

Would she have responded differently, squeamishly, if she'd read her grandmother's love story as a brash, careless twenty-one-year-old? Maybe. Probably. But she would like to believe, instead, that her cruel, selfish younger self might have had the grace to recognise it for the immensity of what it was: hope.

Avril

Avril?

She looks up. The exercise book falls slackly on her lap.

Joley is leaning over her. *Are you all right?*

How to explain her tears are for a girl who walked into the sea more than a hundred years ago? *Fine,* she tries, but it comes out all wrong and she is weeping into the sleeve of the borrowed pastel shirt. She grabs her coat and her cigarettes. A helpless gesture of apology to Joley and she rushes to the stairwell. Inside the confined concrete space, she slumps on the bottom step, still weeping.

What now? she asks herself eventually. You're on the ninth floor, Avril. She contemplates lighting a cigarette but a fire alarm would probably go off if she did. Rubbing her eyes, she walks down to the next floor and takes the elevator to the ground.

There's no-one else by the ambulance bay in the still-dark morning.

... the bloody mess of a barely human thing. Meggie's words.

The wind howls and she squeezes her eyes tight to shut out the image of blood and mucus that was barely the promise of a life. Lost at eleven weeks. No-one knew besides Coop and her sister. There had been words, hospital words, antiseptic and quiet. *All too common. One in four. No-one to blame. One of those things.* Words to soften the only one that mattered. *Dead.*

OK, she tells herself, OK, enough now.

She hunches her back to the wind and struggles with the temperamental lighter, tetchy until that first inhalation. Aaaahhh. Hateful how good it is, how much she needs it to keep her steady through this, keep her going. Laura's right: she should eat. But she has more faith in nicotine.

A siren wails in the distance. Which reminds her.

Pulling her phone from her coat pocket, she dials Ben's number, knowing he'll be at the station, on duty, with his mobile switched off, and all she'll get is the familiar message: *Hear the beep, do your thing.*

It's an excuse, of course, calling to tell him what the doctors said. She wants to know what's going on. Why have they abandoned Coop? Because that's what they've done, no two ways about it. Ever since that article came out in the local paper. So much for *the team.*

Abandoned … She thinks again of Meggie's sister, who had never recovered from her loss. Who'd been abandoned.

Avril's eyes stream as she pulls her coat around her and turns into the wind. How much grief is enough?

~

There's a charge in the air as the elevator doors open on the ninth floor. Something's happening.

Joley rushes out from behind the nurses' desk. *I've been looking for you everywhere!*

She freezes.

It's good news, Avril! Joley's half hugging her, half pulling her towards the ICU.

Laura

As Laura starts gowning up, she can sense the change in her son already, feel it through the glass wall that separates the ICU from the world. He's lying on the bed, in much the same position. She knows his eyes will still appear closed, face too swollen to allow him yet to see. And he won't be able to speak, not until the internal burns heal and the tracheotomy tube is removed. And yet she can feel his awareness, of Avril sitting beside the bed, of the presence of the staff as they move around, of the room and all the paraphernalia keeping him functioning. Even of her. At first glance, you would think him no more conscious than he was yesterday, but she knows her boy is not only physically awake; he is mentally alive.

God help him, she whispers to a god she has no faith in. *Please, God, help him.*

Pulling on the mittens, she sees crescent-shaped gouges on her palms. Her fingernails have drawn blood.

~

The staff prefer only one visitor at a time, but Avril hasn't let go of Laura's hand since she came in. The tests show Cooper is responding to stimuli as he should, there is no mental impairment, and in spite of all the problems ahead, the relief, the joy, of knowing that is so profound that no-one's thinking about rules today.

When Avril finally takes a break, Laura moves in close to the pillow. *Welcome back, my boy.* It's all she can manage, this broken benediction.

Movement beneath the dressings on his face, a faint gurgle from his damaged throat. And it's like she can read it already, this new body language, these signs, this pain.

To distract him, she tells him about the Monarchs, almost ready, now, to be released; about the surprising cat who has taken a shine to her; about Gideon's cooking, which puts hers to shame. Not that that would be hard. *You remember Gideon? You met him once, briefly, when he returned the can of two-stroke. I think you two would get along.*

Martine wheels in a trolley and Laura moves to the end of the bed to get out of her way. There's a whole tray of medications, and Laura wants to know what they're for.

This one's slow-release methadone, Martine says, depressing the syringe into Cooper's IV. *He'll be on this all the time, for neuropathic pain.* She looks around at Laura. *From nerve trauma? Nerves take a long time to regenerate. It's a painful process.*

Laura watches Cooper's face, wondering how much is penetrating the narcotic haze of his sedation. He knows she's there, he can hear her, but do *pain* and *all the time* and *nerve damage* register? As explanations of what he's feeling?

Anti-inflammatories, Martine continues, emptying another syringe. *And steroids to help soften the burn tissue. A half hour before every treatment, we'll be giving him ketamine, too, to help him handle those. Physio, dressings—it's a more intense type of pain.*

Avril slips back into the room and sits beside her.

Martine pats the edge of the bed. *OK, there, Cooper?*

A low moan, gut-wrenching.

Laura glances sideways. Avril's face is the mirror of everything Laura is feeling. She looks like she's about to weep.

Martine carries on briskly, tidying away the plastic packaging, dropping used syringes in a special container, but her voice is sympathetic. *Look, I know how hard this is, but although he's* conscious now, he's still heavily sedated. He's not fully aware. Twilight, they call it, a kind of half dreaming.

Another groan from Cooper, and Avril grips Laura's wrist.

Dreaming? Laura thinks. Nightmare, more like.

Avril touches the pillow with her other hand. *How long before he can talk?*

You'll have to ask Dr Nguyen when she comes in. We like to get the tracheo out ASAP, get them talking, but …

Avril is still looking at her, expectantly.

Cooper's inhalation burns, they're severe. Could be a while yet. She flicks over a page on the chart. *Are you staying round tonight?*

Avril nods.

You'll catch Dr Nguyen, then. But for now, go get some coffee, both of you. Please. He's asleep.

How can you tell the difference between twilight and sleep? Laura asks.

Martine pulls off her gloves and smiles sadly. *They always sleep after being given their meds.*

~

Laura puts the cardboard tray on the table: two polystyrene cups of frothy coffee and two plastic-wrapped sandwiches.

Egg salad. Salad salad.

Avril pulls a face. *You're determined to improve my diet, aren't you.*

She passes over one of the cups. *I'll tell you what I'm determined to do: make you go home.*

Not tonight. I want to be with Coop.

Of course you do. She takes a sip of coffee. Predictably bad. *But tomorrow, Avril, when I come back, you're going home. You're going to sleep in your own bed, eat some decent food, wash your hair, phone Pascale, get yourself back on track. OK?*

Avril shrugs. Then surprises Laura with a resigned *OK*.

After a silence, Avril asks, *Have you read your grandmother's last book?*

No, my eyes ... A gesture of frustration. *But tonight.*
I finished the second one ... A long pause.
The little boy?
Um, yes. And ... and what happened to Kitta. She turns away.
Laura puts her sandwich down. *Avril?*

But Avril is running the sleeve of her shirt across her eyes.
When she turns back, she speaks to the floor. *And what it did to
Meggie. God, when you can't help someone you love. When you fail
them.*

Laura studies her daughter-in-law's pale face, the lids of her
eyes pink and shiny. And then Avril does one of those about-
turns typical of people under stress.

*But Meggie, she makes me laugh too. You know? Some of those
words she uses, and the way she slips in and out of them. Did she used
to talk like that?*

*She did, actually. 'Canna' this and 'canna' that. She always had a
strong accent, though I suppose it must have been even stronger when she
first arrived. I remember how cross she used to get when people asked her
to repeat herself. 'Laik I'm talkin' in anither tongue!'*

A smile from Avril.

But when I think about it now ... how ironic.
What do you mean?

*Well, Grunnie was someone who loved reading, loved poetry. She
found such pleasure in language. But language tied her to people she
apparently never forgave, a place she tried for a lifetime to leave behind.*

Avril picks at her sandwich for a while, disassembling it,
discarding rings of onion, bits of cucumber, lettuce, crusts.
Finally she looks up at Laura.

Do you think it's ever possible to do that? Just leave things behind?
What kind of things?

Avril shrugs. *Bad things.*

Laura watches Avril cleaning her fingers, one by one, with
antiseptic wipes.

After a moment, Avril looks up, and, flushing, seems to cast
about for other words. *I just mean ... Like you said, Meggie couldn't*

completely break away. The way she spoke … it was the language of a man who killed her little dog and thought girls were nothing.

Mmm. Laura frowns, pauses. *But it was her mother's, too, I guess. And her sister's, and Clementina's.*

Avril nods. *I wonder when Dr Nguyen's due.*

Well, sweetie, I'm just going to sit with Cooper a little while longer and then go. Laura stands and kisses the top of Avril's head. *I'll let you know when I'm leaving.*

She turns back at the door of the lounge, torn between wanting to remind Avril—again—to eat and a reluctance to bully her. The dissected sandwich has been pushed aside and Avril is frowning at her hands, scrubbing her palms. She looks up.

Laura? I've been reading Meggie's story aloud to Coop.

A shiver runs through Laura. A gust from the North Sea.

Gut feeling again. But I think, I've just got this feeling, he's been listening.

Avril

Sun is breaking through cloud here and there above the eucalypts. Avril tips her face up to it, and too bad about the UVs. It's too weak to worry about, she thinks, knowing it isn't true; that for her, the sun is never too weak to redden her skin and raise those small shiny spots that itch and burn. But she'll take her chances in return for a blue sky today.

She squints into it, and the clouds become a map of the safe world, the world Before. Her home, the herb garden, the fruit trees arcing round the house. The road stretching west into the village, with its pizza store, deli, fruit and veg market. Five k's in the other direction, halfway down the hillside, her mother-in-law's rustic house, Laura and her butterflies. The arterial road that connects suburbs in the hills and winds down to the city, branching off at the foothills hub: cinema, shopping centres, banks, post office, the fire station where Coop works.

Where Coop used to work.

She pinches the space between her eyes, blinks and the safe world disappears.

A car at the top of the drive. Familiar grey sedan. Oh no.

She dashes into the studio and flicks over the pages of her appointment book. There it is, a hurried pencil scrawl. *Ewan, 11.30.* And she's forgotten to call him.

He'd understand, she knows he would, but it'd be unfair to cancel. It's just lucky that she's here at all, that she'd let Laura persuade her that now, more than ever, she's no good to Coop rundown and exhausted. Besides, she thinks, trying to convince herself, a bit of normality will do her good. A piece of the safe world pulled down from the clouds.

She looks in the mirror over the basin, then through the window. He's limping up from the parking bay by the lemon tree, puffing a little, head down.

Hi Ewan, she calls, flying into the house. *Let yourself into the treatment room, will you? Door's open. I'll be with you in a moment.*

~

After the session, she notices he's standing with a protective hand on his lower back, right. She nods at his hip. *How's the pain?*

OK. Stiff more than sore, he mumbles. *She'll be right. Always good by night.*

Well, put a heat pack on it every few hours. And the gel after that. OK?

Yep, he says. *Righty-o. Good news about yer bloke, Avvie. Tell him good luck from me, eh. Bloody miracle.*

She hands him back his card and receipt but he's easing himself into the chair, making himself comfortable. He's not going.

Reckon he oughta get an award for what he did. He shakes his head. *What-I-mean-ter-say, a medal or something.*

She shakes her head. *He'd hate that, Ewan. He'd tell you he was just doing his job.*

Huh. He got that woman out, god rest her, and that little girl woulda died, for sure. A hero, he is, straight up.

Yeah, she thinks, he is. She stands, and Ewan gets the message.

All right, then, Avvie-luv. Call you next week, eh.

Laura

Laura sits where she has sat these last weeks, watching for breaths, for the rise and fall of her son's strong heart. She becomes aware of a restless staccato, her boot tapping on the lower rung of the bed. No. Stop that. Cooper has enough to worry about without absorbing her unease, too.

Could Avril be right? Is he listening for Meggie's voice, waiting for her story? Laura's boot starts tapping again. She won't be reading him anything, not from this last book. A sudden wave of nausea rises, plummets. To discover this child-uncle, this Steven, and then to read of his terrible death. And her grandfather—she'd known he'd been in the war but not much else, and she can't remember now whether it's because she'd made assumptions and hadn't asked, or because she'd been fobbed off.

Tap–tap–tap.

And Kathryn ... all her mother's contradictions.

She shakes herself, a determined shedding, and concentrates on Cooper, aware but not. In twilight. What is it, this twilight?

Laura looks around the room as if for the first time. Imagine emerging from a void into the shock of this singular space. A blur of moving figures, fixed shapes going in and out of focus, metal and white linen and digital numbers blinking green. Conversations among staff—lives going on as normal—and the realisation that you are the centre of everything and you are nothing, and it matters that you can think but what you think does not matter.

Eyes but no faces. Arms without hands. An occasional laugh, the burr of a phone, the gush of water from a tap. Low-pitched emissions from machines. A persistent, terrible pain, source unknown, suddenly raging violent, until it releases and you drift, carried along, fade-in-fade-out, and you know there's someone by you, someone you love, but you cannot speak and you should know why but you don't, and where are you? What are you?

Mere speculation. She has no idea what Cooper is feeling. But it's not difficult to guess what he would want to know.

Cooper ...? she ventures.

A minuscule movement of his head. He's listening.

She tells him where he is. She tells him why. And she tells him his Avril is OK.

She will not tell him that love is as fragile as a butterfly, that everything disintegrates, nothing lasts.

~

A young woman arrives with what looks like a tub of sewing materials. She introduces herself as Tara and shows Laura a sample of fabric for the pressure suit Cooper will wear twenty-three hours a day for more than a year, perhaps several years.

Laura blanches, and points to the door of the ICU; she doesn't want to have this conversation in front of Cooper.

It looks like lycra, she says in a low voice.

You're right, Mrs Ellery. Tara holds up the swatch, lays it across Laura's arm. *Feel it. A nylon–lycra blend. Very soft, but strong. I use silk thread to stitch the pieces so everything's smooth, no irritations.*

Laura glances over at Cooper's dressings, which protect the newly growing skin knitting itself between the spray-on cells.

Tara guesses what she's thinking. *The grafts are delicate, but soon they'll have taken well enough for the pressure suit, and it will help to keep the tissue pliable and smooth.*

Isn't it painful?

Getting it on and off is, yes, but he'll have extra meds for that. And once it's on, and he's used to it, he won't feel comfortable without it.

She smiles at Laura's disbelieving face. *Honestly. It's what they say. Every burns patient I've worked with.*

How long before he starts wearing the suit?

After I take his measurements, it's about four days to make it. Then it's up to the team to say when he's ready.

Laura looks across at Cooper again, at the multiple dressings that form the shape of her son, that cover the infinitely fragile tenderness in the process of becoming skin. How could he ever be ready?

Tara gently touches her arm. *Excuse me now, will you? I need to talk to Cooper, get to know him, let him get to know me a bit. It's … not easy, being measured.*

From the other side of the glass, Laura watches Tara. She can't hear what she's saying to Cooper, but there's a warmth about her, an air of reassurance. Respect. The curtains are drawn around Cooper's bed, and it dawns on her: the vulnerability involved in *being measured*. The full exposure.

Avril

The phone rings. Pascale. A wrinkle of guilt. She'd meant to phone her sister as soon as she got home, to tell her the news.

Tucking the phone between shoulder and ear, she pushes down the button on the kettle and up-ends a near-empty box of teabags.

They want to keep the trach tube in for a bit longer but Dr Nguyen's going to change it for another kind that will let him talk. If his vocal cords aren't too damaged, that is. He won't sound like Coop but he'll be able to communicate.

His voice will be different, you mean? Why?

Avril pushes back her fringe and frowns. *It's to do with how much air passes across the vocal cords. Something like that.*

Like people with cancer who speak through those box-things?

No, just hoarse, I think. Raspy.

Mmm.

It means the investigation into the fire can be finished. They've been waiting to talk to Coop.

Av? What's wrong?

She's twisting her hair into rat tails. *I don't know. Just … there's something they're not saying. And the guys from the station, even Ben, they haven't been to the hospital in ages.*

Look, stop worrying, OK? There are more important things.

Yeah. But both of them know it's not as simple as that.

A pause. Pascale is building up to something. *Listen, Av, how're you doing for cash? You OK?*

She manages a half-smile. It's always been this way, Pascale looking out for her. *We're OK. Coop's covered through the fund. His wages are still going in. For now, anyway.*

But you're not working, are you, not your usual hours, I mean. No-one's covering you …

We're managing. The mortgage's being met, that's the main thing.

Must be costing you a fortune in petrol, too, driving up to the city every day.

Petrol and parking, but that's about all. She knows it's a mistake as soon as the words are out.

Hmph. Doesn't sound like you're eating! Avril, listen to me——

Sis, stop worrying. But thanks. Love you.

When she hangs up, it occurs to her: has she even looked at the bills this week?

~

By late afternoon she's back at the hospital. Not the day of rest she was ordered to have, but she needs to be with Coop.

She looks into his face and is elated. She can see the blue of his eyes.

His hand moves, as though reaching out.

Oh, Coop.

Impossible to hold him so she wraps him in home, in a skein of words. The herb garden (she doesn't mention how neglected it is) and the moon last night and willy-wagtails in the birdbath. Early buds on the lemon tree and parrots taking the last of the mandarins. Encouraged by the sense he's responding, she tells him about the giant zucchinis that keep appearing on the doorstep, courtesy, she assumes, of Murray and Beth next door—*So thoughtful of them, but how many zucchinis can one person eat?*—and tosses in the argument she's just had about a wrong entry on their credit card statement.

Martine's there, preparing a syringe, but Avril carries on talking as if she and Coop are in the kitchen, cooking dinner, chatting about their day, and not in this place where there is no privacy and no home and only one person talking.

$159, can you believe it? Tran's Fish Spa, Kuala Lumpur! Told them I've never been to KL in my life and I don't understand why anyone would pay to have the soles of their feet eaten by slimy goldfish! God, I'd rather stick pins in my eyes. Damned bank. She peters out, glumly. *Don't think they believed me.*

Martine fills her in about the pressure suit as she injects Cooper's IV. *He's floating a bit. We upped the meds while he was being measured.*

Avril speaks quietly, uncomfortable to be discussing Coop as if he isn't there. *That sort of gurgling noise in his throat—is he trying to speak?*

You mean when you were talking just now? Martine's mouth twitches. *About the bank?*

Mmm.

Martine pats her hand, a sort of dry *there, there* gesture. *I think, my dear, he was trying to laugh.*

~

Avril sinks into the chair at the back of the lounge with a cup of coffee and switches on her mobile. A text message from Laura:

> Hi sweetie. C had hard time afternoon but v alert before then. Have left M's last book in lounge. Troubling. Will talk morning. Lx

Yes, there's Laura's Landcare bag tucked between the chair and the wall.

The exercise book is inside, and the grimy cover's been newly encased in clear plastic, the folds neatly taped on the inside, just like her schoolbooks used to be. Laura. So she won't have to handle it. How well her mother-in-law knows her.

There's a note inside:

> Avril, pretty disturbing stuff in this one—can't help hoping you'll leave it for another time. Let me tell you up-front so

you're not compelled to read just to find out what happened on the 'Lily Maud': the last pages have been ripped out. Seems Grunnie's taken that story to the grave.

Lx

Laura

Laura's nervous when she picks up the phone and dials. It rings and rings, and then disconnects. Reprieve.

She crunches another Gold Seal peppermint but can't get rid of what must be the idea of burning, not the smell of it, because nothing is burning, is it? To convince herself, she goes outside. The moon is high over the dark silhouette of salmon gums—beautiful—and she takes a deep breath of cold, clear night. There's a drift of woodsmoke; most of her neighbours have a slow-combustion stove. But that's not it, not the sweet, fetid trace she can smell.

A thump on the table, then a bump at her elbow. A hello. An enquiry.

She runs her hand along Allee-Cat's warm back. *I could get used to having you around.*

He slips through the door with her when she returns to the house, and she doesn't bother protesting.

She dials again. This time, the phone is answered after a couple of rings.

Hello, Wendy, she says, tentatively. *It's Laura.*

~

A soft knock on the door. Laura puts down her book and looks at the clock over the mantelpiece. Nearly midnight.

Gideon's huddled in an anorak and stamping his boots, and the air that comes in with him carries the promise of frost by morning.

Sorry, late, I know, but you haven't seen …? He looks over to the mat, where the heater is doing its best to warm the room. *Ah, you have.*

Allee-Cat gazes back at him through lazy eyes, smug and purring like a freight train.

Oh, Gideon. What's the matter with me? I forgot he was there!

~

Laura's feeling heavy-limbed, warm from the port. She tops up their glasses, slopping Lamont's Tawny on the coffee table. She'd wanted to ask Gideon about genetics, about Dawkins and Darwin and Haldane, but her brain is too woolly now, too fuzzy and full of different questions.

Can't stop thinking, she says. *Grunnie wrote a list of things she wanted to tell me on the inside cover of the last book. Everything ticked. But the last one, 'Brukie's Sandy', has been torn out. Something from way back, her childhood. She said she couldn't bring herself to write it down at first.*

Gideon frowns, trying to remember something. *'You have often begun to tell me what I am, but stopp'd.'* The Tempest?

Oh yes, Miranda says it. To Prospero. Exactly! Another sip of port. *And then, when Grunnie finally does write it down—well, I'm presuming that's what it is—someone tears it out.*

And your friend definitely doesn't have the missing pages?

She shakes her head, helpless. *She looked again for me, bless her, went through everything in Aunty Clem's trunk, but there's nothing else of Grunnie's.*

Gideon tilts his head, considers. *Makes sense.*

What do you mean?

Whoever ripped them out would have probably destroyed them.

Oh. Laura sighs, deflated, and stares at her glass, the rich red glinting in the light.

Maybe your grandmother tore them out herself.

Laura looks at him, suddenly alert again. *So …*

Which means she was the one who destroyed them?

She shakes her head gently, her glass tipping, spilling port on her jeans. *I don't know. There was something she needed to say.*

The mantel clock chimes twice, and Gideon puts his empty glass on the coffee table. He looks across to the heater. *On that note, sir, time to go.*

Allee-Cat yawns disdainfully over his shoulder and stretches.

Laura's still staring into her glass.

What else's worrying you, Dr Ellery?

She looks up at him, this rangy man with his fisherman's pullover, his wild greying hair, her grandmother's notebooks tucked under his arm. It's late and she's just sober enough to know that what else is worrying her is far-fetched, doesn't make sense.

You're the one who should be worried, she tells him.

How so?

Because one of these days, I'm going to have to cook you dinner.

Avril

It's as quiet as it ever gets in the ICU, early-morning quiet, when Avril slips in to see Cooper. She whispers hello, and knows he hears her, his eyes blinking, the slightest inclination of his head towards hers.

She slumps down in the chair, rakes a hand through her hair. She's dazed from sleepless hours in the lounge, from the accumulation of tragedy, the scream of a child with his mouth full of sand. Coop's great-uncle. Two cigarettes and ten minutes in the wind tunnel between Admin and Emergency couldn't clear her head. Her eyes feel gritty, like they've been floured.

Joley puts a hand on her shoulder. *Avril, physio's on her way.*

Code for *Not a good time, you'll have to go.*

Coop seems agitated, anyway, moaning and restless, and she's helpless, unable even to stroke his face, watching the ebb and flow of chronic pain from tissue inflammation and nerves rebuilding their chains, making new synaptic connections, receiving messages. It's a relief to see the syringe in Joley's tray.

She rests her head a moment beside Coop's on the pillow and whispers, *Back soon, OK?*

There's movement in the gowning chamber, someone already in white, pushing clumsy fingers into cotton mittens, but one of the nurses stops him entering the ICU, gestures towards the door. He begins discarding the gloves, unclipping the gown.

Huh, Avril mutters, *it's about time.*

~

When she gets to the visitors' lounge, he's there, and Laura has just arrived, too. Probably just as well, Avril thinks, because Laura's being her usual calm, generous self, which may encourage her to be calm, too. Which is not how she is feeling.

Hello, Ben. Edgy.

Avril!

He envelops her in a bear hug and she's almost undone. It's like being held by Coop—wrapped up, safe. The rasp of his chin on her forehead, the warmth of his sweatshirt, the soft, worn fleece; oh god, and he smells like Coop, coffee and toast and that paint-stripper shampoo he buys cheap from Priceways. But it's Ben, who hasn't been in for weeks and hasn't phoned and could have told her what he knows and hasn't. Avoiding her, abandoning Coop.

She pushes away from him and sits on the armchair, upright, tense.

He flops down opposite. *Look, I know, I'm sorry.*

Avril puts her head in her hands.

You don't know, Ben. Laura's voice is soft. *She's been waiting, we've both been waiting, and no-one's telling us a thing.*

Avril looks up at him. *Where have you been, Ben? You, his mates. Where have you all been?*

He's silent for a moment, and when he speaks she doesn't understand.

I had to tell them at the debrief. It was my fault, but I've only made it worse for Coop.

What are you talking about?

He took the call on the way back to the station from Training. He was first on scene because of me.

Avril stares at him, confused.

Before the call came, he'd dropped me off at the garage. To pick up my car.

The words settle in silence. *He shouldn't have done that, should he*, Laura says, eventually.

Ben looks down. *My fault he did.* He shakes his head. *Shit, it was five minutes. I got back, he wasn't there.*

Do you know what happened, Ben? Laura's still calm, still gentle.

The neighbour says they could see the woman through the window. She was unconscious and it was a snatch-and-grab, clear entry, clear exit. Low risk. Anyone would've done it. But then the guy tells him there's a daughter, doesn't know whether she's at home or with her father. Means doing a search.

Avril closes her eyes. Standard Operating Procedures. Never do a search without backup. Never go in without breathing equipment. Never go in alone. Oh god, Coop.

The neighbour was at the top of the driveway, waiting for the ambulance. He didn't see Coop go in again. I don't know why he did it. He knows it's … Ben's hands rake at his hair. *This is why they can't complete the investigation. Until he can tell them.*

Avril is intent. *None of this explains why you've all been staying away.*

It's an internal matter until the investigation is complete.

Oh, come on, Ben.

He looks down, hesitates. *It's been … difficult. That newspaper article came out and, you know, all the usual hype—'bravery', 'risking his life'. Calling him a hero.*

Well, you know what Coop'd think about that.

Yeah, but there are a lot of people angry.

It's Laura who interrupts, Laura, whose calm has vanished. *Angry! He rescued that woman and he nearly died saving the little girl. For god's sake! Have you SEEN him, Ben?*

Silence.

Ben?

He glances up briefly, then down again. Avril feels like slapping him. She leans forward, and her voice is acid. *Seventy per cent burns and the other thirty's on the inside of his arms and chest, and do you know why? Ben? You do, don't you. Because he used his own body to protect that child. He was shielding her until the beam hit his head.*

He's still not saying anything. Avril turns away in disgust. He knows all this. They all know.

Laura is direct: *Just who, precisely, is angry—and why?*

There're reasons for SOPs, Laura. Ben looks up at her, then at Avril. *Phil Battersby got hurt, getting Coop out. Getting that beam off him.*

His words are like a punch. Avril feels sick. Laura's looking at her with the same winded expression, because in that instant, they both understand.

Is Phil OK?

It's his back, lower spine. Pretty bad. He's had a rough time.

Why didn't anyone …? Laura's crying.

He's still a hero, Avril thinks, clinging stubbornly to the loop of words repeating in her head. Tell that little girl's family he's not a hero. *He saved a child's life*, she says, but it sounds like a whimper.

Ben nods. *And you should be proud of him. Bloody hell, I'm proud of him. Plenty of guys reckon they'd do the same if they had the guts. But … it's complicated.*

~

I'm not going home, she announces after Ben leaves. *I'm not driving. I'd probably wrap the car around a tree.*

OK, sweetie. Laura's distracted, agitated, hugging herself like she's trying to stop shivering. *Want some coffee?* she adds, as though remembering where she is.

Suddenly Avril's exhausted. She doesn't want coffee. She doesn't want to talk. She gets up and feels in the pocket of her coat for her cigarettes.

When she comes back upstairs, Laura's in with Coop, so she curls up in the armchair, her back to the world, the sweet, comforting smell of nicotine in her hair.

Laura

Twenty-eights shriek and rustle high in the salmon gums, sending down a dust of dry leaves. Laura shivers on the verandah, hugs herself. The smell of burning is overpowering.

Cooper.

He'd been fearless the whole of his life, diligent, strong. Always disdainful of rules that got in his way when he thought he was doing the right thing. Reckless, Jarrad used to say of their son when he took on bullies at school, never afraid to risk a walloping from older boys, bigger boys. But there's only a breath between reckless and brave, isn't there, and in that breath is where you'd always find Cooper.

She goes inside for the bag of peppermints. What's wrong with this family? First her grandmother, then her uncle. And her mother, who would have followed Steven into the well if she hadn't been pulled back. And now her son. Is there a gene for sacrifice? It's like there's some dark strain of altruism, some ancestral compulsion to rush off a cliff, down a well, into a fire for others. And to hell with the risks.

She shivers. Grunnie, what else did you want to tell me?

She remembers what Gideon had suggested, that it was Meggie who had torn out her last story, the one it had taken her so long to write. Something had occurred to her when Gideon said that. She rummages through the kitchen dresser, third drawer down, yanking it out and turning it upside down on the table to search for an enamel keyring with a Lockwood key.

Those missing pages. If they exist—*if*—there's only one place they could be.

She glances at the clock, hesitates before picking up the phone.

Gideon answers on the sixth ring. He sounds distracted. *What are you doing?* she asks.

Making moussaka. I've been told it's deadly, which, according to the grandchild, is a good thing. Give it a try?

When you've finished, how would you feel about giving me a hand to shift some furniture?

~

Gideon turns up with the old blue ute, the one he uses for mulch and fertiliser. *In case you want to bring anything home.*

Don't think I'll be needing a ute for what I'm looking for, she says. *But thanks. Thanks for everything, Gideon.*

He reaches over and rests his hand on hers for the briefest moment and she's surprised and as fluttery as a bird. Stop it, she tells herself. He's just being kind. Just being Gideon.

She tells him what Ben said.

Soooo … Cooper's superiors are probably in a bit of a dilemma because he's a hero but he's broken a few rules?

I'm waiting to hear what Cooper has to say about that.

Will there be repercussions? I mean, will it affect his medical insurance, say, if it's proved he did the wrong thing?

She frowns. *I don't think so. Oh god, I hope not.*

So his colleagues are divided?

Mmm. A lot of them know they would have done the same thing where a child's at risk, but he broke SOPs and one of his team got hurt. It's drilled into them: putting themselves in danger means putting the team in danger. It's supposed to be sacrosanct, a line never crossed.

And being lauded in the press, that must be rubbing the salt.

It's the whole 'bravery' label, public perceptions. A lot of firefighters resent it. And yet the adrenalin rush, the chance to play hero—I've heard Cooper say it's why some of them go into the force in the first place.

She turns her face to the rain whipping at the window. And you, Cooper? What about you? *Ben's right: it's complicated.*

When they cross the railway line, into a bleak industrial suburb, she directs him, by memory, to a low warehouse complex sandwiched between two salvage yards. He pulls into the front car park and lets her out to explain to Security that she has a key but not a code to get past the gates. It's not until she produces an invoice that they're buzzed through.

Laura shivers and winds her scarf around her neck as they run from the car to the units. She's trying to remember the way to 72B, the number engraved on the keytag.

Gideon breaks the silence. *You know, your mother's brother, the one who died in the well …*

Steven?

People would have called him a hero, too.

~

Every year, when the invoice arrives, Laura thinks about getting rid of the storage unit. She'd taken over the rent when Kathryn died, always intending it to be a short-term solution to a problem she wasn't ready to deal with. Her beautiful mother had been in good health, still working, strong—and seventy-seven, that terribly old-sounding number, had suddenly seemed too young for a heart attack, too young to die. The furniture and the filing cabinet, the welding gear, the potter's wheel, the works in progress—all of them went to the unit Kathryn rented for storing her ceramics and stone pieces and what her mother used to call *a whole lot of family junk.* That was twelve years ago. At one point, Laura had almost decided to clear it out and bring in a removalist to shift the rest to her shed, but it was around then that she'd become interested in breeding butterflies. A better use for a shed.

She turns the key in the lock, hoping the barrel mechanism hasn't fused or rusted, but it pops open with a click.

Bloody hell! Gideon's surveying the unit from a clearing in the middle.

She's dismayed, too. *God, I'd forgotten how much is in here.*

On one side, the furniture's been skilfully stacked, using every bit of space, a solid wall of it. But Laura turns to the other side, a loose hotchpotch of bits and pieces.

Actually, I don't think it's as bad as it looks. The packers I got to move the furniture from Mum's house did that stacking. The stuff she already had in here is this mess.

Thank the sodding universe for that!

They begin moving ceramic panels, fantastical mermaids, the wild-haired musical goddesses that were Kathryn's signature piece.

These are exquisite, he says, running a hand down the curve of a whitewashed double bass wearing a necklace of shells. *Your mother was the real deal, I had no idea.*

Mmm, I'd forgotten.

What are you going to do with them?

She frowns. *I should do something, shouldn't I. It's criminal to lock them away. Thank god it's dry in here. At least they're in——hey!*

He's moved a panel, and behind it is a wooden trunk.

Bingo!

It isn't a thing of beauty, ornately carved in camphorwood; it's weathered, of sturdy plankboard, with iron handles worn smooth by many hands. Laura sees a watery girl standing beside it, in pinafore and hat, her hands pressed together, looking out to sea. The girl turns and whispers: *The wide world!*

Something's carved on the curved top slat, between rusty studs. She blows across the surface and uses her sleeve to rub away the grit of decades—dust and spider webs, moth wings, mouse droppings.

Oh! Confirmation in crudely made letters.

MEGGIE DUTHIE

And an addition, smaller, cramped to fit:

TULLOCH

Her grandmother's kist.

~

Laura feels bad about refusing the offer of a late dinner at Gideon's, but she wants to explore the trunk. And she wants to do it alone.

Gideon unloads some of Kathryn's sculptures onto the side verandah and struggles inside with the trunk. Yes, on the rug is fine. Yes, she promises, she'll eat something. No to moussaka and Chianti, but yes to another time. He gives her a quick hug on the way out, an open-palm wave at the door.

Laura kneels beside the kist and tries to prise open the lid. It takes some work to move the hinges but then they lock into place and the lid falls back with a thud.

Disappointment.

Thin towels, once white, neatly folded. She lifts them out, layer by layer, but beneath them is more household linen: sheets, also thin, also with that sludgy look of old white.

And then something tucked down one side. Her hand touches paper. She pulls out a stiff sheaf of pages torn from an exercise book and holds them to her chest, struggling to breathe in smoky air.

April 1975

Dearest lambsie, your postcard just arrived. That beautiful mountain, with its crown of snow. Snow! All these years, but if I lived to be a hundred or more, never would I forget the touch of snow, what it feels like falling on the palms of your hands. I am glad to remember that. Glad you have made me remember. But there are other things, I remember them too.

And so I've closed the slatted window on the autumn sun, on the smell of rosemary and sweet alyssum. I've brought out my notebook again.

This is the last thing I will write for you, my lambsie. The last thing on my list, the thing I promised. I've not told the story to anyone before—not your mother, no, nor Clementina. Not even Magnus Tulloch knew. I was too ashamed at first to tell him and then ... well, it was one more thing, and there seemed already too many.

Is it right to speak of it now, after all this time? I have been thinking on this a long while, and still I don't know. Kathryn has never been one for looking back, and Clementina has told me plain to leave the dead where they canna hurt the living. Finished, done, gone. Perhaps it's true there are some things should never be told, that nought is to be gained by passing them on. Better they die like memory does—held for a time and then let to become ash. Cast on the water, or to the wind, or returned to the earth.

No, I just don't know.

You can decide, lambsie, whether to turn this page and read. But if you have come this far on the journey with me, I canna imagine you will do that. So it is down to me, after all, for good or ill.

I am sorry, my lambsie.

Brukie's Sandy

April 1905—only seventy years ago. It might as well be two hundred or more. That's how it seems when I look back now, like it was a darker century, a primitive time. But in 1905 that small village was edging closer to the bewildering world, thrust into change after centuries of none. Those old ways, all those old beliefs, stirred together with a pinch of God to keep the frown from the pastor's face.

That boy, that Brukie's Sandy, he wasn't like other boys, no. People called him simple. Or blessed of God. 'A great lumpin' gapus,' my brothers used to say. He loved Kitta, he did. She was kind to him, gentle, and he worshipped her for it. Pretty Kitty—that's what he called her.

But you know all this, lambsie, of course you do. I've told you before, aye. What I haven't told you is what else that boy loved.

In another time, he would never have gone to sea, blessed of God or not. But when our men and boys started signing on to the herring, well, beggars could not be choosers and Brukie's Sandy became a fisher boy for the few boats still going out. In the spring of that year, Granda Jeemsie couldn't manage the Lily Maud *alone. He had Brukie's Sandy and Gammy Jock as crew, one feeble and the other lame. Sailor Finney, too, for all the good that old one would have been. With his 'catamaracks', so he called them, he was every bit as dweeble-eyed as Mackie's Peter ever was. And Jeemsie, well, he was not so spry himself.*

That boy, Brukie's Sandy, he was a one for plucking the world from the sea. Driftwood, rope, slimy knots of net and weed, bonxie feathers, odd leather slippers, bits of wool, salt sacks, mittens, wax paper, eggshells,

Dutchmen's caps, syrup tins, skeleton fish, the beaks and broken wings of gulls. Once, he scooped from the swell a hank of long yellow hair with the skin still upon it. Gave them gooseflesh, it did, those hard, tough fishermen, but the boy stashed it away in his bundle like it was worth something.

And once, Jeemsie had to stop him from pulling aboard a half firkin of sodden grain wriggling with rats. 'Ye gaakie lad!' the old man cried. 'What have I told ye about the long-tailed fellers on the Lily Maud!' The kick of Jeemsie's seaboot busted up the rotting staves and flung the lot into the foam. And that boy, that Brukie's Sandy, he hung his sorry head, for he knew as well as any there were things a fisherman should never even say, let alone bring aboard a boat. But still he kept his eyes on the sea, for what it would toss up next.

So there was none surprised at how it happened. Aye, none at all.

This day in April, the day I remember, that everyone in Roanhaven would carry for all of their memory, it was dark as winter sky. The sea was eerie slow in its swell, as though gathering for something big but taking its time about it, aye. With Gammy Jock ailing in his bed, Jeemsie had put to sea the night before with a man short. Maybe he thought twice about going, but more likely he didn't. He lived for the times on the Lily, Granda did, to be turning a seaman's back on those left behind in Tiller Street.

They'd woken before the late dawn, worked the lines by lantern light, and when the lines were cast again the boy sat at the stern of the Lily, watching the sea, watching and waiting.

It was Sailor Finney who told Ma what happened. They didn't know a girl of fourteen was listening at the door.

He was a one, that Brukie's Sandy, a one with the grapplie hook, but this day the prize was just beyond his reach. Prize it was, too, the kind he always knew would come some day, if he was patient, if he kept both eyes on the sea.

A bottle.

And he saw, through the corked amber glass, that there was something inside it. A spiral of paper, a message from the sea. Imagine what faraway place it might have drifted from, what stories it might tell. Imagine!

So that boy, that Brukie's Sandy, he leaned out over the stern of the Lily Maud, *leaned out with the hook in his reaching hands.*

Did I tell you, lambsie, that they never learned to swim, those men, those boys, of the north? It wasn't just the promise of a slow and painful taking until your heart stopped, your blood turned white, if you fell overboard. There were things more terrifying than freezing, aye. Better to drown, it was, a fast decent droonin', than to fight the will of the Witch when she had you in her grasp.

Made hardly a splash at all, that boy, that Brukie's Sandy, when he lost his balance, reaching with the grapplie hook for a message from the sea. He toppled from the stern of the Lily Maud *in his gansey layers, his long oilie, his great hulking seaboots.*

As he fell, a rope from the stern. Snagging an arm.

A lifeline.

It held him there, held him for a time, struggling and kicking against the dragging weight of his boots. His face just clearing the waves. Gasping and gaping, he was, and swallowing the sea.

The sea, the sea, the Witch who must be appeased. For all that the world was changing, wrenching Roanhaven from its own little world, still the old ways held with those well stricken in years. And so it was that Jeemsie Neish, my granda, like those who came before him, believed it unnatural, believed it wrong, to get between the sea and the drowning. Because the sea must have its prey. Because, if cheated, it would take another in its place. Because anyone who interfered would be cursed and bring ruin on all. Aye, this was the order of things. So when that boy cried out and Sailor Finney went soft and grabbed the second grapplie hook to save him, Jeemsie Neish yanked it from the old man's hands and flung it away. 'The sea must have her nummer!' he roared at the old gaak, who knew as well as any, who knew better.

And then Jeemsie Neish stood at the stern of the Lily Maud. *He stood by and did nothing.*

That boy, that Brukie's Sandy, he took his time drowning, as is the way of the young and the strong. He held on, held on. Until the freeze in his fingers. Until the weight of the sodden gansey and oilie. Until the drag of his boots. Until the sea in his lungs. He just held on, crying for the Lord to save him.

And Jeemsie Neish stood by and watched that boy drown.

~

'Accidental death at sea.' That's what the newspaper over in Gadlehead said, and no-one in Roanhaven would say otherwise. They may have listened to whispers, the madman rantings of Sailor Finney. They may have suspected, they may have guessed. But never would they have spoken of it outside the village.

Didn't mean they condoned what Granda did, no. There wasn't one among them would have said that. And none could wipe the horror from their eyes when they looked on Jeemsie Neish, when they looked on any of us, his family. It was 1905, for the love of God, and they did not think themselves barbarians, did they? But they turned their backs on it, aye, they would not face what had been let to pass. It was knitted into the pattern of who they were, see, as much as it was into Jeemsie. To come right out and confront him, condemn him—well, that would be to condemn their old ones, all they themselves had come from.

It has taken a lifetime for me to see that the more afraid people are of the darkness, the further into it they will flee.

I don't know whether that boy could ever have been saved. Two old men and a grapplie hook? No match for the icy North Sea. For the Witch. Mostly likely they would have been pulled in to be drowned themselves. But I'll tell you this: I made a promise to myself that night I heard Ma crying for Brukie's Sandy. I swore that if ever God put chance in my way, I would make up for the wrong Granda Jeemsie had done. I would never turn from saving another to save myself. I would not stand by and do nothing.

~

There it is, lambsie, there it is. The past in all its shame. Writing has been a heavy, wearying thing. I think it may be true you will not thank me. And maybe I will change my mind, after all, and tear the pages from this book, spare you the terrible burden of knowing your family's shame.

But something has gnawed at me for the longest time to make this record of what happened. Maybe to honour that boy who sang silly songs and lolloped over the sands with my little dog, who showed me and Kitta his precious bundle from the sea. Who loved my sister. Aye, maybe that. And maybe because it's only now, now that I have grown old like Jeemsie himself was old, with eyes no longer black nor white, that I can imagine another view of it, a view from Granda's eyes. Could it be he believed himself to be doing the right thing? The only thing? The thing to protect the Lily, the family, the village, not just his wretched self, from the Witch and her curse? Was it torment to stand there, doing nothing? Did it haunt him the rest of his days? Could such a thing be true of Granda Jeemsie?

I don't know, lambsie. I just don't know.

And maybe I have needed to write of this to make my own peace with that shift in the world when everything changed. I look at the pattern of my life, lambsie, with its yarns of many colours—the blue stripes of my mother's apron, the blue of the sea that took me from that place, the other blue of your granda's eyes, the glittering greys of a herring's back, the purple silk that loops around my Kitta, the random greens, pinks, golds that gather Clementina and Stivvy, Steven and your mother, too, into the story. The snaking silver thread that stitches it all together and joins me to you, my beautiful granddaughter. It comes from what happened on the Lily Maud, that shift in the world.

As I sit here with your mountain postcard propped up against all these bottles of pills, hoping I will see you again, it comforts me a little to think of all I have written in these books, the life that I have made from the life given to me. And to see that from the greatest shame have come these things, the greatest joys.

Laura

Black cockatoos cry into the night. Laura looks through the curtainless window at the shapes crossing an outline of trees. She pulls on her jumper and scarf and goes out into the cold. As she shivers, hugging her jumper close to her body, a fleet shape darts from under the diosma hedge and disappears over the fence. Too small and liquid to be Allee-Cat. Too lacking in grace and manners. A rat?

The moon slips behind cloud and she picks her way around to the side verandah, boots crunching on cold gravel. Words sound in her head like verse. *Perhaps it's true/there are some things/ should never be told.* Words in a voice she still remembers, even now. *Perhaps it's true.*

Gideon has positioned the pieces all along the verandah. *Just for tonight*, he'd said. *I don't know how best to store them. You can tell me where you want them tomorrow.*

The moon floats out from the haze, and she can see them in silhouette. They're lined up like dancers, beautiful. *There are some things.*

Gideon's right. Kathryn's art is exquisite. She goes from one to the next, admiring the lines of her mother's goddesses, until it dawns on her that they are not goddesses, not these, not the musical figures with flowing hair that Kathryn was known for. These are from that new series her mother had been working on, was working on when she died. She remembers what Kathryn called them. The Swimmers.

A feeling of claustrophobia grips her. A squeezing of breath. Crouching down, she traces the limbs, the stretching, reaching limbs of a swimmer-child, arms extending upwards, reaching up through water, reaching up for air. A tremor.

It feels ... it feels like desperation. The swimmer is not swimming, the swimmer is drowning.

Perhaps it's true ... No ... There are some things ... This can't be. Her grandmother's words, her terrible story, must be changing the shape of the figures in the dark.

Laura runs her fingertips over the face of the next swimmer and finds it encaged, shielded by arms bent at the elbow, defensively. Desperate too, this one, but not a swimmer. She swings around wildly.

A clanging noise, metallic, hollow, as she trips and knocks one against another in her haste to get up, get away, flee from the figures. None of them are swimmers, none of them.

They are Steven. Her mother's rendering of her brother drowning as she watched. Drowning in sand.

Should never be told.

Avril

Cooper is more alert. He's following the orbit of white around his bed, Dr Nguyen and two interns. Eyes focused, concentrating, and then he looks across at her. Oh god. It's Coop. The real Coop. Come back to her, just as she knew he would. A softening of the iris, so intensely blue, an elongation of white. Silent greeting after long absence:

Hey babe.

Hey y'self.

OK, then, says Dr Nguyen, and Avril realises she's talking to her. *We're all set. The trach has to stay, I'm afraid, until we can get that inflammation down a bit more, but we'll change it to a double tube this week. And then, hopefully, Cooper will be able to talk—in brief spurts, anyway.*

She explains the way it works, that it requires Coop being able to cover the opening with his bandaged hand to allow air to flow over the vocal cords; that the swelling has receded, the inhalation burns healed, just enough to make speech possible.

When? Avril asks.

When will we do the procedure? In the next day or so.

And will he be able to speak straight away?

If it's mechanically possible—by which I mean, providing there's no damage we're unaware of—then yes. When he's ready.

When he's ready. Avril turns to Dr Nguyen, who's smiling briskly and almost out the door. *Will there be restrictions on visitors once he can speak?*

Only the usual. She frowns, quizzical, taking a step back towards Avril. *What's concerning you?*

Um, nothing. Just …

You need to alert the nurses if there's anything they should know, Avril, anything that will affect Cooper's recovery? Her voice rises. A question.

Avril looks back at Cooper.

Laura

Laura eases herself into what she'd always thought of as Gideon's old bomb of a car, without really noticing it. She's only recently learned it's a 1970s Monaro GTS. A prize. Red, of course. Weren't all Monaros red back then, acid red? *Picardy Red*, Gideon corrects.

Where're we going?

He's fiddling with the radio. Doesn't answer. She glances behind her and sees a wicker basket on the back seat, a linen cloth across the top of it. Something smells delicious. Warm pastry and cinnamon. Comfort food.

OK, so we're taking a picnic. Where?

He smiles across at her. *Not far. If Avril calls, you'll be no further from the hospital than if you were at home.*

He takes a turn, away from the highway, and Laura settles back in the seat. The sun, the motion of the car, the smell of cinnamon—soporific at another time. But Laura's fidgety, unable to relax.

Another turn, a slip road.

What's bothering you, Dr Ellery?

She blinks. Uncanny. She glances quickly at him and then at the narrowing road ahead.

Genetics.

Hmmm? He's frowning, quizzical.

Gideon, is there … is it possible there's a gene for heroism?

~

It's Laura's kind of picnic. Olive bread, cheese, ripe pears, an apple tart. A half-bottle of Pinot Gris. *Glass each*, he says.

She looks out over the falls, noisy with last month's rain, while Gideon reads the pages from Meggie's kist. Finally, he puts the sheaf on the blanket, face down.

It's a horrifying story, what the old man did, but your grandmother's message to you—it's beautiful, Laura.

She scratches at the grass with a twig, not trusting herself to speak at first. And then she looks up. *I'm not even sure there is a message, or if it's just the unburdening of some shameful secret. A stab at absolving family sin, perhaps.*

He shakes his head. *There's a stab at forgiveness there, Laura. Forgiveness is always beautiful, don't you think? And, undoubtedly, there's love.*

Laura looks away. *But you see what I mean?*

That it's some family legacy thing? From a biological perspective, no. Although there's an anti-Darwinist defiance in the idea that I rather like.

What d'you mean?

Well, Darwin's theory of natural selection is premised on self-preservation—to maximise the passing on of one's genes and, hence, one's genetic stake in the future.

She shifts restlessly and he waves a hand.

Sorry, you know that, of course you do. Well, the old man's superstitions about letting the sea 'have its prey' can be restated in the most basic Darwinian terms: survival of the fittest. You don't risk saving someone else at a cost to yourself. Meggie's resolve to do the opposite is biologically anarchic. He taps his chin with two fingers and smiles. *Yep, I reckon Allee would have liked that.*

I never thought I'd hear a biologist rejecting Darwinism.

Not rejecting, just acknowledging its reductiveness. Evolutionary biologists will tell you it's a whole lot more complex. Even old Darwin himself suspected that. And you know what? One of the things that stumped him most was altruism. He just couldn't account for it. Why do certain animals sacrifice themselves for the benefit of the group? Insect workers that devote their lives to the queen. A species of monkey that warns others of the approach of predators, making itself the vulnerable one.

He pours the last of the wine into Laura's glass.

Well, the old man toed the Darwinian line, she says grimly. *No problem with pesky altruism there.*

Are you going to give the pages to Avril?

Mmm, she says, frowning. *I don't want to, god knows, but I will. There've been too many secrets in this family.* She hugs her knees, rests her chin there. *And anyway, she'd never forgive me if I didn't. Meggie's real to her, you know? There's a connection there … something …*

Gideon's quiet for a moment, and then he looks up at the sun. *The old man—you know, I wonder whether the whole thing was rather bewildering for him.*

You're defending him?

Hardly. But imagine what it must have been like in 1905, a whole way of life sort of … collapsing. Suddenly you're shunned for upholding beliefs your people held for generations.

Laura swirls the wine in her glass without tasting it. *So you don't think there's a gene for it? This pointless self-destruction, I mean.*

I don't think there's a gene 'for' most of the things that get trotted out as genetic these days. He counts off on his fingers. *Gay gene. ADD gene. Fat gene. Huh. Forget individual variations in biochemistry; forget interactions with the environment, the social world. History. Chance. Choice. Forget the plasticity of living things. It's about as simplistic as the fishermen's superstitions—and look, they evolved as just a way of explaining the natural world.*

He pauses. Laura says nothing.

Comes down to this: something to blame, something to point the finger at, something we might be able to 'fix'. It's not only reductive, it's bad science. He lowers the cheese knife he's been waving around and shrugs, sheepish. *Ah, see, lecturing again. You shouldn't have got me started.*

He uses the knife to slice a pear, offers a wedge to Laura.

To get back to your original question: no, I don't think you've passed on to Cooper some altruistic death-wish gene. That's what you're getting at, isn't it? Look, leaving aside the question of compassion—which is what I think of when your grandmother speaks of 'not standing by and doing nothing'—sacrifice is kind of hardwired into our culture.

She picks at the pear, peeling off bits of skin.

All those men who went to war, like your grandfather. Both of mine, too. A lot of them were just kids, thought they were off to see the world, but many of them understood what they were doing and were ready to die for their country. Who can say where a conviction like that comes from?

Well, there was a lot of social pressure on them, she says slowly. *But patriotism ... I guess it's a kind of cultural inheritance. Like religion. And superstition, for that matter. Tribal. What was that term Dawkins invented for 'cultural genes'?*

Memes, you mean? Gideon snorts. *Now, if you want reductive ...*

But it's uncanny. I can't get past it. This, this LINEAGE. *Meggie, Steven, my mother. And now Cooper, ignoring everything he's been trained to do, going back into that house when he knew ...*

*Laura! There's no issue of lineage here. What about you? You've never—*he splays his hands, palms up, mock dramatic—*I don't know, thrown yourself in front of a mad dog to save a snail, have you? Seriously, your son wasn't listening to some ancestral voice in his head. He was doing his job. And saving a child's life.*

He wasn't doing his job, Gideon. That's just it. He didn't know where the girl was. He didn't even know if she was actually in the house. He just ran into the fire, blind.

Gideon's voice is low. *You don't know that.*

Laura's silent, crumbling a piece of bread between her fingers.

Look, Cooper may have acted a bit recklessly, he continues. *He probably did. But if he'd followed the rules, that little girl would be dead. Simple as that. Like Brukie's Sandy.* He looks at her over the tops of his glasses. *Laura, if he'd followed the rules, he'd have done just what the old man did.*

She stands abruptly, jolting the glass, spilling wine on the blanket.

Gideon joins her at the water's edge.

He nearly died, she shouts above the noise of the falls. *And now he's got so much ahead of him. He'll be struggling for the rest of his life.*

Yes. But never underestimate the capacity of the individual not just to adapt to change, but to flourish. It's one of the truly wondrous tendencies of the living world.

She's quiet as they walk back to gather up the picnic things, hands deep in the pockets of her coat.

A small self-conscious laugh from Gideon. *Hey, I'm sorry, that sounded a bit trite, but I was speaking as a scientist, not trying to trot out some new-age spiel.*

So tell me, as a scientist, what do you make of my grandmother wanting to atone for the old man's sin?

Oh god, Laura, I can't explain the impulse to save another person's life, regardless of risk, any better than Darwin could, or Allee, either. But your grandmother ... His voice softens. *I reckon she was a strong, intelligent, compassionate human being and it doesn't surprise me the least bit that she responded intuitively to a child in danger. If you want to talk lineage, I can list a few things you've inherited from her. And passed on to Cooper.*

She shuffles her feet, looks down. Offers him a peppermint. *But I reckon you'd just be embarrassed.*

~

There's something I want to show you on the way home.

He presses 'play' on the CD and she closes her eyes. David Bowie. 'Life on Mars.' Always surprising, Gideon.

They pull up in the driveway of an old weatherboard house. *Where are we?*

Lucy's house.

She raises a brow.

A friend. She's at work. I asked her to let me know if they came this year ... *Well, come on, it's easier just to show you.*

He gets out and she reluctantly follows, murmuring in protest when he unclips the latch on the side gate.

It's OK, he says, grabbing her by the wrist. *Lucy knows we're here.*

Then why are you whispering?

They are now round the back of the house. An old-fashioned garden of fruit trees and flowers and little paths of broken bricks. He puts a finger to his lips and leads her towards a tree densely leaved in orange and brown. Odd. An autumn tree. In early spring?

He stops, whispers again. *So they don't fly away.*

A hush of recognition that the leaves are not leaves. They are quivering, minutely fluttering, alive.

Oh, Gideon …

Thousands, there must be thousands of Monarchs clustering on the spreading branches of the loquat tree.

I don't believe it!

I know. Incredible, isn't it?

She is drawn forward, stepping cautiously. Bunches of butterflies are hanging like tiny bats, the colour of fire. *I've seen photographs of those forests in Mexico where they fly every year to overwinter, but never here.*

They've been hibernating for a few weeks. Just now beginning to awaken, getting ready to mate.

But …?

Don't know where they've come from. Or why here. You're right, you never see them aggregating like this in Perth. Apparently not anywhere in the West. But they've been coming to Lucy's loquat tree for three years now.

Has she told anyone about this? The museum?

Monarchs are an introduced species, Laura. The museum's not as interested in them as you are. He grins. *And now the novelty's worn off, Lucy's only mildly interested herself. Reckons she's done her bit for science by telling me.*

Laura feels the kinesis, the collective energy of all those tiny flutterings.

There's a Mexican legend about the overwinterers, she remembers.

They say they're the spirits of dead children returning home.

She stretches out her palms towards the light, the warmth of that pulsing life.

And you have no idea why they come?

He shrugs. *Absolutely baffled. But then, that's biology for you.* Another grin. *Never underestimate the element of chance.*

Avril

Two weeks later

Avril feels as though her muscles have turned to string and fibre, pulled taut, tight, out of tune. She can visualise the gnarling of trigger points, their build-up of lactic acid and toxins, up through her back and into the cervical spine. A sideways glance at Laura shows all her tension being held in the hunch of her shoulders. They are a pair. They are in a bad way.

Avril's up on her feet, Laura just behind her, when Tony Hadley puts his head around the door of the lounge. Station Officer, Cooper's boss.

Here you are, good.

He strides in, tosses a plastic file on the table, and takes command of the nearest chair, gesturing for them to sit opposite. He anticipates their anxiety. There's minimal smalltalk.

Well, Cooper went in alone for the child—and without the required personal protective equipment—but you'll be pleased to know he didn't go in blind. He looks from Avril to Laura and back again. *He knew the child was there, and he knew where she was.*

How? Laura demands.

The mother told him.

But the mother died.

In the ambulance. He consults the file and shakes his head. *Asthma attack, smoke inhalation, complications. But she regained consciousness briefly when Cooper brought her out. We knew that from the neighbour's statement.* He runs a finger down a page in the file. *She was coughing and struggling. Turns out, she was trying to tell them about the daughter, urge them back inside. But by then the neighbour's taken off to wait for the ambulance, run up to the road to guide them in. And that's when Coop's figured out the woman's trying to give him a key. Turns out, the key to the laundry door.*

Avril's hardly breathing.

Which explains why the investigator found it melted into the lock. On the outside.

Laura wants clarification. *Cooper went in through a back door?*

Yep. Room next to the kid's. He knew what he was doing. If the roof hadn't collapsed, it would have been straightforward, another snatch-and-grab.

They breathe, the two of them, and Avril clutches Laura's wrist.

He should have waited for backup and PPE but the fire was gaining, he had clear evidence of life in danger, and he used his judgment. Training. He nods vigorously. *Always the training. Proud to say it.*

And relieved you won't get hung out to dry, Avril thinks.

Of course, there's the issue of him being there alone in the first place, he adds, frowning at the file. *Ben Storer has been cautioned. There'll be no further action.*

He's up and shaking their hands, making assurances, expressing sincere regrets. Already moving on. It's clear Cooper's future lies outside his jurisdiction now.

When he's gone, Avril looks at Laura. Quiet, just sitting there. Stunned. She takes her mother-in-law's hand again and squeezes it.

So.

Laura squeezes back.

So.

Avril

Avril rests a hand gently beside his face while he talks to her in a wheeze of words punctuated by rushes of air as his hand lifts on and off the opening in the tube. Miraculous. And she remembers a conversation from yesterday.

The thing about miracles is that they make you hungry for more, she'd told Pascale. *One miracle, then another, and soon you're expecting them, taking them for granted. I'm scared I've used up all my share.*

She'd spoken lightly but Pascale knew. She knew.

Cooper's saying, in little bursts, that he doesn't like having the pressure suit taken off, something they do once a day to bathe him and apply new dressings.

Because it's painful? she suggests, rushing in to complete the breathy explanation.

He's momentarily irritated and she admonishes herself. Let him speak, for god's sake. He's short on breath, not words.

No, he manages. *The pain*—here he falters, and leaves a space, just moves past it. *Because this*—he makes the gesture of patting the suit, here, here—*this … my skin.*

She has to turn her face away.

Laura's on the other side of the glass. Coop's seen her, too, and lifts a hand to wave.

Look at Laura, look at that smile.

Laura waves back and then gestures to Avril, holds up a bakery bag.

Back in a while, babe. She leans down for a kiss—the kiss without touch she always gives him.

Uh-kay.

As she pulls off the gown, she looks through the glass at Coop, her Coop, his new skin protected in the all-body pressure suit they have made for him in three pieces. And she smiles, as she always does, at the colour of the fabric that she and Laura chose for the head piece, startling against the white bedsheets. Everyone who comes in for the first time has something to say about it—*What a gorgeous shade! Err … that's different! Sure brightens up this place!* But they chose it simply because it's Coop. The brilliant, flaming red of his hair.

~

They sit either side of the coffee table in the lounge, cappuccinos and an extravagance of Danish pastries spread between them. Laura's face is pink-and-gold warm. Young.

You know what I saw on the drive in? she says. *You know that burnt-out strip just before the highway …*

A cool shudder along Avril's arms. She nods.

… I caught a glimpse of something scuttling out onto the road. Only just managed to brake in time. Thank god no-one was behind me.

What was it?

Echidna!

Avril shakes her head.

Can you believe it? Life from all that ruin …

She picks up a pastry and breaks it in half. *When will you go back to work?*

I don't know. Laura shrugs. *I guess I should check my emails, though.*

What do you mean?

Well, I told them I was taking the long-service I was due but I didn't exactly wait for permission.

Avril's eyes widen. *Laura!* Her mother-in-law's grin is 100 per cent Coop's.

She's curious when Laura clears a space on the table for her Landcare bag. A clunk, metal on glass.

I found something else in Grunnie's kist, Laura says, leaning forward. *Right at the bottom under everything else.*

A small pulse of excitement.

Laura takes a large tin out of the bag and turns it so Avril can see. Old and scratched, a few rusted indentations. A faded scene painted on the lid—horse and cart, a man in rolled-up sleeves, two smart women with hats and parasols to match their long dresses. The words *Mills & Ware* embossed across the top. Laura uses her fingernails to pop open the lid.

The first thing she picks out is small, a broad cone, dirty white with sepia stripes. Avril takes it from her, feeling its rough outer surface with encircling ridges, the inside powdery smooth.

Limpet, I think, Laura says.

A barefoot girl with a bucket, trudging across the shore, prising shells away from rocks, breaking new ice crusting shallow pools.

Next, two books. The first, *The Girls Forget-Me-Not Annual of Prose and Verse*, covers bound to the spine with industrial tape. And a compact volume of *Underwoods*, well worn, its dog-eared pages furred at the edges. Laura thumbs it open at the frontispiece and hands it to Avril. There's an inscription in small, neat letters:

> To Miss Margaret Neish Duthie
> Never be content with what the world expects of you, Meggie, for you will always be more than that. Good luck!
> Mildred Birnie
> Roanhaven, Buchan, May 1905

Avril gasps when Laura extracts, with a flourish, a broad white feather. She runs the tip of a finger along the yellowing vane, thick as toenails and hollow at the base. It's not the bird her mind conjures—the wings suspended on a northern thermal, merging white with sodden sky—no, not that. It's the girl again, the girl with her arm down a rabbit hole, the girl with the gift of a feather and a promise balanced on the palm of her hand.

Laura unwraps something from tissue paper and passes to Avril a wooden hairbrush, the glaze of its back a web of fine lines. Avril turns it over, feeling the stiff boar bristles, and it takes a minute for her to realise what she has in her hand, what is caught in the vintage lint and dust. *Oh*, she breathes, disentangling one of many long wiry hairs and holding it to the light. Rich, plum-bright, jarrah red.

The last thing in the tin is unrecognisable at first—a dark, decaying pouch of something once soft, perhaps fabric. Avril takes it gingerly from Laura. Yes, fabric, folded over and over into a square, its fibres stiffened with age. You can almost see the shape of the hand that smoothed it flat.

Purple silk, Laura says softly.

And the girl is laughing, her eyes following a swathe of purple shooting into the air, up through the plasterboard ceiling, up through four floors, through the sheet-iron roof of the hospital, up, up into a cold, clear West Australian sky the colour of the North Sea.

Avril hears the cries of gulls on unseen winds. On her tongue, the taste of salt.

Laura

Early spring, a bluesky morning.

Laura carries the nylon box frame from the hatching shed to the far side of the garden, where lantana and plumbago compete wildly for a supremacy of colour. Ten am—her favourite time on a day like this when the air is warm enough for release. Carefully she upturns the box frame on the grass, stands back to give them space.

Dozens of Monarchs cling to the nylon mesh, perfectly still until sun and breeze unlock in them some primeval instinct to enact this last small miracle. Each pair of wings quivers, contracting at the base as though preparing for great effort, and at once the air is a sinuous flutter of honey and amber, black and white. It's over in seconds, this deliverance to the wild, but it's the only ceremony Laura would wish for. Her reward, the breath of diaphanous wings as a cloud of butterflies drifts through her as though she has become porous, a thing of air. Elemental, these small moments of boundarylessness, of finding your place beside butterflies in the order of things.

She closes her eyes, revelling in the untethering of body from earth.

Goodbye, beauties!

She becomes aware of the smell of eucalypts, their earthy bark, medicinal leaves. Her eyes snap open. She sniffs again. Yes, thyme between the stepping stones, its leaflets bruised by the soles of her shoes. And somewhere close by, someone is baking.

Beautiful smells. Good, she thinks, and takes a peppermint from her coat pocket—not because she needs it now but because she's grown to like the taste, hot and sharp and sweet.

One of the Monarchs, dizzy with freedom, lands briefly on the back of her hand. Spectacular, these wings, like stained glass, with their elaborate spots and veins and dappled bands. It lifts on a gust of air, and she is left looking at her hand. Once firm and unblemished, it is beginning to take on the look of parchment, time-weathered, with a history to tell. It's the hand of a woman who has earned her way through life but has not had to do it with a gipper in her hand.

She picks up the now-empty box frame and is heading back towards the shed when she hears a call from behind.

Laura turns to see a figure stumping up the drive with a cloth-covered plate, a shock of greying hair blowing about in the wind, a shapeless cardigan hanging from his back. She laughs. There's something almost biblical about a man bearing a loaf of bread. This man.

I know you, she thinks suddenly.

Glossary of Scots, Doric* and Shetland words

arling	signing on to a curer for the season, a commitment sealed with a small payment; a girl signed up was said to be 'arled'
ay ay	hello (colloquial)
bairnikie	bairn, young child (colloquial)
bannockies	bannocks (flat cakes made of oatmeal or barley)
blether	talk foolishly
bonnie clip	good-looking girl
bonxie	local term for skua, a kind of gull
braes	slopes
bubblyjock	turkey
Buchaner	a native of the Buchan area (Aberdeenshire)
but-and-ben	a simple two-roomed cottage consisting of a living room/kitchen area (the but) and a bedroom (the ben)
canna	can't
ceilidh	party, celebration (pron. kay-lee)
chaifing snipes	cheating swindlers
chuckney	chicken
clooties	rags, bandages
cran	a measure of herring (four baskets; around 1,000 herring)
doughboys	flour dumplings
dreich	dull
droonin'	drowning
dulse	edible seaweed (considered a treat)
dweeble-eyed	weak-eyed
farlins	large tubs or troughs containing herring ready for gutting
fulls	herring over 10¼ inches, full of milt or roe
fulpie	puppy
funcy	fancy
gaak, gaakie	fool, foolish
gansey	pullover
gipper	small knife used for gipping (gutting) herring
grapplie hook	grapple hook
grunnie	grandmother
guizer	performer in disguise who takes part in a festival or celebration
gullie knife	large knife
gweedmen	groomsmen
half-loaves	crude thick sanitary napkins made out of old rags
hash	hurry
hoose, hoosie	house, hut
howdie wifie	midwife

---

* The richly expressive dialect spoken in north-east Scotland.

GLOSSARY

jamaica: give (someone) a jamaica; have a jamaica	shock (someone); have a seizure
jeely pieces	bread and jam
kirk	church
kist	chest
kittlin	kitten
laavie	toilet
large-fulls	herring over 11¼ inches, full of milt or roe
limmer	slut
loon	boy, young man
mannie	man, husband
mattie-fulls	herring over 9¼ inches, full of milt or roe
matties	herring over 9 inches, maturing
muckle	big
mumpin'	grumbling
murlin	wicker basket
neeps	turnips
nummer	number
oilie	oilskin apron
peely; peely-wally	sickly
peenie	tummy
peerie	small
piece	piece of bread
quine, quinie	girl, young woman; 'quinie' is an affectionate form of the word
raickless	wreckless
reddin' the lines	preparing (readying) the fishing lines by cleaning them of old bait
reid-heid, reid-heidit	red-head, red-headed
rooed wool	wool plucked by hand (rather than shorn)
sailing on the back of Sunday	leaving port just after midnight on Sunday (boats couldn't sail on the Lord's day)
scaur	steep, rocky area
selkie	mythical creature (part human, part fish, like a mermaid)
snood	length of cord attached to a main fishing line
solan goose	local term for gannet
spents	herring that have spawned (of lesser quality)
The Sooth	The South (England)
tammie norie	local term for puffin
tatties	potatoes
tinkies	gypsy (Roma) people; travellers
unty	aunty
weel-faurt	good-looking
widdershins	anti-clockwise
wifie	wife, woman
ye	you

Note

Roanhaven and Gadlehead are fictional constructs, although they have geographical and some historical links to several actual places in the north-east of Scotland. All the characters in *Elemental* are fictional.

Acknowledgments

For their kindness and willingness with research assistance, my sincere thanks to: Professor Fiona Wood (The McComb Foundation) and Joy Fong (State Burns Unit, Royal Perth Hospital); Margaret Harris (the 'Butterfly Lady') and Dr David Daniels (butterfly photographer); former 'herring girl' Rita McNab (McNab's Kippers, Lerwick); Paul Ratter (Shetland Catch, Lerwick); Angus Johnson, Blair Bruce, Brian Smith (Shetland Archives, Lerwick); the helpful staff at Aberdeen Central Library and volunteers at the Buckie and District Fishing Heritage Centre; John Casley (Retired Firefighters Association, WA); Denis Brown (Fire and Emergency Services); Dr Terry Houston (WA Museum); Matt Williams (Department of Environment and Conservation); Richard Rossiter (for terrible lessons in fishing and ethics); Berice Todd (for discussions about life in Depression Perth); Val Kamman (for showing me the compilation of her father's letters, *Love to All at Home: Letters from World War I*, W. M. Telford, Sapper, 1st Australian Tunnelling Company); David Buchanan (consultant reid-heid). All responsibility for any inaccuracies, or licence taken, is mine.

I also want to acknowledge the debt I owe to the following influential texts: Steven Rose, *Lifelines: life beyond the gene* (Vintage, 2005); Lee Alan Dugatkin, *The altruism equation* (Princeton University Press, 2006); David Fraser, ed., *The Christian Watt papers* (Caledonian, 1988).

I have had the privilege and pleasure of writing parts of *Elemental* during residencies at Kelly's Cottage, Hobart; Hawthornden International Retreat for Writers, Lasswade, Scotland; and the Tyrone Guthrie Centre, Annaghmakerrig, Ireland. I thank the Tasmanian Writers Centre, Mrs Drue Heinz and the Australia Council for the Arts, repectively, for making these possible. And I thank my fellow residents at Hawthornden Castle and the Tyrone Guthrie Centre for their friendship and inspiration. It was at Tyrone Guthrie that I saw one of sculptor Anne McGill's musical goddesses.

How lucky I am to have had generous, perceptive readers at various stages of writing. Thank you to friends Richard Rossiter, Wendy Bulgin, Susan Midalia, Robyn Mundy and Annabel Smith.

I am honoured that Gail Jones agreed to read *Elemental*, and thank her for her words on the back cover, which mean a great deal to me.

ACKNOWLEDGMENTS

My gratitude to Terri-ann White for her careful reading and her continuing faith in my work, and to the enthusiastic, hard-working team at UWA Publishing—in particular, Linda Martin for her wholehearted engagement with the work and insightful editing, and Anna Maley-Fadgyas for another beautiful cover. Freelancers Deb Fitzpatrick (proofreader) and Keith Feltham (typesetter) are the best of the best.

Thanks to my patient family, who have been waiting for 'the fish book' for a long time. And to Ric, as always, for everything.

WORKS CITED

Browning, Elizabeth Barrett, 'With the breath ...' [p. 299], Sonnet 43, *Sonnets from the Portuguese* (1850).

de Cervantes Saavedra, Miguel, 'All sorrows ...' [p. 353], *Don Quixote* (1605).

Dickinson, Emily, 'That love is all there is ...' [p. 249], *The single hound*, ed. M. D. Bianchi (Little, Brown, 1914); 'There is a word ...' [pp. 206, 276], *Poems by Emily Dickinson*, Third Series, ed. M. L. Todd (Robert Brothers, 1896); 'Hope is the thing with feathers ...' [p. 226], *Poems by Emily Dickinson*, Second Series, eds M. L. Todd & T. W. Higginson (Robert Brothers, 1891).

Owens, Priscilla Jane & William James Kirkpatrick, 'Will your anchor hold?' [p. 101] (1882).

Shakespeare, William, 'A quintessence of dust' [p. 324], *Hamlet*, Act 2, Scene 2; 'You have often begun to tell me ...' [p. 397], *The tempest*, Act I, Scene 2.

Stevenson, Robert Louis, 'From a railway carriage' (p. 151), *A child's garden of verses* (1885); 'Requiem' [pp. 257, 308], *Underwoods* (1887).

Whiting, William, 'O hear us when we cry to thee' [p. 127], hymn (1860).